The Second Son

Andy Blackman

Clink
Street

London | New York

Grenville St Louis Hampton, the eleventh Duke of Hampshire, second son, slowly came awake to the sound of someone chopping wood. It was a methodical chop; although his eyes were still closed, he knew it was daylight by the brightness of the sun seeping through his drawn curtains.

Opening his eyes and quickly looking about, he was surprised to find himself in his own bed, at Hampton Hall. How this happened he was unsure, last night's party in London was a blur – the last thing he remembered was trying to get into Lady Penelope Stanton's panties. Although he was having a slight modicum of success, she still played hard ball, which to Grenville was an annoyance he was prepared to undergo.

"Damn women" made him smile; being the son of a Duke allowed him access to all the right parties and the elite of the social circles, but he knew the rules as well as everyone else in the social circle. You can flirt and go so far but to fully commit you need the ring on the third finger. Stretching like a lion on a sunny afternoon on the open savannah of Africa, Grenville flung back the covers and sat on the end of the bed. His head was surprisingly clear, especially after the amount of champagne he had consumed; he thought to himself, *perhaps I am finally becoming immune to the stuff.* He looked over to where his clothes were neatly folded over a chair and smiled.

Grenville had just finished his first year at Cambridge. His degree is in Land Economy, which was more for his parents than himself; being the second son he had to find his way in life, and even Grenville realised his parents was not going to fund his life style forever. But at the party one of his old-school friends, Jonathan Spencer, was talking about them going to Belize for the summer backpacking. Grenville during a drunken promise agreed to go with Jonathan, and all he had to do now was ask his parents to fund the trip. He was sure they would agree, just to have him out the way for the summer.

He smiled as he was pondering how he had managed to get home, undress himself, neatly fold up his clothes and get into bed without remembering, when he heard a light knock on his door. "Come in," he said, knowing it could not be his mother or father, the Duke and Duchess of Hampshire. They were too upper class to enter his bedroom themselves; in fact, since he had moved to the west wing, he did not even think his mother or father knew or had any idea where his bedroom was.

The door slowly opened and Preston walked in with a tray, and a mug of steaming hot coffee. Preston put the tray down on the bedside cabinet, went over to the large windows and drew the curtains back; Grenville closed his eyes to the full glare of the sun. "Morning Master Grenville, sleep well?" asked Preston.

"Yes, thank you Preston, like a log," replied Grenville, laughing. This also brought a laugh from Preston. "Preston, how did I manage to get to my room?" said Grenville, opening his arms wide to encompass the room.

"Some of the tenants were coming out of the railway tavern last night and saw you stagger from the night train from London. Seeing you were in no fit state to get back here under your own steam, they decided to bring you back to the Hall, where Mrs Preston and myself brought you to your room and put you to bed," said Preston.

"Preston, you and Mrs P are my guardian angels." This brought another laugh from them both.

"No doubt Mrs Preston will have have some breakfast in the kitchen, if you are hungry." Said Preston.

"Thank you, Preston, most kind," said Grenville. As Preston turned to leave, Grenville asked, "Are my mother and father at home?"

"The Duke is still sitting," replied Preston, which meant Grenville's father, the eleventh Duke of Hampshire, was still at the House of Lords sitting in chambers. "The Duchess is in the reading room and has requested your presence once you surface," said Preston.

"Thank you, Preston," said Grenville, "please let my mother know I will be along post haste."

"Of course, Master Grenville," replied Preston. As Preston left, Grenville, showered and dressed, sat in a chair and finished his coffee.

Before going to see his mother, Grenville returned the empty mug to the kitchen, which was the hub of the hall. Grenville always loved the kitchen; it was where the hall's heart and soul lived and breathed. Of all the seventy-eight rooms in Hampton Hall, the kitchen was his favourite.

Smiling, Grenville went up behind Mrs Preston and put his arms around her, kissed her on the neck and whispered, "Morning Mrs P, when you going to leave that old bugger Preston and run away with me?"

Mrs Preston gave a small shriek, and turned to face Grenville. "Be off with you, you're a ruffian," said Mrs Preston, laughing. Mr and Mrs Preston had been part of the family since Grenville was born; they had first served his late grandfather, the tenth Duke of Hampshire, as butler and cook. Now into their sixties, their only son had been killed in the war, so they treated Grenville like a surrogate son.

"Hungry?" asked Mrs Preston.

"Ravishing," replied Grenville.

"Sit yourself down and I will see if I can find you something to eat." This brought a smile to Grenville's face. It was one of Mrs Preston's sayings: "see if I can find you something to eat." Grenville could never remember a time when Mrs Preston had not supplied ample food in minutes. Mrs Preston placed a large English breakfast in front of Grenville, smiled and said, "Tuck in my dear; you look like you could do with it." Sitting at the kitchen table, chatting with Mrs Preston, while eating his breakfast, Grenville caught up on all the family, Hall and estate gossip. The Preston's knew everything and everyone, they were the centre of Hampton Hall; if you wanted to know anything you asked the Preston's.

After clearing his plate and returning it to the sink, Grenville kissed Mrs Preston, and said, "As always Mrs P, outstanding." Mrs Preston shooed him off with her tea towel while smiling.

Grenville made his way to the reading room. As he entered, his mother was sitting by the French windows bathed in sunlight reading a magazine. "Hello mother," Grenville said, going over to his mother and leaning down to kiss her on the offered cheek.

"Grenville, my darling, how are you?" asked his mother. "Come sit with me so I can take a good look at you." Grenville sat next to his mother and smiled. She was still the most beautiful women that Grenville had ever seen, and it still amazed him how his father had managed to bag such a beauty. Grenville once asked her how she settled on his father, as she must have had many admirers when she was young; she had told him, "I had many suitors after my coming out ball, but the first time I saw your father he looked so handsome in his Army uniform, plus he looked like he needed a good woman," which always made them both laugh. It was their private joke.

"Very well, thank you mother," said Grenville.

"Now your first year of Cambridge is over have you decided what you are going to do for the summer?" asked his mother, placing the magazine on the table.

"Mother, Jonathan Spencer is planning a trip to Belize backpacking, thought if I could squeeze a few pounds out of father, I would tag along for the ride, bit of further education, you might say," said a smiling Grenville.

His mother stared at him and looked him in the eyes and said, "I will have a word with your father, I am sure we can sort something."

"Thank you, mother," said Grenville, leaning over and kissing her again on the cheek.

"Your father will be coming down on Friday, with your brother," said his mother, "so we expect you to attend the family dinner, we have special guests, the Farthings. They are staying for the weekend, as guests of your brother Stephan," said his mother.

"Oh mother, do I have to?" pleaded Grenville.

"Well, if you want to see Belize, I suggest you are the attentive son and you make this weekend pleasant for all," smiled his mother.

ಔ·ೞ

Sofia Newton-Jones was the only daughter and child of the Right Honourable James and Marcia Newton-Jones, and according to Grenville's late grandfather, the late tenth Duke of Hampshire, "they were new money." The marriage was agreeable to both families, but was more of a surprise to the late Duke that a beautiful outgoing lady like Sofia Newton-Jones could have settled on his only son, the serious and straight-laced James Julian Hampton, the tenth Earl of Eastleigh; then again women always were a mystery to the Duke, and he tended not to ponder on such topics.

Sofia Newton-Jones had first met James Julian Hampton, the tenth Earl of Eastleigh, at a cocktail party a few months after her coming out ball. It was late November 1944 when she first spotted him; he was dressed in full military uniform, dressed as a colonel attached to the War Office stationed in Whitehall. The war had been raging for five years, but still Hitler could not stop the rounds of cocktail parties and social functions arranged by the upper classes. To cancel a social event was not British, and would send out the wrong message.

Sofia asked her friend Daphnia Degut-White, who had escorted her to the function, who the young serious looking man in the military uniform was standing at the bar. Daphnia explained to Sofia who he was, and with a twinkle in her eye asked Sofia if she wanted her to present her to him. Surprisingly Sofia agreed, much to Daphnia's shock, as she had only mentioned it as a jest; not for one moment did she imagine her outgoing friend Sofia Newton-Jones would be interested in the plain boring James Julian Hampton, tenth Earl of Eastleigh.

Both Sofia and her friend Daphnia made their way to the bar, nodding and speaking as they went. Once at the bar, James had his back to both and did not see their arrival. Daphnia tapped James on the shoulder and said, "James, please may I present my dear friend, Sofia Newton-Jones, who recently came out."

James turned and stared at both ladies. James bowed deeply and said, "Nice to make your acquaintance." Both held out their gloved hand to him. James had known Daphnia since childhood, so took her hand and quickly kissed her gloved hand, and said, "Daphnia, a pleasure as always." James took Sofia's hand and held it for a few moments before kissing it, all the time staring deeply into the most beautiful blue eyes he had ever seen. Sofia stared back into his brown wide eyes, and smiled. James had fallen deeply in love and was lost for words, but managed to mumble out, "The pleasure is all mine, my lady." Daphnia looked from Sofia to James, and knew a spark had been lit that would be hard to extinguish.

There was a whirlwind courtship which was a surprise to some – Sofia was always talkative and outgoing, happy and carefree, where James was always quiet and serious, totally un-suited as a couple, as it had been pointed out on more than one occasion. But it was also pointed out that opposites do attract. The first-time James presented Sofia to his family, even his normally reserved mother the Duchess of Hampshire was impressed, but being a woman knew where Sofia was coming from, and knew as she did that Sofia saw something in her son James that others missed and he was worth investing in, and much to her husband's surprise took to Sofia and welcomed her into the family. Later the Duke asked his wife what she thought of the match.

"Perfect," she said.

"Not beneath him, then," said the smiling Duke.

"Not at all, a nice presentable young lady, I thought," replied the Duchess.

"Family is new money, not blue," said the Duke.

"Sometimes, Julian, you can be an awful snob," said the Duchess, tutting. The Duke tried hard not to laugh at his wife, the most snobbish person he knew.

The war finished the following May and they were married the following February. This was a chance to celebrate, after years of austerity, and the establishment did not disappoint. They were married in the local village church, which caused some delicate compromises on attendance for both sides, as they were aware to snub the wrong family member could cause future problems.

As for the reception, it was held at Hampton Hall, the Hampton family's ancestral home, so invitations were plentiful. The whole society elite were in attendance, including royalty, and the wedding would be talked about for many years as one of the most lavish and fun events since before the wretched war.

James and Sofia moved into Hampton Hall. James was unsure after the war what he wanted to do, but with Sofia's guidance James took to managing the family estate back up to its full potential, which impressed his father and mother. James introduced a new breed of dairy cow, and many new livestock breeds, James liaised with the tenant farmers on crop rotation and stock, making sure that the whole estate was covering the whole spectrum of farming.

After a year, Sofia was pregnant, to the delight of James, but more so to his parents. Sofia gave birth to a fine heathy boy, which they called Stephan Albert. Three years later Sofia gave birth to another heathy boy which they called Grenville St Louis.

ಬಿ·ಲ೮

Grenville only knew his grandfather, as the Duke's wife, the Duchess, and his mother's parents had all died before he was born. Grenville was very close to his maternal grandfather, and since he could walk he could be found sitting with him in his study listening to his stories about his exciting life and travel.

Julian James Hampton, the tenth Duke of Hampshire, like Grenville was not the first born so was not expected to inherit, and so led a life of adventure that had Grenville captivated when he told him his stories. Grenville would sit for hours listening to his grandfather, only leaving when he fell asleep or was dragged away by his governess for food or bath.

When Grenville was seven he asked his grandfather how, after all his adventures, he ended up as the present Duke. His grandfather explained that during World War One, everyone from the estate had mobilised for Kitchener's army; this included his two older brothers and himself. After the war, had finished, the estate had been decimated of local men and his family had lost both his brothers, which had elevated him to the future Duke of Hampshire.

"Did you ever want to say no, grandfather?" Grenville asked one day.

His grandfather took his hand and said, "Follow me." His grandfather led him into the great hall and pointed above the great fire place.

As Grenville stared up, he asked, "What's that, grandfather?"

"That, child, is the family crest of arms and the family motto," replied his grandfather.

Grenville stared at the impressive large shield with a yellow background and a large black eagle clutching a lightning bolt in the middle. "What do the words mean, grandfather?" asked Grenville.

"*Officium antequam glorificetur;* Duty before honour," said his grandfather. "Those words are what us Hamptons have lived by for countless generations," explained his grandfather. "If you are called upon to do your duty, young Grenville, then the family will expect you to do so." Grenville stood nodding his head seriously, while his grandfather smiled down at him.

Grenville and his brother Stephan were never close. Grenville on many occasions tried to engage his brother and have a brotherly relationship with him, but for some reason his brother did not want to spend any time with him. One day Grenville, asked his grandfather about his brother. His grandfather placed Grenville on his knee and said, "Grenville, my boy, it's not you, it's your brother. After I have gone, he will be in line to inherit the title and the estate. Some find the prospect exciting and some, it fills them with fear and dread. Your brother is the latter. And with that fear, he will compensate it with his snobbish attitude, as if everyone was put on this earth to serve him. He reminds me of my later brother Arthur, he was the same as your brother." Grenville nodded, not really understanding his brother's attitude.

When Grenville was nine his brother Stephan was sent to Rayleigh boarding school, to follow in the family tradition of always being educated at Rayleigh then onwards to Cambridge. When Stephan left for Rayleigh School, Grenville was standing with his grandfather who stood lined up outside the house with the rest of the staff to say farewell to Master Stephan. Stephan shook Grenville's and his grandfather hand's but did not speak before he got into the car with his parents; his grandfather said, "Pompous ass," only loud enough for Grenville to hear, but Grenville smiled and agreed. He was still unsure what a pompous ass was, but he would be sure to ask his grandfather later.

Three years later it was Grenville's turn to attend Rayleigh School, but unlike his brother's departure, most of the staff was sorry to see him go. Grenville then clung onto his grandfather, and sobbed, before his father had to physical drag him to the car. Grenville looked out of the rear windows and saw his grandfather waving after him. Grenville waved back with tears in his eyes. On the drive, up to Rayleigh School, his father gave him a list of things to remember, while his mother sat holding his hand also with tears in her eyes. On arrival at Rayleigh School the grounds were full of cars, with parents taking their offspring to school for the first time. Grenville knew that this was a one off; next time, only the chauffeur and his brother Stephan would take him back to school.

Grenville followed his mother and father up the steps into the great hall. The progress was slow as periodically his parents would stop to speak to other parents. Eventually up on the stage a man appeared wearing a black gown, asked for calm, and immediately the room went silent. "Welcome my Lords, Ladies and gentlemen and distinguished guests. I am Mr Yates, Headmaster of Rayleigh School for Boys, and it is a particular pleasure to welcome you all here today with the new intake for Rayleigh School." Scanning the room and smiling, the Headmaster said, "I can see looking around the hall, that most of you are returning with your own offspring." This brought laughter from the room. "Please can you register your son's name at one of the reception desks, they will then be give their house allocation. Thank you for your patience, and once again, welcome."

Before his father moved toward the reception desk area, Grenville asked, "I won't be in Stephan's house, will I father?" This was Grenville's worst fear about attending school.

Smiling down at him, his father said, "No Grenville, siblings are never put in the same houses."

Grenville smiled and stayed with his mother. Eventually his father returned and handed Grenville a white envelope; printed on the front was "Grenville Hampton, Walpole House."

Eventually Mr Yates the Headmaster said, "Parents, if you could finish off your goodbyes." His father and mother stooped down and both embraced Grenville; his mother especially had tears in her eyes, and Grenville was trying hard but failing miserably not to cry as well.

His father said, "You are following in a proud family tradition, Grenville, make us proud." Grenville just nodded, not trusting himself to speak.

His mother looked him in the eyes and said, "See you soon, my darling, and don't forget to write." Once again Grenville nodded. Eventually a bell sounded and parents made their final farewells and departed. Grenville watched the departing backs of his parents, and found he was standing in a crowd of sad looking boys, but he never felt so alone in his whole short life.

Eventually someone shouted, "Boys for Walpole House this way." Grenville looked over to see where the shout had come from, and saw a tall smartly dressed boy waving a blue hanky.

Grenville moved towards the waving boy, and as he approached another boy asked him his name, Grenville replied, and the boy told him to stand with the other five boys already there. As Grenville approached, one of the boys smiled and said, "Hi I am Jonathan Spencer," holding out his hand.

Grenville took the offered hand, and said, "Grenville Hampton, pleased to meet you," and smiled for the first time since his arrival. Another boy introduced himself as Hugo Thorpe, and the three started to chat while they waited. Eventually there were eight boys standing in the huddle.

The boy with the blue hanky said, "follow me to the Walpole House, where we will meet Mr Raymond, the Walpole House Master."

Turning, the boy smartly took off followed by the eight boys. Eventually they arrived at Walpole House, and were told to take a seat in the common room and wait for Mr Raymond. Mr Raymond eventually stepped into the middle of the common room and looked about at the eight boys and said, "Welcome to Walpole House, this will be your house and home whilst you are at Raleigh School, until you leave for future endeavours. I am Mr Raymond, the House Master of Walpole House. I am your first point of contact, if you have any problems or concerns whilst you are at Raleigh School or Walpole House, do not hesitate to contact me or if you require my assistance anytime night or day, my house is next door, please do not hesitate to knock. If I am not about, my wife Margret will know where I am at all times." Smiling, Mr Raymond asked if there were any questions, all eight heads nodded in unison. Mr Raymond went on, "I know for most of you this is the first time you have ever been away from home and all this seems very daunting to you, but I know in a few days this place will seem like home as well.

"In your white envelopes that you are all clutching are the School and House Rules, plus your timetables for your days, evenings and weekends. We at Raleigh School and especially Walpole House expect great things from you freshman boys and I no doubt have the greatest faith in all your abilities to make Rayleigh School and Walpole House proud. That is all for now, I will get Graves here to take you to your new dormitory where your luggage has been delivered, so you can unpack and settle in for the night. I shall meet you all back in here tomorrow morning after breakfast. Graves will be with you in the morning to escort you to the Walpole Dining Hall for breakfast and give you a quick tour of Walpole House, so I will see you all tomorrow morning. Any questions?" And before anyone had a chance to answer, Mr Raymond strolled out of the common room.

Graves stood and said, "Follow me." Leading the boys up three flights of stairs to the top floor, he opened a door onto eight beds with eight lockers; four on each side of the room. At the bottom was a washroom. "Find a bed and I will see you all at seven in the morning for breakfast," said Graves before he closed the door on them.

Grenville took the last bed on the right near the washroom; Jonathan took the one next to him and Hugo the one opposite. The room was totally silent as the boys located their luggage from the assembled pile in the middle of the room. Eventually they all started to unpack and placed all their belongings into the lockers and small bedside cabinets. After a time, Grenville lay on his bed and thought of home and his grandfather, but before he had time to wallow, Hugo had come over and said, "Grenville, my dear chap, got any scoff, I am bloody well starving."

Grenville started to laugh, and that seemed to break the tension in the room and before long, on the table in the middle of the room, a feast had been laid out of all the food the boys had brought with them, and they were all chatting and getting to know each other.

☙ · ❧

The first year went so fast, Grenville did not even have time to miss home or even ponder on life before school. Hugo, Jonathan and Grenville became the best of friends and were always found in each other's company. The three friends were so different, Grenville was getting tall with blond hair, and a natural born leader; Jonathan was slight with dark hair, but a natural statesman, he could negotiate or talk his way out of most situations – on many occasion his oration skills had saved their bacon in a delicate situation made by Grenville. Hugo was the brightest of the three, a natural scholar, and the most sensible of them, for he had a natural ability to think through a problem and come up with the answer. Together they made a force to be reckoned with, and most in the House and school left them alone; others quickly found out if you picked on one of them, then you picked on all three, and so they were left alone. Out of the friendship, Hugo was the enigma of the three, where the other two were extroverts Hugo was an introvert, but the three were always found in each other's company. Never did it occur to them their friendship seemed strange to some, one a Duke's son, one a barrister's son and the other a banker's son.

Summer break was looming, which signified the end of their first year at Rayleigh, and all three friends were sitting in the common room one evening after dinner discussing the forthcoming school break. "So, what you two chaps up to?" asked Grenville.

"Family holiday time for me," said Hugo.

"Not sure," said Jonathan.

"What about you, Grenville?" asked Hugo.

"Not sure," Grenville replied.

"Well, I hope we all have a smashing time, going to miss you chaps," said Hugo, which made them both nod and agree with Hugo.

The summer break finally arrived and the common room was a hive of excitement. The car park was beginning to fill up with cars. Grenville looked out of the window and spotted his brother striding towards the entrance. Grenville went out to meet his brother.

"Greetings brother," said Grenville.

His brother did not even acknowledge him but said, "Newton has arrived, and is ready to depart. Gather your things and let's be off."

"Give me five minutes," said Grenville to his brother's back as he walked away.

Grenville went back inside, gathered his things, and went to say goodbye to Hugo and Jonathan. All three hugged and wished each other a fun-packed holiday. Grenville left to find Newton, the family chauffeur.

When Grenville found Newton, he was standing next to the family Rolls Royce with the boot open ready for Grenville's things. Newton saluted and smiled at Grenville as he approached and said, "Nice to see you again Master Grenville."

"And you Newton, everything OK at the ranch?" asked Grenville, which made Newton laugh.

"Fine, master Grenville, looking forward to seeing you."

From the back seat, Stephan said, "When you two have quite finished, I would like to get home before it gets dark."

Grenville poked his tongue out and Newton rolled his eyes; both then started to laugh, which brought a further tut from the car. All the way down to Hampton Hall Stephan and Grenville did not speak. Grenville tried a few times to engage his brother, but gave up when he realised his brother was just not interested in conversation.

As they pulled up at the Hall, the family and servants were there to greet them. Stephan sat until Newton opened the car door for him; once Stephan had exited the car, he first kissed his mother on the cheek then shook hands with his father and grandfather, and ignoring the servants went into the hall. Before Newton had time to go around and open the car door for Grenville, he had run to his mother's embrace, and kissed her, shaking his father's and grandfather's hands. He then ran to the servants and said he hoped they were all well, and how pleased he was to be home and over the next few weeks, would catch up with all of them all for the local gossip. This made them all laugh, and as they returned to work, they all agreed having Master Grenville back home would certainly liven the old place up.

The summer break came and went, and as promised every day Grenville could be found with a member of staff, in the house or out in the garden helping, much to the annoyance of his brother.

His mother scolded her eldest son one day, and said, "Stephan, you should be more engaged like your brother Grenville," to which Stephan replied, "Mother, one does not socialise with the lower classes," which left his mother speechless.

Grenville could not wait to get back to school to see Hugo and Jonathan again, but knew he would miss everyone at home, especially his grandfather. Grenville was first back in the room and was unpacking when Jonathan came in.

"Grenville, how the devil are you," said Jonathan, rushing over to hug Grenville.

"Jonathan, my dear chap," said Grenville as they hugged.

Hugo rushed in out of breath as usual. "Hello Grenville, Jonathan, hope you are well," said Hugo. This made the other two laugh, as they went to embrace their friend.

It was during a double period of Latin that Grenville was bored as usual; his thinking was, a dead language should remain dead, but he would dare not voice his opinion to Mr Stark the Latin teacher, who Grenville was sure would have a coronary on the spot if he did. There was a knock on the door and a boy passed Mr Stark a note. Not even pausing, Mr Stark gave a quick glance at the note whilst he carried on with the translation of Pliny the Younger's account of the destruction of Pompeii. Mr Stark wandered up to Grenville and handed him the note and said, "*Praepetibus pennis permissum vos rapiunt ".*" Let swift wings carry you off".

Grenville read the note:

Grenville Hampton is to report to Walpole House Common Room, without delay

The first thing Grenville thought was, what had he recently done that could warrant him a visit to Walpole House Common Room during lesson times? Then he realised if it had been trouble then surely, he would have been summoned to the Headmaster's study for retribution, and surely both Jonathan and Hugo would also have been summoned.

Grenville stood. Jonathan and Hugo looked at Grenville; both looked concerned, but Grenville shrugged and smiled as he left the Latin class. On the way, back to the Common Room, Grenville thought hard on why he would be summoned, especially out of a lesson. As he crossed the car park, he spotted Newton standing next to the family Rolls Royce. Newton raised his hand; this made Grenville run as fast as he could toward Walpole House. Grenville was out of breath by the time he reached Walpole House. As he entered the Common Room, Grenville saw Mr Raymond and his mother were sitting chatting over a cup of tea. As Grenville entered, they both stood. Grenville knew it was bad news, especially since his mother had decided to break the news herself.

Grenville went to his mother's embrace; Mr Raymond made his excuses and left them alone. His mother placed him at arm's length, and was surprised he was nearly as tall as she was. "I have some bad news for you Grenville. I am afraid to tell you your grandfather has passed away," said his mother with tears in her eyes.

"When, how?" Grenville asked quietly.

"Yesterday tea time, I found him in the library, he looked so peaceful as if he had just fallen asleep."

Grenville smiled. "I think that's the way he would have wanted to go."

"Yes, I am sure you are right," said his mother, smiling.

"Have you told Stephan yet?" asked Grenville.

"Your father is with him now," replied his mother.

"When is the funeral?" asked Grenville.

"Next Tuesday," said his mother, "but your father has decided not to take you out of school to attend."

"But mother…" Grenville started to say, but his mother took his face in her hands, and with tears in her eyes, said, "It's your father's decision, please respect it." Grenville nodded, his eyes full of tears, and said, "Of course, mother, I will."

His mother took a white envelope from her pocket, and passed it to Grenville. "We found this envelope addressed to you in your grandfather's effects," said his mother.

Grenville took the envelope but, not opening it, placed it in his pocket. There was a light knock on the door, and Mr Raymond poked his head round the door.

"Everything alright?" he asked.

"Yes, thank you, Mr Raymond," replied Grenville's mother.

Grenville was looking out of the window and saw his father striding toward the house. Not wanting to speak or see his father, Grenville asked his mother's and Mr Raymond's permission to be alone for a time. Grenville embraced his mother and after saying goodbye, ran from the Common Room towards his room.

Alone in his room, Grenville sat on his bed and sobbed. He was going to miss his grandfather so much, he was his mentor and when at home his playmate. Remembering the letter his mother had given him, Grenville looked at the front of the envelope and in his grandfather's neat copperplate handwriting was written "Grenville."

Grenville opened the envelope and taking out the letter he read:

My dearest Grenville

If you are reading this, I know you have a heavy heart, as you have just been informed I have departed this mortal realm. Please try and not feel too sad at my passing, my time has ended, as all things in life must end and reach their timely conclusion, my time is now. I want you to know that in my ageing years you were my brightest joy, in future when you think of me only think of the happy time we spent together. You were the reason some days for me to carry on, you remind me so much of how I was at your age, so let me partake in some words of wisdom to you, as my grandfather did to me, on this road you are about to embark on.

Although you might not inherit the title or estate, always remember who you are: you are a Hampton, and have a proud family history to uphold, so always hold your head up high and be proud to be a Hampton. I have always been proud to call you my grandson, and I know you will always make me and the family proud.

Your ever-loving grandfather Julian

Grenville read the letter, repeatedly, until the words were emblazoned on his heart, Grenville lay back on his bed and closed his eyes, and sobbed until he fell asleep.

Jonathan and Hugo found him later that day fast asleep on his bed, still clutching the letter. Jonathan and Hugo gently woke Grenville, and on opening his eyes, Grenville smiled at them, sat up and said, "Read this," passing the letter so both could read it.

Afterwards Jonathan and Hugo both said, "Sorry for your loss, old bean, if you need us shout," as they both left the dormitory to leave Grenville alone once more.

80 · 03

A few months later, Grenville, Jonathan and Hugo were walking towards the school library when they spotted walking toward them his brother Stephan and his odious friend Dexter Simon-Smyth. Once close, Stephan and Dexter stopped and waited for the three to join them. As they approached, Grenville said, "Hello Stephan," to his brother, but it was Dexter who replied, "It is now My Lord, as your brother is now the eleventh Earl of Eastleigh, so show some respect, spare," which made Stephan and Dexter laugh.

Dexter went on, "Another step closer to the title, Stephan."

"Absolutely," said Stephan, speaking for the first time.

"Show some respect," said Grenville. "Grandfather was a great man, and I will miss him."

"Well, I am the Earl of Eastleigh now and some day will inherit, so I will not," said Stephan, which made Dexter and he laugh again.

Grenville stared at his brother and watched him laughing. Grenville felt the blood rise and his anger boil over, and after years of pent up frustration at his brother, all he wanted to do was smash his brother's smug laughing face. He rushed his brother, and with swinging arms landed a lucky punch that made Stephan sit down heavily.

"Why, you little wretch," said Dexter, reaching for Grenville and getting him into a head lock.

"Hey, leave him alone you oaf," said Hugo, who lunged at Dexter, wrapping his arms around Dexter's neck, pulling him to the ground. Stephan looked stunned, sitting on the ground touching his mouth and seeing blood on his hand. The commotion brought others running across to the fighting boys, and two Masters finally parted them all, without any serious injury.

"All of you off to the Headmaster's study. Fighting will not be tolerated under any circumstance in school grounds," said one of the Masters.

As the five stood outside the Headmaster's study, it was a few minutes before the two Masters came out of the study, leaving the door open.

"Come," said a deep voice from within. Mr Yates the Headmaster stood in front of the five boys and said, "So what caused boys from my school to publicly humiliate themselves by fighting like ruffians in a manner unbecoming of the high standards of Rayleigh School?"

Stephan spoke first. "I am the injured party, Headmaster," he said, pointing to his split lip that was still seeping blood.

"Who threw the first punch?" asked the Headmaster.

"I did, Sir," replied Grenville.

"Why?" asked the Headmaster.

"My brother and his friend insulted the memory of my late recently departed grandfather, the tenth Duke of Hampshire," said Grenville, standing a bit straighter as he spoke.

"And your involvement, Simon-Smyth?" asked the Headmaster.

"After the Earl of Eastleigh's brother decided to violently attack him in an unprovoked manner, I felt honour bound to step in and protect the Earl of Eastleigh from further harm."

"Did you now," replied the Headmaster, "and you two," pointing at Hugo and Jonathan, "what part did you play in this Greek tragedy?"

"I stopped Simon-Smyth here from harming my friend Grenville," replied Hugo.

"And you?" asked the Headmaster, pointing at Jonathan.

"Nothing Sir, it all happened in the blink of an eye and was over before I could react," said Jonathan.

"No doubt," said the Headmaster. "You three can go," pointing at Stephan, Dexter and Jonathan, "you two stay where you are." All three turned and left the Headmaster's study; as they went, Stephan and Dexter had a triumphant smile on their faces. Jonathan left the Headmaster's study looking glum.

"Well, obviously, this was a matter of honour, and a personal disagreement between you Hampton boys," said the Headmaster, "but I cannot let a breach of school rules and a lack of discipline go un-punished whatever the circumstances."

Grenville and Hugo nodded.

"Three of the best for each of you." Once the Headmaster had administered their punishment and before Grenville and Hugo left the Headmaster's study, the Headmaster said, "I do hope this will be the last time we meet under these circumstances." Grenville and Hugo both nodded solemnly. As they were departing the headmaster said, "I will be writing to both your parents and will raise your excellent conduct in this incident with them." The Headmaster watched them depart and he smiled and said to himself, "You were right, Julian, my old friend, your grandson will be a credit to you."

As they walked back slowly to Walpole House, Grenville and Hugo were smiling. As they entered the Common Room the place was filled with the entire Walpole House, who as they entered cheered and clapped. Jonathan stepped forward and said, "The hero's return," and hugged them both, the House came and congratulated them, and to the surprise of Grenville he had been elevated somewhat in status for punching his very unpopular brother.

That was the last time any incident occurred between Grenville and his brother. As the years passed, his brother finally went up to Cambridge, which left Grenville free to become Walpole House and Rayleigh School Head Boy, and as he pointed out to his father before he himself left for Cambridge, he was the first Hampton from the family in generations to become Rayleigh School Head Boy.

ℰℴ · ℰℴ

Grenville, Jonathan and Hugo sat in the common room. "Well, our last day at Rayleigh School and Walpole House, going to kind of miss it," said Hugo, smiling.

"Are you?" said a surprised Jonathan.

"Not the place, exactly, us three and the fun we had together."

"I know what you mean," said Grenville.

"We will keep in touch, won't we?" Hugo asked.

"Of course," replied Jonathan.

"No one can break the Walpole boys," said Grenville, which made them all laugh.

"So, what you going to do before you go up to Oxford, Hugo?" asked Jonathan.

"Mother and father are off on a touring holiday around the South of France, so thought I would tag along for the ride," replied Hugo.

"Very nice," said Grenville, smiling.

"What about you, Jonathan?" asked Hugo.

"Father has insisted before Cambridge I work in the family business, learning the workings of chambers before I start my law degree," said Jonathan, looking glum.

"Don't worry old bean, it will all come out right in the end, when you inherit the firm and you are a top law court judge, you will look back and laugh," said Grenville, smiling at Jonathan.

"What you up to then, Grenville?" asked Hugo.

"I am going to help out on one of the tenant farms," replied Grenville, smiling.

"That will keep you busy," replied Hugo, smiling.

"Well, anything to pass the time until Cambridge," replied Grenville. They all stood and hugged each other.

"Don't be strangers," said Jonathan.

"Easy for you to say, you are both off to Cambridge," replied Hugo.

"Don't worry," said Grenville, "we won't forget you."

"As if," said a laughing Jonathan.

৪৩·৫৪

Grenville was not looking forward to the forthcoming weekend. The Farthings who were coming were apparently bringing their daughter to meet his parents; for some strange reason the girl had obviously set her sights on Stephan and the family title. Her parents were as his late grandfather would have put it "new money, not blue." This made Grenville smile, to think of his grandfather, which he often did.

Grenville was reading the paper in the reading room. His mother had disappeared, no doubt to speak to the Preston's on the arrangements for the weekend, and to make sure it all ran smoothly, when he heard the family Rolls Royce pull up in front of the Hall. Looking out of the windows he watched Newton open the car door for his father, the eleventh Duke of Hampshire. Newton then rushed round and opened the door for Stephan, his brother, the eleventh Earl of Eastleigh. "What a dick," thought Grenville; his brother was such a snob.

His father thanked Newton and strolled into the hall; Stephan ignored Newton and followed his father. Grenville noticed father and son were so different in appearance now: his father remained tall and thin, where his brother was shorter and getting rounder by the day and thinning on top, but both had the airs of the upper class. His brother Stephan certainly outshone his father with his arrogant and self-absorbed attitude. Grenville smiled. Being the second son was sometimes a blessing. He was not really bothered, he was left alone most of the time, unless like this weekend where he wanted something so he had to play the polite, attentive second son; but Grenville knew the effort would justify the rewards.

Grenville was ready when he heard the gong go downstairs to announce that dinner was being served in thirty minutes. On entering the lounge, he was the first to arrive, which was a surprise. He was followed by his mother and father. Grenville went and kissed his mothers offered cheek, and shook his father's hand. His father said, "So, my boy, how was Cambridge for the first year?"

"Rather good, thank you father," replied Grenville.

"How is the degree going? Same one as I did," asked his father.

"Yes, father, Land Economy, going rather well thank you father," replied Grenville smiling.

"Your mother informs me you wish to travel this summer," said his father.

"Yes, Jonathan Spencer is planning to spend the summer backpacking in Belize," replied Grenville.

"I am sure it is a good opportunity for Grenville to get some world experience," said his mother, smiling at Grenville.

"Looks to me you have both decided," said his father, laughing.

"Decided what?" said Stephan, as he approached them.

"Grenville here wants to backpack in Belize this summer," said his father.

"Good. Might keep him out of trouble and out of the way," said Stephan.

Just as Grenville was about to reply, Preston opened the lounge doors, and announced the Farthings. "May I present Mr Gerard and Mrs June Farthing and their daughter Sara Farthing." Preston bowed and stepped aside to allow them to enter. Grenville hung back as his parents and his brother went over to greet their guests.

Grenville was on his best behaviour for the whole weekend. He was very attentive, to a point that impressed his parents. "That boy must want to go to South America very badly indeed," said James to Sofia, when they were alone in their room.

"I must admit he has quite impressed me this weekend," replied Sofia.

"I guess we can give him a decent allowance for his trip," said James.

"Thank you my darling," replied Sofia, leaning over to kiss her husband on his lips which made him smile.

Grenville woke with the sound of Preston knocking. "Enter, Mr P," Grenville said. Preston entered with a coffee, and placed it on the table.

"Your father has requested your attendance in his study as soon as possible," said Preston.

"Thank you, Mr P," said Grenville, who jumped out of bed to shower and get dressed. Twenty minutes later Grenville knocked on his father's study, and waited for the, "Enter," before Grenville turned the handle to enter the study.

Grenville was surprised but not shocked to see his brother Stephan sitting opposite his father. "Grenville my dear boy, come in and sit down," said his father. Grenville did as instructed, and sat next to Stephan.

"Morning father, Stephan," said Grenville, but despite Grenville's acknowledgement of his brother Stephan ignored him.

"Morning Grenville, So," said his father, "tell me about this trip to South America you are planning."

"Well, Jonathan Spencer and I have decided to take in Belize," said Grenville.

"For the purpose of?" asked his father.

"Just to see a different culture and to further one's education," replied Grenville.

His father smiled. "Just like your grandfather. Well, your mother has persuaded me that this trip might be the making of you, so who am I to disagree with your mother," said his father with a light chuckle.

His father passed a plain brown envelope over to him, which Grenville placed in his pocket. "Thank you, father," Grenville said.

"All I ask, please do not let the family name down. Or embarrass your mother or me," said his father.

"I promise I will not let down the trust you and mother have placed in me," replied Grenville.

"That's all we ask," said his father, standing and offering Grenville his hand. Grenville shook his father's hand and realised the meeting was over. Nodding to his brother Grenville left the study; once outside, he took the envelope from his pocket, opened it, kissed it and punched the air.

After Grenville left, Stephan said to his father, "Are you sure you've done the right thing, father? After all he is not the most reliable person on the planet.'

"Perhaps not," replied his father, "but for all his faults he is a Hampton, and I cannot see him coming to any harm with young Spencer along for the ride, he is a sensible lad. Plus, I get rid of Grenville for the summer, and I for once am in your mother's good books. For me, win-win all round I think," said his father, laughing.

"Still cannot see any good coming out of this, father."

"Please Stephan, for once have a bit of faith in your brother," replied his father.

"Perhaps," said Stephan too quietly for his father to hear.

Grenville immediately went and telephoned Jonathan to break the good news.

"Excellent," said Jonathan, "leave all the preparations to me, I will get your share of the cost when we meet."

"You sure?" said Grenville.

"Of course, but only if you are good for it," said Jonathan, laughing.

"I am now father came through," said Grenville, joining in the laughter.

The night before his departure the Duchess arranged a family dinner, and she made it clear to Stephan he would attend. The evening went without incident and everyone was in flamboyant moods; even Stephan tried to be civil towards his brother.

Afterwards as they were sitting enjoying a drink, his mother said, "All ready, Grenville?"

"Think so mother, all packed and raring to go," replied Grenville.

"Well, make sure you have a lovely time," said his father. His father and mother both stood, and came over and gave Grenville a hug,

"Well, keep safe, and see you soon," said his mother, smiling at Grenville.

"Remember who you are," said his father.

"Always, father," said Grenville. They both said goodnight to Stephan and Grenville and left for bed. After they had departed, Grenville said, "So what you got planned for the summer, Stephan?"

"That, Grenville, is none of your concern," replied Stephan.

Grenville stood and looked at Stephan and said, "Sometimes, Stephan, it surprises me we are from the same gene pool."

"Grenville, my dear chap, you are a waste of space," replied Stephan as Grenville left the room.

∛ · ∜

Stephan sat and pondered what his brother had said – "from the same gene pool." He was sure he was not too far from the mark; he never had since his birth shown any love for anyone or anything, not even his mother whom everyone loved. He could not feel close to her, and he had no brotherly love for Grenville. He was always an irritant to him, the "family pet"; everyone loved Grenville. When his brother was three and he was six, his parents gave his brother his first puppy, a soft little thing that followed Grenville about every day, which annoyed Stephan no end, so going to the gardener's shed he took some slug poison and then took some meat from the kitchen – making sure that nosy bitch Mrs Preston did not see him, or she would have reported him to his mother – and waiting until the puppy was alone, he poisoned the puppy. He sat on the stairs smiling with a strange feeling as he watched the puppy suffer and gained even more pleasure watching his brother's anguish. Eventually, his grandfather had taken the puppy and gave it a humane ending.

This was the first-time Stephan felt alive and since that day he went out of his way to feed his pleasures. Then again, he himself had never shown any affection to anything; since an early age he was self-absorbed, and knew he had been born into privilege for a reason and he had no intention of engaging with anyone below his social class. Once when he and Grenville were on a term break from Rayleigh School, and wishing he was back at school and feeling bored with Hampton Hall, he had tried to engage a young pretty maid who after a struggle had finally submitted to his advances. Stephan smiled even now at the encounter; not even with the threat of her losing her job did she submit, so in the end he had to get very physical, and afterwards he felt empowered like he had before. He knew after that day, he would have to have a little spice in the encounter to get any sexual gratification.

But this brought a side effect he was not expecting: the girl had been found in tears with a bloody lip by Preston, that old interfering codger of a butler. Many a time he had thwarted his plans for enjoyment, and above all Stephan hated him the most. Preston had report him to his grandfather, the Duke. Stephan was summoned to the Duke's study and he was asked outright if he had molested the girl. Stephan did not even try and deny it, and told his grandfather he could not see what all the fuss was about; after all, she was a servant and he was blue blood so she was there to serve him.

His grandfather looked shocked by his outburst, and it was his grandfather who gave him his first and last thrashing. Stephan learned an important lesson that day, and afterwards made sure he was more cautious in his pursuits. His only friend at school was Dexter Simon-Smyth; although he was well beneath Stephan's class and social standing, Stephan trusted him totally.

Dexter knew him well and pampered to his enlarged ego and self-importance, but best of all he could make sure his needs were fulfilled. After all, Dexter had the same sexual tastes as he did, a true friend. Stephan smiled. Even when the old bastard had died and his brother had attacked him for no good reason, Dexter had come to his rescue, and made sure no further harm had come to himself, a true friend.

As he sipped his whisky he thought about Sara Farthing, who he was sure would agree to marry him when he asked her. After all, he was a Lord and a future Duke, how could she refuse such an offer? Stephan admitted to himself she was a pretty little thing, Stephan had met her father at the club in Soho where Dexter and he had become members. The club catered to men with certain needs. Farthing was also a member. When Farthing mentioned he had a daughter Stephan had invited the Farthings and their daughter down for a weekend, which no doubt had pleased his mother and father; and just as Farthing had said, she was very compliant. She would do nicely: came from good stock, and would no doubt produce the mandatory heir to please his parents, plus he would soon have her broken like a good filly. He had tried a few times to bed her, but she was having none of it. She would eventually enjoy his advances, but for now he would wait until the wedding ring was on her finger and it was too late for her to back out of the arrangement. Now with his odious brother out of the way for the summer, Stephan finally closed his eyes and dreamed of his forthcoming trip to London with Dexter; he had promised Stephan a weekend of delights and pleasure. Dexter was a true friend.

ఈ·ఆ

As the plane was on its final approach, Grenville had his eyes tightly shut, and clung onto the arm rests trying not to panic. To say the flight had been rough was an understatement; since the pilot announced they were on their final approach into Belize International Airport, it was as if the gods were playing with the plane as a child does with a toy one. Finally, the wheels touched down with a bump, and Grenville could imagine the pilots looking at each other and smiling on a job well done. Grenville looked over at Jonathan, who still had his eyes shut, mumbling a silent prayer to whatever god was listening at the time. The plane finally came to a stop and over the speakers came, "British Airways would like to thank you for flying British Airways to Belize International Airport, it is three fifteen local time, and the weather is a warm thirty degrees, I hope you all have a pleasant stay, and hope to see you again when you fly British Airways. Please make sure you exit the aircraft with all your belongings, and have your passport ready for inspection at customs. Once again, thank you for flying British Airways."

As soon as Grenville stood on the top step of the ladder leading down to the ground to the waiting bus, the moisture was sucked from his body, and he started to sweat. The heat was intense and before he had reached the bottom step he was red-faced and breathing heavily. Grenville considered himself fit, but this heat just seemed to suck the life from him. Grenville looked over at Jonathan, who smiled and look just as bad as he did.

Boarding the bus to take them to the baggage reclaim and customs, Grenville was pleased the flight had not been packed, as being pushed into a metal tube like a load of sardines was not an appealing thought. Grenville and Jonathan sat at an open window, but as the bus moved off, realised the wind the bus's forward momentum was producing was not cooling, but producing more hot air which made them sweat even more. Grenville had only been in the country for twenty minutes, but he felt more tired than he had ever been in his entire life. The heat seemed to drain the body of moisture and energy, leaving him feeling lethargic.

Sitting waiting for their baggage, Jonathan said, "Glad you came."

"Will let you know if you have a career as a tour operator tomorrow," said a laughing Grenville. Eventually their backpacks arrived, and they went to stand in line for customs. Customs was not as big an ordeal as they first thought, the customs official looked bored and only glanced at the passports before waving them through without a smile or a word.

Outside the airport was a busy hectic place as all international airports are, but they finally found the taxi rank, and queued up for a taxi. Being third in line they did not have to wait for long. The taxi pulled up and the taxi driver jumped out and opened the boot. With a wide grin, he said, "Welcome to Belize," in English.

Grenville said, "Can you take us to the Hotel Americano?"

"Of course," said the grinning taxi driver. Both Grenville and Jonathan climbed into the back of the taxi, and realised as the windows were down there was no air conditioning; then again, air conditioning was the least of their worries, as the taxi had no seat belts either, and the reason the windows were down was that they had no handles.

Grenville thought this taxi in the UK would not have passed an MOT, or be allowed on the road with other traffic, let alone be licenced to carry passengers. Then again, he wondered if Belize had such things. This was the start of many amazing comparisons they both made daily. As the taxi pulled off into the traffic, they both quickly realised that indicators were not used in Belize; also, Grenville was sure the taxi driver had the brake wired into the horn, as they never slowed but honked a lot as they weaved their way through the heavy traffic.

Turning to Jonathan, Grenville asked, "So where did you find this hotel?"

"Well, I did not actually find it, it was recommended to me by a friend of a friend," replied Jonathan. Grenville stared out of the window at the city speeding past, and wondered for the first time if this trip had been a good idea.

As the taxi pulled up outside the Hotel Americano, Grenville noticed it was a large white marble imposing building, built in the American 1920s style. Jonathan paid the taxi driver, who assured them if they needed a city guide to ring the number on the card that he passed Jonathan.

Entering the building, the interior was decorated, as Grenville suspected, in the American 1920s style. It reminded Grenville of the early black and white Hollywood films. Before they both had a chance to get to reception, a man dressed as a 1920s-film star with a white tuxedo, black tie, hair creamed down, and a pencil moustache approached them. Grenville tried not to laugh, as he thought the man had watched Casablanca too many times.

"Welcome to the Hotel Americano," said the man. "I am Miguel, the manager and your host during your stay."

"Thank you," said Jonathan and Grenville, shaking Miguel's hand.

"Please, let us get you settled in," said Miguel, pointing to the reception desk.

At the reception desk, they both handed over their passports to register. The girl behind the desk was very proficient and its only took minutes to register. Miguel hoovered in the background while his receptionist registered them both. Once completed and both clutching their relevant room keys, Miguel showed them to the hotel lifts, all the time keeping up a running commentary on Hotel Americano. At the lift, just as Grenville suspected, there was a young man dressed in a purple suit, with a pill box hat sat at a rakish angle.

To both their surprise Miguel accommodated them into the lift, and said to the lift operator, "Fourth floor, if you please, Samuel," who replied, "Of course sir, please hold on gentlemen," as the lift proceeded to the fourth floor.

Stepping from the lift and thanking the operator, Miguel turned left towards their respective rooms. Miguel stopped at a door and turned to Jonathan and held out his hand for his key, which Jonathan handed over. Unlocking, he stood back to allow Jonathan to enter first. Turning to Grenville, Miguel once again held out his hand for the key, and repeated the process for Grenville. Miguel followed Grenville into the room. Grenville smiled. The room was large and airy, and the bed looked comfortable, but best of all he heard the deep humming of air conditioning, and felt the cold blast of air.

Turning to Miguel, Grenville said, "My dear chap this is exquisite, and will do me perfectly," in his best English upper class accent.

Miguel beamed his brightest smile, and bowed. "Glad to be of service, my Lord." This made Grenville smile. Passing Miguel, a folded Belizean ten-dollar note, Grenville said, "I am sure your establishment will be most welcoming." Miguel turned to see how Jonathan had fared; both Miguel and Grenville found Jonathan sitting on his bed with his head thrown back and his eyes closed.

Miguel gave a light cough, to which made Jonathan open his eyes and smile at them both.

"All OK?" said Grenville before Miguel had chance to speak.

All Jonathan said was, "Air con," which made them both laugh. Miguel stood looking at the two laughing Englishmen, not getting the joke. Jonathan stood and handed Miguel a folded Belizean ten-dollar note.

Miguel bowed again to Jonathan, and said, "Gentlemen if you ever require my assistance, please do not hesitate to let one of my staff know." Bowing again, Miguel turned and left the room.

"Well," said Grenville, "things are looking up."

"Very nice," said Jonathan.

"He seemed a bit attentive," said Grenville.

"Sorry," said Jonathan, "that might be down to me, he might have gotten the impression you were the Duke of Hampshire. When I booked the rooms, thought it might add some weight to a decent room," said a smiling Jonathan.

Grenville looked at Jonathan and smiled. "To get decent air con in the rooms, my old dear chap, you did the correct thing," said Grenville, mimicking his father's voice. Both rolled on the bed laughing.

"So, what you want to do now?" asked Jonathan.

"To tell you the truth old thing, I am rather tuckered. Could do with a few hours in the sack," replied Grenville.

Jonathan looked relieved. "I am so pleased you said that. I am tuckered myself."

"Good, then," said Grenville standing up, "speak to you later."

"Good, sound like a plan. Tomorrow we will explore this tropical land," said Jonathan, laughing.

"Indeed," said Grenville, as he closed Jonathan's door behind him.

⅚·⅛

Grenville awoke unsure of the time. His watch was still set on UK time; all he knew was that it was daylight, so that did not give him any idea. He sat trying to figure out the time zone difference between UK and Belize, when there was a light knock on his door. Grenville went across and opened his door on a refreshed looking Jonathan.

"Morning," said Jonathan, as Grenville stepped aside to allow him to enter.

"Sleep well?" asked Jonathan.

"Like the proverbial log," replied Grenville. "I was trying to work out the time."

"The UK are seven hours ahead of Belize, old man," said Jonathan.

"Knew you'd know, swot," said a laughing Grenville.

Grenville looked at his watch. "Give it here your useless, and let me change it for you," said Jonathan. Grenville took off his watch and handed it to Jonathan. Jonathan changed the time and handed it back to Grenville. Grenville looked at the time before putting it back on and noticed it was only seven thirty. "Morning," said Jonathan, as if he'd read Grenville's mind.

Grenville smiled and said, "Excellent, good chap. Think we should try and find some breakfast, I am famished."

"Same here," said Jonathan.

Grenville and Jonathan walked to the lift and pressed the button for down. In minutes the lift arrived, and the lift doors opened with a smiling Samuel. Samuel indicated for them both to enter the lift. Still smiling, Samuel asked, "Your destination, gentlemen?" which made Jonathan giggle.

"Wherever breakfast is being served, my good man," said Grenville.

Samuel saluted, closed the doors and pressed the down button. The lift stopped at the lobby and Samuel opened the door, and said, "Dining facilities to the right, gentlemen," pointing in the direction they needed to go. Thanking Samuel, they both made their way to the dining room.

They were met by a pretty girl dressed in a bright yellow dress. "Good morning, my dear," said Grenville, smiling.

The girl smiled back and said, "Good morning gentlemen, your room numbers please."

Both Grenville and Jonathan showed her their room keys, which made her smile. "This way please gentlemen," said the girl. Both followed her into a pleasant, well lit, clean dining room. Each table was set with a crisp white table cloth, cups and plates of white with cutlery. The girl showed them to a two-seater table near the back of the area. Once they were seated, she produced a pad and pencil from her pocket, smiled and said, "Tea or coffee?"

Both in unison they said, "Coffee."

The girl smiled, and said, "Cereal, milk, fruit juice and normal fruit on the table over on the right and on the left, are cooked items, if you want anything else please ask."

Just as she was leaving, Grenville asked, "What about toast?"

The girl said, "The breads at the end of the cooked items, toaster is there as well."

"Thank you," said Grenville to the departing girl's back. Within a few minute the girl returned with a large pot of coffee, milk and sugar. She placed them on the table between Grenville and Jonathan, and then departed without speaking.

"Shall I be mother?" said Jonathan, smiling.

Grenville nodded, while he looked the place over. "Not many in for breakfast," remarked Grenville.

"I would suppose as it's only seven-thirty, most other guests have already acclimatised to the time zone and come at a more leisurely time," said Jonathan, smiling.

"You could be on to something there," said a smiling Grenville.

After sipping their coffees, Grenville said, "Shall we go check out what Hotel Americano has to offer?"

"Absolutely, lead the way old chap," said Jonathan, standing. As they approached the hot food, Jonathan said, "Sure smells nice." The presentation of the food was top class; there were full English breakfast items, including kippers and black pudding.

"Just like home," said Grenville.

"Might be for your upper classes, but for us lowly middle classes its looks like heaven," replied Jonathan.

Grenville laughed. "You mean you don't breakfast like this every morning?" teased Grenville.

"Only when I visited your poor establishment," said Jonathan, laughing; on many occasions Jonathan, had been lucky to have been invited to Hampton Hall.

After a slow leisurely breakfast, both deciding to go back for seconds, and ordered another pot of coffee. They were deciding on what to do with their day. Jonathan sat and studied the tour guide he had purchased before leaving England. "Well, what you fancy?" he asked Grenville.

"To tell you the truth old boy, I am not really bothered," replied Grenville.

"You are not regretting coming, are you?" asked Jonathan.

Grenville smiled. "Not at all my dear chap, just this heat is a bugger, not used to it yet, leaving me feeling rather lethargic, if you know what I mean."

"Of course," replied Jonathan, smiling. "OK, let's just do a nice relaxing city tour on foot, until we get bored or tired and come back."

"Sounds like a plan, my dear Jonathan," said Grenville, smiling.

As they left the hotel the first thing they both noticed was the heat; even now this time of the morning it was stifling, and with no breeze it was soul sucking. They followed the street map Jonathan had; they leisurely strolled about the city exploring the sites, stopping now and again for a rest and to take in the sights. The place was busy. The pollution levels from traffic sometimes made them both feel unwell and they would stop at a road side café for a coffee or a cold drink.

They wandered up to the local market, which like any other market anywhere in the world was a hive of activity selling everything that could be imagined. Jonathan and Grenville both looked for gifts for home. Grenville was not surprised when Jonathan was in his element when he haggled over a price. Grenville decided to leave the negotiations to Jonathan; he told Jonathan what he would like and Jonathan went into action, normally coming away with a good price. Afterwards Jonathan told Grenville, "The art is not to show emotion, always keep your price in your head and remember as the buyer you are in the better position." Grenville was amazed at Jonathan and if the truth be told was always a little envious of his friend's oration talents. After the first day, it was Jonathan who took charge in the planning of their days; not a role he was used to, but Grenville was happy to allow Jonathan the lead.

One night they were sitting in the bar after dinner, when two Americans came in who they had become on nodding terms with.

"May we join you?" one asked.

Both Grenville and Jonathan stood, and Jonathan replied, "Please sit down, can I get you a drink?"

"Sounds good, two beers would be nice."

Jonathan waved at the barman and placed four fingers up, and got a wave back to say he had been understood.

"Let me introduce myself. I am Jonathan and this is Grenville," said Jonathan, holding out his hand.

"Tony and Josh," replied the Americans.

After they had all shook hand and the drinks arrived, Jonathan said, "We are from England."

"No shit Sherlock," said Tony, laughing. "We can tell by your accent, very British."

"I am from common stock, but Grenville here is from blue blood, the aristocracy," said Jonathan, slapping Grenville on the shoulder. "The son of a duke, no less."

Both Tony and Josh stared at Grenville, not sure what to say or do. Jonathan always loved the fact that one of his closest friends was blue blooded; he was never tired of telling people about Grenville, at times much to Grenville's embarrassment.

"So, what do we call you, your grace? My lord?"

"Please, it's just Grenville. My father is titled, I am only his second son and have no title, so please just plain Grenville."

Tony bowed his head in acknowledgement. "So, Grenville, what brings you to Belize?"

"Just a bit of an adventure while on summer break from university," said Grenville.

"Same here" said Josh.

"What part of the States you from?" asked Jonathan.

"Boston," replied Josh.

"Never been to the States," said Jonathan.

"Perhaps one day you will," replied Tony.

"You been anywhere interesting, since you've been here?" asked Jonathan.

"Yes, we've just come back from a three-day trip to a place called Punta Gora, it's down south of the country, on the coast, run down but friendly. You should try it," replied Josh, with Tony nodding in agreement.

"How you get there?" asked Grenville.

"Small island hopper plane," replied Tony. Grenville looked at Jonathan and saw him wince at the small plane part. Grenville smiled. Jonathan was beginning to dread travel.

"We stayed in a really nice B&B right on the beach, at high tide it comes right up to your door," said Josh.

"Sounds idyllic," said Jonathan.

"Cheap as well," said Tony.

"Isn't everything in this country?" laughed Jonathan. The other three agreed with Jonathan.

Tony ordered another beer, and saluted the Brits, to which Grenville said in his best accent, "To the colonies," which made everyone laugh.

Next day Grenville and Jonathan made their way down to the City Airport to see about a flight to Punta Gora. Both had decided to give it a go and have a break from the city and to spend some time on a beach would become a happy change for them both. At the airport, they managed to book a seat on the next available flight tomorrow morning leaving at nine am. "On the dot," said the man behind the counter, making it clear to them both that the plane would not wait. Obviously, they had had people book in the past and not show, so waiting was not an option they did anymore.

Jonathan and Grenville were at the City Airport by eight thirty, ready to go. Since breakfast Jonathan had not said a lot; then again Grenville noticed that Jonathan had had very little breakfast apart from a pot of coffee. A tall well-dressed man appeared dressed as a pilot with a cap on; he stood in front of them and said, "Flight BE125 to Punta Gora is ready for boarding," in a loud voice. Grenville looked around and there were only five people sitting in the reception area waiting for the plane, which made Grenville smile. "Please follow me," said the man, all five followed the tall well-dressed man out to a waiting Cessna two prop plane.

Grenville felt Jonathan tense next to him; Grenville leaned over and whispered to Jonathan, "Chin up, old bean." Jonathan just stared ahead, white faced. Grenville allowed the two women and one local man to board first, then they climbed into the seats behind the pilot, and were luckily enough to see out of the cockpit window.

The tall well-dressed man closed the cabin door, and then climbed into the cockpit. Placing on a pair of headphones and flicking a switch, over the speakers came his deep voice. "I am Captain Mercer, your pilot for this flight from the Belize City Airport to Punta Gora with Island Airways, which will take about approximately just over the hour mark depending on head winds. Please sit back and enjoy your flight."

"Not British Airways, is it," said Jonathan.

"Most definitely not, dear chap," replied Grenville. Just then Captain Mercer switched the engines on, and as the propellers started to turn he revved the engines. Once the engines were running idle and propellers were turning at their optimum speed, he removed the brake and the plane shot off down the runway like a released greyhound. Suddenly Captain Mercer pulled back the stick and the plane shot up into the air and turned south.

After a few minutes the plane seemed to idle back. Grenville finally opened his eyes, and looked over at Jonathan who still had his tightly shut and had gone a strange white colour. Grenville started to laugh. Jonathan opened one eye and said, "What?"

"You, you're a daft bugger," said Grenville.

"Nothing wrong with me old chap, just resting my eyes," replied Jonathan.

"Of course, you are, old boy," said Grenville, still laughing at Jonathan. And as predicted, just after an hour and an uneventful flight Captain Mercer came back onto the speakers to announce that they were descending into Punta Gora and would land in a few minutes. Grenville said, "Hang on dear chap, here we go," laughing and slapping Jonathan's arm. Jonathan remained with his eyes firmly closed and tight lipped.

After a bumpy landing at which even Grenville was feeling relieved once they finally came to a stop, whilst taxing to the staging area, Captain Mercer was on the speaker again. "Welcome to Punta Gora, and thank you for flying Island Airways, and we hope you will fly with us again in the future."

"So how was that for you?" said Grenville.

"Never again," replied a white looking Jonathan. Grenville was trying hard not to laugh at his friend.

Once the plane had completely stopped and the engines shut off, Captain Mercer climbed out of the plane and opened the doors for the passengers. At the exit gate Captain Mercer stood and saluted each of them with a wide smile on his face.

As he passed, Jonathan just gave a weak smile. Grenville shook Captain Mercer's hand and said, "Capital flying, captain," as he strolled out of the exit.

∞·୯3

They spent five wonderful idyllic days in Punta Gora, just lounging about on the beach and sitting in a bar on the beach front.

"You know this is the life," said Jonathan.

"Indeed, it is," replied Grenville. "If this is paradise I can certainly learn to live with it," Grenville went on.

"without a doubt", replied Jonathan, laughing. That evening whilst watching the waves crash the shore, over a tall glass of Jamaican rum, Jonathan said, "Well old bean, we better make our way back to Belize City."

"Do we have to?" said Grenville. "Can we not just remain here?"

"I wish we could old chap, but life states otherwise," replied Jonathan.

"So how do you want to get back to the city?" asked Grenville.

"Well, I've been thinking on that," replied Jonathan, "and I was thinking we could give the coach a try."

Grenville smiled, not wanting to cause his friend further embarrassment. Grenville said, "Why not. Another adventure." Jonathan looked at Grenville and smiled but Grenville could see the relief in Jonathan's eyes.

Next day they went to the bus depot and purchased two tickets for the coach to Belize City. The coach, they were informed, would not leave until one that afternoon, so they had a few hours to spare. Jonathan suggested going to a local bar and have a final drink to Punta Gora. Grenville thought this a fine idea, which seemed to lift both their spirits. They found a little bar just off the main road, near the waterfront. On entering the place, they noticed it was old, but clean.

Going to the bar, Grenville ordered two beers. Sitting at a table near the door, they studied the interior of the bar. The walls were covered with black and white pictures of Hollywood film stars from the forties and fifties; some were signed but Grenville doubted if any of them had ever been in this establishment. Looking around, there were only five others in the bar; the barman who was sitting watching a football match on a little television above the bar, three locals and one man sitting alone. Grenville tried not to stare at the man sitting alone, but there was something about his manner. Although he appeared to be relaxing having a beer, his body and his expression were on full alert, but he had the appearance of being in another world. Jonathan noticed the dart board in the corner and asked Grenville if he wanted a game.

"Why not, it will pass the time," said Grenville. Jonathan went to the bar and asked the barman if he had any darts. Jonathan returned with three different darts. Grenville smiled. "Just like the Black Bull," said Grenville.

Jonathan said, "They were the days," laughing. The Black Bull was the pub just in the village from Rayleigh School, and many a weekend in their last year they were found in the Black Bull playing darts or dominoes.

Jonathan went up to the board and threw all three darts at the board; two stayed in and one fell out. Grenville laughed, "You can do better than that, old fruit."

"Practice," said Jonathan. Jonathan handed the darts to Grenville. "Do your worst, my Lord," said Jonathan. Grenville managed to get all three into the board, but admitted it was nothing like the Black Bull's dart board.

"Shall I go first?" said Jonathan.

"lead on my dear chap," replied Grenville. "At least we have chalk," said Grenville, laughing as he held up a small round piece of chalk.

As the game progressed the three locals were taking an interest in the game, one approached and said, "You want a game of doubles?"

"Why not," said a smiling Jonathan.

Grenville and Jonathan looked at each other as the two locals produced their own darts from behind the bar.

"501, double to finish," said Jonathan.

"Agreed," said the local man. The local men won the first match and Grenville and Jonathan the second.

"Winner take all," said Grenville. The local men just stared at him as he smiled. Jonathan went first and threw twenty-three.

"Come on old man," said Grenville. Jonathan gave Grenville a weak smile; he perhaps had read the situation better than Grenville. The local threw forty-five, just missing the treble twenty with one arrow. "Bad luck old chap," said Grenville, smiling at the local man's miss.

Jonathan tried to get Grenville's attention to let him know that the locals were not impressed, but Grenville was impervious to the atmosphere; to Grenville it was a friendly game of darts with banter.

Grenville stood at the ockey and threw one hundred and put his arms in the air and said, "Yes."

The game progressed and only Grenville was impervious to the heightening tension the game was producing. Both teams were on finishing double. The local man went and just missed the double eighteen. As he went and took out his darts, Grenville smiling said, "Bad luck old bean." The local man did not smile back.

As Grenville went up for his throw he required double sixteen; before he threw Jonathan placed his hand on Grenville's arm and whispered, "Grenville, I think the locals are not impressed with your banter, I strongly suggest you miss."

Grenville waved Jonathan's arms off and said, "You worry too much, old man." Grenville threw his first dart which just landed below the double. Taking his time, Grenville threw again, and this time the dart landed in the double sixteen. Grenville threw up his arms in triumph.

In a flash one of the locals had pulled a knife and Grenville felt a sharp pain in his shoulder.

"Please, someone help us," Grenville said, and he collapsed to the ground. Out the corner of his eye Grenville saw the man who had been sitting alone move with lightning speed towards the man with the knife; he smashed his bottle over his head, and he went down in a heap. Using the momentum of his arm the man chopped the other local man on the neck. He fell just as quickly next to his friend. The other man just stood transfixed at what had happened.

The whole incident could not have lasted more than thirty seconds. The man said in a perfect London accent, "Grab your stuff and follow me if you want to live." Jonathan was the first to react, picking Grenville up, shoving his backpack into his arms, and saying, "Move, follow him," as Grenville and Jonathan stumbled from the bar in the wake of the stranger.

They followed the man down the street towards the jetty, where he jumped onto a small boat. He started the engine and said, "Jump aboard, and can one of you cast off." Grenville and Jonathan jumped aboard the boat and Jonathan casted off. The stranger revved the engine of the boat, and pushed the throttle forwards as the boat picked up speed away from the jetty. Jonathan and Grenville stared at the jetty where the three locals were standing and shouting and making arm gestures towards them.

Once they were out in the main stream of the river, the stranger kept looking back towards the jetty and after an a few minutes realising they were not being followed by another craft, he eased back the throttle to idle and let the river current move them along. Grenville and Jonathan were huddled in the back of the boat, still looking shocked at the turn of events. Minutes ago, they had been in a bar playing a friendly game of darts with two local lads, now they were sitting in a boat with a stranger going wherever.

The stranger came towards them and looking at Grenville and Jonathan he said, "My name is Tom Backer." Holding out his hand towards Grenville, he said, "Can I look at your shoulder? A knife wound in the tropics can become quickly infected if not treated."

Grenville stared at the smiling man who had just saved his life and introduced himself and said, "Grenville St Louis, eleventh Duke of Hampshire, second son," as they shook hands. "Blimey," said Tom, "that's a mouthful, I will call you Duke," to which they both laughed.

Sensing the tension broken, Jonathan shook Tom's hand as well and said, "Jonathan Spencer." Tom told Grenville to remove his shirt. Although there was a lot of blood the wound was not deep; Tom opened his first aid kit, and cleaned the wound with some antiseptic wash and then put some antiseptic cream on it and covered the wound with a large plaster.

"It will be sore for a few days, but no lasting problems," said Tom.

"Thank you so much," said Grenville.

"I have seen some pretty bad knife fights in my time, and most finish with one or the other dying for their wounds, so I think you should count your lucky star's duke," said a smiling Tom.

Grenville again thanked Tom for his help. Tom smiled and returned to steer the boat. Before he left, Jonathan asked Tom where he was from and Tom replied, "Originally the East End of London," but never ventured any other information.

Grenville closed his eyes.

"You in pain?" asked Jonathan.

"Not really, just relieved Tom was there to help us," replied Grenville.

"A true guardian angel," said Jonathan, smiling.

"Indeed, he was," replied Grenville, looking towards Tom.

After a time, Tom returned and said, "It will take about two or three days to get back to Belize City, once there I can drop you off anywhere you want." Jonathan and Grenville thanked Tom with a smile. Eventually the boat turned from the river into the ocean and headed towards Belize City. Jonathan spent the first day hanging over the side of the boat, feeling sorry for himself. Grenville decided to explore the boat. Below was a little cabin area, with a small kitchen and a single cot for sleeping, which could be turned into a small table with a bench. Grenville found the makings for coffee, and made everyone a cup of coffee.

Grenville offered the first mug to Jonathan, who just waved him away without opening his eyes. Grenville smiled at Jonathan. He was not really a good traveller, and he could imagine once Jonathan was back in England he would not be leaving it for a long time. Next Grenville took Tom a cup. When Tom saw the steaming cup of coffee he smiled, and said, "Well done Duke, just what the doctor ordered."

"My pleasure old bean," replied Grenville. "Do you mind if I sit and chat?"

"Of course, not," replied Tom, "glad of the company. How's your friend doing?"

"Not very well poor lamb, don't think he is going to buy a boat any time soon." This made them both laugh. On hearing his name, Jonathan gave a moan and waved his hand.

Grenville asked Tom, "What do you actually do, Tom?"

Tom replied, "Bit of import and export, you know."

Grenville was not sure what that meant but had decided Tom was a bit of a pirate. "How did you end up in Punta Gora?" asked Grenville.

"Was waiting for a contact," was all Tom would venture. Realising Tom was not going to offer any further details, Grenville smiled and let it rest.

After a two-day non-eventful trip, back to Belize City, Grenville had become a success in the galley and managed to produce some decent food for Tom and himself from the supplies he found in the galley. Jonathan did not partake in any substance. Finally, Tom guided the boat off the main route into a side part and docked at what appeared a deserted pier. "Home sweet home," said Tom, finally stepping onto dry land again.

Jonathan said, "Finally, terra firma," and walked down the pier in a zig zag line, to the laughter of Tom and Grenville.

They came to what looked like an abandoned single storey warehouse, which looked like it had had years of neglect. Tom went to a door and pushed it open. "Wait here," Tom said to Grenville and Jonathan and he went into the darkness.

"What you think?" said Jonathan.

"Don't know what you mean, old man," replied Grenville.

"Should we trust him?" asked Jonathan.

"Stop being paranoid Jonathan, if Tom wanted to harm us he would have done it on the boat while you were laid out like a sacrificial lamb," replied a laughing Grenville.

"That's not sporting, old chap," replied Jonathan. "Not very good with boats, not everyone can be Nelson," said a wounded Jonathan.

Just then the outside and interior of the warehouse was illuminated with bright light, and Tom shouted, "Come on in," from somewhere inside.

Grenville and Jonathan stepped into the warehouse and both got a shock to see it was totally different from the outside. The inside was neat and clean and laid out in two halves: one was a small apartment, the other one was stacked with crates of every size. Both Grenville and Jonathan went and sat on the sofa while they waited for Tom to return. Both were unsure where he was in the warehouse. While waiting, Grenville spotted the kitchen.

"Will make myself useful while we wait," said Grenville smiling at Jonathan. Grenville went to find the makings of a coffee. Just as Grenville finished making a coffee Tom returned. He smiled at Grenville as he handed him a steaming hot cup of coffee. Tom toasted Grenville with his cup, Grenville bowed and said, "Glad to be of service," which made them both laugh.

Jonathan looked at both Grenville and Tom and realised they were fast becoming friends. Jonathan admitted to himself he was feeling a bit put out, and felt left out.

"So where do you two want me to drop you off tomorrow?" asked Tom.

"Belize International Airport so we can catch a flight home, I guess," replied Jonathan. This brought a nod, but no comment from Grenville.

Next morning Grenville made breakfast of coffee, toast and eggs; the smell brought the other two into the kitchen area.

"Could get used to this," said a smiling Tom, as he thanked Grenville for breakfast. Tom said, "Will take me about twenty minutes to re-build the Jeep," which brought a surprised look from Grenville and Jonathan. Tom laughed and said, "Follow me." They both followed Tom outside to the back of the warehouse and there was an old rusty Jeep with two wheels up on bricks, no seats or steering wheel.

Grenville said, "You've been robbed, my old son."

Tom went on to explain that if you found a brand-new Jeep outside a derelict building you would snoop about, and nosy people are never friendly, Tom went on to explain that was why he left the place in the abandoned state, to deter uninvited visitors. Grenville and Jonathan both nodded in unison at the logic of his thinking. Grenville and Jonathan both helped Tom to re-build the Jeep which took no time at all. After they had finished they all stood back and Grenville and Jonathan admitted it looked in a better condition than it started.

Tom drove up a covered dirt track, eventually emerging onto a tarmac road. Turning left, they saw a sign that read "Belize City 10 miles." Tom drove fast and with skill through the busy streets of Belize City, eventually arriving at the International Airport. Tom parked in the Departure Drop Off point and turned off the engine. Tom turned to Grenville and Jonathan and said, "Belize International Airport, as requested," with a smile on his face.

Jonathan got out of the Jeep and picked up his backpack, and turned to Grenville who sat still. "Come on slow coach," said Jonathan.

"I am not coming," said Grenville, softly.

"What do you mean not coming?" said a laughing Jonathan.

Stepping from the Jeep, Grenville said, "Look, Jonathan,

what have I got to look forward to? It's not like I will be welcome with open arms."

"I don't understand," said Jonathan.

"It's simple, old bean. If Tom will let me, I am going to stay and have an adventure."

"Fine by me," replied Tom, smiling.

Jonathan looked from Tom to Grenville and smiled. "OK, Grenville, I understand. Come give me a hug," said Jonathan, laughing.

Grenville hugged Jonathan and slapped him on the back. "Do me a favour?" asked Grenville.

"Anything," replied Jonathan.

"Let my mother and father know I am OK and well. And if you see my brother, tell him he is still a prig."

Laughing, Jonathan said, "Of course dear boy, and I hope you find your adventure." With tears in his eyes, Jonathan turned towards the departure doors of the Belize International Airport.

Just as he was about to go through the automatic doors, Tom called and ran after him. "Jonathan, this is my PO box address, if you ever need to contact Grenville."

"Thank you, Tom, and please look after him, he is very precious to me."

"Of course, I will, I promise," said Tom. Jonathan shook Tom's hand and felt better about leaving his friend behind, but he knew he would be well looked after.

Grenville watched Jonathan disappear through the doors of the International Airport, and walk towards the British Airways departure desks, and wondered if he had done the correct thing. It had been done on the spur of the moment and he hoped he did not live to regret his decision.

"What was that about?" asked Grenville, nodding towards the departing Jonathan.

"I gave Jonathan my PO Box number with address, so if you are ever needed to be contacted you can be," replied Tom. This made Grenville feel a whole lot better, and he smiled as Tom drove away. "Got a stop to do on the way home," said Tom.

"Sure," said Grenville.

Tom stopped at a rundown apartment block that had no front door. "Better you stay in the Jeep, for now," said Tom. Grenville was just about to protest but Tom said, "Remember the bar," smiling. Grenville sat back folded his arms and had the look of being hard done by on his face. Tom, laughing, said, "Won't be long," and entered the building with no front door.

Grenville looked about and noticed he was being watched from a few places, but no one attempted to approach the Jeep. Grenville thought Tom could be right, he did feel safe sitting in the Jeep. Five minutes later Tom appeared jumped in the Jeep, and they were off again. Grenville said, "All sorted?"

"Well, my contact was not happy I did not make the pickup, but after I explained I was saving your royal arse, he will set it up again," said Tom.

Grenville turned red and said, "Sorry old chap."

Laughing, Tom said. "No sweat, Duke, only teasing you."

Over the next few days Tom explained to Grenville his life and work in Belize, to which all Grenville could say was, "Wow," and was shaking his head in amazement.

Grenville asked Tom if he could ask some questions just to get the picture clear in his mind, which made Tom smile and say, "OK, but only if I can ask some of mine," to which Grenville agreed.

After what seemed like an age, Tom and Grenville finally stopped asking questions, and they both realised the sun was setting and it was turning dark, so Tom moved over and turned on a side light which although did not illuminate the whole area, gave enough light to be practical.

Eventually Tom said, "God, Duke, I feel like I spent hours in a police integration room," which made them both laugh.

"Yes, but I noticed you only answered the questions you wanted to," said Grenville, smiling.

Tom said, "Let's get some sleep and start afresh in the morning," to which Grenville, smiling, agreed.

ℰ·ℭ

The next morning after a light breakfast, Tom said to Grenville, "Come sit down and let's start," which was making Grenville feel more pensive as time went on. Tom sat staring at Grenville for over ten minutes before finally saying, "First, we got to do something about your appearance. You look like a typical Englishman. Little Lord Fauntleroy, with all those lovely long curly locks." Grenville looked offended but did not say anything. "Plus," Tom went on, "We need to change your whole appearance. The whole Carnaby Street fashion look you have going on is not really going to blend in, especially the places we are going to frequent," which made Tom laugh, and Grenville feel gutted.

Tom went on to explain that if you looked and appeared rich, then most poor people will perceive you as rich; after all, the aristocracy had been getting away with it for years, plus no one noticed poorly dressed people as they all look the same. "You, my friend, in your present state, look like you are a typical English high-born ponce on a road trip," to which they both laughed.

Tom smiled at Grenville and said, "This is going to hurt you more than me," after which he started to cut Grenville's hair. All Grenville could do was close his eyes and think how Mrs Preston would be happy, which made Grenville smile.

After some time, Tom stood back and admired his work and said, "Go look at the new you." Grenville went over to the mirror and hesitantly peered at the new person staring back at himself.

Tom had cut Grenville's hair down to the scalp and coloured it, so it was no longer blond but more a dirty brown. Even Grenville was impressed; he looked a different person. Tom said, "Put some dirt on your face and you will blend in perfectly." Next Tom told Grenville to strip. He then threw Grenville some scruffy jeans and a T-shirt which Grenville immediately tried to protest at, but Tom stood firm and told him once again he needed to blend in. Grenville sighed and realised his parents would have a fit if they saw such dress on their son, but he dressed quickly.

Tom passed him a pair of trainers that had seen better days, and after Grenville had put these on he did a twirl and said, "How do I look?" to which Tom replied, "Not like a stuck-up toffee nose English school boy, that's for sure," which made them both laugh.

Tom looked at Grenville and said, "Just one more thing." Tom moved to a large box, and opening the lid, rummaged for a few minutes before emerging with something rolled up. Passing it to Grenville, Grenville realised it was a webbing belt with a large sheathed knife.

Grenville pulled out the knife, and said, "You have got to be joking," and Tom said, "For protection," but Grenville was not convinced. Putting the belt on and feeling the heavy knife on his hip, he did admit it made him feel a lot bolder and more confident about the place, better in fact since he had arrived in the country all those weeks ago,

After a light lunch, Tom gave Grenville a tour of the warehouse. Apart from the living area, Tom showed him the "control room". Grenville was amazed at the setup: there were twelve monitors, all with different views of the outside and inside of the building, covering the landing pier where the boat was tied up to the road they used to go to the city. Tom explained that in his world it was never a good thing to be caught unawares and a golden rule was "always have a plan". He also showed Grenville the security precautions of the building. The whole building was rigged with explosives ready to blow if compromised, also there were pressure and laser sensors all around the perimeter all fitted with silent alarms connected to a portable device Tom had in his pocket. So, if they had been away and before they arrived back, Tom would know if any intruders had been about or were lying in wait for them. Grenville was impressed at the layout; what first appeared to be a rundown derelict warehouse was in fact a highly technical advanced hideout. Lastly Tom showed Grenville the many products he had stored in all the boxes. Grenville was impressed and said, "Harrods would be so jealous," which made them both laugh out loud.

Next day Tom beckoned Grenville over to the centre of the carpet, and said, "Duke, I think we need to teach you some basic self-defence." Grenville looked at Tom with a worried look on his face. Smiling, Tom said, "Don't worry, I will go easy with you." Grenville still did not look convinced. "Come and punch me," said Tom.

Grenville looked shocked. "Really, old man, I could not do that."

"Listen Duke, I will only tell you this once, the people we are going to be associating with and meeting are dangerous men. They have no morals or honour, there are no rules, and they will not hesitate to destroy you or in some extreme cases kill you if they see weakness in you, or think you are not what you are meant to be."

Grenville moved towards Tom with his hands held up, Tom put his hands on his knees and started to laugh. "Come on Duke, Queensbury rules or what, you learn that stance at public school?"

Grenville felt anger flare up in him and rushed Tom, and tried to punch him, but he punched fresh air. Grenville found himself flat on his back with Tom sitting on top of him. Tom leaned in close and whispered in his ear, "Rule number one, never attack in anger."

Getting off and helping Grenville to his feet, Tom said, "OK, come at me again." This time Grenville made a serious attempt to hit Tom, but once again found himself flat on his back with Tom on top of him, Tom leaned in close and whispered in his ear again. "Rule number two, always mean it, this is a matter of life and death." Standing and helping Grenville to his feet again, Tom said, "Again." This time Grenville moved in a slow circle around Tom, with Tom following him. Suddenly Grenville rushed and found himself back on his back in a blur, with Tom sitting on top of him again. Tom leaned in close and whispered in his ear for the third time, "Rule number three, never let your opponent know your move." Tom helped Grenville to stand up again.

Grenville stood and brushed himself down, looking despondent.

"Duke sit down for a minute", after a pause Tom quietly said "I do not expect you to become a ninja warrior overnight, let me explain something to you, after my family were killed I was consumed with rage and vengeance, I was not thinking straight I was in a dark place surrounded by grief, and I took my Uncle's Ship to Belize to hunt down the people who had killed them", "sorry I never knew", said Grenville, smiling Tom continued "I was oblivious by what people were advising me, and yes I had the backing of my Uncle and the Bratva behind me but all I could focus on was I needed to prepare myself for the following days to come, what I could not rationalise was the fact what did I know about bring vengeance to professional agencies. Yes I wanted revenge when Sebastian was killed, and after my uncles was hospitalised I promised him out of a sense of family honour and commitment to join him in Bratva, and I guess I knew to achieve this I had to became ruthless in my pursuit for those that had killed Sebastian I had to become my Uncles Top Enforcer, but this was because of my family connections, and using my intellect and my ability to enforce allegiance within the organisation, not by what I knew, Natasha understood this and supported me as she was burning with vengeance as well over the death of her brother, and I am sure if she could she would have sought those that had killed him herself", "I am sure she knew what I was getting into but her sense of loss blurred her normal rational thinking", Tom smiled again before continuing "She once told me Family is everything, I never understood this until after she was killed.

So I arrived in Belize full of rage but with family contacts, I met Max, Max was a great help found me this place" said Tom holding out his arms, After a few weeks I had reached the bottom of my depth of despair and had the realisation that while I was in this black abyss, I was inadequate to move forward with the up and coming tasks, yes I had vision and rage to drive me forward, but the actual tools to carry out my plan, I was seriously lacking in practical attitude, Max understood family and the loss I had suffered so Max introduced me to an old man from the small island of Shikoku who was from the Kosa cast of warrior monks, and he eventually agreed to become my master and mentor.

He started off by sitting me down and asking me why I wanted to be trained so I told him about my family and their deaths, he first told me "remember your greatest asset is your mind", I will teach you to become a focus and skilled warrior, but the hard work must come from you and your focus, as we progressed he taught me the three golden rules of combat "Rule one, never attack in anger Rule two, always mean it, this is a matter of life and death Rule three, never let your opponent know your move". With these three guiding principles, he taught me over the months and years how to attack and defend in all forms of hand combat and weaponry, he was a hard task master and a professional in everything he taught me, the underlying principle in any situation is use you mind and remain focus in the task at hand, never let the situation become clouded by emotion always fight with clarity. Smiling Tom said "I don't think in all the time we spend with each other I never saw him angry", Grenville smiled and said "sounds like an impressive chap", smiling Tom replied "that's the point Duke he never did look all that much and you would most probably at your own peril ignore him".

"That was what I came to understand as his greatest asset, he once told me "it is not the roaring lion you have to fear but the quiet one in the background", "become the grey man". Those that have bluster and bravo do so to hide their true nature", never fear them, they are not a threat the man who stands in the shadows looking on is your true enemy". Smiling Grenville said "I think I understand Tom", smiling Tom said "I hope so Duke because in the weeks to come we will meet both types and it is important you recognise them".

"Look, Duke, I am not expecting you to be Bruce Lee in a few lessons, I just want you to be safe," said Tom, smiling.

Grenville looked at Tom and did not see mockery in his eyes but only concern. Grenville smiled back and said, "Sorry, let's try again."

Over the next few weeks, Tom took Grenville through a basic self-defence course, showing him both defence and attack techniques, without weapons and with weapons. Grenville was unsure he could strangle someone with his bare hands, but did not mention this to Tom. Tom took his teaching very seriously so Grenville did as well. Grenville always remembered the first lesson, and if Grenville was not taking it seriously Tom would grab his arm, and throw him over his back, and knocked the wind out of Grenville. It was to remind Grenville they were not playing games, and this was real life and death, and Grenville was left under no illusion that Tom would expect him to uphold his end.

One day, after they had finished for the day, and were sitting under the front porch watching the sun go down, having a beer, Tom said, "Well, I think you are about ready, Duke."

"You think so?" asked Grenville.

"Yes, I think you can hold your own, and look after yourself. Plus, we need to go back to Punta Gora and drop off the merchandise I failed to do last time, before I got distracted and saved your arse. But I am confident you can hold up your end," which made Grenville blush, but he knew Tom was joking, as he was laughing.

Grenville looked at Tom and in his most serious face, held out his hand and said, "Tom, thank you."

"What for?" said Tom.

"For allowing me the privilege of entering your world and sharing it with you, you have also given me the knowledge to be part of your world."

Tom looked at Grenville's face and said, "Oh my god, don't go all mushy on me now," which broke the tension in the air and Tom took the offered hand then slapped Grenville on the back and said, "Beer, my Lord?"

Tom walked Grenville through the security systems and fall back sites – all stacked with enough equipment for a clean getaway if required – until he knew them off by heart, even in the dark. Tom gave Grenville a final test during the day and at night, before declaring Grenville was ready. Tom was impressed by how quickly Grenville had become accustomed to the procedure, but as Tom explained so many times over the last few weeks, "always have a plan" and "sloppy people end up dead people." Grenville wondered why Tom needed such elaborate security, but he did not ask his question. Grenville knew Tom well enough by now that once he was ready he would tell him the truth.

⃝·⃞

Tom and Grenville made sure the warehouse was set ready for their return, and headed down towards the boat. Once on board Tom started it up and Grenville cast off, and before long Tom was navigating towards the busy river estuary and heading out to sea towards Punta Gora. On the way down Tom taught Grenville how to navigate the boat, and after a few days even Tom was impressed at how quickly Grenville had become proficient with the boat.

On the trip down Grenville was feeling apprehensive as the miles went past; he was not looking forward to re-visiting Punta Gora again, after all last time he had nearly died there, but after two uneventful days at sea, they finally made their way up the tidal river towards Punta Gora. Finally, Tom stopped at the jetty, and Grenville jumped off and tied up. Tom looked over at Grenville, and said, "Don't worry, not even your own mother would recognise you, let alone some bar scumbag," which brought a smile to Grenville's mouth, but not to his eyes.

They both made their way up to the local bar, which several months before Grenville and his friend had been entertaining the locals in. Just before they entered, Tom turned to Grenville and whispered, "Better leave the talking to me," which brought just a nod from Grenville. Tom scanned the bar and noticed only two tables occupied; no one raised their heads when they walked in.

Tom went to the bar and ordered two beers, and placed a ten dollar note on the counter which was swiftly removed by the bar keeper in case Tom changed his mind. Grenville turned and headed to the corner table, and Tom smiled and thought, Grenville was learning.

Over the cold beer, Tom and Grenville re-scanned the bar and Tom explained to Grenville, "Always look at the person behind the bar. If they seem relaxed then probably all is well, if they look agitated then it's time to leave."

Grenville noticed the man behind the bar looked bored, or was one hell of an actor. Eventually the bar door opened and two men walked in; one walked straight up to Tom and Grenville's table and sat down and smiled, the other stood by the bar watching. The man said, "You have the merchandise?" Tom nodded and the man stood and turned. The man beckoned them to follow him. Tom and Grenville stood and followed the man, who was joined by the man from the bar, out of the door.

They followed the two men down a dirt track between several shacks. Grenville noticed women and children peering out of the windows as they passed by. Eventually the two men stopped outside a gated yard; just then, a man carrying a gun slung over his shoulder walked across and opened the gate. The two men beckoned them both in. Tom and Grenville followed the men to a side door which was opened for them and they all went inside; the inside was well lit by Florence lighting. A big man in greasy overalls approached and smiled at them, and said, "Shall we do business?" to which Tom lifted his shirt up and removed a belt with several pouches; he then opened and placed the merchandise on an old upturned oil drum.

The big man looked at the merchandise and smiled. With a quick nod of his head, someone from the shadows stepped forward and placed four large plastic bags wrapped in black tape next to the merchandise. Tom quickly took two of the packages and handed them to Grenville and he took the other two, and smiled at the man and said, "Nice doing business with you." Tom was about to turn and walked back toward the open door when the large man said, "You not going to check it, you trust me?" and laughed; this brought on a laugh from the rest of the room. After the laughter, had died down but before the large man had stopped, Tom leaned over and looked at the man and softly said, "If it's not right, I will be back." The man stopped laughing as something in Tom's eyes and manner made him realise this was a very dangerous individual who one didn't cross.

Tom turned and nodded at Grenville to follow. Just then, one of the men grabbed Grenville's arm and bringing his face close to Grenville's, he said, "You sure we not met before?" to which Grenville leaned in and with the fiercest face he could muster said, "Don't think so, and I suggest you try mints," which the man looked puzzled at, but before he had time for a reply Grenville grabbed his hand and twisted it off, and he followed Tom from the building.

Both Tom and Grenville walked quickly, but not appearing to rush back to the boat, closely followed by the two men from the bar. At the boat, Tom jumped aboard and quickly started the engine and Grenville cast off. Grenville did not breathe until he was sure the gap between the boat and the jetty was too big for anyone to jump into the boat.

Once back in the river, Tom asked Grenville, "What was that about?" and Grenville answered, "One of the men from the darts match."

"Oh, I see," said Tom, and was still laughing an hour later.

After a hassle-free trip, back to the warehouse, both Tom and Grenville felt exhausted, and both decided once they had dropped off the packages they would have a few weeks' rest. A few days later, while Tom and Grenville were lazing under a big tree not far from the warehouse, Grenville asked, "How do you know you have a job on?" to which Tom replied, "Follow me."

Tom led Grenville up the trail, to the road. Tom stopped short of the opening to the road, and pointed across the road at a tree, and explained, "When there is a coloured ribbon around that tree, we have a message, so you only need to wander up until you can see the tree, so as not to arouse any suspicion from passing traffic."

"Neat," said Grenville and they both turned back towards the warehouse. Grenville and Tom took it in turns twice a day to check the tree, and after a month a blue ribbon was fluttering on the cool breeze late one afternoon.

∞ · ∞

Driving into town the next day, Grenville asked Tom, "Don't you ever get curious at what you are transporting?" to which Tom replied, "No, I told you curious people are dead people. As long as I get paid I don't care, it's just business."

At the same run-down building, Tom parked the Jeep and they both entered and went up one flight of stairs to a door at the far end of a corridor, knocking once on the door, and after a minute or so the door was opened slightly with the chain still across, and a face appeared and studied them both for a few seconds. The door closed and then re-opened fully to allow them to enter.

Sitting at a table with a cigar stub hanging from the corner of his mouth sat a man who Grenville thought looked like every picture he ever imagined of a Mexican bandit. He smiled and stood and held out his hand and said, "Mr Tom, welcome."

Tom shook his hand and said, "Max, this is Duke, my friend," to which Max smiled at Grenville and held out his hand and said, "Welcome Mr Duke, a friend of Mr Tom's is always welcome in my home." Grenville shook Max by the hand, before both being offered the chairs opposite Max.

Max asked if they both wanted some refreshments; both declined. Max smiled and said, "Mr Tom, always business with you." Max said something to Tom in a language that Grenville did not recognise, but Tom spoke it back to Max like a natural. After some ten minutes of dialogue, Max stood and went into a side room and returned with a large brown envelope and placed it on the table. Max and Tom spoke some more, and Grenville could tell by Max's voice, as he sounded more stressed as he went on, that he was not happy about this.

Eventually Tom and Max stood and shook hands. Grenville stood also and shook the offered hand from Max. As they both turned to leave, Max said to Grenville, "Please make sure Mr Tom is careful, I can tell you are a good friend of his, tell him not to take risks." Grenville nodded and followed Tom from the building and back to the Jeep.

After a silent drive, back, Grenville noticed Tom was deep in thought and did not want to bother him; he knew he would explain once he was ready.

Next day when Grenville woke, he was surprised to find Tom missing. After checking the control room monitors, he was nowhere to be seen; everything else looked all in place, the boat, the Jeep, the perimeter. Just then he spotted on one of the monitors a few boxes being moved at the very end of the warehouse, so Grenville went to investigate. Tom was moving boxes, looking for something.

Grenville asked, "Can I help?" to which Tom replied, "I got it covered," so Grenville shrugged and went to make some coffee. After a time, while Grenville was sitting drinking his coffee, Tom returned carrying a crate which, by the way he moved, looked heavy.

Tom placed the heavy crate on the table and sat down. "OK, I know you are dying to know what's going on," to which Grenville replied, "I was wondering."

Tom explained he had known Max since he had arrived from Russia and was not only his contact but was family. They were speaking Russian yesterday. Tom explained that Max did not only get import/export contracts for him, he also tracked people down and the new name was making Max nervous, as the man with his contacts was extremely dangerous. So, he tried to persuade Tom to forget it. Tom said, "How hard can it be, only dropping in for a chat?" Grenville wondered what form of a chat Tom had in mind.

Next day, Tom said, "We are going on a field trip."

"Excellent," replied Grenville. Tom and Grenville took the boat towards the busy City Marina to fill the boat with fuel. Also, Tom filled several jerry cans, paying in cash. Tom and Grenville were once again heading for the open sea.

During the trip down coast, the large crate that Tom & Grenville had manhandled on board was sitting in the middle. Every time Grenville went past he either caught his toe or knee, which always brought a laugh from Tom after Grenville's profanities, and Tom would always say the same thing: "Language, my Lord," which made him laugh more and Grenville swear more.

After two days of keeping to the coastline, Tom finally turned the boat towards the coast. Grenville noticed he was heading towards a small tributary. Cutting the engine, Tom allowed the boat to drift into the small river mouth and once out of sight of the sea, Tom let the boat ground on the shore. Tom smiled at Grenville and said, "We will camp here," to which Grenville nodded and went to put the kettle on.

Later that night, Tom explained to Grenville that they were meeting a container ship and the man he wanted to talk to was on it. Still smiling, Tom said, "Nice and easy," which still gave Grenville a bad feeling in the pit of his stomach.

While Tom was getting some sleep, Grenville decided to look in the large crate they had manhandled on board. Slipping the locks Grenville opened the crate, and using the light of the moon, looked inside. Grenville was astonished to see it full of weapons and assorted battle-ready equipment, enough to start a small war. Grenville quickly closed the lid and went to lie down. Grenville wondered why Tom would want so much firepower.

Tom watched Grenville open the crate and smiled; he's getting good, I must admit, thought Tom as he closed his eyes again. Next morning over a cup of coffee, Tom was scanning the horizon with a pair of binoculars when he said, "Find what you were looking for last night?"

"Sorry?" said Grenville.

"Last night," said Tom, "in the crate."

"I see," said Grenville, "sorry old man, could not resist. Apologies and all that," looking rather sheepish.

"You only had to ask," said Tom, smiling.

Just as Tom was about to speak again the radio squawked, and Grenville was sure it was Russian being spoken. Tom quickly answered, in the same language, and smiled at Grenville. "On for tonight."

"Deep joy," said Grenville, still feeling uncomfortable.

"So," said Grenville, looking serious, "what do you want me to do?"

Tom said, "Just pilot the boat out to the cargo ship. Wait for me to return."

"And if you don't?" said Grenville with his most serious face, which Tom replied, "Well, Duke, my old flower, you got a bitch of a trip back home without me," and laughed. Grenville laughed as well, but did not see anything funny in it.

Once it had got dark, Tom dressed all in black with his face also covered with black camouflage, opened the crate and put on a combat style vest; also, a double pistol holster, which he placed after checking two hand guns; two thigh holsters with two more checked hand guns in; two short snub machine guns which Tom slung over each shoulder; and finally, he picked up a single short barrel pump action shot gun. "How do I look?" said Tom, smiling.

"Deadly," said Grenville, only seeing Tom's flashing teeth in the moonlight.

"OK," said Tom, "this is what I want you to do. When the cargo ship anchors off the coast, motor out to it, but before you get there, cut the engine, and drift into the ship; you will be watched from the ship. They should lower a ladder down to you, so drift towards it, but take your time. As by then I will have slipped over the side and up the anchor chain onto the ship."

After midnight, Tom and Grenville were watching the ocean for the ship. Eventually a large black object came slowly into view, not more than a mile from their position; they both heard the screw of the ship, and eventually they heard the anchor being slipped and falling into the sea. Tom slapped Grenville on the back and said, "Ready?"

"Not really," said Grenville.

"Don't worry," said Tom, "do your part and all will be fine."

"OK," said Grenville, before switching on the engine and pushing the throttle to forward and slowly manoeuvring the boat towards the large black object stationary at sea.

As Grenville steered the boat towards the cargo ship, Tom was crouched down in the boat. Grenville headed toward the ship, passing under its great arched front. Once level with the ship's anchor chain, Grenville put the boat into idle and let if drift down the side of the ship. Grenville did not hear Tom leave the boat; he was concentrating too much on not hitting the ship with the boat to worry about anything else.

The boat finally came to a halt halfway down the starboard side of the ship, gently kissing the side of the ship with the boat. Grenville felt pleased with himself; he was more than apprehensive about his ability to do what Tom had asked of him, but now he was in position, he felt so relieved.

As Tom, had said, the ship lowered its side ladder; Grenville slowly drifted the boat towards the ladder. As Grenville waited, he tried to see the name of the ship but from where he was it was too dark to make out; as the minutes ticked past, the tension mounted and became anxious. Grenville was sure he heard a soft muffled explosion and gun fire, but was not sure. After thirty minutes while waiting in the dark under the looming ship, Grenville's mind started to ask questions he knew he should not be asking at a time like this. Finally, Grenville said out loud, "Stop it now, you are being stupid, get a grip," to which a voice behind him said, "Talking to yourself is the first sign of madness."

Grenville must have jumped about three feet in the air, as standing there was Tom with a smiling face. "Bloody hell old man, talk about give a poor chap a heart attack."

"Sorry," said Tom.

"Everything alright?" asked Grenville.

"Perfect," said Tom, "let's go home," which Grenville acknowledged with an, "Aye aye captain," and a mock salute, before turning on the engine and pushing the throttle to full and heading back towards Belize City and home. As they were moving away, the cargo ship had already started to pull up its anchor and the ladder and start its engines again.

ꙮ · ꙮ

On the way, back, Grenville asked Tom what happened on the ship.

"Well," said Tom, "first I had a chat with my uncle Ivor, the captain of the ship which is called the Red Star, then a chat with the man in cabin four, who told me everything I needed to know before I killed him."

"You killed him? You said you were going to just chat," was all Grenville could say.

Tom smiled. "Did I? Well, sometimes we start out chatting and then they stop, so they must die. Uncle Ivor will dump the bodies once he is out at sea."

"Bodies?" said Grenville.

"Well, this particular gentleman had three bodyguards, who would have objected to me chatting to their employer."

"So, you killed them and only chatted to one man before you killed him," asked Grenville.

"Yes," was all Tom said.

Grenville nodded and said, "Blimey," whilst staring out of the boat's window pretending to steer the boat, all the time realising that what Tom had just told him was not really a shock anymore, knowing Tom as well as he did now. He saw Tom in a new light and respected him more, but still had a thousand burning questions.

Once they had docked and everything had been stored away and they were back in the warehouse, Grenville was making a coffee and Tom shouted over, "We will go and see Max tomorrow and check the mail box," to which Grenville replied, "Sounds like a plan."

"Oh yes, got us a present," said Tom, throwing Grenville the large over-stuffed backpack.

"Splendid, love presents," said Grenville. Grenville caught the large backpack, and was surprised at how heavy it was. Slowly Grenville opened it and looked in. His eyes nearly popped out of his head as he looked up from the backpack towards Tom, who was laughing.

"See, not a total lost trip, was it?"

Grenville could not believe his eyes as he tipped the entire contents of the backpack on the table. Both stared at the pile of money on the table. "How much you think is there?" asked Grenville.

"Not sure," said Tom, "it's all in difference currencies, so hard to judge."

Grenville just sorted out the English and American, as he recognised the dollars. After a time, he whistled. "500,000 English pounds, and 300,000 US dollars, and if the rest are the same amounts, depending where you exchange them, this is a small fortune," said Grenville, smiling.

Grenville then spotted a large brown pouch that was hidden in the pile of money; taking the pouch, he opened it and for the second time that day was speechless. Tipping the contents of the pouch on the table as well, it formed a heap of pure cut diamonds which sparkled in the sunlight. Grenville just stared at the diamonds, and finally said, "I don't think I have ever seen so many diamonds in one place, not even the queen of England owns this many." Tom laughed, and finally Grenville raised his head and howled, which made Tom laugh even louder.

Tom extracted Max's commission from the money, and placed them in a small backpack. The rest Tom placed in an old battered safe in the Communications Room.

On the drive into Belize City, Grenville turned to Tom and said, "This killing lark is quite lucrative," which made Tom smile.

"I am not in it for the money," said Tom, which made Grenville's brain turn somersaults with theories.

After leaving Max, Tom and Grenville drove to the post office to collect the mail from the PO Box; also, Tom paid the rent for the next six months on the box while they were there.

Once back at the warehouse, Tom was flicking through the pile of mail, when he stopped and said, "Oh this is for you, Duke."

Grenville looked puzzled. "Me, how strange."

Grenville did not recognise the writing on the envelope, which made the mystery even greater. Grenville opened the letter and then stood and went outside.

∓·∔

The Duke and Duchess of Hampshire were sitting in the reading room. "I've been a bloody fool" said the Duke to his wife.

The Duchess took his hand and said, "It was not you my darling, he is our son."

"I know, my love, but I cannot understand why he is acting in this manner," said the Duke.

"I cannot either," smiled the Duchess.

"Why does he hate us so?" asked the Duke.

"You know Stephan, he marches to the beat of his own drum," said the Duchess.

"We have given him everything and he is still hell bent on destroying the family," said the Duke, putting his head in his hands. The Duchess felt so sorry from her husband; for the life of her she could not understand her son's attitude and why he was so determined to destroy his own family. This, she knew, was the thing that hurt her husband the most, knowing his own son was going to destroy the family name after countless generations.

Sofia could not understand why her eldest son had no feeling for the family name as if it meant absolutely nothing to him, and this was making her husband ill, which was more of a concern to her. She had tried so many times to engage and make her son understand what he was doing to his father and the estate, but last time he sat and laughed at her and for the first time in her life she felt like slapping him hard across the face.

Just then Preston knocked and opened the door. "Yes, Preston," said the Duchess, smiling.

Preston bowed and said, "The Chief Constable, your Grace."

Still smiling, the Duchess said, "Please show him in, Preston."

The Duke and Duchess both stood. The Duke said, "Wonder what Giles could want." As the Chief Constable entered, the Duke approached with his hand out and said, "Giles nice to see you again, how are things?"

"I do apologise, your Grace, for the untimely intrusion, but I have grave news," said the Chief Constable, shaking the Duke's hand. The Duke beckoned him to an arm chair and sat back down next to the Duchess. The Chief Constable looked at both the Duke and Duchess and said, "I do apologise but I am the bearer of terrible news for you both about your son."

Both the Duke and Duchess looked at each other without speaking, and if the truth be known they both had harboured the same horror on hearing bad news about their second son, Grenville, after all he had been away so long now and they knew that bad news would eventually arrive. The Duchess said, "We appreciate you coming to inform us about Grenville." The Duke nodded.

The Chief Constable said, "Sorry, you do not understand, it is Stephan I am here about, not your other son," he said quietly.

The Duke and Duchess took each other's hands and the Duke said, "Please continue, Giles."

"I am here to inform you that Stephan was in a major road traffic accident on the road leading to the estate and I am sorry to say he was pronounced dead at the scene by the emergency services," said the Chief Constable.

"What happened?" said the Duke quietly.

"Apparently with the initial findings at the accident scene, it looks like he was speeding, swerved to avoid something, maybe an animal, due to the wetness of the road skidded and lost control and hit a tree."

"Oh dear," said the Duchess.

"Was anyone else involved?" asked the Duke.

"He had his fiancée in the car, Miss Sara Farthing," said the Chief Constable.

"Was she injured?" asked the Duchess, looking concerned.

"Apparently just minor scrapes and a few minor bruises, she has been taken to Southampton General Hospital, along with the body of your son," said the Chief Constable.

"We must go and see Sara," said the Duchess, standing up.

The Chief Constable stood as well. "Of course, and we would ask if you could formally identify the body of your son," he said quickly, "just for the official paperwork."

The Duke stood and shook the Chief Constables hand and said, "Thank you Giles, I understand these situations are never easy."

"I do apologise for the intrusion and once again please can I offer my condolence on your sudden loss," said the Chief Constable before he left the room.

The Duke looked at the Duchess and could see in her eyes her loss. They both embraced and started to cry. Eventually, the Duchess said, "Now we must go and see Sara."

"Yes, of course," said the Duke, striding from the room. Over his shoulder, he said, "I will go fetch Newton."

The Duchess watched her husband depart and thought to herself, poor James, he must be in a terrible place, he is going to mourn the loss of his son, but on the other hand try and not show the relief he would feel over it. She also felt the loss of her child but could not really feel bitter loss that a mother should feel.

Taking a deep breath, she walked from the room to join her husband and let the staff know their loss, but she was sure no one in the hall would mourn.

ᘒ · ᘓ

On the drive, down to Southampton General Hospital the Duke and Duchess did not speak, both lost in their own worlds, trying to come to terms with the turmoil of the event. Eventually they arrived at the hospital.

"Should not be too long, Newton," said the Duke.

Newton saluted and said, "Will be here when you are finished, your Grace."

Arm in arm, the Duke and Duchess went into the hospital and were directed to Sara's room. On seeing Sara, the Duchess looked concerned; Sara lay with her eyes closed, and her face and arms were covered in deep blue bruises. As they approached Sara opened her one good eye and tried to smile.

Smiling back, the Duchess said, "How are you feeling, my darling?"

In a soft whisper, Sara said, "Feeling lucky." The Duchess was unsure if this was because of the accident or the death of her son.

"Do you need anything?" asked the Duke.

"No, mother and father are on their way," said Sara.

"Well, we won't stay long," said the Duchess, smiling.

"Thank you for coming," said Sara, smiling.

"Do you remember anything?" asked the Duke.

Sara shook her head and said, "Everything is a blank."

"You know about Stephan?" asked the Duchess.

"Yes, they told me at the scene," said Sara.

Patting her hand, the Duchess said, "Well when you are up for it, please visit us both."

"Absolutely," said the Duke, smiling.

"Thank you, you have always been so kind to me," said Sara, closing her eyes.

The nurse who was hovering said, "I think she has had enough for now."

"Of course," said the Duchess.

"If she needs anything, please let us know," said the Duke as they both left the room.

Once in the corridor they were met by a Doctor. "Your Graces," he said, smiling.

The Duke said, "Is there a problem with Sara?"

"No, not at all, she is on the mend, should be up and running in a day or two and the bruising will fade quickly," said the doctor smiling.

"That's good news," said the Duchess, smiling.

"How can we help?" asked the Duke.

The doctor said quietly, "I am here to escort you to see your son."

"I see," said the Duke.

The doctor escorted them to the mortuary. On seeing the sign, the Duchess gave a shudder; she had always hated that word. The Duke misread her actions and squeezed her hand in support.

Before they entered, the doctor said, "Are you both ready?"

The Duke and Duchess both nodded and the Duke said for them both, "If you please." As they entered the room the curtains were drawn. Eventually they were slowly drawn back and they both stared at the prone body of their son, Stephan James Hampton the eleventh Earl of Eastleigh.

"Is that your son?" the doctor asked.

The Duke said, "Yes, I can confirm that is my son." The Duchess gripped his arm and began to sob.

The doctor said, "Thank you, I will leave you both, please, when you are ready I will be outside."

"Thank you," said the Duke as the doctor closed the door behind them.

Both the Duke and Duchess stared at their son. Eventually the Duchess said, "James, I want my Grenville home with me."

The Duke nodded and said, "I know you do, my love."

"Please make it happen," the Duchess said as she left the room.

Standing alone, the Duke had tears in his eyes as he looked for the final time at his son and said softly, "You bastard," before he left to join his wife.

 හ · ලෂ

Jonathan Spence sat at his desk looking out of the window. After gaining his degree he had joined his father's law firm as a junior partner. He loved the law, but sometimes, he wished he had had the courage of his best friend Grenville who had decided to stay in Belize after their summer trip. He had the odd postcard over the years from him. They were always full of hope. Looking at the rain hitting the window, Jonathan smiled and wished his friend well. There was a sharp knock at his door and before he could speak, the door opened. Clive Manners, one of the other solicitors, poked his head around the door and said, "Jonathan, the old man wants to see you."

"Thanks Clive," said Jonathan, smiling, as Clive closed the door. Jonathan wondered what his father could possibly want.

Jonathan hated going to his father's office. It always reminded him of the headmaster's study at Rayleigh School. Jonathan smiled as the memory of school always brought back fond memories. Grenville, Hugo and himself, the three Walpole Boys. That reminded him – he must see if Hugo was available for lunch, they had not met up in a few weeks. Jonathan knocked on the door and heard the muffled, "Enter." On opening the door, his father said, "Jonathan come in and take a seat." Jonathan closed the door behind him and entered the office. Jonathan noticed his father was not alone but had the Duke of Hampshire with him. His father said, "Jonathan, you know the Duke of Hampshire."

As the Duke stood, Jonathan said, taking the out stretched hand, "Nice to see you again, sir."

"Likewise, my boy, how are you?" smiled the Duke, sitting down again.

"Very well, thank you sir," said Jonathan as he took the seat opposite the Duke.

His father said, "The Duke has a request of you, my son."

Looking at the Duke, Jonathan thought this must be to do with Grenville. He could not think why the Duke would seek him out for a matter of law when his father Judge Malcolm Spencer was sitting in front of them. "As you know," said the Duke, "my son Stephan died recently."

Jonathan said, "We were all saddened by your loss, sir."

Smiling, the Duke said, "Thank you."

"But not sure how I can help?" asked Jonathan, now knowing what was coming next.

"It's Grenville, his mother and I are most desperate to have him home," said the Duke, looking at Jonathan.

His father said, "We were hoping you could know how the Duke could contact his son."

Jonathan looked at the Duke and pondered whether to tell him, eventually Jonathan said, "I have a contact address for him."

"Excellent," said his father.

"I would like you to do me a favour," asked the Duke.

"If I can," said Jonathan.

Taking a piece of paper out of his inside pocket and passing it to Jonathan, the Duke said, "Please could you write a letter to my son and let him know he is required to come home."

Jonathan studied the piece of paper and realise what was being asked of him. Smiling, Jonathan said, "Of course Sir, I will get onto it straight away."

Both standing, the Duke shook Jonathan's hand again and said, "Thank you my boy, I knew I could rely on you."

After Jonathan, had departed the Judge said, "I will speak to the FO on your behalf, see if we can speed things along."

"Thank you, Malcolm," said the Duke, smiling.

Once back in his office Jonathan read the Duke's note again. Jonathan smiled at its contents and was torn between his duty to Grenville and to his father. Yes, he understood Grenville's parents wanted him home after their tragic loss, but was he a true friend if he contacted Grenville? Jonathan remembered what Tom had said to him, "My PO Box address in case you need to contact him."

Jonathan took a piece of paper and started to write the letter. After he had finished it, he re-read it several times, and hoped his friend would forgive him, for as he saw it he was betraying their friendship.

∞·∞

After it had gone dark, Tom wondered where Grenville could be. Going looking for him, he found him sitting on the front porch. "Everything OK, Duke?" said Tom.

"Not really," said Grenville, "here, read this, it will explain it." Tom took the letter and read:

My Dear Grenville

It is with a heavy heart I write to you, and I apologise for being the bearer of bad news.

It gives me great pains to inform you your older brother Stephan was killed in a car accident on the way back from London to Hampton Hall; also in the car was his future bride who fortunately survived the car accident.

Your mother and father have asked me if I knew how to contact you, and persuaded me to write to you, and let you know the terrible news that has befallen your family; you are now the rightful heir and next in line, both your parents are eager for you to return as soon as possible, so you can rightfully take your place as the future Duke of Hampshire.

Your father asked me to point out the family motto to you: "Officium antequam glorificetur", "Duty before honour." He knows you will do the right thing.

Your friend

Jonathan Spencer

Tom folded the letter back up and passed it back to Grenville, who placed it in his top pocket. "Sorry," was all Tom could say. He patted Grenville on the shoulder, stood and went back inside.

Also, included in with the letter was Jonathan's business card. After reading it, Grenville smiled and thought of home for the first time in years.

Grenville sat and thought about his family motto, "Duty before honour". Grenville instantly thought of his late grandfather, and smiled. He remembered the time when he was a little boy, and his grandfather had first shown him the family motto at Hampton Hall; Grenville frowned as he imagined his father having a hand in the letter of Jonathan's. Old bastard, thought Grenville, just like him to tug the heart strings to get his own way. He had never really seen eye to eye with his father, always in Grenville's eyes he was a disappointment; he never really fitted into the role he was meant to be. Second sons of Dukes are meant to go and slip quietly into the shadows; all Grenville wanted to do was to be free from all restraints. He was pleased in some way to be the second son, no pressure to achieve, unlike his brother Stephan who was constantly reminded he was the heir, and depended upon to do the right thing always. But now, just like his grandfather, Grenville had been elevated to become the future Duke of Hampshire. Grenville still felt unsure how this made him feel.

He had been away nearly five years now. At the last family dinner before he left for Belize, the last thing his brother said to him was, "Grenville, my dear chap, you are a waste of space." Grenville smiled when he remembered that; he probably was, but now he was a rich waste of space.

Grenville tried to feel sad at his brother's passing but could not conjure any emotion. He felt nothing, and not even a tear, but he did feel sad when he thought of his mother and father. They would be feeling the loss, and no doubt his mother was anxious for him to return home. Also in the letter Jonathan said that in the car with his brother was his future bride; he never knew his brother had any feelings apart from the one he had for his own self-importance, to have feelings for someone enough who wanted to marry him. Then Grenville smiled. Grenville remembered the weekend before he left for Belize, the Farthing girl, what was her name? Something beginning with S, he was sure... oh yes, Sara. So, she finally agreed to marry Stephan, thought Grenville, then again looks like she had a lucky escape. Grenville felt bad about thinking that but he knew his brother well, and wondered if she did.

༄ · ༃

Next day Tom found Grenville staring into space, and asked what he was going to do. Grenville said, "To tell you the truth, Tom, I am not sure." Tom did not push the matter, as he knew what Grenville was going to do, even if he did not; Tom knew people, and Grenville would decide to go home and become what his family required of him. Tom felt a bit sad; he would miss Duke; they had become very close.

As they both drove into Belize City to visit Max, Tom asked Grenville, "You know you must at least write home, or contact your family, to prove you are still alive before your father sends the cavalry to find you?"

"I know, I know," said Grenville, sounding annoyed, which made Tom smile but he did not speak again until they reached Max's place.

When they arrived at Max's place, they were both surprised to see a police car parked outside. They both entered the building and went up to Max's apartment. A policeman asked, "Yes, can I help you?"

"Friend of the family," said Grenville. Silva, Max's wife, noticed Tom and Grenville and smiled, she spoke to the policeman at the door, who stood aside to let them both enter.

Grenville went directly to Silva, who looked like she had been crying, as her eyes were red and puffy. Grenville sat next to her and took her hand in his and asked gently, "What's going on, Silva?" to which she replied, "Max is dead."

Tom stared at Silva, not believing what she had just said. The policeman standing next to Tom said, "We found Max's body in a dumpster outside the Flamingo club, do you know it?"

"No," Tom lied.

"To us it looked like a robbery, nothing was on the body apart from this piece of paper with a name on it." The policeman passed the paper to Tom and he recognised his own handwriting on the bloody piece of paper immediately. "Do you recognise the name?" asked the policeman. Once again, Tom lied. The policeman said, "If there is anything thing else you can remember," passing a card to Silva, "please contact us." Silva showed the two policemen out and came and sat back down next to Grenville.

Tom said to Silva, "OK, tell me everything."

Silva went on to explain that after he left last time, Max made a few phone calls and last night told her he was on to the name that Mr Tom had given him; he said he had to meet a man at the Flamingo club at seven pm. Tom asked, "Did Max mention who he was meeting?"

Silva nodded. "Yes, Juno Broutini."

"Never heard of him," said Tom.

"He was one of Max's contacts," said Silva. Tom looked at Grenville, who shrugged.

Tom took out a large wad of money and passed it over to Silva. "What is this for, Mr Tom?" said Silva.

"It is what I owed Max," replied Tom.

"Thank you," said Silva, "he loved working for you, Mr Tom. As Max always said, family is important."

"Too true," said Tom. "If you ever need anything, you will let me know."

"No, it's OK Mr Tom, Max left me and the children well provided for. Just be safe, Mr Tom." Tom and Grenville left Silva with a smile.

Back at the Jeep, Grenville turned to Tom and for the first time saw pure rage in his eyes, and said, "Poor Max, he seemed a nice man."

"He was," said Tom, quietly, "plus he was family, so this makes this even more personal."

"So, I take it we are off to the Flamingo club for a few drinks and a snoop?" asked Grenville.

"Got it in one, partner," said Tom with a smile that did not reach his eyes.

Arriving at the Flamingo club, Grenville said, "Not the Carton Club, is it?"

"Carton Club?" Tom asked.

"In London, very exclusive, one day, old man, I will treat you to lunch there."

"Sounds like a plan," said Tom. "Bet it looks better inside," said Tom, smiling.

"That I doubt," said Grenville, laughing.

Walking up to the main door, Tom pushed and found it was locked. "Perhaps it's too early for opening hours?" asked Grenville.

"Doubt it," said Tom, "more like it's members only." Tom knocked on the door and a hatch opened. "Two please," said Tom, passing some notes through the hatch. The hatch closed and the door opened and they entered.

"Money talks," said Grenville.

"Always," said a smiling Tom.

Tom was wrong; the inside was no better than the outside. Along one wall was a bar, the other side a stage and several tables with chairs scattered about. The place was quite empty now which was not surprising for the time of day. Also, dimly lit, it was hard to see the entire room. They both walked up to the bar, as Tom smiled at the oncoming barman. "Two large rum and Cokes," said Tom.

"Large?" said Grenville in a whisper. "Pushing the boat out a bit, aren't we?"

"Drinks in memory of Max," replied Tom.

The barman retuned with the drinks, and said, "Twelve dollars," which Tom handed over. Tom passed one of the drinks to Grenville.

"For Max," said Tom, taking a gulp of his drink,

"For Max," replied Grenville, also taking a good drink. Grenville turned and walked towards the table in the corner, sat down and realised Tom was still talking to the barman.

Eventually Tom joined Grenville at the table. Grenville said, "Everything OK, Tom?"

"Yes, Juno Broutini is not in yet so we will wait," replied Tom, smiling.

Eventually Tom looked at Grenville and said, "So what you going to do, Duke?"

"Well old man, I think it's best if I return home to face the music."

"Thought as much," said Tom, smiling.

"Really," said Grenville, "am I really that predictable?"

"Yup," said Tom, "after all this time I must admit, I am going to miss you."

"And me you, old fruit. But I have been wondering about that."

"Oh really?" said Tom.

"Yes, I think I can help you even from the UK," said Grenville.

"What do you mean?" said a shocked Tom.

"Now Max is dead, you will need help in the future so what if I become your contact, tracker-down of people for you?"

"Hang on a minute my Lord, I cannot ask you to do that."

"Of course, not, that's why I am asking you, after all, who would suspect the heir to a dukedom helping you?"

Tom thought about it, and said, "OK, let's discuss this when we are back at base."

Just then the barman nodded to the door; a small, scruffily-dressed man had just entered the bar with another man. They sat at a table near to Tom and Grenville and one of the men went to the bar and brought back two beer bottles to the table.

Tom told Grenville to stay put, and look out for any surprises; not sure what kind of surprise Tom was referring to, Grenville said, "OK," and watched as Tom casually walked over to the table where the two men were sitting. Grenville watched Tom sit at the table of the two men, when Grenville noticed one of the men flop forwards as if he had fallen into a deep sleep. Watching the other man Grenville noticed he was looking scared, but then Grenville thought he would look scared if someone like Tom was asking him questions in his mood. Once again Grenville smiled; he was so glad Tom was on his side.

Grenville noticed Tom smile at the man and then tap his face, then the man slumped forward like his friend, then Grenville noticed Tom nodded towards the exit. Grenville stood and followed Tom out of the building; on the way, out Grenville glanced at the two men and realised they were both dead.

Once outside Grenville said, "Well, what happened in there?"

"Max was definitely set up by that scum bag in there," replied Tom. "But the plot thickens; Max seemed to have opened a hornet's nest asking about the name on the piece of paper I gave him, and the wrong people got to hear about it, and did not like it, and had Max killed."

"So, what happens next?" asked Grenville.

"Well, my friend, we shall go home, and further discuss your proposal."

"Sounds like a plan," said Grenville, which made them both laugh.

∝·∞

Next day Tom came back into the room and handed Grenville a battered looking box file. "In here will explain it all," said Tom, smiling. Once Tom had handed Grenville the box file, he said, "I will leave you to it," then left Grenville alone. Grenville slowly opened the box file and removed the contents.

There were not many documents from the box file, but most of the pages looked new as if they had not been handled much. The first document, which was an official looking document obviously written in Russian, looked like a trading licence for a company. Although Grenville could not read Russian, he worked out the company was called S&T Imports, and it was a Russian company, but it was owned by a Tom Backer and a Sebastian Sharapova. Grenville wondered who they both were. Grenville placed the document down and picked up what looked like a marriage certificate for a Tom Backer and a Natasha Sharapova. Grenville knew that Tom had been married. Grenville picked up another document; this was a birth certificate for a Grace Sharapova. Grenville suddenly realised that Tom had changed his name from Backer to Sharapova and taken his wife's name. Grenville also knew; Tom had had a child, but he had never mentioned it was a girl called Grace, if fact apart from the one-time Tom had never mentioned his lost family.

Grenville picked up another document that was stapled with another. Reading both, Grenville worked out they were both death certificates for a Natasha and Grace Sharapova. Grenville now understood why Tom did not speak of his wife and child much, Finally, Grenville picked up several press cuttings obviously cut from newspapers. Flicking through them, although they were in Russian, and Grenville could not read them, they were obviously about a car crash as the pictures with the articles showed an upturned car that had obviously been in a major car crash. The pictures showed in graphic clarity the aftermath of the crash with emergency service personnel standing around the crash site. The last document was the most interesting to Grenville, as it was written in English, Grenville noticed the hand writing was beautifully penned, and filled five double sided pieces of A4 paper, and was titled "Tom Sharapova."

As Grenville read the document, he realised it was Tom's life so far, how he left England after being accused of murder, heading for Odessa, on board the Red Star, the heartache of leaving his mother, arriving in a strange country not knowing what the future held, setting up his trading company with his new best friend Sebastian, marrying his sister Natasha, taking her name once they were married, and the child that was born to them which they called Grace after Tom's mother, then Grenville read the tragic death of Sebastian and then the deaths of both Natasha and Grace. Grenville had tears in his eyes as he read; the author, who he suspected was Tom, was laying out the facts in a logical and clinical way void of any emotion, just concentrating on the facts. Although the narrative was very well written, it did not comment or venture any comments or try and embellish anything, just the pure facts. The document finished with Tom arriving in Belize and his mission to find the people responsible for the death of his family.

After reading the document Grenville closed his eyes and tried to process all the facts the documents had laid out. He tried to place himself in Tom's shoes: how would he have reacted to the tragedies that had befallen Tom? He now understood Tom better and his drive. The part Grenville struggled with was how Tom had gone from a happy married man with a child with a successful business to a ruthless killer void of any emotion, but Grenville realised that not everyone in this life is the same, and everyone handles loss in their own unique way. No doubt to some, seeing their wife and child die in front of them within minutes, knowing they were helpless to help, would have sent some spiralling into a pit of despair full of darkness, never to return – eventually leading to ending their own life, knowing that there was no escape from the pain of the loss they had endured. Others would have accepted what life had dealt them, drifting through life void of colour, not having the courage to end it all but waiting for death to finally come; but for a rare few like Tom, they would be burned up with vengeance and anger, leaving all emotion behind, tuning their hearts from one full of love to a heart full of hatred and anger. Grenville was unsure how he would have coped with the tragedies that had befallen Tom, but suspected he would have taken the first option rather than the latter, but he now understood Tom's drive and commitment on finding the people who had caused him to lose his family, and bringing them to his own form of justice.

Grenville reasoned that to Tom he would have convinced himself that his cause was just, and he must kill them all, but to achieve this he had to change his whole personality and being, circumstances had turned Tom into a cold-blooded killer.

∞·∞

When Tom returned, Grenville was staring out into space with tears in his eyes. He turned to Tom and said, "My dear chap, I had no idea. You don't know how sorry I am."

Tom waved it off and said, "It's who I am and the way I am."

Grenville nodded and said, "I totally understand."

Grenville asked Tom, "So what happened after you left Odessa?"

Tom said, "We found out the two-people involved in the assassination attempt on my uncle had fled Odessa on board a ship bound for Belize, so the hunt for those involved started here. As Uncle Ivor was shipping out to here, I tagged along, Max was the family contact in Belize and he found me this place. The rest, as they say, is history."

Grenville asked, "What happened to S&T Imports?"

"Well, technically it's still trading," said Tom. "We registered it under Russian law, so it's still a viable company."

"Good, good," said Grenville.

Tom looked at Grenville, and Grenville could see by Tom's puzzled expression that he was confused. "Don't worry," said Grenville, "I have a brilliant plan, just need to work out some details."

Over the next few days Grenville and Tom worked on the plan. As the pieces fell into place Tom was impressed with Grenville's enthusiasm and flair; Tom in a million years would never have thought of half the things Grenville was suggesting. Then again, he had known one other person like that many years ago; this brought a smile to his face.

"So," said Grenville finally to Tom, "first things first, once I am back in the UK I will register S&T imports as a private company and register it in the UK. I will also open a UK bank account for S&T Imports which we both can add and withdraw funds from, and with the money we have already, and the money we will make, we will create a world class import and export business, delivering worldwide, above the radar or under the radar, depending what the client wants. We will become the name to be trusted to deliver anything anytime anywhere, and as we build we will expand. In the shadows, I will create a clandestine operation to rival any top government intelligence agencies. I will employ the very best programmers and analysts; none will know the whole picture, or what they are doing; as far as they know, it will all be working towards the import and export business, but only you and I will know the real reason for S&T Imports. As you pass me a name, I can find them, check them and pass on their profile within months, possibly weeks, or even days, and 'hey presto', we are in business. What you think then, Tom?"

Tom stared at Grenville and realised he was not joking he was serious and started to believe Grenville's commitment.

Grenville said, "The money in the safe is easy to move, but the other stuff like the diamonds, gold and other trinkets you have acquired over the years will be more difficult; it will take me some time to finally shift it all, and convert it into cash." This brought a smile to Tom's face.

Grenville went on, "You need to get in contact with your Uncle Ivor and ask him when he is next planning a trip to the UK. I am sure we can make a run to the UK worth it."

"I'm sure we can," said Tom, smiling. "What has uncle Ivor got to do with this?"

"He, my dear chap, is going to smuggle all the gold into the UK for us."

"Trinkets."

"Sorry?"

"And trinkets," said Tom, laughing.

"Yes of course, trinkets," replied Grenville seriously.

"On paper the plan looks excellent and well thought through," said Tom, smiling.

"I can feel a big but coming," said Grenville, laughing.

"I applauded your enthusiasm Duke, but this is not a game to me, it is serious, and I will not stop until it is over," said Tom quietly.

Grenville smiled, "Tom, I do not understand your commitment but I understand what drives you, but you have given me something to dedicate my life to, sink my teeth into. Before I went home I was worried and wondered what life held for me, now I know. You have your quest, I now have a chance to become part of that quest," Grenville continued, "and together we will track down the rest of the people responsible for the death of your family, and make them pay," he said, looking Tom directly in the eyes.

Tom could see Grenville was serious and finally said, "OK then, put it there, partner," as he held out his hand. Grenville waved the hand away, and opened his arms and leaned in for a hug. They both hugged and started to laugh. "So, give me the piece of paper with the name on it, I saw you fail to give it back to the policeman," said Grenville, smiling.

"Not yet, you get set up then once we both decide you are ready you can have it, deal?" said a smiling Tom.

"Deal," said a reluctant Grenville, taking Tom's outstretched hand.

ᘒ·ᘓ

Next morning, Grenville told Tom that he needed to go to the British Embassy to get a new passport and sort some things out. Tom looked confused. "What about the one you have already?"

"I need an excuse to get into the Embassy. Once they realise who I am, they will be falling over to help me, and I need their help to get my large holdalls through customs via the diplomatic route."

"Sneaky," said Tom.

"Practical," said Grenville. "If there is one thing I have learnt from you after all this time, is always have a plan."

Tom dropped Grenville at the British Embassy gates, and went to the docks to see if the Red Star was in, or if she was likely to return soon.

Watching Tom depart towards the docks, Grenville went up to the buzzer and in his best accent said, "I would like to speak to someone about a lost passport." Eventually the door buzzed and opened a fraction and Grenville entered the British embassy. Grenville went up to the front desk, smiling.

"Can I help you," said the girl behind the counter with a smile that did not reach her eyes.

"I wish to talk to someone about a lost passport," said Grenville.

"Of course," said the girl. "Please take a seat," indicating to the seating area.

Grenville smiled. "Thank you, most kind." Grenville went and sat down. There were already a few people waiting. No doubt by the looks of them they were locals waiting for a UK visa. After about ten minutes, a man went to reception and spoke to the girl who indicated to Grenville. Grenville smiled; here comes the fun.

The man walked over and said, "I am Mr Forbes from the Embassy, Mr…" letting the Mr hang in the air.

Grenville stood and held out his hand and said, "I am the Earl of Eastleigh, son of the Duke of Hampshire." Mr Forbes stared at Grenville and was not sure what to say. He just stood and was trying to work out if the scruffy man in front of him was genuine or raving mad. Grenville went on. "I do apologise for my appearance, old man, but had a hard few days since I was robbed down south."

Forbes decided to err on the side of caution. "Please, my Lord, will you follow me."

Grenville smiled and said, "Thank you, old man." Grenville followed Forbes through the security cordon into a back office.

Opening the door, Forbes said, "Please can you take a seat, my Lord, so we can determine the facts correctly."

Grenville sat as Forbes closed the door and left. Grenville smiled and knew "determine the facts" meant to make sure he was who he said he was and if not, Grenville was sure he would most probably be shot for wasting Embassy time.

After about fifteen minutes Forbes returned and Grenville could tell by his attitude the news was good. "I do apologise, my lord, for the delay, but protocol and all that," said Forbes.

"Understand absolutely, old bean," replied Grenville, smiling.

"Please can you follow me, my Lord, the Ambassador will see you now."

"Thank you," replied Grenville.

Forbes led Grenville through the maze of the Embassy, eventually arriving at an open door. Knocking, Forbes said, "Ambassador, the Earl of Eastleigh."

"My lord," said the Ambassador, coming from behind his desk to greet Grenville, holding out his hand. Grenville took the offered hand. "James McLeish" said the Ambassador, smiling. "This is a lucky encounter," said the Ambassador.

"Really," replied Grenville.

"Yes, only got word this week from the FO to find you."

"Excellent," said Grenville, trying hard not to laugh.

"I went to school with your father," said the Ambassador.

"Really, you are a Rayleigh boy as well, how wonderful," replied Grenville.

"When you get home please give my regards to your father, the Duke," said the Ambassador.

"I will pass on your best wishes and let him know how helpful you were to an old-school friend's lost son and a fellow Rayleigh boy."

This made the ambassador grow a few inches in height and have a huge smile on his face. "Where are my manners, can I get you anything?" asked the ambassador.

"Would love a decent cup of tea," replied Grenville, smiling.

"Forbes, tea for two if you please," said the ambassador.

"Coming right up," replied Forbes as he departed.

"I must admit, my Lord, you do not look like the picture they sent us of you."

"I know, was down south in Punta Gora when I had all my luggage stolen, luckily for me met a really nice American couple who lent me the bus fare back to the capital. Once I arrived, I came straight here, hence my appearance," replied Grenville, smiling.

"How dreadful," replied the ambassador without further comment.

"How much have you been informed, may I ask, Ambassador?" asked Grenville.

"We know about your brother's death and your father's asking the government to urgently track you down so you can come home to take up the mantel, shall we say," said the ambassador.

"Excellent," said Grenville, just as Forbes returned with the tea.

"After tea, can we get you to have a quick wash up for a photo for your new passport?" asked the Ambassador.

"That would be wonderful, most kind," replied Grenville, sipping his tea.

"Should only take a day or two for a replacement to be issued," said the ambassador, smiling.

"You are very efficient," replied Grenville, smiling.

"Once finished, please could you follow Forbes here, he will take you for your photograph," said the ambassador.

Grenville placed down his cup and saucer and, standing, said, "Lead the way, Forbes old chap."

Forbes led Grenville to a wash room. "If you pop in and freshen up a bit I will go find the photographer," said Forbes.

"You are most kind, old man," replied Grenville. Grenville entered the washroom, and went to the sink and stared into the mirror and the face staring back was not him. He smiled and said, "Oh well, back to the rat race." Looking about he noticed shower gel, shampoo and a towel by the shower and a fresh set of clothes hanging up on a coat hanger, with a new pair of trainers.

Grenville stood in the shower for five minutes letting the hot water cascade over him. Part one of the plan was now complete; he needed a few more things to fall into place and the plan would be complete. Quickly drying and dressing, Grenville started to laugh at himself; this was the first shower in ages where he would not have to dirty his hair and face again.

Grenville was surprised on the sizes, but no doubt Mrs Preston would have given then the correct sizes, which made Grenville smile. He was now looking forward to seeing everyone again after his absence. The trousers hung loosely from him, but the shirt was tight against his chest and arms; even Mrs Preston would be surprised at how much he had changed.

As Grenville left the bathroom, Forbes smiled and said, "Feeling better, my Lord?"

"Much," replied Grenville.

"Can you stand against this white wall, please, my Lord," said Forbes.

As Grenville, did as requested the photographer quickly stood in front and said, "Look directly into the lens, sir."

The photographer then clicked three times, and said, "Thank you sir, most kind."

Grenville nodded his thanks. Forbes said, "This way my Lord, I will take you back to the ambassador."

"Lead the way, old man," replied Grenville, following in Forbes's wake.

Back in the Ambassador's office the ambassador smiled at Grenville and said, "Spoken to the FO that we had located you, and they are going to inform your father."

"Most kind, Ambassador," replied Grenville, taking the offered chair. "Was wondering if I could send the parents a quick email, in person, if that's OK?" asked Grenville, looking down.

"Of course, cannot see why not," replied the Ambassador, moving to his desk and pressing a button on the phone console. "Forbes, can we arrange for the Earl of Eastleigh to send a private email to his parents, to let them know he is well and homeward bound."

Forbes immediately replied, "Will arrange it now, ambassador." Once the line went dead, the ambassador returned to sit with Grenville.

After a pause, Grenville said, "Ambassador, I was wondering if you could do me a small favour."

"Please ask away, my Lord," replied the Ambassador.

Reaching into his bag, Grenville extracted the handwritten paper Tom and he had previously drafted for the transfer of S&T Imports. "I have a document from an old friend that I need endorsing, and I was thinking, who better to ask than one of my father's old school friends?"

The Ambassador beamed with pride and said, "Would be delighted to." Passing over the document, the Ambassador went to his desk; as the document was in Russian, Grenville showed the ambassador where to enter his name and sign, but without really reading the document the ambassador signed it and placed his office stamp on it and returned it to Grenville smiling, and said, "There you go, my Lord."

"You are the embodiment of diplomacy," replied Grenville, smiling. After studying the document, Grenville folded it up and placed it in his bag; phase two of the plan was complete.

Just as Grenville placed the document into his bag, Forbes knocked and entered and said, "Ready for you, my Lord."

Grenville stood and said, "Thank you, ambassador."

"Take your time, see you before you go," replied the ambassador, standing.

Grenville followed Forbes to a nondescript room; opening the door, Forbes said, "Jenkins here will show you the ropes."

"Thank you, most kind," said Grenville.

"Jenkins here will escort you back to the Ambassador," said Forbes.

"You have been most helpful, dear chap, most professional," said Grenville, smiling. Forbes bowed slightly and left.

Turning, Grenville smiled at Jenkins and said, "Most kind of you to show me the ropes, old man."

Sitting beside Jenkins, he explained to Grenville the laptop and how it worked. He explained it was a top of the range encrypted laptop. "You enter your password here, and see the envelope icon? If that is flashing, you have a message. Open the message and it will be all encrypted. To de-crypt so you can read it, select the hand like a hammer and it will ask for a password. Enter the password and it will open the message. Everything done by a biometric algorithm programme, and same for the reverse: type your message, then encrypt it and then send it to the email address. Things to note is the passwords need to be changed every thirty days, the laptop password and the de-crypt password can never be the same, and for extra security, if you enter an incorrect password for either of the two passwords three times, the whole laptop will wipe." Suddenly Jenkins stopped talking. "I apologise, my Lord, rambled on a bit there. But obviously, you only need to send a simple email," said Jenkins, smiling.

"Amazing stuff and I admire your enthusiasm in your job," said Grenville, smiling and formulating a new part of the plan.

Once Jenkins went over the laptop with Grenville, he said, "Do you want me to help you, my Lord?"

Grenville noticed Jenkins take a sneaky look at the wall clock. Realising it was lunchtime, Grenville decided to push his luck. "No thank you old man, rather personal to the Duke, all things considered." He was not sure how much Jenkins knew, but was sure Forbes would have explained who he was and needed VIP treatment.

"Of course, my Lord," replied Jenkins, sliding his chair to another desk.

"Look Jenkins old man, I am sure I can handle this, I am sure I can find Forbes to escort me back to the ambassador office. I don't want you to miss your well-earned luncheon waiting for me, that would make me feel really awful," said Grenville, smiling.

"You sure, my Lord?" replied Jenkins, smiling.

"Our little secret, old man," said Grenville, winking at a smiling Jenkins. Without further comment Jenkins stood and left the room. Grenville stared at the blank screen, and started to laugh. He did not even have a clue what his mother's or father's email addresses were, or even if they had one. He could not even remember seeing a computer at Hampton hall.

Grenville closed the lid and traced the power supply and placed both into his bag. Quietly closing the door behind him, he traced his steps back to the Ambassador's office. Once there, Grenville gently knocked and he heard, "Enter." Grenville opened the door, smiling, and entered the room again. The Ambassador came from behind the desk, smiling, and held out his hand and said, "All sorted, my Lord?"

Grenville took the offered hand and said, "Yes, thank you, feel so much better, have emailed the Duke." Forbes returned to the Ambassador's office and was surprised to see Grenville already there.

"My lord, your passport and first class flight ticket back to England will be ready in two days' time," said Forbes. "Where are, you staying?" asked Forbes.

"Hotel Americano, do you know it?" asked Grenville.

"Yes, of course," replied Forbes smiling, "I shall arrange for a car to pick you up at eight in the morning on Wednesday, and take you to the airport," smiled Forbes.

"Do you require anything else, some money until you leave?" asked the Ambassador, smiling.

"No not at all, and fine but thank you for asking," replied Grenville. "One last indulgence?" asked Grenville. "I have two duffle bags with some items for my father, the Duke, any chance they can go diplomatic?" asked a smiling Grenville.

"Of course, old chap, Forbes will sort that out, won't you Forbes."

"Of course, Ambassador."

Standing, the Ambassador said, "Well, my Lord if nothing else, I have to crack on, diplomacy waits for no man." He laughed at his own joke. "Forbes here will see you out."

Holding out his hand, Grenville shook the Ambassador's hand and said, "You two are the epitome of why there is still a Great in Britain. Once I am home I will get father to mention you both in the House of Lords," said Grenville, smiling.

At the exit, Forbes shook hands with Grenville and watched Grenville go through the gate of the Embassy, and thought to himself, somehow the future Duke of Hampshire has made right mugs of the embassy staff, but for the life of him could not figure out how.

Smiling, Forbes closed the door. As he did so, Grenville spotted Tom waiting on the other side of the road.

"Well, don't you scrub up well," said a laughing Tom. "Everything OK?" asked Tom.

"All as per the plan," said a laughing Grenville. Back at the warehouse, Grenville explained to Tom, "The plan went better than even I imagined, and you are right, don't embellish the story, stick to known fact, that way you cannot be tripped up," which made them both laugh.

"Two days," said Tom.

"Yes, old bean. Tomorrow is our last day together."

Tom slapped Grenville on the back and said, "Well, we better make it a good one," to which Grenville agreed.

Tom and Grenville finalised the plan, and the way to contact each other. Grenville said, "The old PO box is a bit outdated and long winded and time consuming, we need something modern," at which Grenville produced the laptop and placed it in front of Tom. Grenville opened the laptop and turned it on. "Got this little beauty while I was at the embassy, asked to use a laptop to send a secure message to the folks, bent over backwards to show me how it works. Top of the range encrypted laptop," said Grenville. "Let me show you how it works."

Afterwards all Tom could say was, "Amazing."

"Technology, my dear friend. But before we get connected you need to get a phone line run into the place and a modem," said Grenville.

"I will sort that as soon as you leave, set up an email address and send it to you," promised Tom.

Grenville said, "In the future we can communicate in minutes rather than days by post, and all from the comfort of your own home." Grenville gave Tom the two passwords for the laptop, and made sure he was conversant in its use before he let it rest.

Tom looked at Grenville with a smirk and said, "So you stole this laptop."

"Not at all," replied Grenville. "I simply recruited it to our cause," Grenville went on, smiling.

"Will the embassy not miss it?" asked Tom.

"Well, it was in the office when I left, if I am asked," said Grenville, "and I don't think they would ever consider or accuse a future Peer of the Realm to be a light-fingered thief. Just not cricket, old boy, bad form," which made them both laugh.

Tom went on to explain he had sent three crates homeward bound with uncle Ivor; he was expected to be in England in three months or so. Tom gave Grenville the password he had agreed with Ivor, and made sure Grenville realised the importance of remembering it; if not, their little endeavour would end before it got off the ground.

That night Tom and Grenville stayed up until nearly dawn, drinking and talking, both trying not to think about the day after next when they would finally go their separate ways. During a silent period, Grenville said, "I want to thank you, Tom."

"What for, Duke?" said Tom, smiling.

"You have given me your friendship and loyalty and since I have been here, your trust." Turning to Tom and looking sincere, Grenville said, "I promise you Tom, I will never let you down, you can always count on me for anything. This I promise on my family name." Tom knew what Grenville had said was most probably the most sacred oath he could have made, and it was not given lightly.

Tom smiled at Grenville. "I knew there was a reason I saved your upper class sorry arse," replied Tom, which set them both off laughing.

The day for Grenville's departure arrived and Tom drove Grenville to the Hotel Americano and parked up.

"Well," said Tom.

"I know," said Grenville.

They both hugged and slapped each other on the back.

"Be safe," said Tom.

"You too," said Grenville. Grenville lifted his two large duffle bags from the Jeep and walked towards the embassy's waiting car.

Tom shouted, "Thank you, Grenville," using his given name for the first time.

Grenville turned with tears in his eyes and shouted back, "Get that email sorted, you old pirate," before moving towards the car with the boot open. The chauffeur saluted Grenville and took his bags off him and placed them into the boot. Once Grenville stepped into the car, he closed the car door behind him. The driver did think it was strange that his passenger had come from the opposite direction from the hotel and not from the hotel lobby; but then again, he had worked for the Embassy long enough to know not to ask questions, or ponder on things that did not concern him.

Tom watched the car drive off towards the airport and as he watched it disappear into the distance, Tom had a smile on his face. He put the Jeep into gear and headed towards home with a new hope for the future.

ⅎ·ℴ

As the plane touched down at Heathrow International Airport, Grenville opened his eyes, and smiled. Although he was pleased to finally be home, he knew he was going to miss Tom, but his new quest would drive him on.

An air hostess came and told Grenville to please stay in his seat until the plane had been disembarked by the other passengers; there were two other diplomatic passengers who stayed in their seats as well. Eventually the air hostess came and asked them to depart the aircraft. At the end of the ramp, a British Airways employee showed them down a flight of stairs to waiting cars. At the bottom of the stairs, Grenville smiled as he saw the family Rolls Royce, with a waiting Newton.

Grenville smiled as he approached Newton, who stood to

attention and gave a smart salute. "Welcome home, my Lord," said Newton.

"Thank you, Newton, how's things at the ranch?" replied Grenville.

Smiling, Newton replied, "Not good my Lord, not good."

"Better get back then," said Grenville.

"I have your luggage already loaded, so we can leave at your convenience," said Newton as he held the back door open for Grenville. Grenville slept most of the way down to Hampton Hall. Just as they entered the gates, Newton gave a loud stage cough and said, "We have arrived, sir."

Opening his eyes, Grenville smiled and said, "Thank you Newton, good chap." As Newton pulled up the staff had been assembled and his parents were also waiting. Grenville was not looking forward to this one bit. He felt quite guilty that he had spent such a long time away, plus he was only back because of the death of his older brother.

Newton pulled up at the entrance and stopped, and the door was opened by a footman, who bowed deeply as Grenville exited the car. Grenville went straight to his mother and embraced her, and shook his father's hand, who said, "Welcome home, my boy."

"Thank you, father," replied Grenville. Grenville turned to the staff and thanked them all for being there and no doubt he would catch up with them over the following days, Grenville noticed Preston and nodded. Preston smiled back. Preston turned and ushered the staff off to their chores. Taking his mother's arm, Grenville followed his father into the hall.

Once in the drawing room, his mother spoke for the first time. "Come sit next to me, and let me look at you." Grenville did as she asked and went and sat next to her and took her hand. Grenville stared into her eyes and noticed that, although still a beautiful lady, the recent events had taken their toll and she was beginning to look her age.

Grenville smiled at his mother and said, "You look well, mother."

"You are sweet, my darling, to say," replied his mother, "you look so different from when I last saw you. I cannot quite put my finger on it but you have changed," as she stared intently at him. "What do you think, James?" she asked, looking at her husband.

Grenville father had been studying his son, and his wife was correct: something had changed in Grenville. He was more confident and relaxed, his time away had made him a man. "I totally agree, my darling, our son is a changed man," said his father, smiling at them both.

After some idle chit chat, Grenville broached the subject that was in the air but no one was prepared to speak of. "I am sorry that my return was only because of Stephan's death," said Grenville, "but if not too distressing I would be grateful if you could give me all the details." He looked from his mother to his father. His mother looked down at the ground and his father stood and went to look out of the big bay windows. After a pause his father began to speak.

"Your brother was returning from London in the early evening last month, and according to the police report swerved to avoid something, probably a deer or some other animal, whilst driving down the narrow lane leading to the estate. Due to his speed, he lost control on the wet surface and hit a tree. As he was not wearing his seat belt, plus the speed he was travelling at, he went through the wind screen and he was killed instantly."

Grenville's father walked across and stood behind his mother and put his hand on her shoulder, and she placed her hand over his. Grenville could see although they were both still traumatised by the sudden loss of their son, there was something else bothering them deeply. "Jonathan's letter said Stephan had his fiancée in the car as well, and she survived?" asked Grenville.

"Yes, Sara. She was fortunate to have had her seat belt on and only suffered minor injuries," replied his father.

"Why did Stephan not have his seat belt on?" asked Grenville.

"You knew your brother Grenville, never would conform," replied his mother, with a light laugh. That was the first time in his life that Grenville had ever heard his mother speak ill of his brother.

Grenville tried not to smile, but said, "Yes I did, mother."

"We buried him in the family plot next to your grandfather, it was a small affair with just family and a few friends in attendance."

From this, Grenville took that due to his standoffish attitude towards people not a lot attended the funeral or were saddened by his death.

"So, my boy," said his father, "you are home ready to take up the mantle of Earl of Eastleigh and future Duke of Hampshire."

Grenville looked at his parents and both had the look of expectation in their eyes. Grenville said, "Father, I will do my duty."

His father went across and hugged him, and to Grenville's surprise, whispered in his ear, "Thank you, my son."

"Well, I have things I need to attend to," said his mother, "see you at dinner, my darling." As she stood and hugged him and kissed his cheek she whispered, "Glad you are home." Grenville and his father waited until she left before speaking again.

"She took it hard, you know," said his father, "but she does not show it."

Grenville nodded and said, "I cannot imagine your loss, father."

"Tomorrow I have Stevens the family lawyer coming down, to settle some estate business, and now you are back we can tie up a few formal loose ends on your inheritance," said his father.

Grenville said, "Of course, father, whatever you wish. Now, if you'll excuse me I have a touch of jet lag, so could do with a few hours' sleep before dinner, if you don't mind."

"Not at all my boy, we can talk later," replied his father.

Before returning to his room for a quick nap, Grenville decided to pop in and see the Preston's. On entering the kitchen, it was a hive of activity as usual. Grenville spotted Mrs

Preston and holding out his arms, said, "Mrs P, come give me a hug."

Smiling, Mrs Preston went to Grenville and gave him a big hug. "Here, let me look at you," said Mrs Preston, holding him at arm's length. "You look well, lost a bit of weight as well, suits you, as for the hair, much better."

"At least you don't look like a ponce anymore," said a voice from behind him. Grenville turned to see a smiling Preston with arms outstretched. After hugging, Preston said, "Glad you are home, lad, been a bit fraught around here lately." Mrs P stood and nodded in agreement.

Grenville laughed at Preston's comments and said, "Surprised you are still here, father not put you out to farm yet?"

"As if," said Preston, smiling. "But seriously glad you are home, place was never the same after you left. But we have time to discuss all of that when you have settled in. You look bushed," said Preston.

"To tell you the truth, it's been a bit of a tense homecoming," replied Grenville.

"Well, you get off to bed for a few hours' sleep. I will give you a knock before dinner," said Preston.

"As always, Mr P, you are a star. Mrs P, as always, a pleasure," said Grenville as he bowed deeply to Mrs Preston.

"Be off with you, you're a young rake," she said, laughing.

Grenville left the kitchen, laughing, to finally get some sleep.

As they watched Grenville depart, Mrs Preston said, "I don't think I have ever seen such a change in a person as Master Grenville."

Nodding, Preston said, "You are right my dear, young Master Grenville has finally become a man."

Grenville opened his door and stood in the doorway; the room was the same as he had left it apart from his baggage stacked neatly in the corner. Grenville smiled. "Part one complete," he said to himself, as he lay down on the bed fully clothed. He was fast asleep before his head hit the pillow.

�∞·⁣�∞

Grenville opened his eyes when he heard the light knock on his door. One thing that he had learnt during his time in Belize was how to react to every noise and movement. Sitting up, Grenville said, "Enter."

The door was opened by a smiling Preston holding a steaming cup of coffee. "Preston, my dear chap, most welcome."

"Sleep well, my lord?" asked Preston.

"Like the proverbial log," replied Grenville, smiling. "What time is it, Preston?"

"Just after eight," replied Preston.

"AM or PM?" asked Grenville.

"AM," said a laughing Preston. "It was your mother's idea not to wake you last night for dinner, so we let you sleep."

"Must have needed it," replied Grenville.

"Indeed, you did," said Preston. "Do you want me to sort out your luggage?"

As Preston moved over towards the luggage, Grenville was out of bed and rushed over and placed his hand over Preston's and said, "No need, I can do it."

Preston stared into Grenville's eyes. "Master Grenville, I have known you all your life. I have seen you grow and develop into the man you are. I know when you have something to hide. Even as a child, you were crap at it."

"Preston, sit down, let me tell you about Belize."

Preston took a chair and held out his hands and said, "Well, tell me."

Grenville sat opposite Preston. Ever since Grenville was a little boy, he could never get one over on Preston. It was like a sixth sense he had, he always knew when Grenville was in the wrong, or he was innocent.

Grenville decided to tell Preston about some of his time away, so Grenville went on to explain some of the things that had happened whilst he was in Belize. After Grenville, had finished he smiled at Preston, who remained silent. Eventually

Preston said, "Well, my Lord, quite a story."

"I would appreciate if you could keep it to yourself?" asked Grenville.

"Mum's the word," replied Preston. "If I can help in anyway let me know," said a smiling Preston. Grenville felt better he had told someone and he knew Preston was the correct person to have told. Grenville always knew that Preston and his grandfather were the only two people he trusted in the world. Grenville showed Preston the contents of the two bags stuffed full of money and jewels.

Preston gave a loud whistle when he saw the content of the bags. "Well, you certainly had a rare old time whilst you were in Belize, and very profitable," said Preston, laughing.

Grenville replied, "I have a ship docking in England in about three months with three crates full of stuff."

"OK, I will arrange transport for us," said Preston.

"Us? I don't want you to compromise yourself, Preston. After all, it's not quite above board."

Preston smiled. "Don't worry, my lord. At my time of life an adventure now and again can lift the spirits."

Grenville held out his hand, which Preston shook. "Thank you, Preston, knew I could rely on your discretion," said Grenville.

"Always, my lord," replied a still smiling Preston. "Just one more thing, perhaps it's not my place to say," said Preston.

"Please, Preston, we don't have secrets." This made Preston smile again.

"I think your brother has run the estate down."

"What do you mean, Preston?" asked Grenville, feeling concerned.

"Well, and bear in mind this is what I have observed and estate rumour," said Preston.

Grenville knew that nothing happened around Hampton Hall without Preston knowing about it, plus if it was estate rumour as well then it was accurate. "Please go on, tell me your concerns," said Grenville.

"Your father handed over the running of the estate and hall to your brother a few years ago, and he made some pretty bad investments. A few of the tenant farmers and house staff are concerned. I think by the time your father found out the damage was done, and I am sure he is hiding it from your mother, which is not like him so it must be pretty bad," said Preston.

Grenville said, "Thank you, Preston, for bringing this to my attention. Please let the staff and the tenant farmers know, and that I will sort it."

Preston stood and said, "I always knew you would not let us down." Smiling, Preston left the room.

Once Preston had left, Grenville sat and wondered how bad his brother had left the estate. This made Grenville angry. "Bloody idiot," said Grenville out loud. Grenville quickly showered and dressed and went down for breakfast.

On entering the dining room his mother looked up and smiled. "Nice sleep, darling?" she said.

"Yes, thank you, mother, I needed it," said a laughing Grenville.

Grenville went and gave his mother a kiss on the offered cheek. "Father not appeared yet?" asked Grenville.

"He was up early, I think he is in his study," replied his mother.

Grenville caught the worried look in his mother's eyes when she spoke. "Mother, is something bothering you?" Grenville asked.

His mother smiled and said, "Why do you ask that, darling?"

"Mother, we have never had secrets, so I know you are keeping something from me."

"I am worried for your father," she said.

"You mean the state of the estate," replied Grenville.

His mother looked shocked. "How did you know?" she asked.

"Preston and rumour control around the estate."

His mother smiled and said, "Your father does not know I know."

"How did you find out, mother?" asked Grenville.

"Your brother came to me a few months ago, with his begging bowl," she said.

"Oh mother, why?" said Grenville.

"What could I do? He was my son and it was for the family estate," said his mother. Grenville knew his mother had been independently wealthy in her own right as the only child of her late parents; they left her with a sizable inheritance.

"How much, mother?" asked Grenville.

His mother tried to laugh it off. "Nearly all of it," she said.

"Which was?" pushed Grenville.

"Close to a million pounds," she softly said.

Grenville looked shocked; if his brother had borrowed close to a million from his own mother then how much had he lost on the estate? No wonder his father was worried. Grenville went and sat next to his mother. Taking her hand, he said, "Mother, don't worry, I am home now and I will sort out this mess, and save the family."

Grenville's mother placed her hand on his face and with tears in her eyes said, "I wish your brother was more like you, my darling."

Grenville kissed his mother and said, "Please don't worry, mother, it will be OK."

She smiled at him again and said, "I have every faith in you, my darling."

After breakfast Grenville went for a walk in the garden to clear his head. What Preston and his mother had told him came as a shock. No wonder his father was worried; the estate had been in the family for countless generations. Grenville cursed his brother for being a fool, an arrogant bloody fool; if he had not returned when he had done, and his brother was still alive, would there still have been an ancestral family estate for him to return home to? Plus, he was sure he would not have been welcome. Smiling, Grenville thought how life can twist and turn and throw you a life line. With his brother's death and his new-found circumstances, he would save the family, and still smiling he could feel his grandfather's presence. "Don't worry Grandpa, I will sort it," he said out loud.

Grenville spotted Stevens the family solicitor's car coming up the driveway. Grenville walked towards the entrance to meet Mr Stevens. "Mr Stevens, how the devil are you, old chap?" said Grenville, approaching Mr Stevens with his hand out.

Mr Stevens shook Grenville by the hand and said, "Young Grenville, nice to see you again. Sorry they are not in better circumstances."

Grenville smiled and said, "Indeed." Holding out his arm, Grenville said, "Shall we? I think father is in the study."

"After you, Grenville," replied Mr Stevens.

Grenville lightly knocked on his father's study, and heard, "Enter," before standing aside to allow Mr Steven to enter first. Grenville's father came from behind the desk and said, "Stevens, nice to see you again, how are you?"

"Very well thank you, your Grace," replied Stevens, shaking the offered hand.

"Please sit down. Coffee?" asked Grenville's father.

"Most gracious, your Grace," said Stevens, bowing.

"Grenville," said his father, pointing to the seat next to Stevens.

After Preston, had brought in the coffee and served, the meeting started.

"Shall I start?" said Stevens.

"Please," said the Duke, clearing his throat.

Stevens went on, pulling out an official document from his briefcase, "I just need Grenville and yourself to formally sign the act of Hereditary Peerages passing the title of Earl of Eastleigh and the future title of Duke of Hampshire from yourself, your Grace, to your second son, Grenville St Louis Hampton. This will supersede the one signed by you and your late son Stephan, so only Grenville as the Earl of Eastleigh can have claim on the family title, Duke of Hampshire."

Grenville's father smiled at Grenville, and said, "Good, all legal and above board."

This statement made Grenville feel intrigued as to why had his father rushed to make sure he was the next in line, unless someone else had a claim that he did not know about. After they both signed, Stevens placed the document back in his suitcase. "Congratulations," said Stevens, bowing slightly at Grenville, "you are now sanctioned the twelfth Earl of Eastleigh and the future twelfth Duke of Hampshire."

"Thank you, Mr Stevens, most kind," replied Grenville. Grenville looked at his father, who was smiling at him. Grenville smiled back and said, "Mr Stevens, I am sure you did not drive all the way from London just to make me sign that document." Stevens fidgeted in his chair and cleared his voice.

"Grenville," said his father, "we have estate business to attend to, nothing to worry you about."

"Oh, but father it does, I know what has been going on."

Both his father and Stevens stared at Grenville. Stevens tried to look away, and his father placed his head in his hands and said, "I am sorry, my boy."

Grenville smiled. "OK, Mr Stevens, give it to me straight, and please do not sugar coat it. I need to know everything."

Stevens look at Grenville's father, who held out his hands and said, "OK, tell him Stevens."

Stevens nodded at the eleventh Duke of Hampshire and said, "My Lord, it is not a pretty tale. Some years ago, your father passed the managing of the estate over to your brother Stephan. As your brother took up the reigns of the estate he brought in his personal advisor, a Mr Dexter Simon-Smyth, and between them they made some very bad investment calls so they started to plunder the estate accounts, liquidating assets and borrowing heavily against the estate."

Grenville looked at his father, who had his eyes closed. Mr Stevens continued. "So, it was one bad investment after another, until the bank refused a credit line, and then your brother went to the extraordinary length of actually having the estate valued for sale. This of course was done without anyone's knowledge."

"But surely he could not legally sell the estate?" asked Grenville.

"He had every right, as your father had handed over the running of the estate to him, in a legal document signed by both parties," replied Stevens.

"So, what is the state of play now?" asked Grenville.

"The estate is over budget by four million two hundred and fifty-seven pounds and thirty pence."

"So, what are our options?" asked Grenville.

Mr Stevens smiled. "There are no options, My Lord, the account needs to be settled by the end of next month."

"Or?" asked Grenville.

"Or the estate will be placed on the market to cover the debt," replied Mr Stevens.

"Which bank was my brother dealing with? Obviously, it was not the family bank," asked Grenville.

"There lies the rub, the bank is run by Mr Dexter Simon-Smyth, Easington Investment Bank," replied Mr Stevens.

"How much did my brother lose?" asked Grenville quietly.

"Well, as a rough estimate, just short of twenty million. Before your brother took over management, your family and especially your grandfather and father had built up quite a profitable estate," said Mr Stevens.

"Sorry my boy, looks like I only have my title to pass on to you," said his father quietly.

Grenville smiled and turned to Mr Stevens. "Mr Stevens, anything else?"

"Now you are home, next week I have summoned all parties for the reading of your brother's will".

"This will take place here?"

"Yes, of course," said the Duke.

"Good, when next week?" asked Grenville.

"Next Wednesday," replied Mr Stevens, "if that is suitable to you, your Grace," looking at Grenville's father.

Grenville's father nodded and said, "Of course, old chap, perfect."

"Mr Stevens, before then I would like you to do me some detective work," asked Grenville.

"Of course, my Lord, if it is legal and above board," replied Mr Stevens, looking hard at Grenville.

Grenville smiled. "Don't worry, Mr Stevens, I would not ask anything that would jeopardise your office," replied Grenville.

Mr Stevens bowed his head at Grenville in acknowledgement. Mr Stevens took a pen and legal pad from his briefcase. "What information do you require, My Lord?" asked Mr Stevens.

"First I want to know the exact amount the estate owes, and any daily interest it is occurring whilst the debt is running. Can you find out the exact date the debt must be cleared by, and the legal document my father signed to transfer over the estate to my brother's running; now he is deceased, could his will legally transfer the estate to someone else, or does it revert to my father. And finally, if any other debtors are chasing payment against the estate."

Mr Stevens wrote everything down that Grenville had requested. "I will have the information next Wednesday, when I visit to read your brother's will," replied Mr Stevens.

"Mr Stevens, that might be too late, so please can I ask you ring this number," he said, passing Mr Stevens the card Jonathan had included in his letter to Grenville. "This is Mr Jonathan Spencer, my lawyer and close friend, if you can pass on to him the information I have requested," said Grenville.

Mr Stevens said, "As soon as I have the information, I will pass it on."

"Anything else?" asked the Duke. Both Mr Stevens and Grenville shook their heads in unison. "Good, until next week then."

He held out his hand to Mr Stevens, who took the offered hand and shook it and said, "Until next Wednesday, your Grace." Turning to Grenville, he said, "My Lord, a pleasure," as he shook Grenville's hand.

After Mr Stevens left, Grenville said, "Father, I don't know how you could let things get so bad."

His father looked tired and said, "Grenville, I trusted your brother to do his duty towards the family," holding up his hands. "I know I was wrong for trusting him, but in my defence, he was my son and a Hampton."

"You know about mother's inheritance," said Grenville quietly.

"Yes, my boy, I do," replied his father. "She does not know I know, but your brother told me one night, after dinner. That was when we had an argument and the whole rotten truth came out. I was shocked by the extent of it all," said his father.

Grenville looked at his father and felt sorry for him; to have a son dishonour the family name as his brother had was one of the most heinous crimes in his father's eyes. His father said softly, "You know the thing that hurt the most, Grenville?"

"What, father?" asked Grenville.

"That he sat and laughed when he told me like he was not bothered, that the family name and title meant absolutely nothing to him."

Grenville stood, held out his hand and said, "Father, I will restore the family honour and fortune."

"Your grandfather was right," replied his father, as he shook Grenville's hand.

"Oh?" said Grenville.

"He once told me that Stephan would be our ruin but you, Grenville, were a true Hampton and would honour the family." After Grenville left his father's study he went and stood in the main hall, looking up. Grenville stared at the impressive large shield with a yellow background and a large black eagle clutching a lightning bolt in the middle. Grenville remembered his grandfather's words, "*Officium antequam glorificetur*", "*Duty before honour*". "Those words are what us Hamptons have lived by for twelve generations. If you are called upon to do your duty, young Grenville, then the family will expect you to do so."

Next Grenville went to find Preston. He found him in the kitchen reading a newspaper and drinking a cup of tea. "Preston my dear chap, need you to do something for me."

"Ask away, my Lord," replied Preston.

"I now know the full extent of my brother's betrayal of the family." Preston smiled as Grenville went on, "Mr Stevens said that my brother had liquidated certain family items and tried to asset-strip the hall.

"Now, I know he could not have done this without you knowing about it," said Grenville smiling.

Preston gave a chuckle. "Oh, he tried to my Lord," replied Preston, taking a folded piece of paper from his pocket and passing it to Grenville. "Here is the list of the exact items he removed from the hall."

"Preston, sometimes I could kiss you," replied a laughing Grenville. Taking the list, Grenville went to find his mother and father. Finding them both in the reading room, Grenville showed them the piece of paper that Preston had given him; after they both studied the list, the Duchess said, "Three paintings and two statues."

"Got off lightly," the Duke said. "One Gainsborough, one Constable and a Degas."

"He took three of the most expensive, did not know he was so up on art," said the Duchess.

"More his friend than him," replied the Duke.

"And the statues?" said Grenville.

"One was a Constantini Brancusi, and a Henry Moore," said the Duchess.

"I will speak to Stevens to see if any have come up for auction yet," said Grenville. "Don't worry, I will try and get them back."

"I know you will, son," said the Duke.

"I need to take a trip to London; any chance I can use Newton and the car?" asked Grenville.

"Of course, you can," replied the Duke.

Later that day Grenville sat in his room and formulated a plan. Grenville smiled as Tom always drummed it into him. "Always have plans," he said out loud, smiling Grenville decided to first sort out the family's problems, and then he would tackle the S&T Import part. first, he made three phone calls: one to Jonathan and one to Hugo, who both agreed to meet him tomorrow for lunch. The third was to Directly Enquires. He knew the money he had in the Hoddles would raise a few eyebrows and possible attract the wrong interest if he wandered into a bank and tried to deposit over two million pounds in different currencies. So, he decided to sell the diamonds Tom had acquired during his time in Belize. Once he had the number he rang Liebermann diamond exchange. He made an appointment for tomorrow morning as a seller, which Grenville was surprised was easier than he expected. Then again, he did not actually tell them the quantity he had to sell. Smiling, he was going to look forward to seeing their faces.

80·03

Next morning after breakfast, Preston announced that Newton was waiting outside ready to depart. Grenville thanked Preston. "Hope all goes well for you today," said the Duchess, smiling.

"So, do I, mother," replied Grenville, kissing her on the cheek.

"Good luck," said the Duke.

Grenville smiled at his father, shook his hand and said, "Hopefully I shall return with good news."

Watching the Rolls disappear down the drive, the Duke turned to the Duchess and said, "Our boy has changed, so confident and focused."

"His time away was certainly well used, and educational," replied a smiling Duchess.

"Strange," said the Duke.

"Strange why, James?" asked the Duchess.

"I believe Grenville actually can restore the family's honour and estate."

The Duchess walked over to her husband and placed her arm through his. "Never in doubt, my love, he is a true Hampton, just as your father predicted." The Duke smiled and patted his wife's hand, feeling more confident and happier that he had done in many months, and for some strange reason felt less worry now his second son was home.

∮·∱

Grenville climbed into the Rolls Royce and said to Newton, "Hatton Gardens, London, old chap."

"Of course, my Lord." As Newton put the car into gear and moved away, Grenville closed his eyes and tried to find any pitfalls with his plan.

Once they arrived in Hatton Gardens, Grenville said, "Not sure how long I am going to be, Newton."

"Don't worry my Lord, I have some shopping to do for some of the staff, so I can drop you off and return."

"Splendid. As it's now ten, shall we say midday?" asked Grenville.

"Plenty of time my Lord, will be back at midday to pick you up."

Grenville watched Newton merge back into the London traffic before turning to the door that said Liebermann Diamond Exchange. On entering, Grenville went to the reception desk and smiled at the pretty receptionist, and said, "The name is Hampton, I have an appointment."

After checking her computer screen, she said, "Yes sir, I have you here, please take a seat and someone will be with you shortly."

Grenville sat as instructed and picked up a copy of an outdated *Tatler*. Before he had flipped through five pages, a man appeared in front of him and said, "Mr Hampton."

Standing, Grenville smiled and said, "Absolutely," shaking the offered hand.

"I am James Yoshie, junior partner in Liebermann. Please can you follow me."

Grenville followed Mr Yoshie into a well-lit plush room. "Please take a seat, Mr Hampton," said Mr Yoshie, indicating a chair opposite. "So, down to business," said Mr Yoshie. "You have a diamond to sell, and you require an appraisal on it," Mr Yoshie continued.

"Not quite," replied Grenville.

Mr Yoshie looked confused. "Oh, sorry, I was told you had a diamond to sell," said Mr Yoshie.

"Not one, but many," said Grenville, and he placed two pouches on the table and smiled.

Mr Yoshie said, "May I?" pointing at the pouches.

"Please, be my guest," replied Grenville. Mr Yoshie opened each of the pouches' drawstrings and opened out the top. His eyes nearly popped out when he saw the number of diamonds in each pouch.

Mr Yoshie stood and said, "I need to speak to a senior partner. Please wait here, Mr Hampton."

Grenville said, "Of course old chap, no worries."

Mr Yoshie left the room. Grenville placed the pouches back in his pocket, placed his hands behind his head, smiled and waited. Within ten minutes Mr Yoshie returned and said, "Please, Mr Hampton, will you follow me?"

Mr Yoshie took Grenville to the lift; Mr Yoshie stood to one side to allow Grenville to enter the lift first, and once inside Mr Yoshie pressed the eighth button for the top floor. As they ascended to the top floor, soft music was playing in the lift. The lift stopped on the eighth floor, and as the lift doors opened another man was waiting for them.

"Mr Hampton," said the man as Grenville stepped from the lift; Grenville shook the offered hand and smiled. "I am Mr Fisher, assistant to the senior partners, please follow me." Mr Fisher led them down a long corridor to the bottom where a large set of oak doors were closed.

Gently knocking on the doors, a voice from the interior said, "Enter." Mr Fisher opened the large oak doors and entered, followed by Grenville and Mr Yoshie. There, sitting at the top of a table, were three old gentlemen all dressed in Jewish attire. Mr Fisher showed Grenville to the chair opposite, and Grenville sat down and smiled at the three men.

The middle man spoke first in a European-accented English voice. "So, Mr Hampton, let me thank you for picking our establishment to check your merchandise first," said the man. Grenville smiled and nodded as the man went on, "Please can we see what you have to offer?" This time Grenville did not place the pouches on the table but emptied the contents of both pouches onto the soft fabric that covered the table. First the pouch full of cut diamonds that made a neat pile, second the seven uncut diamonds; the smallest was bigger than a human knuckle.

The three men did not show any emotion, but Mr Yoshie and Fisher both took an audible intake of breath. The middle man leant back and spoke to the man standing behind him, who quickly left.

"Well, Mr Hampton," said the middle man.

"Grenville, please," replied Grenville.

"Grenville," smiled the old man, "you have quite a stash here. May I ask where you acquired such a large collection?"

"I can assure you that they are not stolen, if that's what you think," said Grenville.

"Don't worry, if we thought that, we would have had the police here by now," said the old man to the right.

"I have been abroad travelling in Central America and a friend and I acquired them. Unfortunately, due to work commitments, he is unable to be in the UK now," said Grenville with a smile.

"Indeed," said the middle old man. Just then a light knock on the door where the middle old man said, "Enter." In walked a small rounded old man with thick glasses, who came to the table and bowled deeply.

"You asked for my assistance, Mr Liebermann," he said in a light whisper.

"Bernard what do you make of these seven stones, and can you give us a quick appraisal?" Pointing to the table, Bernard stared at the pile of cut diamonds, but was not interested; his eyes were drawn to the seven uncut diamonds. Taking a seat and producing a small magnifying glass, he picked up each diamond and examined them. After about ten minutes he said, "Central American, flawless, uncut, over 10 carats per diamond. Excellent quality as well," he whispered and smiled.

"Thank you, Bernard, for your appraisal," said the old man on the right, smiling. Bernard stood and bowled and left the room.

"Please, Grenville, if you would step outside for a moment while we discuss your merchandise and make a judgement?" asked the middle man.

"Of course, my pleasure," said Grenville, standing, and with a slight bow, left the room accompanied by Mr Yoshie. Grenville took a seat outside while he waited to be summoned back in.

After twenty minutes Mr Fisher opened the door and said, "Mr Hampton, please," indicating to the interior of the room. Grenville went and sat in the same chair. The middle man had a brown thin folder in front on him.

"Obviously, we have done some checking, my Lord," said the middle man, smiling. Grenville bowed his head in acknowledgement. "You have not been totally honest with us, Grenville," said the man to the left.

"I don't understand," said a worried Grenville.

The man continued, "You are Grenville St Louis Hampton. Earl of Eastleigh and future Duke of Hampshire, your brother Stephan who recently died left your family estate in quite a mess. And you have recently returned from a time in Belize," said the man, smiling. "We like to know who we are dealing with, my Lord," said the man.

Grenville opened his hands and said, "You are correct, I am who you say I am," replied Grenville, "but I am trying to put back together my family and restore my family estate."

The man to the right spoke for the first time. "Family, we can understand that."

"So down to business," said the man in the middle. "These we will take off your hands now," he said. "The uncut, we would like to keep and appraise properly," he said. Before Grenville could speak, he said, "Of course we will give you a holding payment, and once we have decided on a correct price give you the balance." The man opened the folder in front of him and extracted a white banker's draft, and, face down, slid it over to Grenville.

Grenville took the banker's draft and turned it over, and the figure even made him look twice. The figure on the banker's draft was for twenty million.

"Of course, the uncut diamonds should treble the figure once they have been correctly cut and polished," said the man.

Standing, the man in the middle held out his hand to Grenville. "Let's hope we can be of use to each other in the future," he said, smiling.

"I think we can do more business," replied Grenville. The three men were smiling as Grenville left the room. Grenville stood outside Liebermann and took in a deep breath and closed his eyes; that went better than expected, he thought to himself. "Phase one complete, onto the next phase." Just then Grenville heard the honk of the Rolls Royce as Newton came around the corner and stopped next to him.

"East India Club, St James Square," said Grenville as he got into the Rolls Royce.

Newton said, "As you wish, my Lord," and once Grenville was settled pulled away from the curb. As the Rolls Royce departed, the three men watched from the upper window of Liebermann. One said, "So what do we make of young Hampton? A lucrative business opportunity, I suspect."

The other two nodded in agreement. "If the rumours are true and he has more items to sell, we should do well," said one of them.

"But we need to be cautious, we all know who he is aligned with now," said the third man, "and we all know how dangerous they can be, so let's keep faith with young Hampton."

"Agreed," they said in unison.

⊗⋅⊘

Arriving at the East India Club, Grenville noticed Jonathan was already waiting. As the Rolls Royce pulled up, Jonathan opened the door and allowed Grenville to exit. "My dear fellow," said Jonathan, as he embraced Grenville. Grenville returned the hug, and slapped Jonathan on the back.

"Good to see you again, old bean," said Grenville.

"Let me look at you," said Jonathan, holding Grenville at arm's length. "You look well, Belize obviously agreed with you."

"It was amazing, Jonathan," was all Grenville said in reply.

Grenville turned to Newton and said, "Can you return and pick me up at four?"

"Of course, my Lord," replied Newton as he indicated to merge back into the traffic.

"Before Hugo arrives, let me apologise about the letter," said Jonathan, looking sheepish.

"No need to old chap, I understand you were put in a no-win situation by my father," smiled Grenville.

"Thank you, old bean. I was rather put under pressure to write to you," said Jonathan softly.

Grenville hugged Jonathan and said, "You have always been a true friend," laughing. After a few minutes chatting a taxi pulled up and Hugo Thorpe got out.

Grenville smiled. Hugo had not changed one bit; a little rounder but still with a smile on his face. Hugo hugged both Grenville and Jonathan. "Dear chaps, so good to see you both, and all three of us together again after all these years," said Hugo. "I have booked a private room for lunch," he went on. "Follow me."

Smiling, both Grenville and Jonathan followed Hugo to the private room in the club. After ordering drinks and taking a comfy chair, each toasted Rayleigh School, and each other. "So," Hugo started, "although it is lovely to see you, Grenville old bean, I got the feeling your invite was not totally social."

"Astute as usual," replied Grenville, smiling.

Grenville continued, "I don't know how much Jonathan has told you about our trip to Belize and our recent acquaintance, Tom."

"Jonathan gave me a good grounding on your recent activities in Belize, up to the time he left," confirmed Hugo.

"Excellent," replied Grenville. "Putting that aside for one moment, what you might not be aware of is the state my brother has left my family in."

"We have heard the rumours," said Jonathan, as Hugo nodded his head in acknowledgement.

"Easington Investment Bank," said Hugo quietly.

Grenville said, "So you have heard of it."

"It's the talk of the city," said Hugo. "Easington Investment Bank as a traditional investment bank only did financial advisory work. For example, a big corporation might ask for the bank's help if it wants to borrow money in the bond markets, or float itself on the stock market, or buy up another company.

"In this capacity, the investment bank acts as an impartial adviser – like a solicitor or an accountant – using its expertise to help its client in return for a fee. But since Dexter Simon-Smyth took over the reins, Easington Investment Bank have changed track; they are dealing directly in financial markets for their own accounts. They are buying financial assets from one client, and then selling them to another – often with a hefty mark-up," continued Hugo. "To help boost their credit, your brother became an investor with the bank using his, or your family's, money."

"So, they are losing money now?" asked Grenville.

"So, the City rumour mill is speculating, and no one is touching them," replied Hugo.

"How much is the family estate in for?" asked Jonathan.

"Roughly five million," Grenville said, "but we estimate he lost just under twenty million."

"My dear chap, I never knew it was that bad," said Hugo.

"Water under the bridge now, old chap," replied Grenville.

"But you are going to be OK?" asked Jonathan.

"Of course, dear chap, us Hamptons are made of sterner stuff," smiled Grenville.

"Well, if you need any advice," said Hugo.

"Now you mention that, old chap…" said Grenville, smiling at then both. "Jonathan, old chap, did Mr Stevens get in contact with you?"

"Now you mention it, he did indeed," replied Jonathan, taking a folded piece of paper from his pocket. "First, the exact amount of debt owed by your estate to date is four million, four hundred and seventy-eight pounds, which will not change until the end of next week, where two per cent will be added for another week," said Jonathan. "The exact date the debt has to be cleared by is three months' time, but obviously the debt can be called in by Easington Investment Bank anytime," continued Jonathan, "and as for the legal document your father signed over the estate to your brother it is now forfeit, I suspect your Mr Stevens was very clever in the wording as it was a contract between the Duke of Hampshire and the Earl of Eastleigh, so as no names were used, only titles, once one of the titles changes hands then the original document becomes void. Plus, as far as Mr Stevens can determine no further claims have been made against the estate, so only Easington's have a claim," said Jonathan, smiling.

"Thank you very much, Jonathan," said Grenville, "now back to my original topic."

"Your friend Tom," replied Hugo.

"Exactly," said Grenville. Grenville went on to explain in part his plan for S&T Imports and the setup of his new business venture. "I would like you both to help me set it all up," said Grenville, "of course I am not expecting your expertise for free, and I know you are both busy in your present employment."

"No problem on my part, old man," said Hugo, smiling.

"Thank you, Hugo, old chap," replied Grenville.

"Well, I can help out as and when I can, of course," said Jonathan.

"Thank you, Jonathan, I understand your law practice is your main concern, but any help you give would be invaluable," said Grenville, smiling. Grenville explained what he wanted them both to do for him before their next meeting. "Hugo, I want you to register S&T Imports as a private UK company, and set up a bank account," said Grenville, as he passed over all the relevant documentation he had gotten from Tom to Hugo. Hugo scanned the paperwork, nodding.

"No problem old bean, will do that for you," said Hugo smiling.

"Jonathan, as S&T Imports' new solicitor I want you to find me creditable office space here in London for the company to trade from," asked Grenville.

"That it? No worries old bean," replied Jonathan.

"Now, shall we eat?" asked Hugo. Both Jonathan and Grenville smiled at Hugo, as nothing stopped him from eating; he was the same at school and would never change.

Last stop, Grenville had Newton take him to the family bank. On entering the bank, Grenville went to reception and smiled at the pretty girl behind the counter. The girl smiled back and said, "Yes sir how may I help you?"

"I am the Earl of Eastleigh and was wondering if I could have a quick word with Mr Sacks."

The girl said, "Of course my Lord, if you take a seat over there I will see if he is free." As the girl picked up the phone, Grenville smiled and went and sat down. Mr Sacks had been the family's personal manager for many years. Grenville still remembered the day his father had brought him into the bank to open his first bank account in his own name.

Just as Grenville was reminiscing, he spotted Mr Sacks come through the door and walk towards him. Standing, Grenville smiled and held out his hand. "Mr Sacks, so good of you to receive me at such short notice."

Mr Sacks took the offered hand and said, "Of course, my Lord. Please come this way," indicating to a side office. Once the door was closed and they were both settled, Mr Sacks said, "I am sorry for your recent family bereavement."

"Thank you, most kind," replied Grenville, smiling.

"And of course, your elevation to the title," said Mr Sacks.

Grenville nodded and smiled. "Don't worry, Mr Sacks, I am aware what my brother did to my family's estate's bank account."

Mr Sacks smiled and said, "Sorry, but your brother, shall we say, would not take any advice from me or the bank, so in the end we had to terminate the estate's credit line."

"I totally understand," said Grenville. "Just as a matter of interest, can you tell me how much the family estate account is overdrawn by?"

Mr Sacks turned to the computer and after several keystrokes looked at Grenville and said, "Just short of six hundred thousand pounds, my Lord. We have of course allowed your father to pay the estate wage bill, for the last few months."

Grenville understood from the tone that the bank would not allow this state of affairs to carry on indefinitely. "And my personal account?" asked Grenville.

After a few more keystrokes, Mr Sacks looked up, smiled, and said, "You are in the black by four hundred and twenty pounds."

"Thank you, Mr Sacks, most kind." Taking the banker's draft from his inside pocket, Grenville passed it over to Mr Sacks and said, "I would like to deposit this banker's draft into my personal account and clear off my family estate account's overdraft."

Mr Sacks picked up the banker's draft and Grenville could tell by his face he was having trouble digesting the figure on the banker's draft.

"Any problems?" asked Grenville casually.

Without taking his gaze from the banker's draft, Mr Sacks said, "Of course not my Lord, no problem at all." Standing, Mr Sacks said, "If you could wait here my Lord, I will go and process this banker's draft for you."

"My dear chap, take your time," replied Grenville, smiling.

Once Mr Sacks had left, Grenville closed his eyes and thought, at least the bank was on the ball in seeing Stephan's madness, and closed the family estate account down quickly. Just short of six hundred thousand pounds was to Grenville not bad, as he knew without the bank's quick intervention it could have been much worse. His father would be pleased to have the family estate account back in credit with the bank.

A smiling Mr Sacks returned and sat behind the computer once again. After a few taps, he looked up and said, "Do you wish to clear all the overdraft, my Lord?"

"Just transfer a million from my account to the family estate account, if you would be so kind," smiled Grenville.

After a few taps Mr Sacks looked up and said, "Your family estate account is now back in the black, anything else I can help you with today, my Lord?" asked Mr Sacks.

"There is just one more thing, can you let me have a banker's draft for four million, four hundred and seventy-eight pounds, drawn from my personal account" smiled Grenville.

"I will send it down to the estate by courier tomorrow," said Mr Sacks bowing his head.

Standing and holding out his hand, Grenville said, "Mr Sacks, as always you been professional and a credit to the bank."

On the way home to Hampton Hall, Grenville closed his eyes and went over the day. He was sure he had not missed anything from the plan, but he must admit the plan went better than even he had anticipated. He was mildly surprised how easy it was to sell the diamonds and he was sure by what was said at Liebermann's that anything else Grenville had to sell would be considered, and receiving a cheque before he had left was an unexpected windfall. This made Grenville smile. Still smiling, Grenville thought about Jonathan and Hugo; it was brilliant to see them both again, neither had changed one bit, and he realised he had missed their company. Now they were both on board and were going to help him set up S&T Imports as a UK company, he felt a lot easier as he knew that if anyone could make S&T Imports a success Jonathan and Hugo would; also, they would steer Grenville in the right direction, and would advise him on what needed to be done. The bank was also a surprise, although

Mr Sacks was stunned by the size of the banker's draft he had presented, and cashed it without any questions. Grenville was pleased he had cleared the estate's account and placed it back into the black; this, he knew, would please his parents. Grenville thought about next Wednesday and the reading of his brother's will. Smiling, Grenville was sure he would not even be mentioned in it, but Grenville was going to look forward to the show down with Easington Investment Bank and especially that toad Mr Dexter Simon-Smyth. All in all, a very good day, and from now on Grenville knew he would be able, as he had promised to Tom, to help him continue his quest.

ଓ · ଔ

The next day Grenville found his father in his study. "Father, can I have a word?"

"Of course, my boy, what is on your mind?" asked the Duke.

"I popped into the bank while I was in London, said Grenville.

"The estate account," said the Duke.

"Overdraft cleared and back in the black," said a smiling Grenville.

"How?" said a shocked Duke.

"Just, shall we say, it was a windfall from Belize."

The Duke stared at his son. "What you got there?" asked the Duke, spotting the holdall Grenville was holding for the first time.

"A means to an end," Grenville replied. Opening the holdall, Grenville placed the content on his father's desk. His father sat and stared at the growing piles of money that Grenville was placing on the desk.

"Where did you get so much money?" asked the Duke.

"Shall we say, my trip to Belize was not all fun," said a smiling Grenville. "It was your friend James McLeish, the ambassador of Belize, that allowed me to bring it through in the diplomatic baggage," said Grenville.

"That was good of old McLeish," said the Duke.

"Well, I did kind of lay it on strong that you would be most grateful that he had helped his friend's son and a fellow of Rayleigh School," said Grenville, smiling.

"I am not going to ask any more. How much is here?" said the Duke.

"About a million, give or take a few notes," said Grenville, smiling.

The Duke stared at the piles of money, finally lifting one from the desk and holding it. "I don't understand," said his father.

"To pay the house staff and estate workers a bonus," said Grenville. "I am sure they have all been worried about the state of the estate, and this may restore their confidence in the family. A bonus is always welcome," continued Grenville.

"Thank you, my boy," said his father softly. Grenville noticed his eyes watering.

"Plus, I am sure any left over, you and mother could put to good use and place your personal accounts back into the black. Look on it as a gift from a grateful son," said Grenville softly.

The Duke looked at his son and came around the desk and hugged him. For the first time in his life, Grenville felt close to his father. "Can I tell your mother, or is this our secret?" asked his father.

"Please tell mother, I don't want any more secrets in this family," said a smiling Grenville.

"You are so right, my boy," replied his father, smiling as well.

Later that day Grenville helped his father place the money into bonus envelopes for the estate staff. The Duke placed the remaining money into the safe, and said he and the Duchess would take a trip to London and deposit the money into their personal accounts. The Duke said, "My son, you have made me so proud once again."

Grenville smiled at his father and quietly said, "*Audere est facere.*"

The Duke smiled back and remembered the school motto as well: "To dare is to do."

80 · 03

Next day Preston had been requested to gather all the staff for an announcement from the Duke himself. Most were under the impression that it was going to be bad news; some of the younger members of staff were not bothered as they were young enough to find other employment, but most of the staff had been with the family and house for years, some second and third generations of family, so Hampton Hall and estate was family, not a job, to some members of staff.

All the staff was gathered in the great hall. There was a soft murmur amongst them. The eleventh Duke of Hampshire stood on the third step up on the grand staircase looking down on them; standing by his side were the Duchess and his second son the twelfth Earl of Eastleigh.

The Duke started, "Thank you all for attending this short gathering. I know you are all extremely busy, so will not keep you long. As you all know by now, that there were certain rumours bandied about that Hampton Estate was in a state of financial flux, and I know you all have been worried about your future employment at the Hall and around the estate. Well, let me assure you all here and now, that your employment is safe and there is no risk to the Hall or the estate, now or in the future, this you have my word on." This brought a soft murmur from the gathered staff. The Duke went on, "You will all be receiving a cash bonus, and I hope this will go some way in setting your minds at rest, and I apologise if any miscommunication has been spread by the rumour mill. I would ask if anyone in the future asks you about Hampton Hall, then you tell them we are buoyant and as always a happy family." This brought a round of applause from the gathered crowd. "Preston will send you in as and when we call you forward, I would appreciate your patience until you are called and let me finish by saying that on behalf of my family and I, we thank you for your loyal service to us, and hope you will continue to loyally serve the family and the estate."

The Duke with the Duchess and Grenville went into the study where they sat behind the desk waiting for the staff to appear. Mr and Mrs Preston went in first. After a light knock they entered the study.

"Preston and Mrs Preston," said the Duke, smiling. After handing them their envelopes the Duke said, "Without you two, Hampton Hall would never be the same, thank you for your support and future endeavours."

"Our pleasure," replied Preston for them both, slightly bowing.

"We have and always will serve the family," said Mrs Preston.

"Thank you both," said the Duchess.

"Now, Preston, if you could send them all in one at a time, I would be most grateful," asked the Duke.

Preston bowed and said, "My pleasure, your Grace."

After three hours Preston appeared and said, "That was the last one, your Grace."

"Thank god for that," said the Duchess softly. Grenville smiled. It had been quite enjoyable for him, watching his mother and father engage each member of staff as if they were family and not staff, asking about personal things, making them feel special, and all the time remaining the Duke and Duchess of the estate. It was an art form, not taught.

Grenville's mind wandered back to a time when he was a small boy. One day Grenville and his grandfather were walking in the grounds, and they spotted a gardener. They approached the gardener and as they did, his grandfather said, "Hobbs my dear chap, how is the wife?"

The gardener stopped what he was doing and removed his cap and said, "On the mend, thank you for asking your Grace, and she loved the basket of fruit you sent."

"Well, send her my regards, won't you," said Grenville's grandfather as they strolled off.

After a short time, when they were alone again, Grenville asked, "How did you know about Hobbs and his wife, grandfather?"

"Grenville, it is your place to always know what is happening on the estate, the people are not just staff, they are family, and so you should let them know now and again that you are interested in their wellbeing. Plus, it makes them happy knowing that even though you are blue blooded you do have a heart and care," said his grandfather, smiling.

"I understand, grandfather," said Grenville.

After they were alone, the Duke said, "That went well, I thought."

"I think they all went away happy," replied the Duchess, smiling.

"Well done, son," said the Duke.

"Yes, my darling, you have made both your father and I proud," added the Duchess.

"Glad to be of help," said Grenville, smiling at them both.

"Wednesday to get out of the way now," said the Duke.

"But at least now we go into it with a positive attitude," replied the Duchess. Both Grenville and his father nodded at the sentiment and smiled.

⁖·⁗

Wednesday came and Grenville was up bright and early, as his parents were as well. At breakfast the Duchess said, "I hope this is over with quickly."

"I cannot see Stephan having much of a will," replied the Duke.

"It's seeing that odious man again, his friend Dexter," said the Duchess. This made Grenville laugh. "Never could take to him, unlike Jonathan or Hugo, he always reminds me of a smiling snake," the Duchess continued. "But at least Sara will be here, so there is a silver lining," said the Duchess, smiling. Grenville never considered his brother's betrothed would be in attendance, but then he never did ask who was attending.

"Do you know who is actually attending the reading, father?" asked Grenville.

"Not really, never thought to enquire of Stevens who was coming," replied the Duke.

Grenville was looking out of the window as cars started to arrive. On spotting Stevens pull up, Grenville went to meet him. "Mr Stevens, how the devil are you?" asked Grenville with his hand out.

Mr Stevens took the offered hand and said, "Very well, my Lord, hope you are well."

"Splendid," Grenville replied. "Thank you for passing on the information I asked for, most helpful," said Grenville, smiling.

"Glad to be of service, my Lord," said Mr Stevens.

"Absolutely," said Grenville, still smiling.

Grenville spotted Dexter Simon-Smyth pull up; not wanting to speak to him, Grenville followed Mr Stevens into the hall. Grenville went into the reading room to find his mother. She was sitting chatting to a pretty young blonde lady who Grenville did not recognise.

"Grenville," said his mother as she spotted him.

Grenville smiled at them both. "Mother," he replied.

"You remember Sara," said his mother, smiling.

Grenville took the offered hand and kissed it lightly and said, "The pleasure is all mine, Miss Farthing."

"Sara, please, my Lord," said Sara.

"As you command. And please call me Grenville," replied Grenville, smiling.

"Thank you, Grenville, most kind," Sara said, looking intently at Grenville. Sofia watched the exchange with a deep satisfaction. Sofia had to admit Sara had been far too good for Stephan, and if she had married him she would have had a dull life, always in the background without an opinion, and totally miserable. Sofia also suspected it was more her father than her pushing the union.

Grenville was love-struck as he gazed into her blue eyes and for the first time in his life he felt he was falling in love. All he could do was smile at Sara. Sara smiled back, and Sofia tried not to laugh at them.

The Duke came in and broke the spell and said, "They are ready for us now."

"Good, shall we?" said the Duchess, as all four went into the library for the reading of Stephan's will. As they took their places, Grenville looked about and apart from Mr Stevens, who sat at the front, Dexter Simon-Smyth sat with another man both dressed in suits – the man with Dexter looked like a lawyer to Grenville – apart from his father, mother and Sara, there were two other men present. Grenville wondered who these men could be.

Mr Stevens started, "Good morning. Thank you all for coming to the reading of the late Stephan James Hampton, the eleventh Earl of Eastleigh's last will and testament." Mr Stevens continued, "The late Stephan James Hampton made me sole executor of his last will and testament." Mr Stevens looked up and gave a slight nod to Dexter Simon-Smyth, who returned the nod with a smile. As Grenville looked at his face, the sly smile looked like to Grenville he knew exactly what was in his late brother's will, and to Dexter Simon-Smyth it was all good news.

As Mr Stevens went on with the legal parts of the will, Grenville took a sideways look at Sara who sat there next to his mother and smiled. She had changed so much since he had last seen her. It was the weekend before he left for Belize, she had come down for the weekend with her parents. Grenville's memory of that weekend was blurry at the best of times so he could not remember what impression he had made upon her. Grenville looked up as Mr Stevens was starting the beneficiaries of Stephan's will. "To my good friend, Mr Dexter Simon-Smyth, I leave my entire estate as well as my peerage."

Grenville's father was on his feet in a flash. Mr Stevens, before the Duke had time to speak, held his hand up and waved him down. The Duke sat down just as quick. Grenville noticed Dexter Simon-Smyth was sitting with a smug look on his face. So, that was his game, the title and the estate from Stephan. Mr Stevens went on leaving various bequests to family and friends. After an hour, Mr Steven look up and closed the will. "That concludes the reading of the will of the late Stephan James Hampton, the eleventh Earl of Eastleigh."

Dexter Simon-Smyth spoke first. "Thank you, Mr Stevens elegantly carried out. But I am afraid that this may be your last commission for the Hampton Estate." The man with him smiled at this and he gave a slight giggle.

"Why do you say that, Sir?" Mr Stevens asked.

"The will, man, Stephan passed the title to me, you old fool."

"Sir, the late Earl of Eastleigh passed you nothing but his worldly goods." Everyone was engrossed in the exchanged between Mr Stevens and Mr Dexter Simon-Smyth.

"What are you talking about you old fool, talk sense," said Dexter Simon-Smyth, raising his voice.

Mr Stevens ignored the verbal abuse and quietly said, "Mr Stephan James Hampton was the Earl of Eastleigh by birth and hereditary title only given to him by the Duke of Hampshire, his father, so Stephan James Hampton was never the titled Duke of the realm, he was only heir apparent." The room was silent. "And as such, could not pass on the title he only had by bequest from his father, the Duke of Hampshire," said Mr Stevens. "But," he went on, holding up a document, "here is a copy of a legal formally signed act of Hereditary Peerages passing from the still living Duke of Hampshire to his remaining living second son, Grenville St Louis, who has become the twelfth Earl of Eastleigh and the next in line to inherit the Dukedom of Hampshire. This will supersede the one sign by the late Earl of Eastleigh Stephan James Hampton, so only Grenville St Louis Hampton can have a claim on the family title. So, Mr Dexter Simon-Smyth, as I first correctly stated, you only get Stephan James Hampton's worldly goods," said Mr Stevens, smiling for the first time.

Dexter Simon-Smyth stood and ripped the document from Mr Stevens' hand and passed it to the man with him, who quickly studied the document. "This is all bull shit, Stephan assured me the title was mine," said Dexter Simon-Smyth.

"And no doubt it would have been if he had been the actual Duke of Hampshire," said Mr Stevens softly. The man spoke to Dexter Simon-Smyth in a dull whisper. Grenville knew by the look on Simon-Smyth's face it was not what he wanted to hear.

Dexter Simon-Smyth nodded to the two strange men and said, "I did not want it to come to this on such a day but you have forced my hand."

The two strangers went to the Duke and said "Your Grace, we are High Court Enforcement Officers," holding out a white bundle of papers. "This is a High Court writ brought against your estate by the Easington Investment Bank to the sum of four million, four hundred and seventy-eight pounds, payable today," said the High Court Enforcement Officer.

Dexter Simon-Smyth said, turning to the man with him, "I win, I think. At least I get the estate." The man nodded and smiled.

"Wait." Everyone turned towards Grenville. "Gentlemen, I have a banker's draft here for the full amount," said Grenville, smiling. The High Court Enforcement Officer said, "Of course, my Lord. We just need a few minutes to clear the banker's draft with head office."

"Excellent," said Grenville. "Anyone got a pen I could borrow so I can sign it over?" he asked, holding up the banker's draft.

Dexter Simon-Smyth looked totally shocked by the turn of events. The Duke went to him and said, "Sir, if you have finished your business, I will ask you to leave my estate."

Dexter Simon-Smyth glared at the Duke, realised everyone in the room was looking at him, smiled, gave a small bow and said as he was leaving, "This is most definitely not over."

Grenville signed the banker's draft and after thirty minutes the High Court Enforcement Officer returned and handed a receipt to Grenville and said, "Thank you, my Lord. That concludes our business, the debt raised by Easington Investment Bank against the Estate of the Duke of Hampshire has now been cleared, and the matter is now closed," said the man as he passed over the bundle of papers to Grenville, "thank you for your time." Both men slightly bowed to the Duke and the Duchess and left.

After they left, Grenville, his mother and father all started to laugh. Sara joined in, even Mr Stevens who was normally so traditional was smiling and said, "That felt so good."

The Duke slapped Mr Stevens on the back then said, "You were outstanding, my dear Stevens."

Mr Stevens said softly, "A solid answer to everything is not necessary, blurry concepts influence one to focus, but postulated clarity influences arrogance."

Grenville went to his father and held out the bundle of paper the High Court Enforcement Office had given him and said, "Father, your estate is returned to you."

Smiling, the Duke took the papers from Grenville smiled and said, "Words cannot express how I feel right now." He had tears in his eyes as he hugged Grenville. The Duke passed the bundle of papers over to Mr Stevens and said, "Can you keep these with the other family documents?"

Taking the bundle of papers, Mr Stevens said, "It would as always, your Grace, be my pleasure." Mr Stevens bowed deeply to them all. Just before he left, Mr Stevens said softly, "I now feel confident about submitting my bill." This made everyone laugh.

After Mr Stevens left, the four of them were sitting in the lounge. Mr Stevens was correct, said the Duke.

"In what way, my dear?" asked the Duchess.

"The arrogance of Simon-Smyth. He was so sure he had the title and estate in his grubby hands," the Duke went on.

"Always have a plan," said Grenville softly.

"Sorry, what did you say darling?" asked his mother.

"Nothing, just something a friend told me once," replied Grenville, smiling.

"Fancy a walk in the grounds, Grenville?" asked Sara.

"Love to," replied Grenville, standing.

After they left the Duchess said, "What do you think, my darling?"

"Sorry, not with you, my love," replied the Duke.

"Grenville and Sara, a nice match."

"Well, she cannot do any worse than her first choice," said the Duke.

"That's what I was thinking," replied the Duchess, smiling as she looking out of the window, and watched them walk away together.

ဆ · ၶ

Grenville and Sara walked in silence, until they reached the stone gondola on a small rise, out of sight of the hall. Sara took a seat. Grenville went and sat next to her.

"I killed him," Sara said in a whisper.

"Sorry, what did you say?" said Grenville.

"Your brother, Stephan, I killed him," she said a little louder.

"It was an accident, the police report said so, no need to blame yourself, Sara," said Grenville, smiling.

"I know what the police report said, I was there in the car," said Sara, putting her head in her hand. She started to sob.

Grenville placed his arm around her and said gently, "Tell me the whole story."

After a silence, Sara started to speak. "I never really loved Stephan, it was my father who pushed for the match, a good match, a titled husband. But I found him arrogant and aggressive, treated me like he did any servant. You know what he actually said to me after we became engaged?"

Grenville shook his head, not wanting to speak for fear of stopping her flow.

"He said my sole job was to produce an heir to further the family line, apart from that he did not see any use for me."

"But I thought he was going to pass the title to his friend Dexter," said Grenville.

Sara started to laugh. "Stephan was going to change that once he had his heir. He only agreed to Dexter's plan because he was so in debt to him, and giving him the title in his will was a way he played to Dexter's ego. Stephan never showed love or loyalty to anyone," said Sara. Grenville nodded in agreement, thinking of his brother. Sara continued "The evening we were driving down to Hampton Hall, I had decided to finish with him. He tried on many occasions, especially when he was drunk, to have his way with me, but I always managed to fight him off. The last occasion he was in such a rage that he said when we were married, he would beat me if I ever tried to refuse him, as it was his right as my husband, and not a court in the land would disagree.

"As the wedding got closer I was losing my nerve, so I decided to tell him it was all over. As we drove down he was in his usual bullish attitude, saying some awful things about your parents and Hampton Hall. It was like he hated them and the place."

Grenville nodded and said, "My grandfather once told me there are two types of future heirs to the title, some find the prospect exciting and some it fills them with dread. Stephan was the latter."

Sara nodded at Grenville's words, and continued, "As we continued driving down, I told him I wanted to break our engagement. He went red in the face and went mad, I have never seen him so angry. He started to swerve over the road. I got scared as he turned to me and said, 'Listen bitch, you try and back out now and make me look foolish in front of everyone at this late stage and I will kill you'." Sara put her head in her hands and started to cry.

"It's still not your fault, Sara," said Grenville, "he lost control and by what you have told me he was out of control."

"You don't understand, Grenville," said Sara softly, "while he was ranting and raving at me, I unbuckled his seat belt and grabbed the steering wheel. He tried to punch me in the face, but he missed and as he only had one hand on the wheel something ran out in front of us. As he swerved, he hit a wet patch and he lost control of the car and we hit the tree and as we bounced off. The last thing I remember was Stephan going through the windscreen."

Grenville took Sara in his arms and let her cry her sorrow out. Grenville knew she would feel so much better now she had unburdened herself with the story to someone. Grenville was glad it was him she trusted enough to tell her story to. "Have you told anyone else this story?" asked Grenville softly in her ear.

"No, no one," she replied.

"Good," said Grenville, "it will be our secret." Taking her face in his hands Grenville kissed her. She returned the kiss. After a time, she rested her head on his shoulder, and felt happy for the first time in many months. There both sat like that until the last of the sun was just dipping over the horizon. Finally, Grenville stood, took Sara's hand, and they both made their way back to the Hall.

The Duchess was looking out of the windows and noticed them approaching and said, "Excellent," and smiled.

"Sorry, did you say something?" asked the Duke.

"Nothing important, darling," she replied, still smiling.

"You are so different from your brother," said Sara.

Grenville smiled and said, "I do hope so."

Sara went on, "Since we first met that weekend you seem different, more self-assured, hard to put my finger on it."

"For better or worse?" replied Grenville, laughing.

Sara laughed as well. "Last time I thought you spoiled and immature."

"And now?" asked Grenville.

Squeezing his hand, Sara said, "Definitely for the better," which made them both laugh.

As they were sitting chatting to his parents, Preston announced that the Earl had a phone call from Mr Jonathan Spencer.

"Must take this," said Grenville, as he went and followed Preston from the room.

After Grenville left, the Duchess turned to Sara and said, "You two seem to be getting close."

Sara went red, and said, "He is so different from his brother."

"Indeed, he is," replied the Duchess.

"And changed, since last time we met," Sara said.

"I know what you mean dear, he has become a man instead of a lost boy."

"Totally," replied Sara, smiling. "So, you don't mind if we carry on getting to know each other?" Sara asked.

"You have my blessing," said the Duchess, leaning over to kiss Sara on the cheek.

"Thank you," replied Sara.

"Jonathan, my dear chap how the devil you fairing?" Grenville asked.

"Very well, thank you Grenville for asking," replied Jonathan. "Good news old bean," Jonathan went on, "Think I found you the perfect premises, Bombard Street. Used to be an old insurance company building. Been on the market for years. Plus, it's a snip at just over the million mark."

"Why so cheap?" asked Grenville.

"There is the rub, my dear chap. It's tucked away down a side street so not very easy to find," said Jonathan.

"Sounds promising. Can you set me up tomorrow afternoon for a viewing, old chap?" asked Grenville.

"Of course, will do. Let's say three," replied Jonathan.

"Perfect, and can you have Hugo meet us as well?"

"Of course, old chap, see you tomorrow."

"Bye for now, and thank you, Jonathan," said Grenville, setting down the phone. Returning to the lounge, he could see his mother and Sara in deep discussion. "You two look like you are scheming," said a smiling Grenville. Before they could answer, Grenville said, "Got to go to London tomorrow, Sara, would you like to accompany me?"

"Sounds intriguing," said Sara, laughing.

"Jonathan has found a property for my new business venture so thought a woman's eyes cast over it cannot harm," replied Grenville.

"It's a date, only if dinner is thrown in," said Sara, smiling.

"You drive a hard bargain, Miss Farthing," said Grenville.

"Get used to it, Mr Hampton," replied Sara, which made them all laugh.

୫୦ · ଓଃ

Next morning, Grenville and Sara took the train to London. After a leisurely lunch, and using a map, they made their way to Bombard Street. Grenville spotted Hugo loitering in the street. "Hugo," Grenville shouted. Hugo waved back. Grenville and Hugo hugged. "Hugo, let me introduce Sara," said Grenville.

"Hello Sara, nice to meet you," said Hugo.

Sara smiled and said, "You too, Hugo."

Just then they spotted Jonathan coming down the street. Once he arrived, he hugged both Grenville and Hugo. Grenville said, "Jonathan, you remember Sara?"

"Of course, nice to meet you again my dear," said Jonathan, smiling.

Sara smiled back. "You too, Jonathan," she replied.

Hugo turned to Jonathan and whispered, "How do you know Sara?"

"She was Grenville's brother Stephan's fiancée and in the car when he died," replied Jonathan.

"Intriguing," smiled Hugo.

"Definitely," replied Jonathan.

Just then a taxi showed up and an elegant lady got out. Jonathan went across and said, "Miss Hughes."

The lady smiled and said, "Please, Mr Spencer, call me Anna."

Jonathan smiled and said, "Please call me Jonathan, Anna." Jonathan introduced everyone and Anna shook hands with them all.

"So, Anna, tell us about this lovely building," asked Grenville.

Anna went up the steps and opened the double doors onto a dark spacious reception area. Locating the light switch, Anna switched the lights on and they all stood in a magnificent reception area designed in the late Victorian/early Edwardian era.

Anna started, "Welcome to Bombard House, originally used by the Bombard Insurance Company, who went into liquidation during the Lloyds list scandal. The property is of late Victorian/early Edwardian period covering five floors, with three internal lifts, and stairs, also having a private car park to the rear for ten or so cars. The building conforms to all the current fire, health and safety regulations."

"How flexible are the building regulations?" asked Grenville.

"I can find out," replied Anna, "but normally, they tend to baulk if you try and change exterior rather than interior, so interior has more flexibility by building control."

"Super. if you could liaise with Jonathan on the points we raise, that would be most helpful," smiled Grenville.

Anna smiled back, "Of course," she replied.

"Jonathan, old chap, do you mind taking lead on this?"

"Of course, old bean," replied Jonathan. Both Grenville and Hugo smiled; there was no way Jonathan was going to pass up a chance to get to know the lovely Anna more.

"Shall we start at the top and work down?" suggested Grenville. Everyone agreed as they moved towards the stairs. After a guided tour of the building, which took over two hours, by the time they reached the reception area again Grenville had already made up his mind.

"Anna, thank you for a wonderful fully briefed tour of the property, your knowledge was excellent," said Grenville.

Anna blushed and said, "Thank you my Lord, most kind." The others agreed with Grenville's sentiments.

"What is it on the market for, Anna?" Grenville asked.

"Just over the million," she replied.

"And you've had no more interest?" he asked casually.

"Now you come to mention it," she said, "only this morning we had another party asking about this property."

"I bet you did," said Grenville, smiling, which left everyone else looking baffled. "Thank you, Anna, for being open," said Grenville. "Can I ask," Grenville went on, "can I have twenty-four hours first refusal on the building?" asked Grenville, smiling.

"I should check with head office," Anna replied.

"If you would, my dear?" asked Grenville, still smiling.

Anna left the building to make her phone call. "What was that about?" asked Hugo, asking what they were all thinking.

"Dexter Simon-Smyth," said Grenville. "He obviously knew Jonathan was looking for properties in the London area, and when Jonathan used my name with them, it must have raised a flag to him, so to try and muddy the water he will no doubt try and stop me getting this property," said Grenville.

"What a rotter," said Hugo.

"Not really, my dear chap. We can find out how much he is prepared to go, to try and stop me."

"Is that not dangerous?" asked Sara.

"Not really," said Grenville, "he came across the Walpole Boys once and lost," which made Jonathan and Hugo laugh. "Sorry, my dear," said Grenville, seeing Sara was looking confused, "that's what us three called ourselves at school, and together we are unbeatable." Sara smiled but did not look convinced.

Anna returned from her phone call. "Bad news, I am afraid," she said. "Head office cannot give you a first refusal, due to other interest," she went on. "I am so sorry," she said.

Grenville smiled. "Not your fault, my dear. Let me thank you once again, and as the saying goes, we will be in touch."

They all stood on the pavement while Anna relocked the building. Smiling, Anna wished them good luck and left. "Well what do you think?" asked Grenville.

"Very nice," said Hugo.

"Certainly, got character," said Jonathan.

"And you, Sara?" asked Grenville, turning to Sara.

"I think it has potential," she said, which made them all laugh.

"Spoken like a true female," said Grenville. "it's been a long tiring day," said Grenville, "how about we all gather at Jonathan's work place, at say ten tomorrow?"

"Can we make it eleven, old chap?" asked Jonathan.

"Fine by me" said Hugo.

"Until tomorrow," said Grenville. "Now Miss Farthing, I promised you dinner," said Grenville, turning to Sara.

Smiling, she said, "Anyone else want to join us?" Both Hugo and Jonathan read the situation correctly and declined. "Let's walk for a bit," said Sara, so saying their farewells to Jonathan and Hugo, they strolled down the road arm in arm.

"So, your opinion?" asked Hugo.

"Needs a lot of work," replied Jonathan.

"Not the building you daft bugger, Sara," replied Hugo, laughing at Jonathan.

"I think our friend Grenville is now smitten," said a smiling Jonathan.

"Poor lamb, and he won't even see it coming," replied Hugo which made them both laugh. "Share a cab, old bean?" asked Hugo.

"Why not, you can drop me off on the way," replied Jonathan.

"Excellent," said Hugo as they both walked down the road in the opposite direction to find a cab.

℃·ℂ

As they walked arm in arm silently down the road, Grenville finally said, "Sara, I also have a confession to make."

"Oh, sounds mysterious," she replied smiling.

Grenville went on to tell Sara all about his time in Belize, meeting Tom and the new quest he was on for his friend. Sara did not say anything during Grenville's confession, but noticed they were near a nice little Italian restaurant.

"This will do," she said, smiling. Entering, Grenville asked for a quiet table, smiling at the waitress, who smiled back with understanding. She showed them to a little corner alcove, and after ordering a glass of wine, Grenville said, "So what do you think?"

"It's quite a story, Grenville," said Sara.

"All true," said Grenville, laughing.

"I don't doubt you," said Sara, laughing as well. "Thank you for trusting me enough with your secret," Sara said softly.

Taking her hand, Grenville said, "Since the first moment we met the other day, I knew I could trust you."

"Thank you, Grenville," she said with tears in her eyes.

"Why the tears?" asked Grenville, looking worried.

"No, it's not you," said Sara laughing, "it's me being silly, they are tears of joy. For so long I have felt so alone and lost, I find you and my life changes," said Sara quietly.

"For the better I hope," said Grenville, trying to make it light again.

Sara stared into his eyes and smiled and said, "Definitely for the better."

"So now we both know each other's secrets," said Grenville. Still holding her hand, he squeezed it and said, "I would love you to be part of my quest."

Still staring intently into Grenville's eyes, Sara said quietly, "Nothing in this world could stop me. Now let's order, I am famished."

"Absolutely," said Grenville in reply.

After they had eaten, Sara said, "So, what happens now, Grenville?"

"Well, I think due to the lateness of the hour, we find accommodation, until tomorrow's meeting." Sara giggled. Grenville went red. "I did not mean anything by it," said Grenville, too quickly.

"I am teasing you, Grenville," said Sara. "But I have a London flat, we could stay there, if you like," Sara said softly.

Taking her hand again, Grenville said, "I will be the perfect gentleman."

"Not too perfect," said Sara, laughing, which made Grenville go red again. Paying the bill and leaving the restaurant, they hailed a cab, and Sara gave the address to the driver.

On entering the flat Grenville noticed it was not full of personal things, so he surmised Sara did not spend a lot of time here. Just as he was thinking this, Sara said, "My parent bought this for me, but I must admit I don't use it much."

Grenville started to laugh, and said, "You read my mind."

"Coffee?" said Sara. "I think I can manage one of them. "

"Splendid," replied Grenville, smiling. While Sara made the coffee, Grenville had a look about the place. It was a nice neat one-bedroom flat, clean and tidy. Grenville wondered if Sara had a cleaner pop in for time to time to have a quick going over. Sitting on the settee, Grenville waited for his coffee, which was not long coming.

Sara placed the tray of steaming coffee on the table and said, "Sorry, only got powered milk."

"Don't worry, had worse," replied Grenville, smiling. "No biscuits?" asked Grenville.

Sara smiled. "Sorry, all out."

Grenville picked up his coffee and took a deep sniff. "Wonderful," he said.

"Fibber," said a laughing Sara.

Grenville smiled at Sara and said, "Strange how life turns out."

"How so?" replied Sara.

"Well, I was trying to think about the first time I met you before I went to Belize, and for some strange reason it's all a blur."

"So, I never made that much of an impression on you then," said Sara, laughing.

"To tell you the truth, no," Grenville replied, "but then again in my defence you were my brother's guest."

"Please don't remind me," said a laughing Sara.

"I never really knew my brother. Yes, we were brothers, but we were never brotherly or close, if you know what I mean," said Grenville.

"Yes, I totally understand, Grenville," said Sara. "It was my father who decided it was a good match. Met Stephan at some function or other, so I was the grease that my father used to worm his way up the social ladder," said Sara. "That weekend was the first time I met Stephan and during the weekend he was quite charming, and attentive."

"Charming?" said Grenville.

"I said quite charming," replied Sara, smiling.

"I stand corrected," nodded Grenville. "Why did you agree to marry him, if you knew his character? "

"There is the rub, in the weeks leading up to his proposal, he was a totally different person. Plus, my father was pushing for me to say yes, so stupidly in the end to make everyone happy I reluctantly agreed. It was only after I had the ring on my finger that I found out his true nature, of how arrogant and spiteful, he was. By then, my fate was sealed, as they say," said Sara with tears in her eyes.

Grenville placed his arm around Sara and said, "All in the past, we have our future to look forward to now."

Sara kissed him on the cheek and said, "Thank you, Grenville."

To lighten the mood Grenville asked, "So, what do you think of my parents?"

"Your father is, how shall we say, the archetypical Peer of the Realm," said Sara, smiling.

"Good one," said Grenville, laughing.

"Oh, but your mother is charming, and a good listener," said Sara. "It was on her insistence that I told Stephan I wanted to break the engagement."

"Really? Go mother," said Grenville.

"Your mother gave me the fortitude to carry on sometimes. She once found me in the reading room sobbing my eyes out after a quite awful row with Stephan. After she made me tell her everything, it was like a burden was lifted and I had a friend who understood me," said Sara. "Sound weird?"

"Not at all," said Grenville. "Mother is like that," he carried on. "If I ever find a younger mother, I will marry her on the spot," said a laughing Grenville.

Sara laughed as well, and said, "I still cannot believe that you and Stephan were actual brothers."

"I know, always amazed me as well," said Grenville.

"You know your mother saw us when we went for our walk yesterday," said Sara.

"Did she, and what did she say?" asked Grenville.

"Her exact words were 'you have my blessing'," replied Sara softly.

Grenville took Sara by the hand and said, "Who am I to disagree with my mother," as he leaned in to kiss Sara for the first time.

Afterwards, Sara stood, held out her hand and said, "Let's go to bed."

Grenville smiled at Sara, and said, "Your wish is my command, my lady."

₧·₨

Next day after a leisurely morning, both Sara and Grenville arrived at Stephan's offices by ten forty-five. At reception Grenville asked for Jonathan. The receptionist smiled at them both and said, "Please take a seat, I will let him know you are here."

Just as Sara and Grenville sat down, Jonathan appeared. "Grenville, Sara how are you both?" He hugged them both and kissed Sara on the cheek. "Follow me, Hugo is already here."

Sara and Grenville followed Jonathan to his little corner office where Hugo was waiting. As the door opened, Hugo stood and smiled at them both; with little room Hugo shook both their hands. All three sat opposite Jonathan's small desk.

"Tea, anyone?" asked Jonathan, more out of politeness. When all three declined, Sara gave a small smile and could see in Jonathan's eyes that making tea would have been a major task. "So, down to business," said Jonathan. "I have rung the lovely Anna this morning and as prophesied by Grenville there was another bid placed against Bombard House."

"How much was the offer?" asked Grenville.

"Unfortunately, Anna would not specify, but I got the feeling it was for the asking price," replied Jonathan.

"Jonathan, I want you to go back and place a counter offer, for, let's say to make it interesting, a million and a half," said Grenville.

Jonathan nodded, and Sara and Hugo stared at Grenville. "So, Hugo, tell us how you got on?" asked Grenville.

Placing his battered briefcase on his knee and extracting a large blue folder, Hugo said, "With the documents supplied, I have registered S&T Imports as a private company with hopefully offices in the UK, so in about three weeks, once the official government paperwork has been complete, the company will be ready to begin trading."

"Do you foresee any problems?" Grenville asked.

"No, not at all, if we keep the tax man happy and conform with all the current UK business regulations, we will be fine," smiled Hugo. "I have also set up a UK bank account in the name of S&T Imports," said Hugo. "By the way, I had to open it up with a deposit of ten pounds for the account, so you are in debt, Mr Hampton, to a sum of ten pounds." This made every one laugh.

Grenville slapped Hugo on the back and said, "Well done, old bean."

"Sara is now in the picture about S&T Imports, so we can talk freely in front of her," said Grenville, Jonathan and Hugo looked at Sara and smiled.

"Welcome to the madmen club," laughed Hugo.

Grenville went on, "You three are the only people who know what S&T Imports is all about, so I would ask for your discretion when talking to anyone outside this room with regards to S&T Imports."

Sara, Hugo and Jonathan nodded and Sara said, "I think you can count on our loyalty, Grenville," taking his hand and smiling. Both Hugo and Jonathan watched their exchange and they both smiled.

Grenville said, "Hugo, I want you to make me Chairman and Jonathan legal Director, yourself Financial Director and Sara Procurement Director, the four of us will make up the board. Keep it in house, as they say. Any questions?" asked Grenville, looking at each of them in turn.

All three nodded but Sara said, "You sure, Grenville? I am not very business savvy."

Grenville smiled at Sara and said, "Don't worry, I am sure Hugo and Jonathan will help."

"Absolutely," said Hugo.

"Without question," Jonathan said.

Sara smiled at them all and said, "Thank you both so much."

"So," Grenville said, "anyone got anything they want to add?"

"Yes," said Sara. The three looked at her. "Next meeting can we pick somewhere more spacious?" and this made everyone roar with laughter.

"Next meeting at Hampton Hall, shall we say next Wednesday?" said Grenville, smiling at Sara. Both Hugo and Jonathan looked in their respective diaries and both nodded.

"Seems fine by me," said Jonathan.

"Super," said Hugo, smiling.

Leaving the office and saying goodbye to both Hugo and Jonathan, Grenville turned to Sara and said, "What you want to do now, my lady?"

Sara smiled at Grenville and said, "I could do with a little lay down."

Grenville was just about to say something and noticed the smile on Sara's face. "Will go and urgently flag down a taxi," said Grenville, smiling.

Grenville and Sara spent the rest of the week in London at Sara's flat, not venturing out much, only for supplies or urgent purchases. One thing Grenville did have in the front of his mind was to purchase a laptop, the same type he had obtained for Tom from the British Embassy.

As Grenville was deep in thought on how best to procure a laptop, Sara walked in and said, "Penny for them."

"Sorry, deep in thought with a problem," replied Grenville, smiling.

"Tell me, after all a problem told is a problem halved," said a smiling Sara.

"Well, it's this bloody laptop. I need urgently to get a message to Tom, so I can let him know everything is going to plan. I feel conscious as the days go by I am letting him down without any contact," Grenville said.

"I am sure Tom will understand, by the way you talk about him and if I have judged him correctly," replied Sara.

"I know, Sara, but I do worry sometimes," Grenville said.

Smiling, Sara went over and sat next to Grenville and put her arms around him. "Don't worry Grenville, together we will sort it. Don't suppose you took the model number of Tom's laptop?" Sara asked.

"To tell you the truth, Sara, the last few day in Belize were manic. We had so much to arrange and sort out, it never entered my head," replied Grenville.

"We could always ask the FO where they get their embassy laptops from," said Sara.

"Could do, but I don't really want to draw any attention to it, as it is Tom's lifeline to me. Plus, shall we say, I did not come by it via a legitimate source," said Grenville.

"I understand that," said Sara. "Oh dear, why did I not think of this before?" said Sara, jumping up.

"What?" asked Grenville, looking confused.

"Carole Burke," said Sara.

"Sorry Sara, you lost me," said Grenville, laughing.

Sara sat back down again and took Grenville's hand. "Let me explain," said Sara, smiling. "Carole Burke is my closest and dearest old school friend, and a total wizard at technology. She was refused entry to Oxford to study her doctorate in computer science, even though she was top of her class."

"Why was she refused?" asked Grenville.

"Let's say she is rather outspoken, and I think she rubbed the male egos of Oxford up the wrong way too much for their liking," replied Sara, smiling. "But if it's technology we are after, she is your woman," said Sara.

"Can we trust her?" asked Grenville.

"With my life," said Sara, quietly.

"Good enough for me," said Grenville.

"OK, I will give her a ring to see if she is free for lunch."

"Excellent," said Grenville. "I will make us a coffee while you do," said Grenville.

When Grenville returned from the kitchen with the coffee, Sara was just finishing her phone call. "Excellent news," said Sara. "Carole is free and coming here for lunch at about one."

Looking about, Grenville said, "We better do some house work."

Sara smiled and said, "Better had. Let's start in the bedroom," she said over her shoulder as she slipped off her dressing gown and walked toward the bedroom.

At one sharp the doorbell rang. Sara went to open it and all Grenville heard from the hall was girly shrieking, which made him laugh. Finally, Sara and her friend Carole entered the lounge arm in arm.

"Grenville, this is my best friend in all the world, Carole," said Sara. Grenville stood. "Carole, this is Grenville," said Sara.

Grenville shook the offered hand of Carole and said, "Nice to meet you Carole, Sara has told me a lot about you."

"Only the good bits, no doubt," said Carole, laughing.

Grenville laughed and said, "Are there any bad bits?"

Still laughing, Carole said, "Sara, you certainly landed a charmer here." Sitting down, Carole said, "So where did you two meet?"

"Carole, this is Stephan's brother," said Sara. Carole looked shocked. Sara placed her hand on Carol's arm, and went on, "Don't worry, he is totally opposite from Stephan, and we do not have any secrets."

Carole looked at Grenville seriously and said, "Grenville, if you treat my lovely Sara and make her as unhappy as your bloody awful brother Stephan did, this time," she looked at Sara, "despite her plea not to get involved, I will castrate you, Earl or no Earl."

Grenville smiled and said, "Carole, I believe you would," giving a nervous laugh.

Taking Sara's hand, Carole said softly, "Your brother nearly drove my best friend to end it all, and this world would have been a duller world without her."

Looking at both Sara and Carole, who had tears in their eyes, Grenville said, "Carole I love Sara, and promise you I will always keep her safe."

Sara said, "You love me?"

Smiling, Grenville nodded and said, "Since the second time I saw you," which made them both laugh. Not getting the joke, Sara explained to Carole their first and second meetings.

After lunch, Sara said, "Carole, we need your advice on something."

"Ask away."

Grenville and Sara both looked nervous.

Carole said, "Come on, you two, out with it."

Grenville turned to Sara and said, "I guess if you trust her that much we can let her in on the team."

"Thank you, Grenville," said Sara. Taking Carole's hand, Sara said, "I am going to tell you something but before I do, I want you to promise me that whatever you hear in this room you will never divulge to anyone apart from the team."

"You know you can trust me, Sara," said Carole softly.

Sara went on to explain part of Grenville's story and his plan for S&T Imports, and during Sara speaking Carole kept looking at Grenville and smiling. After Sara finished, there was a long quiet pause. Eventually Carole said, "Grenville Hampton, you are a dark horse," which made them all laugh.

"So, you in?" asked Sara.

Carole looked at both Sara and Grenville, smiled, and said, "Count me in."

All three stood and hugged, and started laughing. Carole leaned into her bag and took out a laptop. "This is what I think you need, a top-of-the-range encrypted laptop all done by a biometric algorithm programme, enables you to send and receive encrypted emails from one email address to another without being intercepted and read."

"Exactly," said Grenville, smiling.

"But will Tom in Belize have the same software to open and send emails?" asked Sara.

"Let's give it a go," said Carole.

"Really?" said Grenville looking shocked.

"No time like the present, if Sara has paid her bill and the connection works," said Carole, laughing.

"What is Tom's email address?" asked Carole.

"I think I need to set up an email name first," said Grenville.

"Of course, I understand," said Carole, "so what do you want it to be?" After she had explained the composition of the email address, Grenville thought then smiled and gave Carole the email address. Carole smiled. "Excellent choice, Grenville," said Carole. Carole then took ten minutes to program the laptop with Grenville's new email address. "OK, Grenville, what is your friend's email address?"

Grenville extracted the telegram from his wallet and passed it to Carole. Carole passed the telegram back to Grenville and said, "Best if you do it Grenville, for the practice."

Grenville took the laptop from Carole and said, "I hope I can remember what to do."

"Don't worry, I am here to guide you," said Carole, laughing.

"While you two techno kids are having fun, I will make a coffee," said Sara, laughing. After ten minutes with Carole's guidance Grenville had produced his email:

Hi Pirate

Everything going well here, plans are progressing as well as can be expected, S&T Imports will be up and running soon, getting together a good trusted team, trinket sales going well, bank account set up and has funds coming in, apologise for the delay in contacting you, but had a few family problems to sort, email again soon.

Duke

"Sent," said Carole, "just wait for a reply now."

"Not sure how quick, depending if Tom is at home or away on business," said Grenville.

"In that case, you keep the laptop," said Carole.

"You sure?" said Grenville.

"Just call it a gift to the cause," said Carole, smiling.

"Thank you so much," said Grenville.

Sara returned from the kitchen with the coffee, and said, "Everything sorted?"

"Absolutely," said Grenville, holding the laptop to his chest.

"Boys and their toys," said Carole, laughing. Carole turned to Grenville and said, "So what's next?"

"Wednesday, Hampton Hall, where you can meet the other two in the team," said Grenville.

"Looking forward to it," said Carole.

After Carole, had left, Sara said, "A weight off your mind."

"It was a worry and I feel so much better now I have contacted Tom," replied Grenville.

"So, what do you think of Carole?" asked Sara.

"Most impressed," replied Grenville.

"You think she will be a good addition to the team?" asked Sara.

"I think we can safely say she will be a top asset, well done you," said Grenville, taking Sara in his arms and smiling.

"Now earlier," said Sara, "You told Carole something about me."

"Did I?" said Grenville, smiling.

"Yes, you did," said Sara, poking Grenville in the ribs and laughing.

"I love you," said Grenville, quietly.

"I love you too," replied Sara. "Now take me to bed and prove it," said Sara, standing and holding out her hand to Grenville.

$$\text{ℬ} \cdot \text{ℬ}$$

On the Tuesday Sara and Grenville returned to Hampton Hall. As the taxi drove away and before Grenville had time, the front door opened and Preston stood smiling. "Welcome back My Lord, Lady Sara," said Preston, bowing.

"Nice to be home," said Grenville. "Are the parents home, old man?" asked Grenville.

"Both in the lounge, my Lord," replied Preston.

"Any chance you can rustle up some coffee, old bean?" asked Grenville.

"My pleasure," said Preston, smiling.

Entering the lounge, Grenville said, "Mother, father, how are you both?"

Standing, the Duke came over and kissed Sara on the cheek and shook Grenville's hand. "Lovely to see you both, and I must say you both look well," said the Duke smiling, which made Sara turn a light red. The Duchess was watching the exchange and smiled, as she knew that things had progressed between them both since last time she had seen them.

"Mother, how are you?" said Grenville, going to his mother and kissing the offered cheek.

"Very well now you are home, my darling," said the Duchess, smiling. "Sara, come sit next to me and let me look at you," said the Duchess. Sara did as she was asked, and sat next to the Duchess. Taking her hand, the Duchess said, "Sara, I do believe I have never seen you look so radiant, you are positively glowing," which made Sara giggle and go red. "My son must have a good effect on you," she went on. Leaning in, she whispered to Sara, "Sometimes I love being correct about people." Sara smiled. Just then, Preston entered with coffee.

Once Preston returned to collect the coffee tray, Grenville said, "Preston, dear chap, can you show Sara to her room?" Grenville winked at Sara.

Sara looked puzzled but played along with it, and said, "Thank you, Preston, most kind."

After Preston and Sara had left, Grenville said, "Mother, father, I love Sara and would like your permission to ask for her hand in marriage."

The room fell silent. Eventually, the Duke said, "Grenville, if Sara will consent, I think your mother and I could not think of a better match."

Grenville looked at his mother, who was nodding. Grenville went and shook his father's hand, and kissed his mother. As he did so, she said, "Well done my son, you made us both proud. Do you mind if I ask a question?"

"Please ask away mother."

"When you going to ask Sara?" she asked.

"I need to get a ring first, it was a kind of the spur of the moment decision," replied Grenville, laughing.

"Thought as much," said Sofia, pulling the bell cord.

Finally, Preston arrived and said, "You rang, Your Grace."

"Preston, please can you ask Mary to go and fetch the little purple box on top of my dressing table and bring it to me."

"At once, your Grace," said Preston, bowing before closing the door again.

Once Preston returned and had passed the purple box to Sofia, he bowed and departed.

"Come sit next to me, Grenville." Handing the purple box to Grenville, he looked puzzled. "Open it," she said. Inside was the most beautiful large diamond ring Grenville had ever seen. "It was your grandmother's, on your father's side," said his mother. "I had it sent down the other day from the bank."

Grenville looked astonished.

The Duke said, "Once we realised what your brother was up to, we had a few choice family items removed to our safety deposit box at the bank."

"Clever you," said Grenville, which made them all laugh.

"But how did you know, mother?"

"Grenville, once I saw you and Sara together the other day, I knew," she said, leaning over and kissing him.

"I don't know what to say to you both," said Grenville.

"Let's hope she says yes," said the Duke.

"Never in doubt," replied the Duchess, smiling.

After Grenville, had left, James went and sat next to his wife and said, "I am please he is going to do right by the girl."

"I am just pleased it's our Grenville she will marry and not Stephan," she replied. "I nearly offered him that ring once," said Sofia.,

"Oh, you never said."

"I said nearly. But when I mentioned it to Stephan all I could see was pound signs in his eyes instead of love, as I saw in Grenville's eyes."

Taking her hand, James said, "Where did we go wrong with Stephan?"

Smiling, she said, "We never did. They were both treated equal, Stephan's failures were his own making, he never let anyone close. Your father once told me," she continued, "Stephan would never make as good a Duke as Grenville would."

"I think out of everyone he understood the situation. He was a wise old buzzard," said James, smiling.

After dinner that evening they all gathered in the drawing room for coffee. The air was electric with expectation. Everyone noticed it; eventually the Duke said, smiling, "Is it warm in here or is it me?"

"You OK, Grenville? You look worried," said Sara.

Grenville took a deep breath and went and knelt in front of Sara. "Sara, I know we have only known each other for a few weeks, but that second meeting, that's all it took for me to know. I fell in love with you, and I know in my heart I will always love you. I know you have not had a happy association with my family, and I hope you know I am so different from my brother Stephan, and I promise to always love and respect you. So, will you consent and become my wife?" Pulling the ring box from behind his back, he opened it and showed her the ring.

Sara's hand flew to her mouth and she started to cry, but managed to say, "I will, I will." Leaning over, she hugged Grenville. Grenville gently pushed her away, and taking the ring from the box placed it on her finger. As he did, both his parents clapped.

The Duke went and slapped Grenville on his back and said, "Well done, my boy." The Duke hugged Sara, and said, "This time I am very pleased to welcome you to our family."

The Duchess hugged and kissed her son and hugging Sara, said in her ear, "I am so happy for you both."

ଝ · ଔ

Next day, they were having breakfast, when Grenville smiled at Sara, who was every so often looking at the ring on her finger and smiling. "You will wear it out if you keep looking at it," said Grenville, laughing.

"Never will get tired of looking at it," said Sara, laughing as well.

"Taxi arrived," said the Duke, looking out of the windows.

"Showtime," said Grenville.

"Have fun you two," said the Duke, as they got up and left the dining room.

Just as Hugo and Jonathan got out of the taxi, Sara and Grenville were coming down the steps. They all hugged. "Just waiting for one more person," said Grenville. Just then another taxi came up the drive.

"Come on you two, let's go in, Sara can meet our guest."

"Intriguing," said Hugo, smiling. Grenville led Jonathan and Hugo into the library where coffee was waiting for them. Just as they were having coffee Sara entered with Carole, arm in arm.

"Hugo, Jonathan, may I introduce Miss Carole Burke, our latest recruit," said Sara. Both Hugo and Jonathan smiled and introduced themselves.

"Congratulations, Grenville," Carole said, smiling.

"For what?" said Hugo, looking puzzled. Jonathan nodded in agreement with Hugo.

"Their engagement, men are bloody useless at spotting things in front of their noses," said a laughing Carole. Sara held up her hand and showed Hugo and Jonathan her ring.

"My dear chap, well done," said Hugo, shaking Grenville's hand and hugging Sara.

"Well done my dear, I am so pleased for you," said Jonathan, who shook Grenville's hand and hugged Sara with tears in his eyes, and was unable to speak again.

Eventually they all sat down and finally Grenville said, "OK, down to business. Hugo, Jonathan, let me formally introduce Miss Carole Burke to our team. She has been fully briefed on our forthcoming adventure, and is in the picture with recent events, also she is a technical wizard so Hugo," said Grenville, turning to Hugo, "can you make Carole Director of Information Technology, and no doubt she will be giving you lots of hard times asking for money."

Hugo nodded to Carole and smiled.

"Good," said Grenville, carrying on. "Jonathan, how we doing with Bombard House?" asked Grenville.

"Well, I spoke to Anna and gave her our offer of one and a half million, and it was like they were expecting it, so I upped our offer to two million and am awaiting a phone call as we speak," said Jonathan smiling.

"Well done old man, excellent," replied Grenville. "You look shocked, Carole," said Grenville.

"It's just you say two million like it's a small amount," she replied. This made every one laugh.

Hugo said, "One pound or a million pounds, it's all relative if you've got it."

"If you put it like that," said Carole, smiling.

"Well, without Bombard House we cannot move forward, so I will give you a few tasks to get your teeth into. Jonathan, I am prepared to go to three million on Bombard House, so I will give into your judgement and negotiating skills over it," said Grenville, "but in a worst-case scenario and under the radar this time, as we now know what we are up against, can you also look for some other building suitable to our needs? But I have kind of fallen in love with Bombard House, so do your best, old chap," said Grenville, smiling.

Jonathan finally looked up from writing and said, "Leave it to me old, bean."

"Hugo."

"Yes, chairman," said Hugo, using Grenville's title for the first time. Everyone smiled.

"I want you to find out the state of play with Easington Investment Banks, how close are they to closure, and can they possibly be in line for an aggressive take over." The room was silent. Grenville carried on, "It's time to stop playing at this and starting to act like an international company." Everyone around the table nodded, and everyone now understood the drive and passion Grenville had for his project.

Hugo said, "Of course old bean, will have a full report next meeting."

Grenville went on. "Carole, I would like you to get a list together of equipment you will require to set up the IT Department."

"Of course, but you do realise this equipment is not cheap," said Carole, looking about. This brought smiles from around the table.

"Of course, it will not be, but fortunately we had a good financial grounding, and money now is not an issue," said Grenville. "Sara, I am not letting you off the hook, but until we have a permanent residence for the company there is not a lot you can do," said Grenville, smiling.

"After all, the poor girls got a wedding to prepare for," said Carole.

Both Hugo and Jonathan said, "Well said," in unison, which made everyone laugh. From under the table Grenville placed the second large holdall he brought back from Belize on the table. Everyone just looked intrigued at the holdall.

Opening the holdall, Grenville said, "I know and am aware up to now I have asked a lot of all of you, looking around the table, and most of the time and effort you have contributed so far has been by the goodness of your own hearts and…"

"Not at all, Grenville," said Jonathan.

"Glad to help," said Hugo, holding up his hand.

Grenville said. "Please let me finish. I think it is time efforts should bring rewards," Grenville went on. To this end, he took a bundle of money from the holdall and placed it in front of each of them. Everyone stared at the pile of money in front of them and Grenville answered the question that was on everyone's mind. "In front of you is fifty thousand pounds, payment for your efforts so far and to cover any further costs soon," said Grenville, looking about and smiling.

Carole was the first to speak. "I don't think I have ever seen so much money in my life, in one place."

Hugo and Jonathan just stared at the money.

Sara just said "Grenville."

Grenville went on, "As I said I want to build the best of the best in a company, and I believe that the people around this table are the brightest and best to help me achieve this. Plus, I have your trust."

Hugo softly said, "And loyalty, dear chap," which the others echoed with an, "Absolutely."

"Now," said Grenville, "Hugo."

"Yes, Grenville."

Passing the holdall to Hugo, Grenville said, "Let me know how much is left in there. I know some is foreign currency but do your best, old chap."

"Of course," said a smiling Hugo, moving to another table. Hugo set to work stacking and counting all the remaining money. After a time, Hugo joined them again and said, "Well, with my rough calculations, we have about five million pounds, give or take a few currency exchange fluctuations." Everyone in the room gasped, and looked at a smiling Hugo.

Grenville said, "Will you have a problem banking that amount of money?"

"Should not think so, old man," replied Hugo.

"Good," said Grenville, "place it all in the S&T account, if you would be so kind."

"Of course, old chap, will do."

"OK for now we have a working capital of five million, so I would be grateful if when deciding what you require to move forward you are mindful of this for now." Everyone shook their heads in agreement. "Anything else?" asked Grenville. Once again everyone nodded around the table. "OK, shall we say meet next month, same day, here?" asked Grenville. Hugo, Jonathan and Carole checked their diaries and after a few minutes nodded in agreement. "Good," said Grenville. "Lunch, I think, and no doubt Mrs Preston has done us proud. Shall we all move to the dining room?" Everyone got up in unison and followed Grenville into the dining room.

After Jonathan, Hugo and Carole had left to return to London, Sara said, "You are really going to make a go of this?"

Taking Sara's hand and looking deeply into her eyes, Grenville said, "Sara, Tom saved my life and let me into his world, gave me his trust and friendship, without asking anything from me. If it was not for my brother Stephan's death, I would still be in Belize with Tom. But after a few strange events, life gave me an opportunity to repay Tom, plus give my life some meaning."

Sara could see Grenville's eyes had watered and she knew that everything Grenville had said was from the heart, and holding his face in her hands, Sara said, "I will always support you. I love you."

Grenville smiled and said, "Suppose we better go see your folks and let them know recent events."

"Your mother has already been proactive on that front, she has invited them down for the weekend," said Sara.

"Clever mother," said Grenville, smiling.

"Well, you know your mother, she sees things others miss," said Sara.

"Too true, my love, too true," replied Grenville, smiling.

℘·℃

Next day Grenville was delighted on the laptop to see "You Have Mail" flashing on the laptop.

Opening the email Grenville read:

Duke

Good to hear from you, sorry for the delay, but been down south on business, glad S&T Imports progressing well, and account set up for funds, sorry to hear about family problems, but please sort them before company.

As you know I have all the time in the world.

Take care

Pirate

Next day Grenville was studying the local shipping news, when he spotted the arrival he was looking for. "Red Star docking Milford Haven docks this Friday." Smiling, Grenville stood and went to find Preston. Grenville found Preston in the study talking to his father. "Apologies for the intrusion but Preston, my dear chap, can we get our wagon for Friday morning?"

Smiling, Preston said, "Will be ready for nine if that is convenient with you, My Lord."

"Super," said Grenville, as Preston bowed to the Duke and left the room.

"What was all that about?" asked the Duke.

"Company business," said Grenville.

"Understand," said the Duke and went back to his paper, smiling.

Later, when they were all gathered in the lounge, Sara said, "As you and Preston are going to gallivant secretly on Friday, then your mother and I are going wedding shopping."

"When do you want, the church booked for?" asked Sofia.

"To tell you the truth, I don't think we have ever discussed an actual day, have we Grenville," said Sara, turning to Grenville.

"Not really, been a bit of a rush," replied Grenville, smiling.

"Well, we can decide once your parents are here this weekend," said Sofia.

"If you don't mind," said Sara, "Grenville and I would prefer a smallish affair."

Sofia smiled and said, "I totally understand, we will do our best," which brought a soft laugh from behind the Duke's paper.

ಬಂ·೦ಚ

The Friday came and as promised Preston was waiting by the garages in a white transit van.

"Morning, Preston," said Grenville as he approached.

"My Lord," said Preston. Grenville thought how different Preston looked out of his normal butler uniform.

"All ready to go?" asked Grenville.

"Waiting on your word," replied Preston.

Climbing in, Grenville said, "Milton Haven docks it is, Preston."

"As you command, My Lord," said Preston as he put the van into gear and drove off.

At the gates of Milton Haven docks, Preston asked for the pier where the Red Star had docked. The gate guard asked them to report to the harbour master's office first. Preston drove as instructed and parked up. "Hopefully will not be too long, old chap," said Grenville, getting out.

"No worries, My Lord," said Preston, turning off the engine. Grenville went into the harbour master's office and noticed it was a busy office, with phones ringing and people generally dashing about. Grenville smiled at himself. This was going to be a doddle.

Walking up to reception, a young girl approached and smiled. "Can I help you, sir?" she asked.

"Hope so," replied Grenville. "I am the Earl of Eastleigh, son of the Duke of Hampshire, and I am here to see the Captain of the Red Star recently docked, is that possible?"

The girl, on hearing Grenville speak and his title, changed her attitude from bored to compliant. "Yes, my Lord I will check." After a minute, she returned to the counter. "Red Star docked this morning, she is berthed at pier twenty-seven. Follow the yellow route and you will find her," she said.

"You have been most helpful my dear," smiled Grenville, as he left the office.

As the girl returned to her desk, her friend opposite said, "Who was that?"

"An Earl, son of a Duke no less," she replied.

"He was handsome for an Earl," said her friend.

"Out of your league, Janice," she replied, laughing as she looked out of the window at the departing white van.

Preston followed the yellow route all the way to pier twenty-seven, and parked up in the loading bay. "Now for the hard part," said Grenville.

"You want me to come with you?" asked Preston.

"No, it's OK old chap, only need one of us to get killed today," said Grenville, smiling. Preston looked at Grenville and realised he was not joking.

Grenville went to the gangplank, looked up and remembered the last time he saw this ship; it was at night and pitch black and he never knew its name, until Tom had told him when they were back home.

Grenville shouted up, "Permission to come aboard."

"Granted," said a deeply accented Russian speaking English from the shadows. Grenville took a deep breath and went up the gangplank. At the top, he was confronted by the biggest man he had ever seen, with a scar running down the side of his face.

"Captain Ivor Sharapova, I presume," said Grenville, holding out his hand.

The Captain looked at the hand and decided to take it and said, "Yes, that is me."

Grenville smiled; he was exactly as Tom had explained him, down to the hand shake like a vice.

"I find you funny?" said the Captain, looking annoyed.

"No, sorry, you are the same as Tom explained you to me."

On hearing the name Tom, the Captain stiffened up and said, "And who is Tom to you?" still on the offensive.

"I am his best friend Duke," said Grenville, smiling.

"Anyone can say that," replied the Captain.

Grenville swallowed hard. The next part could mean him leaving or not. "Tom sent me to pick up Grace's belongings," said Grenville.

Captain Ivor Sharapova stared at Grenville for a few moments then a smile spread across his face and he said, "Welcome to my ship," holding out his arms. Grenville and Ivor embraced. "Tom told me you would be along for your merchandise, and I must admit you are exactly as he described you," said Ivor, laughing. "Is that your white van down there?" asked Ivor, pointing towards Preston who stood next to the van.

"Yes, it is," replied Grenville.

"Good, I will get my men to load the cargo for you," said Ivor.

"Most kind," said Grenville.

"In the meantime, come have a drink with me."

Grenville smiled and said, "Why not." Before Grenville followed Ivor into the ship he waved at Preston to let him know all was well. Ivor lead Grenville to his cabin, and told Grenville to sit. Ivor placed two glasses and a bottle of vodka between them.

Pouring the two glasses and handing one to Grenville, Ivor picked up his glass and said, "To Tom," to which Grenville replied, "Tom," and drank the neat fiery vodka down in one.

Ivor laughed and poured two more glasses. This time Grenville took a sip and placed the glass back on the table. "How is Tom, have you seen him recently?" asked Grenville.

"Not since you left Belize," replied Ivor. "We are hoping to return that way next month," he continued, "if you require anything taken over let me know."

"Most kind, Captain," said Grenville.

"Nonsense," said Ivor, "anything for family." Grenville nodded; this he understood. After a silent pause, Ivor said, "So you are to help our Tom in his quest."

Bowing his head, Grenville said, "I am, and I volunteered to help, after all Tom has done for me."

"Last time I saw Tom he seemed more alive and energetic than I think I have seen him since the tragedy, which I suspect was down to you, Duke," said Ivor, using his name for the first time.

"Captain," said Grenville.

"Please call me Ivor, after all we are family now," replied Ivor, interrupting Grenville.

Grenville smiled. "Ivor, I think Tom and I needed each other to complete ourselves, if that makes sense," said Grenville.

"Perfect sense," said Ivor, smiling. Just as they were chatting a crew member knocked on Ivor's door and spoke to him in Russian. Ivor said something back in Russian and the crew member disappeared. "Your three crates have been loaded onto your vehicle," said Ivor.

"Thank you, most kind," replied Grenville.

Following Ivor back to the gangplank, Grenville and Ivor shook hands and embraced again. Grenville said, "Until next time, Ivor."

"Be safe," said Ivor, before turning and disappearing into the ship.

Grenville approached the van and smiled at Preston. "All OK old chap?" said Grenville.

"Excellent," said Preston, smiling and holding up the cargo manifest. Grenville smiled at the cargo manifest. "Tractor parts" was on the manifest and the name was for the Duke of Hampshire; hopefully, no customs official was likely to delve too deeply. Following the yellow route back to the harbour master's office, once again, Grenville entered.

On spotting, him the same girl came over and smiled. "Back already, my Lord," she said.

"Just picked up some tractor parts from the Red Star, so I now need a stamp to clear port," replied Grenville, smiling.

"Two seconds, you need customs, I will go get them for you," said the girl.

"Thank you, most grateful," said Grenville with a slight bow. This made the girl giggle as she went off.

She returned with a customs official dressed in a smart uniform. Smiling, he asked, "Can I help you, my Lord?"

"Just picked up three crates of tractor parts from the Red Star for my father the Duke of Hampshire, just need your permission to leave port, if you can arrange that my dear chap," said Grenville, as he passed over the paperwork.

Taking the paperwork and studying it for several minutes, the customs official smiled and said, "Please wait here for a second, I will just go and get this authorised and stamped." After several minutes the customs official came back, and handing the paperwork back said, "All compete my Lord, just hand the pink copy into the front gate, and the yellow copy is for your record, have a nice day."

"Thank you both so much, so kind and professional," replied Grenville before he left the office. Preston stopped at the barrier, and an official came out and Grenville handed him the pink copy of the authorised cargo manifest. "There we go old chap," said Grenville in his most upper class voice he could muster. Even Preston smiled.

"Thank you my Lord, have a pleasant day."

"You too, old man," replied Grenville as the barrier opened and Preston drove out of the docks.

On the way, back to Hampton Hall, Grenville fell asleep. Preston smiled at the softly snoring future Duke of Hampshire. Back at the hall Preston reversed back into the garages, and Grenville and Preston manhandled the crates off and stacked them on a low bench in the corner of the garage. Preston took a tyre iron from the bench and opened the first crate; on top was just as the manifest said, "tractor parts". Removing these down to a layer of plastic, underneath was a hoard of silver and gold. Preston opened the other two crates and, once again, to a casual inspection they contained tractor parts.

Grenville said, "A lot of gold and silver there."

"Indeed, my Lord," replied Preston, "are you going to take the items up to London, to Liebermann?"

Smiling, Grenville replied, "I am sure Liebermann will be able to give us a good price for the lot." Grenville continued, "Preston, I will leave you to sort out the crates and place the items in suitable containers ready for transit, if that's OK old man."

"Of course, my Lord, leave it all to me," said Preston, smiling. Grenville turned and started to walk back towards the house.

ℰ·ℭ

Later that evening after dinner, Sara asked Grenville how his day went.

"Most profitable, my love," was all he would say. Sara never pushed him for any further details.

Next day just after breakfast, they heard a horn being honked looking out of the windows. Sara said, "It's my parents," rushing from the room.

"Be nice," said Sofia to the Duke, "always," as she followed Sara out to meet her parents.

"Cannot stand the fellow," said the Duke, "bloody social climber," he went on.

"It's for Sara and mother," said Grenville.

"Lucky then, or I would chase them off with a bloody twelve gauge." Grenville smiled and followed his father out of the room. Grenville was in no doubt he meant it.

Sara was hugging her mother and father, as Grenville and his father joined the reunion on the hall steps. "Welcome," said the Duke, shaking hands with Sara's father and mother.

Sofia said, "You remember my other son, Grenville," she said, introducing Grenville to Sara's parents.

Grenville shook the offered hands. Grenville smiled and said, "Pleased to meet you, Mr and Mrs Farthing."

"Please call us Gerard and June," Sara's father said, smiling.

"Lovely to meet you both," said a smiling Grenville.

"Pleasure is all ours, my Lord," said Mr Farthing, smiling. Sara was watching the exchange between her father and Grenville and smiled. Grenville was a different entity to Stephan and his father would have a harder time trying to win over Grenville as easily as he did Stephan.

Grenville smiled at Sara's mother and realised who Sara took after; even now she was still a good-looking lady, and far more friendly and open than her husband.

"Shall we?" said the Duke, pointing to the Hall doors. "Preston, please can you arrange for the Farthing's luggage to be sent to their room?" asked the Duke.

"Of course, your Grace," replied Preston, bowing.

In the lounge, Sara sat next to her mother and Grenville sat next to his mother, while the Duke and Gerard stood by the unlit open fire place.

The Duke asked, "Good trip down?"

"Light traffic," replied Gerard.

"Dinner will be at eight," said the Duchess. "Hope that is acceptable with everyone," she continued, smiling.

"Excellent," said the Duke, and the Farthings smiled and nodded in agreement.

Grenville stood and beckoned Sara to his side. Sara's parents looked puzzled. Grenville said, "Mr and Mrs Farthing, Gerard and June, this weekend was not just a social visit, we had an ulterior motive to invite you down to the Hall this weekend, as I have something to ask you." Both Gerard and June looked at each other in confusion. "I have fallen in love with your daughter, and would like to ask your permission for her hand in marriage." The Farthings looked totally stunned by Grenville's speech.

Sara's mother was the first to speak. "Sara, is this what you want?"

"I love him," said Sara, taking Grenville's hand in hers.

"Who are we to stand in the way of love?" said Sara's father. Grenville looked at his face and could see total relief that his daughter was still going to marry well.

Sara's mother started to cry and say, "Oh my darling, I am so pleased for you, come here and give me a hug." Sara went to her mother and hugged her, placing her ring back on her finger and showing it to her mother.

Grenville took the offered hand from Sara's father. The Duke and Duchess congratulated the Farthings and once again welcomed then to the family.

"Have you set a date yet?" asked Sara's mother.

"We been waiting for your visit to discuss it," replied the Duchess.

"Most kind," said Sara's mother. "Do you have anything in mind?" asked Sara's mother.

Sara looked at Sofia and smiled. "What about next July?" said Sara.

"Excellent," said Sara's mother.

"Give us a good time to plan, and of course you must hold the reception here at the Hall," said Sofia, smiling.

Gerard said, "That is most kind of you both."

"Yes, thank you," smiled Sara's mother.

After dinner, the men retired to the Duke's study. "How is business?" asked the Duke, smiling.

Gerard replied, "Very well, the furniture industry is doing rather well in this current economic climate. I heard a rumour that your estate was struggling until recently," Gerard asked casually.

Grenville looked at his father and smiled; so here it was, Farthing had begun fishing. Grenville wondered if he was in league with Dexter Simon-Smyth. The Duke smiled. "Just spiteful rumours put about by nasty people," said the Duke, smiling at Grenville.

Gerard looked at Grenville and said, "I also hear your time away was most profitable and you had a lucky windfall, my Lord."

"I think the luck was me returning when I did," said Grenville, smiling.

"Still, a great relief to everyone, now the rumours are found untrue. After all losing the family home would have been devastating," said Gerard, Grenville wondered if Farthing would have been after Hampton Hall for himself. Grenville decided to give Farthing a test.

"Simon-Smyth and his bank tried to default the estate with a court order, but we were able to fend off his attempt," said Grenville.

"I did hear that," said Gerard with a smile that did not reach his eyes.

"Do you know Simon-Smyth, by any chance?" Grenville asked casually.

"Only as an acquaintance of your later brother Stephan," replied Gerard, much too quickly for Grenville. So, he did know about Simon-Smyth's plan to obtain the hall, thought Grenville; now for the bait.

"Of course," Grenville said, "we as a family are not going to take this lying down, I personally am going to ruin anyone that had anything to do with trying to take my family estate away from me."

"Brave words, can you back them up?" said Gerard with a light laugh.

"Yes, I can, fifty million times," said Grenville, staring at Gerard without a smile.

Gerard looked shocked and finally said in a joking voice, "Well, lucky we are going to be family." Grenville hoped he would report back to Simon-Smyth with what had been said tonight; the battle lines had been drawn.

80·03

Next day after breakfast Grenville excused himself and went to find Preston. Finding Preston in the kitchen having a cup of coffee, Grenville sat down opposite and said, "So how was your sorting?"

Preston passed Grenville a folded piece of paper and said, "Two holdalls under the work bench in the garage office, one full of trinkets, one full of gold, ready for you to take to London."

Grenville looked at the piece of paper and smiled. "Excellent job, Preston, my dear chap."

"Always glad to help you, my Lord," said Preston smiling.

Next day Grenville announced he was off to London on some business, and could he borrow Newton and the Rolls again? Sara said she would stay at the Hall and go over some arrangements with Sofia, and her mother, the Duke and Farthing were off to do some shooting.

Before he left, Grenville made two phone calls; one to Liebermann to book another appointment for that afternoon.

After a short pause the receptionist said it was convenient for twelve noon. The second call was to Hugo to enquire if he was free to meet him at Liebermann's for the appointment. Hugo agreed to meet him there at the appointed time. Newton loaded the two holdalls into the car before they set off for London.

Once in Hatton Garden, Grenville asked Newton if he had any shopping to do.

Newton smiled and said, "What time would his lordship like to be picked up?"

"Shall we say two?" replied Grenville.

Newton took the two holdalls into Liebermann's reception for Grenville, saluted and said, "Until later, my Lord."

"Thank you, Newton," replied Grenville as he watched Newton return to the Rolls and drive away.

Grenville smiled at the Liebermann receptionist and said, "Hello," but before Grenville had a chance to say anything else she replied, "Good day my Lord. Mr Fisher is expecting you, please take a seat and I will see if he is free," she said, smiling. Grenville did not take a seat but stood staring out of the doors of Liebermann, as he was expecting Hugo any minute. Smiling, Grenville spotted Hugo walking towards the Liebermann building.

On seeing Hugo, Grenville went out of the building to greet Hugo. Embracing, Grenville said, "Thanks for meeting me on such short notice, old boy."

"My pleasure, dear chap," replied Hugo.

"Shall we go in?" said Grenville. Hugo gestured Grenville to lead the way; on entering, Mr Fisher was already waiting for them.

On seeing Grenville, Mr Fisher smiled and said, "Welcome back my Lord, hope all is well with you."

"Thank you, very well indeed," said Grenville, "may I introduce my financial advisor, Mr Hugo Thorpe?"

Holding out his hand, Mr Fisher welcomed Hugo and smiled. "Before we continue, is there an office Mr Thorpe and myself can use for a minute to discuss some urgent private business?"

"Of course, my Lord, please wait here a moment," said Mr Fisher.

A few moments later Mr Fisher returned with Mr Yoshie, who Grenville first met on his first visit. Smiling, Mr Yoshie bowed slightly and said, "Welcome back, my Lord."

Grenville said, "Thank you, sorry to cause such a fuss, I know you must be busy."

Smiling, Mr Yoshie said, "Always a pleasure, my Lord. Can I take your bags, and please follow me?"

Mr Yoshie took the holdalls and walked towards his office. Mr Yoshie placed the holdalls in the room, bowed slightly and said, "When you are ready, please let me know and I will take you back to Mr Fisher."

"Thank you, most kind," replied Grenville, smiling.

Once the door was closed Hugo said, "Why the cloak and dagger?"

Grenville replied, "Wanted you to take a quick glance over the merchandise first old bean, to see if you can shift anything." Not sure what Grenville was on about, Hugo nodded and smiled and took a seat.

Opening the holdalls, Hugo looked in and said, "Blimey," which made Grenville laugh.

"So, what do you think?" asked Grenville.

Hugo studied the contents of both holdalls and after a few minutes said, "I guess I could shift the gold, but it has a set standard price, plus it might raise a few flags within the banking community, so I would leave it to this lot if they can shift it. But the other items, would not have a clue, old man."

"Thank you," said Grenville. "At least we are both in the dark," he said, laughing.

Hugo started to laugh and said, "The blind leading the blind."

"Well, let's go see," said Grenville.

As Grenville opened the door, Mr Yoshie was waiting, smiling, and said, "All finished, my Lord? Can I take your bags up to the fifth floor?"

Grenville smiled and said, "Please lead the way, old man."

Once again as they stepped from the lift Mr Fisher was waiting for them. Smiling, he said, "This way my Lord." Turning, he moved down the corridor towards the large oak doors at the bottom. Mr Fisher knocked once and heard, "Enter." Opening the door, he stood aside to allow Grenville and Hugo to enter first. Grenville nodded to the three men sitting on the top table. Grenville went and sat at a vacant chair across from them, Hugo took the seat next to Grenville.

After Mr Yoshie, had placed the two holdalls next to Grenville, the middle man said, "Welcome back my Lord. First, down to previous business. The diamonds and un-cut diamonds you left with us last time, we have appraised and cut and polished and we estimate your share will be thirty million pounds. I hope this is acceptable."

Grenville smiled and said, "Thank you, most generous, sir."

The man opened a folder and slid a banker's draft over to Grenville. Grenville nodded and picked up the banker's draft and without looking at it, handed it to Hugo. Hugo sat staring at the banker's draft, before placing it in his briefcase.

The man to the right said, "So what have you brought us this time, my Lord?"

Grenville and Hugo both placed the contents of the holdalls on the table in front of the three men. Even they seemed impressed with the contents. "I understand that this is not your normal field of expertise and an appraisal today is out of the question as you will need time to examine and study them," said Grenville, gesturing over the items on the table.

"Thank you, most kind," said the second man.

"Once you have made your appraisal and have come to a fair price, can I ask you contact Mr Thorpe here," said Grenville, pointing at Hugo, "he is my financial advisor and has my compete confidence."

The man in the middle smiled and said, "Of course, my Lord. Please, Mr Thorpe, can you give the contact details to Mr Fisher before you leave?"

Hugo nodded in agreement. Grenville and Hugo stood, and Grenville said, "Thank you once again for your indulgence, gentlemen."

"Our pleasure," said the middle man.

Once outside, Hugo turned to Grenville and said, "Thirty million."

"I know," said Grenville, "nice little fund top up."

"I need to go to the bank, having this much money on me is insane," said a laughing Hugo.

Grenville hugged Hugo and said, "Until next meeting at the Hall."

"Absolutely, old chap," said Hugo as he flagged down a passing taxi.

Grenville did not have to wait long until he spotted Newton and the Rolls coming down the street. Grenville smiled to himself; a nice day's work. Newton pulled up to the curb and Grenville got in. "Home, Newton, if you please," said Grenville.

"As you wish, my Lord," replied Newton as he merged back into the flowing traffic.

Once again, the three men watched Hugo and Grenville depart. "Young Hampton has done better than even I expected," said the middle man.

"Most lucrative dealings," said the left man.

"Let's still keep an eye on him," said the other man.

"Agreed," said the other two in unison.

∞ · ∞

Back at the Hall, Grenville found everyone in the lounge, apart from Sara's parents. Kissing Sara and his mother and shaking his father's hand, Grenville said, "Everyone have a good day?"

"Excellent," said his father, smiling. "Bagged a few grouse for the pot."

Sara said, "We have made a few plans for our wedding."

"Wonderful," said Grenville smiling.

"But I suspect like your father and our wedding planning, you would like to leave it to us ladies," said his mother, smiling.

"Mother as always your powers of perception are amazing and you know me so well," replied Grenville, laughing.

The rest of the weekend went too quickly for Sara and eventually they were on the steps bidding her parents goodbye. "Keep me posted on any plans," said her mother as she hugged Sara.

Shaking Grenville's hand, Gerard said, "Until next time, my Lord."

Grenville nodded and said, "Until next time, Gerard."

Grenville kissed Sara's mother. Gerard hugged his daughter and said, "My darling, be safe." Farthing honked as he drove down the drive towards the main gate. Grenville took Sara's hand and smiled as they waved at the departing car. Grenville smiled to himself, and decided this was perhaps one little secret he should keep from Sara; after all it had been an enlightening week.

Wednesday came and Sara and Grenville were in the dining room waiting for the others to arrive for their monthly meeting. Sara said, "You know one thing you need to do?"

"Really, cannot think," replied Grenville.

"You need to go see Tom's mother and tell her about Tom," said Sara.

"Oh, dear yes, totally forgot," said Grenville, "how did I ever live without you?"

"Badly," replied a laughing Sara.

Grenville took her in his arms and kissed her. "I love you, Miss Farthing," said Grenville.

"I love you too, Mr Hampton," Sara replied. Looking out of the window, Sara said, "A taxi has arrived, must be them," taking Grenville's hand and leading him towards the front doors. This time all three of them arrived in the one taxi.

Grenville and Sara waited on the top step. Carole was the first to greet them, hugging both Sara and Grenville. Hugo and Jonathan were more leisurely in their greetings. "Shall we?" said Grenville, pointing to the house. Turning, they all followed Grenville into the library.

Sara and Grenville served coffee. Once they were all seated around the table, Grenville said, "Shall we start?" which brought a nodding of heads. "Jonathan want to kick us off," Grenville said, smiling.

"Absolutely," replied Jonathan. Standing, Jonathan continued, "First, some good news and bad news," which brought a low murmur around the table. Still smiling, Jonathan said, "The good news is we have purchased Bombard House for two million five hundred pounds." This brought a round of applause from the group.

"Surely there cannot be any bad news," said Sara, laughing.

Jonathan continued, holding up his hand. "The bad news is that someone has been muddying the water with Historic England and has put in an application to Historic England to have Bombard house listed as a building of interest."

"And I bet we can all guess who has done that," said Hugo, smiling.

"That bloody man," said Grenville. "So where do we stand on this?" asked Grenville.

"Well, I have a meeting with Historic England next week, so hopefully we can get a positive outcome," said Jonathan.

"And if we don't?" asked Sara.

"Well, there are two grades of listed buildings. Grade 1 is of exceptional national architectural or historic importance, which means we could be buggered and not change a lot to the building, second is Grade 2 of national importance & special interest, which will be more flexible to building change. But it is up to Historic England to make the recommendation to The Secretary of State for Culture, Media and Sport who is responsible for compiling the statutory list of buildings of special architectural or historic interest. Hopefully due to the location and age of the building, they won't deem Bombard House suitable as a listed building," said Jonathan, sitting down.

"Thank you, Jonathan," said Grenville. "Hugo," said Grenville, smiling.

Hugo stood and said, "We now have a working capital of thirty-five million," which brought a round of applause from everyone. Hugo smiled and said, "Moving on, Easington Investment Bank. Did some digging about and called in a few favours in the City, and I can say that they are to put it poetically up shit creek without a paddle," which made everyone laugh.

"What do you recommend, Hugo?" asked Grenville.

"Well, we have two options. One is to invest in the bank then raise a vote of no confidence in the current Chairman Mr Dexter Simon-Smyth, or I would suggest we quietly go about buying up shares and get enough to have a seat on the board."

"Any suggestions?" asked Grenville.

"I prefer option two myself," said Jonathan.

"How is the share price looking now?" asked Carole.

Taking a piece of paper from his briefcase Hugo said, "Five pounds fifteen pence."

"So, it could work out cheaper for us with option two," Carole said.

"Plus, option one is a big risk," replied Hugo.

Grenville said, "Shall we vote who is in favour of option one?" No one put their hand up. "Option two?" Everyone raised their hand at once. Grenville smiled. "Option two it is then. Hugo, see how many shares we require for a place on their board and see if you can purchase them for Easington Investment Bank," said Grenville.

Hugo nodded and said, "Up to the value of?"

"Will leave that up to you, old chap, if we get on their board," said Grenville, smiling.

Hugo nodded and sat down.

"Carole," said Grenville, smiling.

Carole stood and smiled. "I will not bore you all with details but to set up and have a secure computer system, we are looking at just over a million." She passed each of them a piece of paper. "On the paper, I just passed you is a breakdown of equipment and services we require," said Carole.

"Any questions?" asked Grenville. Everyone shook their heads. "Thank you, Carole," said Grenville. Carole sat down, smiling. "Now we have purchased Bombard House, and notwithstanding the problem with Historic England, I think it's time we call in a suitable architect to draw up plans to make Bombard House workable," said Grenville. "Sara, can you and Carole cover it?" he asked.

"Of course, we can," said Sara, looking at a nodding Carole.

"Excellent," replied Grenville, "once you have a workable plan, we will all meet at Bombard House to discuss it." Grenville went on, "Anyone got anything to add?" Everyone shook their head, smiling. Grenville said, "Lunch then," and stood up.

After lunch Sara told Grenville she would be returning to London with Carole to begin looking for a suitable architect, plus she would complete some important wedding planning. Grenville smiled as he watched the taxi depart. He would miss Sara, but they all had important tasks. Thinking of his, he went to find his father. Finding both his parents in the study, he asked his father if he could possibly use Newton and the Rolls tomorrow. His father agreed even without asking the reason why.

⁎

Next morning Grenville went to the garages to find Newton. Grenville found Newton sitting in his office having a cup of coffee and listening to the radio. "Newton my dear chap, there you are," said Grenville, smiling.

Newton stood and said, "I apologise for my attire, my Lord," standing up in his rolled-up shirt sleeves.

Grenville smiled and waved his hand. "No need to apologise my dear chap, it was my fault for coming and tracking you down."

"How may I be of service, my Lord?" asked Newton.

"I need you and the Rolls for a quick trip to the East End of London," said Grenville.

Newton smiled. "I will be ready in ten minutes, my Lord," replied Newton.

"Excellent, meet you in front of the Hall," said Grenville, turning and returning to the Hall.

As promised Newton was ready with the door to the Rolls open before Grenville came out of the Hall. As Grenville climbed into the Rolls, Newton asked, "Where we off to, my Lord?"

"Not sure." He passed the piece of paper to Newton with Grace Backer's address on it.

Newton smiled. "I know it well, my Lord, was brought up a stone's throw away from there myself."

"Excellent," said Grenville, smiling.

Newton made good progress to the East End of London. All Grenville could see were derelict and abandoned buildings, and his thoughts turned to Tom who grew up around here and he wondered if he played in the places there were passing. Grenville smiled. This place helped Tom become the man he is today, shaped him. How different from his upbringing, surrounded by opulence, compared to people around here. He spotted a few ragged dressed children staring at the Rolls Royce as it passed as if it were an alien space ship.

Grenville, still smiling, said to Newton, "You grew up around here, Newton?

"Yes, my Lord, not far away from where we are heading."

"Was it tough?"

"Not really, my Lord, we knew no different so we had nothing to compare it with," said Newton, laughing. Grenville nodded and contemplated what it would have been like living around this place. "Just coming up on Brick Lane now, my Lord," said Newton, which brought Grenville out of his daydream.

"Thank you, Newton," replied Grenville. Turning into Durant Street Newton stopped outside number twenty-seven. The curtains in the street were twitching and some had even come out to look; groups had gathered along the street, and were staring at the beautiful blue Rolls Royce. Everyone was speculating why it was here; a group of children just stood metres from it, staring at the car.

Newton got out and opened the door for Grenville. "Twenty-seven Durant Street, my Lord," said Newton quite loudly, so the gathered crowd could hear. This brought an audible intake of breath from the assembled group.

Grenville smiled and said, "Thank you, Newton," as he stepped from the Rolls Royce. Turning, Grenville said, "Please wait for me Newton, not sure how long."

"Take your time my Lord, I will keep an eye on the Roller," he replied, Grenville smiled at the thought of any one trying to touch Newton's pride and joy.

Grenville knocked on number twenty-seven, and after a pause he realised perhaps Mrs Backer was not in. He felt himself turn red for being so arrogant as to think everyone was at his beck and call. He was just about to leave when he heard a bolt being pulled across the door. The door opened a fraction and a face peered out at him and said, "Yes, can I help you?"

"May I presume I am addressing a Mrs Grace Backer?" Grenville asked.

"Who wants to know?" the face replied.

"Sorry, let me introduce myself," Grenville said.

"Please do," replied the face.

"I am Grenville Hampton, Earl of Eastleigh," said Grenville bowing slightly.

"I am Grace Backer, what can I do for the Earl of Eastleigh?" replied Grace.

"I was recently abroad and met a new acquaintance," said Grenville.

"And what has that got to do with me?" replied Grace.

"His name was Tom, and he asked if I could look you up when I was back in England," said Grenville very softly.

Grace opened the door wider without giving anything away by her expression. "Please come in, my Lord," said Grace, standing back to allow Grenville access.

"Please, Mrs Backer call me Grenville," replied Grenville.

"Thank you, Grenville, please call me Grace," said Grace, smiling for the first time. Once seated in the kitchen, Grace asked, "Would you like a cup of tea, Grenville?"

"Most kind, Grace."

After Grace made tea she sat opposite Grenville and smiled. "You know this will be the talk of the street for days to come," said a laughing Grace.

"Why, do you not get a lot of Rolls Royce down your road?" said a laughing Grenville.

Grace looked at Grenville and saw his smiling eyes and knew they were going to become friends. "So, Grenville, you mentioned a name that has only been mentioned in whispers for years around these parts," said Grace softly.

Lowering his cup, Grenville went on to tell Grace his story of how he met Tom and the time they spent together.

Grace continued to ask Grenville questions about Tom and his life since leaving Russia, and Grenville answered them all with honesty. Grace could see from his face that he was being open with her. After a time, Grace, with tears in her eyes, said, "Thank you Grenville, you have made an old lady very happy."

"My pleasure, Grace." Taking Grace's hand, Grenville went on. "I promised Tom I would visit and let you know he was safe. Plus, I promised Tom I would look after you," said Grenville, smiling.

"Do I need looking after?" replied Grace, laughing.

"I think we can find you somewhere better," replied a smiling Grenville.

"The area around here has become a bit run down, and it's definitely not safe to go out at night," replied Grace.

"More reason to find you somewhere where you feel safe," said Grenville. "Leave it with me, Grace, and I will find somewhere suitable," said a smiling Grenville. "I know this time I was lucky to find you in my ignorance, for thinking you would be in, so is there any time you would rather me not call?" asked Grenville.

"Only day I am really out is Wednesday morning when I go to collect my pension, apart from that I am always in," said Grace, smiling.

"Excellent," replied Grenville. As Grace walked Grenville to the door, and as she opened it, it seemed the whole street was standing around the Rolls Royce. Grenville kissed Grace on the cheek and said, "Will be in touch soon."

Grace smiled and said, "Thank you, my dear."

Newton held the door open for Grenville. People looked at Grenville with wide eyes; he was sure he was the first Earl that some had ever seen. Grenville smiled at the crowd and gave a wave, to which most of them just stood and stared. Grenville thought that Grace would be having a lot of visitors when he left, wanting to know who he was and what he wanted with her, and knowing Grace she would be playing it close to her chest, revelling in the attention.

After Newton got in, he turned and said, "Where to now, my Lord?"

"Home, I think, Newton," Grenville replied, to which Newton said, "Home it is, my Lord." As he placed the car in gear and pulled away, the children chased the car all the way down to the main road.

∞·℃

Back at the Hall Grenville went to find his mother. Finding her in the reading room, Grenville kissed her on the offered cheek. "Hello darling, what you up to?" asked his mother.

"Looking for you, and your sage advice," replied a smiling Grenville. Sitting next to his mother, Grenville said, "I told you about my friend Tom," to which his mother nodded and smiled. "Well, his mother lives in a rundown part of London, now retired so we need to get her somewhere safe, and I know it will please Tom knowing his mother is safe," said Grenville.

"So, what do you need from me?" asked his mother.

"Well, I know in your various projects and committees you come across various places."

"What is she like?" asked his mother.

Grenville said, "Grace is, how shall we say, very independent and street wise and I don't think she suffers fools gladly."

"OK," his mother replied.

"In fact, she reminds me a lot of you, mother, in her attitude," smiled Grenville.

"Well in that case, my quest will be easy," said his mother, laughing.

"Thank you, mother, knew I could rely on you," said Grenville, leaving over and kissing her again on her cheek.

Wednesday of the following month came quickly and Grenville had been up since dawn. He was not sure whether it was seeing Sara again or getting updates from the team, but he was feeling excited, and kept looking out of the window after breakfast looking for taxis. Eventually he spotted a taxi coming up the drive. Grenville went and stood on the steps watching it arrive. Smiling, he spotted Sara, who was waving frantically at him and smiling. As soon as the taxi stopped she was out and into his arms. Kissing him deeply, she said, "Boy, have I missed you."

"Likewise," he said into her mouth.

Carole was the next to greet him with a hug, then Hugo and Jonathan. "Shall we?" said Grenville, pointing towards the Hall.

"After you, old man," said Hugo. With Sara on his arm, he led the way towards the library.

Once they had all been seated and coffee served Grenville said, smiling, "Shall we begin?"

Without being prompted Jonathan stood and said, "The purchase of Bombard House has been finalised," which brought a round of applause from them all. Jonathan continued, "I had a meeting with Historic England and convinced them that Bombard House was not a real potential to be a listed building on the scale of Blenheim Palace," this brought laughter from the others, "so as far as we are concerned we are good to go," said Jonathan, sitting down.

"Well done old boy, mightily impressed," said a smiling Grenville, which brought a "hear, hear" from the others.

Hugo stood next. Smiling, Hugo said, "We now have a company working capital of fifty million pounds." This brought a hush from the others.

"How much?" said Carole.

"Fifty million pounds," said Hugo more loudly.

"That's what I thought you said," Carole replied.

"That is the balance after taking off the purchase for Bombard House, and the purchase of stock for Easington Investment Bank."

"How much stock?" asked Jonathan.

"Approximately fifteen per cent, which gives us the right to push for a seat on the board, as we now have ten per cent ownership in the bank," said Hugo.

"What name did you purchase the shares in, Hugo?" Grenville asked.

"S&T Imports," replied Hugo, smiling.

"Excellent," said Jonathan, "so he won't know it's us," Jonathan continued.

"Can he not find out?" asked Sara.

"Surely he will be curious to know who has been buying up all their stock?" asked Carole.

"No," said Hugo. "S&T Imports is a private company, registered in the UK for tax purposes, so unlike a UK company we don't have to list our board or structure, if we keep the taxman happy, and conform to UK business regulations," said Hugo, smiling.

"When can we find out about their next board meeting, and get a place on it?" asked Grenville.

"We can formally write to Easington Investment Bank asking to join the board as soon as we like," replied Hugo, sitting down.

"Well done you," said Carole, smiling at Hugo. It did not go amiss from the others; the smile Carole gave Hugo or the shy smile he gave her back.

To hide his embarrassment, Grenville said, "Hugo, a star as always," which brought another round of laughter from the others.

Sara stood. "My turn," she said, smiling.

"Go for it girl," said Carole, smiling.

Sara carried on. "I have been to see a reputable architect to draw up some plans, after Jonathan and I showed him over Bombard House, and he should have them ready for our approval early next month. But as a basic plan, I suggested we have the fifth-floor management and conference rooms, fourth floor HR and Administration, third floor Accounts and Sales and Marketing, second floor Legal and Procurement and first floor IT," said Sara, scanning the room.

"Most impressive," said Grenville, smiling.

"Also," said Sara, carrying on, "I have spoken to a few recruitment agencies within area and gave them a list of our basic employment requirements, so they can start getting together suitable candidates for the departments." Sara sat down, smiling.

"Well done you," said Hugo; this brought another round of applause for the others.

Sara went red with embarrassment, which made them all laugh. Grenville leaned over and whispered, "I knew you had it in you."

"Thank you my love," she replied, smiling.

Carole stood up. "My turn," she said, "Since we last met, I ordered the following items of IT equipment," holding up her hand, "and before you all say anything, these items due to their, shall we say complexity, may take a few months to arrive, so I have already ordered them."

"Good planning," said Grenville, smiling.

"So, we have a few months to get Bombard House up to scratch before the equipment arrives," Carole said.

"What about normal IT equipment?" asked Jonathan.

"Most we can get bought off the shelf, plus if you buy in bulk, say three hundred PCs, then a discount will be forthcoming," Carole replied.

"Discount, I like discount," said Hugo, smiling, which made every one laugh.

"I think we are moving on quite well," said Grenville, which everyone else nodded at. "Shall we break for lunch?" he asked, standing up.

80 · 08

Grenville stared out of his office window. The last three months had been dedicated to the re-modelling of Bombard House, and between them setting the staffing levels for each department. It was during these sessions and over a few heated arguments that Grenville smiled and realised he had a good team moving S&T Imports forward. Each of them had put heart and soul into the project. Grenville and Sara stayed in Sara's London flat during the week, only going to Hampton Hall at weekends. Hugo and Carole had become closer and although they tried to hide it, Grenville smiled; it was a poorly kept secret to anyone who knew them. Jonathan was the only one still not working full time for S&T Imports, and as he told Grenville on more than one occasion, he had a certain allegiance to his father and his firm, and he was expected to take over the mantle once his father retired, but this in no way distracted him from Grenville's vision, and he would dedicate his time and effort as and when needed. This made Grenville smile again. He always knew since they had first met that Jonathan was destined to follow in his father's footsteps and become, like him, a High Court judge, but he had a good trusted team around him, and he felt he was finally moving forward.

The person who had surprised him the most was Sara. Considering she was the first to admit she had no business brain compared to the others, she had on some things outshone the others with her organisational ability and the flair she had to recruit people, and to make quick decisions: from colour scheme in the reception, to layout of each floor restroom, she had the touch, as Hugo called it. All the top managers were now in place, all the departments were up and running, some more than others. Carole was finalising the IT network but Grenville did not interfere or hassle her over it, as even Grenville realised they needed a state of the art system, and they don't appear overnight. But she had recruited some pretty impressive people in her team, and Grenville was sure she would overcome any foreseen problems, and she told him last time they met some of this stuff was just theory until now.

The buzzer on his phone brought Grenville out of his daydream. Picking up the phone, he said, "Yes Michelle."

"Mr Jonathan Spencer on line one, Chairman."

"Thank you, Michelle, please put him through."

"Jonathan my dear chap, how are you?"

"Fine thank you, Grenville."

"To what do I owe this pleasure?" Grenville asked.

"It's about Easington Investment Bank. Had their company solicitors on the phone and they have convened a board meeting for next month, and they were wondering who was the S&T Imports name."

"Think this should be a team decision, old man. You free for lunch?"

"Let me check," said Jonathan, "yes, can be with you at one."

"Excellent, I will gather the others in the board room."

"See you at one," said Jonathan as he put the phone down.

Grenville picked up the phone again and Michelle immediately said, "Yes, Chairman."

"Michelle, please see if it is convenient for Miss Farthing, Mr Thorn and Miss Burke to meet me in the boardroom for one, and ask Miss Farthing to organise some sandwiches and coffee please."

"Of course, Chairman, straight away."

As Grenville put the phone down he smiled. Michelle was one of Sara's finds, and he knew that Sara had picked her with age and status in mind. Michelle was a contented married middle-aged grandmother of four, and very discreet; a perfect personal assistant for a Chairman.

At one Grenville went to the board room. Jonathan and Hugo were already there. Grenville hugged Jonathan and shook Hugo's hand.

"How you two doing?" asked Grenville.

"Very well," said Jonathan, smiling.

"Busy," said Hugo. "Our chairman is a task master," he went on, laughing, which made Grenville and Jonathan laugh as well.

As they were laughing, Carole and Sara came in. "Private joke?" said Sara.

"Not at all," said Grenville. "Hugo was just telling Jonathan his chairman is a task master."

"He is loveable though," said Sara, going over and kissing Grenville.

"Easy for you to say, you are marrying him," said a laughing Carole, which started them all off laughing again.

There was a knock on the door and one of Sara's team wheeled in a trolley with coffee and sandwiches. "Thank you, Lisa," said Sara, smiling. Lisa smiled back and left.

"Shall we?" said Grenville, pointing to the table and chairs. After they were all seated, Grenville said, "I apologise from tearing you all away from your busy schedules, but I thought what Jonathan had to discuss should be for the Board." Everyone smiled around the room. "Jonathan," said Grenville, holding out his hand.

Jonathan stood up. "Thank you, Chairman. As I informed the Chairman this morning, I have had contact with Easington Investment Bank's solicitors asking for the name to be included on the bank's board, as they have a board meeting set for next month."

"So, do we say it's me and tip our hand?" asked Grenville. "Or give them someone he does not know," he went on.

"Well, I don't think he can harm us now, can he?" asked Carole.

"Not really, we are too financially secure for that," replied Hugo, smiling.

"I think we should let him squirm," said Sara.

"My sentiments exactly," said Jonathan.

"After what he tried to do to your family, let him know you are coming for him," said Sara.

"OK," said Grenville. "Let's vote. All those in favour of naming me as the S&T Imports representative?" Four hands shot up. "OK then," said Grenville, smiling. "Jonathan, can you inform Easington Investment Bank solicitors that the Earl of Eastleigh would be delighted to attend their forthcoming board meeting, on behalf of and as the representative of S&T Imports," smiled Grenville.

"Plus, we are all too busy," said Carole, laughing. "Well, you are all thinking it," she said, which brought a round of laughter from the table.

⅒·⅓

Dexter Simon-Smyth sat staring at the letter he had just received from the bank's solicitors. "The Earl of Eastleigh will be the representative for S&T Imports for the forthcoming board meeting." How in the hell did this happen? He was aware S&T Imports were buying up bank shares, but never in a million years did he connect S&T Imports with the boy Hampton; this was a puzzle that needed solving. Also, Hampton had out played him twice now: once over Hampton Hall, and the second time over Bombard House, but what annoyed Dexter more was, how in the hell did he get enough money to clear the debt, and become a big player within S&T Imports? He had tried to get information on S&T Imports, but his contacts were either playing dumb or had been warned off delving too deep. Dexter was not concerned with the boy Hampton, even at school apart from the one incident with his brother Stephan he had nothing to do with him, plus Stephan always said his younger brother was a total waste of space and would not amount to anything. He had been out of the country for several years, doing god knows what; of course, he blamed Stephan Hampton, stupid prig, getting himself killed just as things were going his way. Plus, he had lost the title which Stephan had promised him, which annoyed him more. Farthing was uncontactable which did not come as a surprise as he had heard that young Hampton and the Farthings' daughter were to marry. How this had happened was a mystery to Dexter, but no doubt Farthing was pleased by the outcome, but he wondered if Hampton knew how much of a player his future father-in-law had been in trying to bring down the Duke of Hampshire and his estate. He was deep in it, up to his neck, over the debt against the Hall; he was going to part purchase it after the present Duke had forfeited the debt, they were ready to swoop in and give the going rate for the place, and with the sale of the estate Dexter would have just about saved his bacon from gathering creditors.

Picking up the phone, he said, "Can you show Grimes in?" After a minute, there was a silent knock and Dexter said, "Come in." Grimes entered and walked slowly up to where Dexter was sitting. Dexter loathed the man, he was an odious creature, but was excellent at his work.

"Grimes, have a small task for you."

Grimes smiled a sly smile and said, "It will be a pleasure, Mr Simon-Smyth."

Without making eye contact, Dexter passed Grimes a piece of paper, which Grimes picked up, read, and placed back on the table. "I want you to find out everything you can about that person, where he been, how he made his fortune, and any other relevant information," said Dexter.

Grimes bowed and turned without speaking before he left the room. Dexter said, "Grimes, this is a top priority, I expect a report in a few days." Grimes half turned, and gave a slight bow in recognition. Dexter sat back and smiled. By next week, hopefully he could have some dirt on the Hampton boy. Dexter refused to call him the Earl of Eastleigh, after all that should have been his title, and the fact still left a bitter taste in his mouth.

Grimes kept to the shadows. He hated crowds, preferring his own company. Being a second-rate private investigator had its drawbacks, but since he had gained employment from Mr Simon-Smyth things were looking up. Now he even had money to spend; before, he lived from hand to mouth, sometimes even sleeping rough. His first assignment for Mr Simon-Smyth was by pure chance. He had spotted the advert in the local paper: "looking for an investigator, no questions". Grimes knew no self-respecting private investigator would apply. He, of course, had no morals and applied at once. Grimes hated Mr Simon-Smyth the first time he saw him, and he knew the feeling was mutual. At least he did not try and be something he was not. Mr Simon-Smyth was a stuck-up toffee nose oaf, who thought the world was there to grant him his every wish, he on the other hand knew exactly his station in life, and was happy with it. After his successful completion of the first job, he was put on a retainer by Mr Simon-Smyth and used from time to time, which for Grimes become quite lucrative; so, started their strange working relationship.

A week later Grimes was sitting in his local pub nursing a pint of bitter. Although it was only eleven thirty and the place had just opened, he felt he needed it. He was feeling frustrated; his underworld connections were normally good with forthcoming information but his normal sources had either been unavailable or scared to talk to him once he mentioned the name Grenville Hampton, Earl of Eastleigh. This was a conundrum that needed a pint of beer to ponder over.

Grimes knew Mr Dexter Simon-Smyth would not be happy with his lack of progress and he would soon be hassling him for information. He was unsure why people were not willing to even discuss the Earl of Eastleigh; he had done his preliminary work in Who's Who and public records, which only described his family tree and his school record up to dropping out of Cambridge after the first year, returning when his brother had died to take up the mantle of Earl of Eastleigh and the next Duke of Hampton. It was the fact he dropped out of Cambridge and then returned several years later that intrigued Grimes. During that time, something major had happened and he was going to find out, as that was the key to the mystery.

As Grimes studied his pint, pondering what to do next, a fresh pint appeared in front of him. Looking up, a large smartly dressed man smiled and said, "On me, Mr Grimes," and sat down opposite.

"Can I help you?" asked Grimes.

Ignoring Grimes, the man smiled. "You been asking about the Earl of Eastleigh?" Grimes nodded in acknowledgement. "The Earl of Eastleigh is off limits, Mr Grimes," said the man quietly. "You are going down a dangerous path, Mr Grimes," he continued. "The Earl of Eastleigh, how shall we say, is protected by some very powerful friends, who do not like people like you asking questions about him." Grimes felt the sweat trickling down his spine as the man smiled at him. Eastern European, thought Grimes. "We suggest, Mr Grimes, for your own health and safety you cease your present line of inquiry, and forget you ever heard the name of Earl of Eastleigh, and perhaps even take a long overdue holiday," said the man, still smiling. "Let's hope my colleagues and I do not have to re-visit this conservation," the man said, gesturing over his shoulder at the three large men staring intently at Grimes. Standing, the man said, smiling, "We will be watching, Mr Grimes, and if we hear any whispers, we will return and next time you won't get a free pint on us." The man turned. He nodded to the three men standing at the bar, and as all four left, Grimes sat and stared at their departing backs.

Grimes quickly took a gulp of the offered pint. His mind was racing. What had Mr Simon-Smyth got him into? No way was he now going to ask more questions about the Earl of Eastleigh. The threat, although subtle, had spoken volumes, and no way was he going to jeopardise his life for Mr bloody Simon-Smyth and his meagre payment. Quickly formulating a plan, Grimes quickly finished his pint and left the bar, keeping to the shadows back towards his lodgings. Once or twice he stopped in doorways to look behind him but could not see anyone, but that did not mean they were not watching him. Grimes started to sweat heavily and his breathing was becoming laboured. Calm down, he told himself, after all they gave you a free pint and a warning.

Once back at his lodgings Grimes quickly packed a suitcase with his personal belongings, which did not take long, then moved aside his chest of drawers and under a loose floorboard removed the money he had saved. Counting it, it came to just close to three thousand pounds, enough to get him far away from this place. Closing the door behind him, Grimes crossed the road just as the bus for Waterloo Station arrived. Grimes brought a single ticket to Waterloo Station. Grimes sat on an unoccupied seat and closed his eyes and for the first time in an hour breathed normally.

From the shadows, the man who spoke to Grimes in the bar watched Grimes board the bus. Once the bus was out of sight, he smiled and turned and walked away in the opposite direction.

Dexter Simon-Smyth was in a fury. It was the day of the board meeting and still he had nothing concrete on the boy Hampton. Grimes had vanished off the face of the earth. Despite ringing the emergency number Grimes had left with Dexter, it just kept ringing out. Dexter had even sent someone round to his shabby flat, which was empty. Asking about, they were told that no one had seen Grimes in a few days. Where the hell could he have gotten to? It was not like Grimes, he loved money too much not to get in contact.

Dexter closed his eyes and pondered on the next course of action he needed to take. The board were manageable, he could sweet talk most of them; after all, most of them owed him their good fortune, which Dexter had no qualms in letting each of them know. Hampton was an unknown force. If Dexter knew his game plan he could head it off, or even come up with his own plan of attack. He hated this present situation. He always had the ability since school to manage situations and manipulate them and people to his own advantage, but this new situation with the boy Hampton was new ground, and for the first time in his life was unsure how to proceed.

There were now seven members on the Easington Investment Bank board. Dexter himself as the Chairman, one

Executive Director, Forbes who also ran the bank's Procurement Branch, two inside Directors, Manning and Herbert both from associated banks within the City, and three outside directors, Cross, Baker and now the boy Hampton. Dexter was sure he could still control an overall vote of the board with the layout as it was, but Hampton could muddy the waters if not checked.

Dexter smiled at the men sitting around the boardroom table, but the smile did not reach his eyes. As he stared at a smiling Hampton, Dexter turned to Forbes and said, "Please, Duncan, the minutes of the last meeting, if you please." Forbes stood, and read the minutes of the last meeting, after finishing Dexter said, "Anyone object to these being a true account so we can pass them as read?" Everyone around the table raised their hands except Grenville. "Item two," said Dexter, "the welcome of the representative from S&T Imports as the seventh board member due to their company's investment into Easington Investment Bank."

Grenville stood without being asked and said, "Thank you chairman, I hope I can make a worthwhile contribution to the Board." A "hear, hear" came from around the rest of the table. Dexter glared at Grenville with hatred in his eyes. Grenville sat with a smile; round one to me, he thought.

The next item on the agenda was the financial statement, which Grenville was most interested in. Dexter said, "At present, the bank is treading water on its own."

"What exactly does that mean?" asked Manning.

"Well, we are holding our own, in the present unstable financial climate," replied Dexter.

"Still does not tell us anything," said Herbert. Forbes had gone white and had a noticeable sweat on him.

Dexter smiled and said, "Gentlemen I can assure you the bank is stable."

"If it is stable, give us the figures," said Grenville, smiling.

Dexter glared at Grenville, and said, "Duncan if you please."

Duncan Forbes got shakily to his feet, and tried to clear his throat, but his voice was still squeaky. "At present, with some assets which the bank is unable to sell on, we are in the red by just under two million pounds."

"Of course," Dexter said quickly, "these are assets that if we sell, we can make a handsome profit on, so I suggest gentlemen this is just a temporary setback for the bank."

"How many purchases are we talking about?" asked Cross.

Forbes looked at Dexter before softly saying, "Five."

"Five," said Baker.

"And how many have current interested parties do we have considering them?" asked Manning.

"Possible one, maybe two," replied Forbes, wishing the ground would open and swallow him.

"But gentlemen, we are actively pursuing buyers," said Dexter, quickly. "Now is not the time to have doubts, we must let our long-term strategy come to fruition," he went on, smiling.

"Can we have a list of the five assets?" asked Cross.

"Absolutely," said Dexter, smiling. "Duncan, can you sort that out for the board members," said Dexter without looking in Forbes's direction.

"I think we should give the chairman the benefit of the doubt, and let his plan run," said a smiling Grenville. Continuing, Grenville said, "Let us wait until the next board meeting in three months' time. I for one have every faith that the chairman can bring about a quick and profitable outcome for the bank with these assets."

"Shall we take a vote," said Herbert. "All those in favour of no action until the next board meeting, raise your hand." Five were in favour and two against.

"Carried," said a relieved sounding Forbes. The rest of the board meeting was taken up with mundane points, which were quickly voted on with little or no discussion, and after two hours, Dexter declared the board meeting closed.

Back in his office Dexter was furious. "Well, you were all but bloody useless," he screamed at Forbes.

"Hang on now," said Forbes, "in my defence, if I am asked I have to tell the truth," Forbes went on.

"Not the actual truth, you bloody moron," said a red-faced Dexter.

"Well, if you kept me in the loop, then perhaps I would know what to say," said Forbes.

"Just get out," said Dexter. Forbes stood and left the room quietly. Dexter placed his head in his hand and knew time was not on his side, and as for Hampton he was surprised he was ready to support him. What was his game plan? But Dexter Simon-Smyth knew he had only three months until the next board meeting to turn things around or they would be after his blood.

Grenville knocked on the closed door, and heard a quiet, "Enter." Opening the door, a fraction and placing his head around the door, Grenville smiled at Hugo and said, "Time for a chat?"

"Absolutely old man," replied Hugo. "Coffee?" asked Hugo.

"No thanks old bean, meeting Sara for lunch and cannot be late."

"What can I do for you then?" asked Hugo, smiling.

"Just thought I would drop this off," he held up a brown folder, "the minutes of Easington Investment Bank board meeting I had yesterday, plus my observations added."

"Will give them my undivided attention," said Hugo.

"No rush, next team meeting will do," replied Grenville.

"Until lunchtime then," said Hugo, smiling.

"Not with you, old man," said a puzzled Grenville.

"Carole and I are lunching with you and Sara," said Hugo.

"Excellent," said Grenville as he closed the door on a laughing Hugo.

Sara found Grenville sitting in his office with a sad face. "What is the matter, my love?" she asked.

"Don't worry, it's me being silly," replied Grenville.

Sitting on his lap and placing her arms around him, she said, "Tell me what's wrong."

"It's nothing really, I just get the feeling I am a spare wheel lately around here, everyone is going about their tasks with gusto, even you are busy, but I seem to be in the way."

Sara took Grenville's face in her hands and said, "Listen here, Earl of Eastleigh, you started this, you had the drive to start and give it life, it's now growing and growing fast, but it still needs guiding by you, as you are the one with the overall vision, which we all look up to. So, we might be busy but we definitely need you." Sara kissed him deeply and said, "Now stop acting like a lost school boy and act like a chairman, and take me to lunch," she said into his mouth. This made Grenville smile and say, "By your command, my love."

୫୭·ୡଓ

Grenville was staring out of the windows, and was thinking how to proceed with Easington Investment Bank and especially Mr Dexter Simon-Smyth, when the buzzer on his phone brought Grenville back to the present. Picking up the phone, he said, "Yes, Michelle."

"A Mr Smith in reception from Sharapova Investments," said Michelle.

Grenville, trying not to sound shocked, said, "Thank you Michelle, please ask reception to escort Mr Smith up."

"Of course, Chairman," replied Michelle before the line went dead.

Still holding the phone, Grenville's mind was racing. This was a turn of events. Placing down the receiver, Grenville took a deep breath, stood and went to greet the mysterious Mr Smith from Sharapova Investments, and wondered what he possibly wanted.

There was a light knock as the door was opened by Michelle, who smiled and said, "Mr Smith, Chairman."

"Thank you, Michelle," replied Grenville as she closed the door behind her. Grenville stared at Mr Smith, a large man neatly dressed in a black long overcoat with highly polished black shoes, but the thing Grenville noticed was that Mr Smith wore tight black leather glove, and a face like granite.

Moving forward, Grenville held out his hand and said, "Mr Smith, how can I be of assistance?"

Mr Smith ignored the offered hand hanging in the air and moved past Grenville and sat in a chair opposite his desk. Grenville returned and sat behind his desk, and once he was seated Mr Smith said, "I do apologise for the abruptness of my visit, my Lord, but a few lose ends have been encountered and I was instructed to seek your guidance on the matter." Mr Smith smiled for the first time but Grenville noticed the smile only stayed on the lips, as if it was a strange gesture for him, and smiling was not natural. Grenville noticed that his accent was most East European; Grenville relaxed as he was sure that if this man had come to kill him, he would have been dead minutes ago, without any conversation.

"You are from Sharapova Investments?" asked Grenville.

Mr Smith gave a slight nod of the head and replied, "We were asked to keep a watching brief on you and your activities and only to assist if necessary."

"So, what has changed that requires a visit?" replied Grenville, smiling for the first time.

"It has come to our notice that a certain gentleman of our mutual acquaintance had a private investigator ask some, shall we say, penetrating questions about you. We have of course removed this problem," said Mr Smith.

Grenville was not surprised that Simon-Smyth had tried to poke about and ask question especially after he had found out that the new board member of Easington Investment Bank was Grenville. "So how can I help?" asked Grenville.

"Our mutual friend was aware that two gentlemen, once your brother was dead, tried to still ruin your family." Grenville stared at Mr Smith. So, as he thought, Farthing was also behind the takeover of Hampton Hall. Mr Smith had just confirmed his suspicions. "Our mutual friend does not like complications getting in his way," said Mr Smith.

"But surely, they are both no longer a problem to us," replied Grenville.

"One gentleman perhaps, as your recent engagement can attest, but the other gentleman is a different fish, and one we feel will not be so easy to placate."

"Sorry, I am not following you," replied Grenville, looking confused.

"It is simple; they both require, how shall we say, removed from causing further problems to us all."

Grenville looked totally shocked at what Mr Smith was suggesting; yes, Grenville was annoyed about the family estate but to go as far as murder, he was sure he would never have considered that option, however desperate things had got.

Staring intently at Grenville, Mr Smith said, "I can see you are shocked, as our mutual friend said you would be, but he told me to remind you of what he said about people and the three rules he taught you when you first met."

Grenville sat back in his chair and remembered what Tom had told him;

"The people we are going to be associating with and meeting are dangerous men; they have no morals or honour, there are no rules, and they will not hesitate to try and destroy you and in some extreme cases kill you if they see weakness in you, or think you are not what you are meant to be. Rule number one, never attack in anger. Rule number two, always mean it, this is a matter of life and death. Rule number three, never let your opponent know your move."

Grenville looked up at Mr Smith and quietly said, "You have my blessing to do whatever you feel warranted to keep our venture true."

Mr Smith stood and nodded to Grenville and said, "We will make sure that these gentlemen are no longer a problem." Just before he touched the handle on the door, Mr Smith turned and said, "We will be watching," before turning and leaving the room.

Grenville sat and closed his eyes. This is a secret he could not share, not even with Sara. He was sure Sara was not as close to her father as she was her mother, and he suspected she never really forgave him for forcing her to marry his brother, but he was sure she would not look too kindly on Grenville if she knew he had just possibly signed her father's death warrant.

໒ঠ·ল৪

That weekend whilst they were down visiting Hampton Hall, Grenville was sitting in the reading room. His mother entered and said, "There you are darling, was looking for you."

"Now you found me, mother" replied Grenville, smiling.

Sofia sat next to Grenville and handed him a colour brochure.

"What's this?" asked Grenville.

"Grace's new home, Peaches Retirement Home," replied Sofia, smiling. "I have searched and I think this is the most suitable place for a still independent lady," Sofia went on.

"Mother, you are a marvel. I will go see Grace and give her the good news," said Grenville. Leaning over, Grenville kissed his mother on the cheek and said, "I am lucky to have you."

Smiling, Sofia said, "I am the lucky one, my son."

Next day at breakfast Sofia asked Grenville if she could accompany him when he went to see Grace and perhaps take her to look at the Peaches Retirement Home. Grenville smiled at his mother and thought it a capital idea. She told Grenville she was curious about Tom's mother. "You are most welcome to come as well, my darling," Grenville asked Sara.

"Please don't worry about me, my love, I have plans today, some wedding shopping with my mother," replied a smiling Sara.

Newton drove them both as before to the East End of London, and as before Grenville was amused that he was still in England. The area looked alien to him, but he was reminded that the class system still ruled in England, and there would always be the haves and have nots; he was lucky to have been born into privilege. Parking once again outside Grace's house, Grenville knocked on the door and this time it was immediately opened by a smiling Grace. "Grenville, welcome back," Grace said, giving him a hug and a kiss.

"Grace, may I introduce my mother, the Duchess of Hampshire."

Grace smiled at Sofia, and shook her hand and said, "Welcome to my humble abode, your Grace."

Sofia knew the greeting was sincere as the smile rose to Grace's eyes. "Please call me Sofia," said a smiling Sofia.

Standing back, Grace said, "Please, both of you, come in." Once they were all seated in the kitchen, Grace asked if anyone wanted a cup of tea.

"Grace, we might not have time."

"Oh, why is that?" Grace asked.

"Because we are here to take you to view your new home," said Sofia.

"Really, how lovely," replied Grace, smiling. "And do I get to ride in that lovely big car of yours?" she asked, laughing.

Sofia said, "Of course you do, my dear," laughing as well.

"Never been in such a posh car in my life," Grace said, "can you give an old lady ten minutes to make herself look presentable?"

"Take your time, we are in no rush," said a still laughing Sofia.

Twenty minutes later Grace reappeared in the kitchen dressed in what Sofia assumed was her finery. Grace even had a hat on. "Stunning," said Grenville, bowing.

"Get away with you and your silver tongue," said Grace laughing. "You have certainly raised a gallant young man, Sofia," Grace said, smiling.

"I am very lucky to have such a wonderful son," said Sofia, smiling as well.

"Shall we?" said Grenville to hide his embarrassment, holding out his arm for Grace. As they stepped out of the house, there was quite a large gathering again; this time, everyone was silent as Newton opened the rear door and saluted as Grace climbed in followed by Sofia and Grenville.

Once they were all seated, Newton asked, "Where to, your Grace?"

Sofia said, "Peaches Retirement Home, if you please, Newton."

"Of course, your Grace," replied Newton as he put the car in gear and pulled away from the curb, everyone just stood in astonishment as the Rolls Royce pulled silently away from the curb and proceeded down the street. While they drove towards Peaches Retirement Home, Grenville handed Grace the brochure for Peaches Retirement Home, which she studied in silence during the drive. As the car pulled up in front of the admin block of the Peaches Retirement Home, there stood a greeting committee of three. Grenville smiled; one of his mother's assistants had obviously phoned ahead of their appointment, to inform them the Duchess of Hampshire was visiting.

As they all stepped from the car, a smartly dressed lady approached, curtsied, and said, "Welcome your Grace, I am Mrs Pritchard, manager of the Peaches Retirement Home."

"Thank you, Mrs Pritchard, lovely to be here," smiled Sofia, holding out her hand. "Please let me introduce my son, the Earl of Eastleigh, and Mrs Grace Backer." After being introduced to everyone, Mrs Pritchard led them into the large reception area, where coffee was laid on.

"So down to business, Mrs Pritchard," Grenville said.

"Of course, my Lord," replied Mrs Pritchard.

"We require new safe accommodation for Mrs Grace Backer here," said Grenville, nodding at Grace.

"I am delighted you chose our establishment for consideration," said Mrs Pritchard, smiling.

"It was mother, the Duchess of Hampshire, who suggested your complex," replied Grenville, pointing towards Sofia. Mrs Pritchard gave a smile and a nod of the head in acknowledgement. Grace sat and smiled at the exchange between Grenville and Mrs Pritchard, Grace knew by Grenville's attitude that he was a true friend to her Tom, as he was so concerned for her wellbeing, which made her feel loved.

Mrs Pritchard gave a short presentation on the complex. "Fifty-three individual one bedroom self-contained bungalows, for singles or retired couples, in a private estate, with their own private parking spaces. Every bungalow comes with help-assist buttons in every room, linked back to the admin centre which is manned twenty-four hours a day. The complex also has a full-time on call doctor and day and night carers who will cater for all the residents' needs. It also has private security patrols, foot and mobile twenty-four hours a day, to give the residents the feeling of community and security. The main admin centre caters for all the resident's needs, from meals if required to many social clubs and entertainment, all voluntary of course for the residents, so they can either partake in the community or not, it is their choice. One of the carers will make contact daily to make sure there are no problems. We have a monthly magazine distributed to all residents on the forthcoming week's activities." After the briefing Mrs Pritchard said, "Would you like to go look at a bungalow?"

"Excellent, please lead the way," said Sofia.

Mrs Pritchard led them to a bungalow next to the admin centre which was obviously the show place. After they had viewed the bungalow, and were back in the admin centre, Mrs Pritchard said, "I will leave you to have a private discussion on the complex." Smiling, Mrs Pritchard left the room, closing the door behind her.

Before the door was fully shut Grace said, "Lovely as it is, Grenville, I think this place is out of my price range on my pension."

Grenville went and sat next to Grace, holding her hand, and said, "Grace I promised Tom I would look after you, and look after you I will, so let us worry about the money, all you've got to decide is do you like the place?"

Grace smiled at Grenville with tears in her eyes and said, "Grenville thank you so much, I love it."

"That's decided then, we've just got to work out now what type of view you want from your sitting room," said Sofia, smiling. Grenville admitted he did not think of that, and was glad he brought his mother along for the female touch.

Mrs Pritchard returned as promised, and Grenville said, "Mrs Pritchard, after much discussion we have decided will take one of your lovely bungalows."

"Thank you my Lord," replied Mrs Pritchard.

"We just need to work out which one," said Sofia.

Mrs Pritchard opened a folded map of the complex, and pointed out the bungalows that were vacant. As they studied the map, Sofia smiled at Grace and they both pointed to the same one, which made them both laugh.

"I think Mrs Backer has found the one she wants," said a smiling Grenville. Mrs Pritchard asked Grenville to accompany her to the office to complete the paperwork. "Won't be long," he said to Sofia and Grace, who both smiled as he left.

After Grenville left, Grace said, "He is a lovely remarkable young man, Sofia."

"And so, changed since his return, and I have no doubt that was down to your Tom's influence and guidance," said Sofia. "Grenville is one in a million."

"My Tom is very lucky to have a friend like Grenville," said Grace.

"Grenville sees it the other way around," said Sofia.

"Well whoever is right, they are both lucky to have someone special to depend upon," said a smiling Grace.

Grenville entered the room, and handed Grace an envelope. "Signed, sealed and delivered," he said, smiling. "You can move in whenever you like," said Grenville.

"That fast? Was not expecting that," replied Grace.

"I think we will both feel better once you are settled," said Grenville.

Grace understood the use of the "we" that Grenville used. Smiling, Grace said, "But what about Durant Street?"

"Leave it all to me Grace, I will sort it all out," said a smiling Grenville.

"Thank you my dear," said a smiling Grace.

"As the place is fully furnished, and you will only need personal items and your treasured possessions from your old house, do you want to come and spend the weekend at Hampton hall with us?" asked Sofia.

"Capital idea," said a smiling Grenville.

"I don't want to impose, plus I do not have anything for a weekend visit to a posh country house," said Grace, laughing.

"Do not worry, Grace, leave it all to us," said Grenville.

"A new beginning demands new things," said Sofia. "Plus, I would love an excuse for a good shopping trip in London," said Sofia, smiling.

"Sounds like a good plan," said Grace, which made Grenville and Sofia laugh.

Grenville got Newton to drop him off in the centre of London, and he told Sofia and Grace he would meet them back at Hampton Hall that evening, as he had a few errands to run. Grenville watched the Rolls pull off towards Oxford Street, and smiled. Mother and Grace were becoming firm friends, which made him feel better, knowing Grace was becoming part of the family, which of course would please Tom, which he would convey in his next email. Grenville had agreed to meet Carole and Hugo at Bombard House, so hailing a cab he proceeded to tell the driver his destination. Using his pass to open the front door and entering the lobby of Bombard House always made Grenville smile; his vision was coming together. He had to admit Sara had a flair for interior designing. The place looked professional but comfortable, and the S&T Imports sign that Sara had made for the reception was impressive and let you know whose building you were entering.

Smiling to the two receptionists as he passed, Grenville took the lift to the fifth floor. As he passed his PA, she said, "Chairman, Mr Thorpe and Miss Burke are inside waiting for you."

"Thank you, Michelle," said Grenville as he entered his office.

"Hugo, Carole, how are you both?" said a smiling Grenville.

Both hugged Grenville and said, "Busy, but well," which made them all laugh.

"Sorry it's just us three and not the full team but Jonathan is at the Old Bailey representing some innocent party," which made them all laugh again.

"And Sara?" asked a smiling Carole.

"Afraid doing some Wedding Shopping with her mother."

"Lucky her," said Hugo.

"Never had you down for a shopaholic," said Grenville, smiling.

"Never get the time nowadays if I wanted to," replied Hugo, smiling.

"Stop it Hugo, you get the weekends off," said Carole, winking at Grenville, which made Hugo go red.

"Looks like work is a rest, old man," said Grenville, which made them all laugh again. "Before we begin, can Sara and I expect you for the weekend at Hampton Hall?"

"Absolutely, old bean," said Hugo, speaking for both.

"Mother has invited Tom's mother Grace for the weekend, so should be a fun weekend."

"Excellent, cannot wait to meet Tom's mother Grace," replied Carole, smiling. Hugo nodded in agreement.

"Right, down to business," said Grenville.

"Before we start," said Carole, "follow me." Grenville looked at Hugo, who shrugged, but both followed Carole who led them both to conference room three. Once in conference room three, Carole went to a newly installed wall panel and pressed a green button. A whirring noise was followed by part of the ceiling opening and a glass cube ascended, which eventually joined another cube emerging from the floor. Once both parts met, they merged into one solid glass cube.

Carole smiled at Grenville and Hugo, who both looked shocked. Smiling, Carole waved for them both to follow her. The glass cube had fitted neatly over the small conference table and chairs.

Once Carole, Grenville and Hugo had stepped into the cube, Carole pressed a button, and the door was merged into the glass cube, with a hydraulic hiss.

"Impressive," said Grenville.

"An evil requirement, currently." Carole went on, "State of the art soundproof room both ways, with air temperature monitors and enough oxygen for ten hours of use, totally secure."

"Are you not worrying about being trapped in here if you forget the time?" asked Hugo, looking worried.

Carole laughed. "Not at all, the room also monitors everyone in the room's vital body functions, and if any one present shows signs of stress the room will automatically unseal.

"Look," said Carole, and she showed Hugo a head up display on the wall of the cube, monitoring all three of them, their vital stats, plus the room temperature and the amount of air remaining, and a countdown clock to unseal.

Once again, Grenville said, "Very impressive, Carole, well done."

Grenville, Hugo and Carole sat at the conference table. "Now we can discuss anything we like and no one can eavesdrop on our conversations."

"I like it," said Grenville.

"Let's keep this to the few," said Hugo.

"Agreed," said Grenville.

"I can now confirm our IT operation is up and running," said Carole. "We can at present monitor all networks worldwide overtly or covertly, depending on what information we need."

"And are your staff reliable?" asked Grenville.

Carole smiled. "Oh yes, I have recruited some pretty savvy people, who love to poke about other networks. I trust them completely, and can honestly say, they are looking forward to getting their teeth into our system and seeing what we can do also running an import/export business with no questions asked, sometimes below the radar, which they think is cool."

"Well done Carole, I am impressed," said a smiling Grenville. Turning to Hugo, Grenville said, "So Hugo, how is business?"

"Grenville, I was surprised at how much business we are generating, from small contracts to large ones. At this rate, it is going to be cheaper to purchase our own air cargo company."

"Well, if that is your recommendation, my dear chap, then put a presentation together for the next board meeting."

Hugo nodded and said, "Excellent."

"I want you to purchase some real estate, Hugo," said Grenville.

"What you after, Grenville?"

"I want you to purchase three apartments for S&T Imports use," said Grenville.

"And of course, they need to be off the books," replied Hugo, smiling.

"I do believe you are catching on, old bean," replied Grenville, which made them all laugh. "Anything else?" asked Grenville. Both Carole and Hugo shook their heads in unison. "Good, see you at the weekend," said Grenville, standing up. "Now, how in the hell do I get out of this bubble?" which made Carole but not Hugo laugh.

Carole went and pressed a red button on the panel and smiled at Hugo and Grenville. The glass door opened then, and after a hydraulic hiss the glass ceiling and glass floor returned to their hidden positions, and conference room three retuned to its normal state. Opening the conference room door, Grenville said, "Most impressive, Carole," and he went back towards his office, laughing.

ℬ·ℭ

The weekend was one of the best in years that James and Sofia could remember having. They were sitting alone in the reading room. "Grace is a live wire," said James, laughing.

"She definitely is that," replied Sofia, laughing as well.

"She certainly had a packed life," James said.

"I admire her, she certainly has many amusing stories about being a nurse, plus she still possesses a positive attitude," said Sofia.

"Our Grenville and Sara are taken by her," said James, smiling.

"I think Grace is one of those people who possess that rare ability to put people at ease," replied Sofia.

Just then Grace entered the room. "Sorry, am I disturbing you?" said Grace.

206

"Not at all, please come sit down," said James, standing up.

"Here, come sit next to me, Grace," said a smiling Sofia.

"Thank you, most kind. The youngsters have gone for walk with the dogs around the estate," said Grace, smiling and sitting down, "and my long walk days are over. You have a lovely house, James," said Grace.

"Thank you, Grace, it's been in the family for generations."

"I had a personal tour by Preston, your butler, most impressive," said Grace.

Sofia leant in and whispered, "To tell you the truth, there are some parts I rarely visit," which made Grace laugh.

"I can imagine, my dear," replied Grace.

"You enjoying your stay?" asked James.

"It's lovely, not used to being so pampered and treated so well," said Grace, smiling.

"Have you lived long where you are now?" asked Sofia.

"Since I was married," replied Grace.

"A long time then," said James, laughing.

"Yes, although the German Air Force tried to bomb me out during an air raid," said Grace in a soft voice. Sofia saw the tears well up in Grace's eyes.

Placing her hand on Grace's, Sofia said, "Please, if it's too painful."

Grace tapped Sofia's hand and, smiling, said, "No Sofia, it's OK, I think sometimes it is good to remember what makes you stronger." Both James and Sofia nodded in agreement. Grace went on to explain the air raid, losing her mother-in-law and the baby in one horrific night, then she went on to tell them of Tom's death. After she had finished there was total silence; the only noise was the ticking of the large grandfather clock in the corner.

Sofia leaned over and hugged Grace and softly said, "I don't know how you endure after so much pain."

Grace replied, "It was war time, what else were we supposed to do? Time is a great healer."

"You are a remarkable lady, Grace," said James.

"Thank you, James, so nice of you to say," replied Grace, smiling, "but you two have had your own tragedy."

"Yes, our son Stephan," said Sofia.

"But you raised a lovely compassionate young man in Grenville," said Grace.

"He is special," said Sofia.

"And changed since he met your Tom," added James.

"Tom has that effect," said Grace.

"Well, we are grateful that he did," said Sofia, smiling.

"It is strange how opposites can attract and become intertwined," said Grace.

"Absolutely," said James, smiling.

"We are both proud of our sons," said Sofia.

Grace took her hand and said, "Strange how life can take us down new paths."

∞ · ∞

A few days later Dexter-Smith was still in a foul mood after the board meeting; annoyed with himself, more for letting the Hampton boy outmanoeuvre him in the board meeting. It had taken all his composure not to let his guard slip, but he was surprised Young Hampton had agreed to allow him to continue until the next board meeting. He smiled; he would not have been so magnanimous if he was in his position. Picking up his phone, he said, "Have my car brought round to the front," before replacing the receiver. Putting on his overcoat and picking up his brief case Dexter thought he need a distraction to take his mind off the current problem before returning home. He would visit his private club for a little pleasure; Mrs Han never failed to make sure his every pleasure was fulfilled. Last time she told him she had some new girls coming who might enjoy the same perverse pleasures as he did. This made him smile and forget all about young Hampton. Passing his secretary, he did not stop but said, "I won't be back today."

As he left, his secretary said once the door was closed, "Good riddance, you, ignorant wanker."

Dexter's car was waiting and the chauffeur had the door open. Not even bothering to look or speak to his driver, he climbed into the back seat of his Rolls Royce. As the driver got in and started the car, Dexter said, "My club," before settling back and closing his eyes.

He quickly opened his eyes when he realised the car had turned left instead of right. Pressing the intercom button, he said, "You bloody idiot, you've gone the wrong way, I said my club," but the car just speeded up. "You listening to me?" said Dexter. Thinking the intercom could be on the blink, he leaned across and said, "Norton, you listening to me?"

The car suddenly stopped and Dexter was thrown back on his seat. Dexter was furious and was just about to give Norton the bollocking of his life when both back doors opened and two men climbed in and sat opposite him. Dexter looked shocked. Both men closed the doors and the car moved off again. The whole incident had taken less than thirty seconds and to any passing stranger they would not have noticed anything out of the ordinary.

Looking scared, Dexter said, "Who the hell are you and what do you want, do you know who I am?"

The man sitting opposite said, "Of course we know who you are, Mr Dexter Simon-Smyth, that's why we are here."

"What do you want?" said Dexter, trying to make his voice sound normal.

"A mutual friend of the Earl of Eastleigh has sent us." This made Dexter nearly hyperventilate and it took all his composure to try and remain calm. "Just sit back and relax, we are going for a short ride," the man said. Dexter just stared at the two men with total disbelief; finally, the car pulled into an old abandoned warehouse and stopped.

"Please, I have money, I can pay," pleaded Dexter.

"This is not about money, Mr Simon-Smyth," replied the man sitting opposite.

"I don't follow," said Dexter.

"This is about family and honour, something you are seriously lacking in your life."

"I still don't understand," said Dexter.

"Nor will you ever, Mr Dexter Simon-Smyth." This was the last thing that Dexter heard before the side of his head exploded across the back seat of the Rolls Royce. The shot had come from the driver, who had shot between the two men with a silenced pistol. Both men left the car, and walked toward a waiting car. The driver picked up the spent cartridge and casually tossed it in the back at Dexter Simon-Smyth's feet. He then got out, removed the silencer from the pistol and placed the gun in the hand of the slumped body of Dexter Simon-Smyth. Staring briefly into the back of the car, he made sure all the doors were closed and nothing was left or looked out of place. He then smiled, closed the door and moved towards the waiting car as well.

₭ · ₮

Detective Chief Superintendent Albert Cross pulled up just short of the yellow tape, turned off his engine and sat for a few minutes. He smiled. His old stomping ground; he had been born and raised not a stone's throw from where he sat now. Albert was an old-fashioned copper, joined as a constable, when the only entrance criteria where you had to be big and have brawn. Not like nowadays, where to get on in the police you need a degree. It still amazed him how a degree in geography could make you a better candidate for promotion than someone with life skills. Even his new boss was twenty-three, came out of university and was fast tracked to his present position. It still made Albert smile knowing that he still could run rings around him. Sure, he had the procedures and theory all down to pat, but actual police work he was clueless. But after over thirty years as a copper, he did not dwell on things; he was known as a hard-old-fashioned copper but fair and decent.

Looking up, he saw his inspector striding towards the car. Even he was a university graduate and no doubt in a few years Albert would be reporting to him, but for now Albert was top dog. Exiting his car, Albert said, "What we got, James?"

"Looks like a posh suicide, boss."

"OK, show me," replied Albert, as they moved toward the car. James kept up a running commentary on the situation as it stood.

"Car was found this morning by two kids playing in the area, once they saw the body they reported it, patrol car was here within fifteen minutes and had the area cordoned off."

"Nice car," said Albert.

"Belongs to Easington Investment Bank, we found the deceased's wallet on him and we can confirm the body is a Mr Dexter Simon-Smyth, Chairman of the company."

"Strange place to come," said Albert.

"Bit off the beaten track," replied James, stepping under the yellow tape.

Albert said, "Morning Doc, what we got?" Dr Sam Wright, the police forensic officer, stood up as Albert and James approached.

"Morning Albert," she said, smiling. "Body been dead for at least fourteen hours. Single gunshot wound to the side of the head, dead on impact I would say," said Sam, smiling. "Will let you have the full autopsy later today, once I get him back to the lab."

"Thank you, Doc," said Albert.

"Can we remove the body now?" asked Sam.

"Of course, Doc, if your people have finished." Albert moved around the car and stood at the front. "Did anyone report him missing?" asked Albert.

"Not that I am aware," replied James.

"Well, find out. He was a chairman of an investment bank, these people are not normal every day working class," said Albert.

"Will do, boss," replied James, writing in his notebook.

Albert went on, "Find out why he drove his own car

yesterday, these people do not do things for themselves. Get the team to find out where he lived and speak to his secretary and his work colleagues, and especially his driver. Let's build up a picture of Mr Dexter Simon-Smyth."

"What you thinking, boss?" asked James.

"It's all too neat, and tidy for me," replied Albert. Albert had a nose for crime, and this scene stank of bullshit. It had just started to lightly run.

"Not a lot more we can do here, let pick this up in the morning."

"Fancy a pint, James?"

"Absolutely, boss," James replied as they both walked back toward Albert's car.

Next morning Detective Chief Superintendent Inspector Albert Cross sat at his desk reading the autopsy report from Dr Sam Wright, the police forensic officer. Not suicide. Simon-Smyth had been murdered; the single shot had come from someone sitting in the driver's seat, entering the left side of the temple, which means he had his head turned and was talking to someone sitting next to him just before the shot was fired. That's why, due to the position of the wound and the fact his hand was found on the pistol, it looked originally like a suicide. Plus, no internal or external forensic evidence found, which to Albert's thinking was looking like a professional hit. The bullet was from a Russian made weapon: a Makarov, which was first designed in the 1950s by Russian Nikolai Makarov. The Makarov was a semi-automatic pistol that was used by the Russian military in 1951. Due to its simplicity, affordability, ease of use and stopping power, it remained a standard military weapon till 1991. If it was a professional hit, this left Albert with an uneasy feeling. The pistol was rare; not the normal weapon the average lowlife of the underworld can get hold of. Albert leant back in his chair and thought, who could Simon-Smyth have pissed off severely enough to have a professional hit put out on him? This was not good. Albert did not want professional hit men operating on his patch. That could only lead to trouble.

Just then his inspector James Cabal knocked on his door. Albert motioned for him to enter. Taking a seat opposite, James said, "Have you read the autopsy report on Simon-Smyth?"

Albert held up the buff coloured folder in acknowledgement.

"What you think?" asked James.

"Not sure yet," Albert said.

"Must have pissed someone off big time, for them to hire a professional," said James.

"My thoughts exactly," replied Albert. "Where are we with the background check?"

Looking at his notes, James gave a brief outline of Dexter Simon-Smyth's life up until his murder. "Sound a right charmer," said Albert, smiling, after James had finished.

"Cannot find anyone who had a good word for him," said James.

"What about his driver?" asked Albert.

"Douglas Norton, been an agency driver for just over three years, did not hold his employer in high esteem," said James. "While he was having his lunch, he was approached by a man who gave him an envelope stuffed with money, asking him to leave the keys in the ignition and take the rest of the day off."

"Description?" asked Albert.

"Smartly dressed man with an East European accent, was all he could remember."

"How much in the envelope?" asked Albert.

"Two thousand pounds," replied James.

"Tidy sum," said Albert.

"I agree, and just enough to make him walk away, especially with no loyalty," said James.

"Well, you cannot fry bacon twice," said Albert, smiling.

James looked at Albert and tried not to smile. Sometimes Albert's sayings baffled him. Not having a clue what that one meant, he went on. "Flat never turned up anything, and we are still interviewing the staff, but nothing has yielded anything substantial yet," said James.

"OK, keep the troops on it, and let me know if anything else comes to light," said Albert.

James nodded stood and left the room. Albert watched James depart and thought to himself, "This is turning into a right royal mystery."

ಬ·ಡಿ

Life for Gerard Farthing was looking up again. After the death of his daughter's fiancé, Stephan the late Earl of Eastleigh, he was sure his boat to further success had sailed, then a strange turn of events had happened. He and his wife were asked back to Hampton Hall for another weekend where he learned his daughter had somehow latched on to his brother, the new Earl of Eastleigh, Grenville Hampton. How this happened he was unsure, but it made the future more promising, and again having a future Duke as a son-in-law made sure closed doors would open once again.

He did not like Grenville. On their first meeting, he thought him guarded and something about him made him seemed unreadable. Gerard always had a knack of reading people, but young Hampton was not all he seemed and to Gerard he seemed dangerous. He was pleasant enough but the conversation about his brother and the family estate left him in no doubt that if Hampton found out his involvement, his daughter or not, he would try and destroy him. That was why he decided to ignore Dexter Simon-Smyth's phone calls and emails. Like his hero, the Earl of Warwick, the kingmaker in the War of the Roses, he would change sides to feather his own nest.

Smiling, he did miss Stephan. He was a pompous upper class twat, but he opened doors. He had first met him in a club the Eastern Delights in Soho, which catered for men with certain sexual gratification. Stephan and his friend Dexter had the same tastes as he did, and like them had to go to specialist places to find them. He learned early on in his marriage his wife did not enjoy his passions and that side of the marriage was dead, especially after his daughter was born; but to Gerard, like his hero, the kingmaker Earl of Warwick, he would use his daughter to further his empire.

After getting to know Stephan he mentioned his daughter, a pretty, submissive, well-educated girl, who would make a fine trophy wife for a future Duke, and to Gerard's surprise his family were invited for a weekend at Hampton Hall, the ancestral home of the Duke of Hampshire. This delighted Gerard no end and as he explained to his wife and daughter, the weekend was special and could open opportunities for them all. Gerard could not remember the Duke's second son during the weekend visit; sure, he was there, but in the background, so Gerard never paid any attention to him. What delighted him the most was Stephan had taken a shine to his daughter and had eventually proposed to his daughter Sara, and after some strong arm twisting and emotional blackmail on his part she accepted. This made him ecstatic with future possibilities. His wife on the other hand was not so taken by his plans and it had caused a god-almighty row between them, which seemed to widen the gap in their relationship.

Striding into the bar of the golf course, after a pleasing round with the Chief Constable, the mayor and a leading businessman, he was feeling good; doors closed to him were now opening after the news had filtered through about his daughter's engagement to the Earl of Eastleigh and the future Duke of Hampshire. Moving to the bar, he ordered a double Grouse while waiting for his fellow players and their lunch engagement.

Studying the young man behind the bar, Gerard said, "You are new."

Smiling, the young man said, "Yes sir, started yesterday, the name is Jason."

"Well, Jason, a good tip for you, keep me and my friends happy and you will prosper in your job."

"Thank you, sir, will make a note of that," replied Jason, smiling.

As Jason moved away to serve another guest, Gerard thought to himself, "Bloody East Europeans, everywhere now."

Not giving it another thought, a hand slapped him on the back and the Chief Constable said, "My round I think Gerard, well played."

Jason noticed Gerard was the only one drinking double Grouse; this made his task so much easier and he would be out of this assignment sooner that he expected. Being a servant for the pampered middle classes was something that made his skin crawl. Taking his phone from his pocket he sent a quick text, just before a waitress came to the bar to order another round of drinks for table six. Smiling, Jason said, "No worries, will get onto it straight away." The waitress turned away to study the room for any other requests.

Quickly making a double gin and tonic and two halves of Diet Coke, the last drink was a double Grouse. Just before he placed the drink on the tray, this time he removed a small glass vial with clear liquid in. Snapping the top, Jason tipped the clear liquid into the whisky and mixed it in. The waitress smiled as she picked up the tray and returned it to table six. After distributing the drinks, she returned with her tray to her waiting station.

Gerard picked up his glass and acknowledged the toast made by the Mayor. "Gerard the next club president." The other two acknowledged the toast with a "hear hear". Feeling good, Gerard took a large sip of his drink.

Gerard was feeling for some strange reason unwell. The room started to spin and he could feel himself get hotter and start to sweat and he felt a sharp pain in his chest. The Mayor was talking to him, and it was like he was trying to hear underwater. Everything was going in slow motion; he did not feel the hand of the Chief Constable asking if he felt OK. Gerard felt his life ebbing away. Everything was becoming blurred and sounds were distant; he clutched his chest and eventually his head hit the table.

The Chief Constable was the first to react. "Someone ring an ambulance; the man is having a heart attack." The Mayor rang the number and everyone rushed to help. They laid Gerard down on the floor, loosened his tie and collar. Gerard was deathly white and was panting hard.

The ambulance arrived within five minutes. The paramedics worked on Gerard for twenty minutes before one of them stood and said, "Sorry, he has gone." Jason picked up a crate of empty bottles and went out the back door of the bar. Placing the crate down next to the door, he moved toward the waiting car with the back door open.

On closing the door, and just as the car was pulling away, the man next to him in the back said, "Everything OK, Janus?"

"Went like clockwork, Ivan," the man smiled as they pulled out of the golf club car park back towards London.

As Grenville entered Hampton Hall, Preston was waiting for him. "Hello Preston, what's the matter?" Grenville could tell by Preston's face that something was amiss.

"It's Miss Sara, my Lord, she has received some very bad news," said Preston.

"Where is she, Preston?" asked Grenville.

"She is in the reading room with your mother, my Lord," replied Preston. Without asking anything more, Grenville quickly rushed to the reading room. On entering, Grenville saw his mother holding Sara, who was quietly sobbing on her shoulder.

As Grenville moved across the room, Sofia said, "Here is Grenville now, Sara." Sara looked up and saw Grenville and rushed into his arms and started to cry again.

Grenville held Sara for several minutes to let the grief out, before holding her at arm's length and asking, "What is the matter, my love?"

Sobbing, Sara said, "It's daddy, he is dead."

"Oh, my poor love," said Grenville, "how, when?"

"He had a heart attack, at the golf club while having lunch today," replied Sara through sobs.

Leading Sara back to sit on the settee and still holding her hand, Grenville said, "How is your mother holding up?"

"It was she who rang me, the police informed her earlier. In fact, it was the Chief Constable who was having lunch with daddy, so he broke the news to mother," replied Sara, still sobbing.

"Well, you must go to your mother," said Sofia.

"you must my love," said Grenville, moving to the wall and pulling the cord.

After a few minutes, Preston entered the room and said, "Yes, your Grace."

"Preston, please ask Newton to bring the car around. He is taking Miss Sara to her mother's," said Sofia.

"At once, your Grace," replied Preston with a slight bow before he left, closing the door behind him.

Grenville asked, "Do you want me to come with you, my love?"

Sara considered Grenville's offer smiled weakly and said, "No, I think I better do this alone with mummy."

"As you wish, make sure you ring me if you want anything any time, night or day," said Grenville.

"I promise, my darling," Sara replied as she leaned in and kissed him full on the mouth. "I better go and fresh up and get ready to go," said Sara as she stood and left the room. Sofia had been watching her son through the exchange between him and Sara, and now she stared intently at Grenville.

"Why you looking like that at me, mother?" asked a fidgeting Grenville.

Softly, Sofia said, "Grenville, you did not look shocked when Sara told you about her father."

"I did," replied Grenville, too quickly.

Smiling, Sofia cupped his face and said, "Grenville, even as a small boy I knew when you were not telling me the whole truth and up to no good, now go and see to Sara."

Grenville smiled at his mother and said, "I love you, mother."

Sofia replied, "You are and always will be my son and I will always protect you, now go."

Standing, Grenville leaned over and kissed his mother before leaving the room. Sitting alone, Sofia smiled and thought to herself, "Looks like Farthing tried to underestimate my boy."; Still smiling, Sofia picked up her magazine and started to read.

ༀ·ༀ

Grenville had his eyes closed but was listening to Hugo and Jonathan having a heated debate about the current state of travel, which made Grenville smile. Hugo was an ardent traveller and Jonathan was not. There were on a boys' night out in readiness for Grenville's forthcoming wedding at the weekend, which Grenville was still surprised was going ahead after the death of Sara's father, but it was on the insistence of her mother that the wedding should not be stopped, which was a surprise to Sara as much as it was to Grenville. Where had, the time gone? It seemed like only yesterday he had proposed to Sara and they had set the wedding for July. That was over seven months ago, since then, Grace had been installed into her new accommodation, and Grenville and Sara visited her at least once every two weeks, time permitting. Grenville also knew his mother visited Grace as well, as they had become firm friends. The company had grown from strength to strength. Grenville had been in contact with Tom and kept him up to date with developments, which by Tom's emails back were full of optimism for the future. Not a day went past without Grenville reassuring himself he was on the right path and his quest was just; not that he needed it.

With the death of Dexter Simon-Smyth, Easington Investment Bank had no longer become a problem, and it was now run by the competent Forbes who had been Dexter Simon-Smyth's unappreciated second in command and as the new chairman had steered it back to its correct path. The death of Dexter Simon-Smyth still left Grenville feeling guilty, but Grenville could not complain. The company had had some good acquisitions from the venture.

"What do you think, Grenville?" asked Hugo.

"Sorry old man, was miles away," replied Grenville, smiling.

"I asked about cruises," said Hugo.

"All in favour old man, in fact that's what Sara and I are doing for the honeymoon, flying down to the Bahamas, then a cruise around the islands," said Grenville. Looking at Jonathan whose face was a picture, he held up his hands. "I know, Jonathan, not your cup of tea," which made Hugo and Grenville laugh.

"Well, I cannot see why people cannot holiday in the British Isles, it is a wonderful place," said an indignant Jonathan, which made Hugo and Grenville laugh even more.

"Jonathan, you are priceless," said Grenville.

"Clueless, more like," replied Hugo.

"It's not my fault if people cannot not see the beauty of their own country," said Jonathan.

"Spoken like a true Englishman," said Hugo.

"Or someone who is afraid to travel," said a laughing Grenville.

"Not at all," replied an indignant Jonathan. "If I want to travel I will, just don't see the point in it," Jonathan went on.

"See, Grenville," said Hugo, "rather that the sunny Bahamas you could go to Blackpool for your honeymoon."

"Now you are just being crass, and twisting what I am saying," said Jonathan. Grenville smiled at his two friends as they bantered back and forth. Since school, they had always been like this and Grenville learned early on not to take sides or comment too much. Grenville sat watching them argue with a smile on his face; he was a lucky man to have two loyal friends as good as Hugo and Jonathan.

❧ · ❧

Grenville woke with an air of expectancy. Today he was getting married. "Wow," he said out loud. Who could have predicted what he had achieved since leaving Belize? He had been in contact with Tom on a regular basis, he had turned S&T Imports into a global company, he had settled Tom's mother Grace, saved his family name and estate, and most of all fell in love and was to marry the woman of his dreams. The last was the amazing feat; never had he thought himself as the marrying kind. Not even before he went to Belize did he imagine himself getting married. But once he saw Sara for the second time, he knew he had found his soul mate.

Just as Grenville was thinking, there was a soft knock on his door. Grenville did not hear the knock but noticed the door slowly open, and Hugo's head appear around the door, smiling. "Oh good, you are awake, old man," said Hugo, stepping into the room followed by Jonathan, holding a tray of steaming coffee.

"Come in, chaps," said a smiling Grenville. Standing aside to let Jonathan enter with the tray, Hugo closed the door softly behind him.

Placing the tray down, Jonathan said, "How you feel, old man?"

"Jonathan, feeling rather good."

"Oh dear, that bad," said Hugo.

"Don't know what you mean," replied a puzzled Grenville.

"Well, if you are not nervous, then it has not hit you yet," said a laughing Hugo.

"No, not nervous," said Grenville.

"Then, my dear chap, the enormity of the forthcoming event has not hit you yet," said Jonathan.

"Nope, still not feeling it," replied a laughing Grenville, taking one of the cups of steaming coffee and taking a sip.

"Well, in six hours you will be standing in front of thousands of people waiting for Sara to walk down the aisle," said a sombre Hugo.

"I know, well excited," replied a smiling Grenville.

"The man is not normal," replied Jonathan, shaking his head.

"Must be love," said a laughing Hugo.

"Thought you two were supposed to be cheering me up as my best men," said a laughing Grenville.

"As your oldest friends, we are here to point out your folly and guide you," said Hugo.

"But…" said Jonathan.

"If you are determined to carry on this foolish path…" said Hugo.

"Then we can only make sure you arrive on time and stand by your side for this madness," said Jonathan, which made them all laugh.

The little church of Hampton was full. Organ music was softly playing in the background and a low audible murmur could be heard around the seated guests. Grenville turned and smiled at his parents and Grace sitting in the front row. They all smiled back.

"Still not nervous?" whispered Jonathan in Grenville's ear.

"Not," replied Grenville, turning and smiling at Jonathan.

"Still not too late to do a runner," said Hugo quietly, smiling. Just as Grenville was about to reply, the Wedding March started and the doors at the bottom of the church opened and in stepped Sara's three bridesmaids: Carole as the maid of honour, and Sara's two small cousins. All three walked slowly to the altar. Grenville looked over them to see Sara and her mother coming towards them. Sara was dressed in a beautiful flowing white gown with her veil covering her face.

At the altar, the three bridesmaids stood to one side. Grenville smiled at Carole, who winked at him, just before Sara arrived with her mother. Sara had insisted her mother walked her down the aisle. Grenville, Hugo and Jonathan all took in a breath. Grenville had a tear in his eye as he looked at Sara; he knew he would always remember this moment, as Sara looked so beautiful. Grenville smiled to himself. He knew all brides were meant to look beautiful on their wedding day but to him Sara looked sensational.

The wedding went without a hitch and to Grenville it was over too fast for him; he wished it could have lasted longer. Back at the reception, the speeches were received with loud clapping and cheering, especially Jonathan's best man speech, which Hugo had agreed he should do as he was after all the better advocate for speaking. Hugo did have a slight hand in the writing of Jonathan's speech; it was full of humour and love for Grenville and Sara.

Once Jonathan finished, Grenville stood to a round of applause. "Thank you everyone for attending our wedding, and on behalf of my wife and myself, we thank you." Grenville had tears in his eyes and was tongue tied.

Sara stood and took Grenville's hand, smiled, and said, "We both thank you all," which brought on the loudest round of applause of the afternoon.

Later that evening the Duke and Duchess were sitting together having a quiet time, as the disco in the ball room was in full swing, and the music "far too loud" as the Duke put it.

"It's lovely to have the house full of laughter again," said Sofia.

"Totally agree, my love," replied James. "Been too long without it," he continued.

"It has been a wonderful day," said Sofia.

"One for the record books," replied James, smiling.

"Remember our wedding day, James?" asked Sofia, smiling.

"Like it was yesterday, my darling," replied James, also smiling.

"If I remember rightly, your father said the exact same about our music," said Sofia, laughing.

James cocked his head and heard the music change to a slow number. James stood and taking Sofia's hand said, "May I have this dance, my lady?"

"How gallant," said Sofia. Standing and taking James' arm, they walked towards the soft music and flashing lights.

Grenville found Jonathan and Hugo deep in a drunken discussion. Smiling, Grenville sat down just as Jonathan poured him a glass of champagne. Holding up the glass, Grenville said, "Gentlemen, as always you have done me proud." Jonathan and Hugo held up their glasses and all three emptied them in one quick swig. As they banged them back on the table, all three started to laugh. "So which one of you reprobates is next?" said Grenville. Both Jonathan and Hugo violently shook their heads.

"Never," said Jonathan.

"Nor me," said a slurring Hugo.

"Carole looked lovely today," said Grenville quietly.

"She is an angel," said a nodding Hugo.

Grenville slapped Hugo on his back and said, "Don't worry old man, she will let you know when you are to ask her." Hugo placed his head in his hands, as Jonathan and Grenville started to laugh.

ℬ · ℭ

Grenville opened his eyes as the pilot came over the intercom to inform them they were ready to descend into Grand Bahamas International Airport, and could everyone fasten their seat belts and place their tray in the upright position. Grenville felt Sara squeeze his hand. Turning, and opening his eyes he met a smiling Sara.

"Hi, sleepy head," said Sara.

"That went fast," said Grenville, still feeling sleepy.

Sara laughed. "You've been asleep for the last eight hours."

"Well, I have had a couple of busy days," said Grenville, smiling.

"You sure have," said Sara, smiling back.

Sara and Grenville sat on the hotel veranda watching the sun dip over the horizon. "This is the life," said Grenville.

"It's lovely," replied Sara.

Just then they heard a voice from behind say, "Move and you will die, I want your wallet." Sara reached for Grenville's hand and went rigid. Sara turned to see Grenville who was smiling. Sara was shocked that Grenville was remaining so calm over the threat from behind them.

Then to Sara's surprise, Grenville started to laugh and said, "Hope you've got a good escape plan." Sara heard a laugh from behind her. Grenville turned and his eyes met a smiling Tom. Standing, Tom and Grenville embraced and were still laughing when Sara turned around to face them both. "What in the hell are you doing here?" asked Grenville.

"Missed the wedding, heard you were here on honeymoon so thought I would come and congratulate you in person," Tom replied.

"Tom, this is Sara, my wife," said Grenville, pointing to Sara.

"Lovely to finally meet you, Sara," said Tom, smiling.

"Sorry, still in a bit of a shock," replied Sara.

"Sorry about that, but wanted to make sure old Duke here was still on the ball."

"That I am," replied a laughing Grenville.

Sara held out her hand to Tom. Tom smiled and said, "Come here and give us a hug." Afterwards, holding Sara at arm's length, Tom said, "You are a very beautiful lady, too good for this rogue."

"Thank you, Tom," replied Sara, smiling.

"Drinks, I think," said Grenville. Once the drinks had arrived, Grenville said, "What a lovely surprise this is, Tom."

"Well, I could not let my best friend get married and not congratulate him in person, could I? Emails are so impersonal," said Tom.

"Well I must say, this has made my week," replied a smiling Grenville. Sara watched Tom and Grenville interact and realised that they were very close, more like brothers than friends, Sara sat smiling at them both as they chatted and laughed together. "Sorry to ask," said Grenville, "but how long you here for?"

"Only the night," replied Tom, "got a job to do in Belize." Tom did not elaborate nor did Grenville ask.

Grenville turned to Sara and said, "I do apologise, my love, if we talk shop."

"Don't be silly, I understand," said a smiling Sara, "in fact I am going to leave you boys to it and go and have a long relaxing hot bath."

"Please don't go on my account," said Tom, smiling.

"It's OK Tom, I have the next two weeks with Grenville, you only have tonight and have a lot of catching up to do so your time is short."

Tom hugged Sara and said, "Thank you, Sara."

Sara gave Grenville a hug and whispered, "Take all the time you need, my love."

"Love you," replied Grenville.

Tom and Grenville watched Sara depart, and after she had left Tom said, "She is lovely and understanding, Duke, where did you find her?"

"Remember my brother Stephan's fiancée," replied Grenville.

"No way, really," said Tom laughing.

"Yes, strange how life takes you down a certain path," said Grenville.

"I will drink to that," said Tom, raising his glass and toasting a smiling Grenville.

"So down to business," said Grenville seriously. "S&T Imports are now fully operational," said Grenville, smiling at Tom.

"Never doubted you for one minute, Duke," Tom replied, holding up his glass and taking a swig of his drink.

Grenville continued, "I have a really good team about me and for obvious reasons, only Sara knows the real reason for S& T Imports."

"Really," said Tom.

"Yes of course, strictly family," said a smiling Grenville.

"Drink to that," said Tom, smiling.

"Well, we have a pretty impressive set up, and to not rouse suspicion every contract big or small I have insisted on a full profile on the client, for our records of course," said Grenville, taking a sip of his drink.

"Of course," replied Tom, laughing.

"So, if I pass a name, everyone will think it's a new potential client," said Grenville.

"Most impressive, my old mate," said Tom smiling. "How is my mother?" Tom asked.

"Wonderful, she loves her new retirement home, and when we can Sara and I visit, plus my mother does as well; the Duchess and your mother have become quite good friends," said a smiling Grenville.

Tom threw back his head and laughed, "My mother and a Duchess good friends, who would have thought it? But seriously, Duke, thank you for looking out for her," said Tom quietly.

"My pleasure old man, she is family after all," smiled Grenville. Grenville stared at Tom and smiled. "So, you got a name for me?" asked Grenville.

Tom eventually took an old folded piece of paper from his pocket and passed it to Grenville. Grenville looked at Tom. "Yes, the same piece of paper I originally gave to Max still with his blood on, and the one the police found on his body," said Tom, reading Grenville's mind. "I did say years ago, I would only give you this when I thought you were ready," smiled Tom. Grenville read the name on the paper, then passed it back to Tom, who placed it over the flame of the candle on the table. The paper quickly caught fire and turned to ash, and Tom used his finger to crush the remains of the ash.

Smiling, Grenville said, "To the continuing quest."

Tom raised his glass and said, "To justice."

Grenville said, "Will have the information as soon as I can, old bean."

Raising his glass and saluting Grenville, a smiling Tom said, "I have every faith in you, Duke," which made them both start to laugh again. After a few hours of chatting Tom said, "Well, better make a move if I am going to catch my flight."

"So, quick," said a despondent Grenville.

Tom started to laugh. "You are on your honeymoon, enjoy yourself," said a laughing Tom.

"Come here and give us a hug, then," said Grenville, standing up with his arms open.

Tom stood and they embraced. "Take care Duke, and look after that beautiful wife of yours," Tom whispered into Grenville's ear.

"You too, you old Pirate," replied Grenville. Moving apart, Tom and Grenville had tears in their eyes.

"See you soon," Tom said as he turned and walked away.

Grenville watched Tom disappear and whispered, "I hope so my old mate, I sure hope so." Grenville finished off his drink then with a smile went to find Sara, to begin their honeymoon.

80·CB

As the plane finally touched down, Grenville turned to Sara and said, "Glad to be home?"

Smiling, Sara replied, "Actually I am," and smiling, Grenville said, "Yes, I know what you mean, no place like home." As they came down the steps, Newton was waiting with the car with the back door open. As Grenville approached, he noticed Newton looking glum with no smile. Grenville thought that Newton would have welcomed them with at least a smile.

As they approached, Newton saluted and said, "Welcome home my Lord, Lady Sara."

"Everything OK, Newton?" asked Sara. Grenville thought, even Sara had picked up on Newton's sour demeanour.

Newton shifted on his feet and said, "It's your father, my Lord, his Grace has been taken seriously ill."

Both Sara and Grenville looked shocked on hearing the news, and all Grenville could say was, "Better get back to the ranch then, Newton, and don't spare the horses."

Once they arrived back at Hampton Hall, Preston was on the steps to welcome them. Even Preston had a tight smile on his face when he welcomed them home.

"How is he?" asked Grenville.

"Not good my Lord, doctor is with him now."

"Thank you, Preston, can you deal with the luggage, we will go straight up."

"Of course, my Lord." Turning, both Sara and Grenville proceeded to his parents' room. As they came down the corridor they noticed the Duchess sitting outside the bedroom.

Rushing to her embrace, Grenville said, "How are you, mother?" to which she replied, "I am well, thank you my son, better now you are both home," hugging Sara as well.

"How is he, mother?" Grenville asked.

"The doctor is with him now, so we should know in a few minutes."

"How did it happen so quick?" asked Grenville.

"It was last week, we were walking the dogs around the estate. It was a lovely sunny day, when we got caught in a nasty heavy downpour. By the time, we got back to the house we were dripping wet."

"Oh dear," said Sara.

The Duchess went on, "Next morning, your father woke with a frightful cold that after a few days he could not shake, so I sent him to bed and called the doctor. He did some tests and he returned today to see your father."

Holding his mother close, Grenville said, "Don't worry mother, father is a fighter."

"I do hope you are right, my darling," she whispered back.

Just then the Doctor came out of the bedroom, and closed the door behind him. "Can we talk somewhere, your Grace," he said, looking at the Duchess,

"No, tell me here, my son and his wife need to hear as well," she said.

The doctor bowed and said, "As you wish, your Grace. I am afraid the Duke has caught a serious bout of pneumonia."

"The prognosis?" asked Grenville for them all.

"Not good, my Lord," replied the doctor.

"Out with it man," said Grenville raising his voice. Sara placed her hand on his arm and smiled. "I apologise, doctor, for my outburst," said Grenville.

"Please don't worry, my Lord, I understand it a stressful time for you all," smiled the doctor. "I am afraid it is not good, I give him twenty-four hours, two days at the best."

The Duchess slumped back down in the chair and placed her head in her hands, Sara bent down and held her. "What am I going to do without him?" she said.

"We will get through it as a family," was all Sara could say, looking at Grenville with tears in her eyes, not quite sure what to say to Sofia.

"Is there nothing that can be done?" asked Grenville.

"Sorry my Lord it is too far along, even the antibiotics I am giving him are not working now, so it's a matter of time. I have given him something for the pain, so he is resting now. He will have periods where he is lucid, others where he will sleep," said the doctor.

"Thank you, doctor, for all your efforts," said Grenville.

"I shall return tomorrow," said the doctor. "Your Grace, my Lord." Bowing, the doctor walked toward the staircase.

Just then they heard a muffled voice from behind the closed door. "Is that my son I can hear?"

opening the door fully, Grenville took a deep breath and entered the room. Looking up the Duke smiles and said "There you are my son, have a nice honeymoon?"

"Excellent, thank you father," replied Grenville. Going to the bed and shaking the outstretched hand, Grenville was shocked at how much weight and how pallor his father looked.

Smiling, Grenville said, "How do you feel, father?"

"Hanging in there, my boy," replied his father, smiling. "Sofia my love, and Sara, how lovely to see you Sara," said the Duke as they both approached the bed.

"Glad to be home," was all Sara could say with tears in her eyes.

"Now come on, no tears," said the Duke, smiling at them all. "These things happen, we cannot stop the march of time."

"That's what grandfather said to me in his letter," said Grenville.

"He was a wise old man," smiled the Duke.

"You want anything, my love?" asked Sofia.

"Not really, my darling, got all I need here with my family," smiled the Duke just as he closed his eyes and gently started to snore.

"You two go rest, after your trip," said Sofia, "I will sit with him for a bit."

"You sure, mother?" said Sara.

"Of course, my darling," said Sofia, patting Sara's hand. Sara took Grenville's hand and led him from the room, closing the door behind them; Grenville took Sara in his arms and cried. Over the next twenty-four hours they all took turns in sitting with the Duke. Sometimes he was awake and lucid, others he was asleep. The place was in a sombre mood; even the staff knew the gravity of the situation and noise was kept to a minimum.

It was during the last time Grenville sat with his father and he was awake, the Duke turned to Grenville with tears in his eyes and said, "Please take care of your mother for me, son."

Taking his father's hand, Grenville said, "Of course I will, father."

"I am proud of you, my boy, and the man you have become," said his father quietly.

"I have been proud to be your son, father," replied Grenville.

"Your grandfather was right about you all along," said his father, smiling. "He always said you would be the family saviour if in the future times got bad."

"Well, I am glad you were here to see me restore our family honour," replied Grenville.

"Talking about your grandfather," said the Duke.

"All in the past," replied Grenville, smiling.

Continuing, the Duke said, "I know it caused a rift between us that I would not let you come to his funeral."

"I understand now, father," said Grenville.

"Your grandfather spoke to me a few months before he died, and he asked me not to let you attend his funeral, as he did not want the last memory you had of him was lying in a wooden box," said the Duke, "so I agreed to his wishes, knowing that it would distance you from me, but I was prepared to have you think less of me rather than your grandfather," continued the Duke. "Please forgive me, my son," said the Duke.

"There is nothing to forgive, father."

The Duke closed his eyes and Grenville said quietly for the first time in his life, "I love you, father." Grenville felt his father squeeze his hand and smile. Grenville squeezed back and sat smiling with tears in his eyes.

The Duke was still alive the next morning when the doctor came. Sofia, Grenville and Sara were standing around the Duke's bed as the doctor made his last examination of the Duke. As he stood, he shook his head towards Grenville. Sofia took her husband's hand, leant in close and spoke to him in whispers. Grenville and Sara stood back a pace, as this was her final farewell to her husband and they wanted it for her to be a special goodbye. Eventually, Sofia stood up and said, "Grenville, he wants to talk to you."

Moving forward Grenville leaned over and said softly, "I am here, father."

From half-open eyes the Duke smiled, and tried to lift his hand, which Grenville took. "You are now the Duke of Hampshire, my son, keep the family true," the Duke said in a whisper.

"I promise father, I will," Grenville said softly. Just then the Duke smiled and breathed his last breath. The doctor leaned over them both and after testing the Duke for life, declared the eleventh Duke of Hampshire dead.

❧ · ❧

It rained on the day of the funeral. Everyone from the estate was in attendance, plus a host of family and friends. The Speaker of the House of Lords gave the elegy, which was full of humour and love for his father. They laid him in the family crypt, where generations of Hamptons had been laid before him. One of his friends from the Lords commented, "He is with good company," which made Grenville smile.

Grenville was quite shocked at how many people came to pay their respect to him. He never realised how popular his father was or how many friends he had. This above all made Grenville proud to be his son. Eventually, Grenville went to find Sara and his mother. He found them both sitting in the reading room. "Here you are," said Grenville smiling, kissing his mothers offered cheek. "How you doing, mother?"

"Darling, good thank you, of course Sara been a rock." She smiled at Sara.

"My pleasure, mother," said Sara, smiling.

"You are a good girl," said Sofia, tapping her face and smiling.

"A lot still here?" asked his mother.

"Not really, most have left."

"Good," said Sofia, "I came in here for a rest, only so much condolences you can take."

"I know what you mean, mother," said Grenville. "I spoke to Stevens and the reading of the will and he will be here on Tuesday, if that's convenient, mother?" asked Grenville.

"Of course, darling."

"Stevens did hint that it was straightforward, no surprises," said Grenville, smiling.

"Never doubted it for a minute," said Sofia, laughing.

Just then Preston came in and said, "Can I have a word, your Grace?"

After a minute, Sofia said, smiling, "Preston is addressing you my son, you are now the Duke of Hampshire." This realisation was the first-time Grenville had thought of himself as the Duke of Hampshire.

"Sorry Preston, what can I do for you?" replied Grenville.

"Lady Barnett from the Lords would like a word."

"Thank you, Preston, please inform her I will be along post haste."

"Very well, your Grace," replied Preston, bowing and leaving the room.

"Please excuse me," said Grenville, kissing Sara and his mother before he left.

"He will make a fine Duke," said Sofia.

"He was born to it," replied a smiling Sara.

"And of course, you are now a Duchess," said Sofia, smiling at Sara.

"I feel far too young to be a Duchess," she said, which made them both laugh.

"Don't worry my dear, you will be a natural."

"I will need your help," said Sara.

"Of course, my dear, always," said a smiling Sofia.

Grenville spotted the leader of the House of Lords, Lady Barnett, speaking to the Bishop of Hampshire. Smiling, Grenville went over and said, "Apologies if I'm butting in."

"Not at all, Grenville," replied the Bishop, "I will let you two to House business." The Bishop bowed and left.

"I am sorry for your loss, Grenville," said Lady Barnett, "your father was a voice of calm in the house."

"Thank you, most kind," replied Grenville.

"I know this is probably not the time, but I have been asked to seek you out," said Lady Barnett.

"Please, what is on your mind, Lady Barnett?" said a smiling Grenville.

"We hope that when you take your father's place in the house we can still rely on your support as we did his," she said.

"To tell you the truth Lady Barnett, I have not really had time to think about it," said Grenville.

Smiling and patting his hand, Lady Barnett said, "It's OK, take your time, and let me know what you have decided."

"Most kind," replied Grenville, bowing. "Now if you'll excuse me, I must find my mother."

"Of course, dear," smiled Lady Barnett.

Grenville found Sofia and Sara still in the reading room deep in conservation.

"What did Lady Barnett want?" asked Sofia.

"Wanting to know if I follow father's political allegiances."

"She was quick," said Sara.

"Politics does not respect death, my dear," said a smiling Sofia.

"What did you tell her?" asked Sara.

"Nothing really, told her I had not decided," replied Grenville.

"But you are going to take your seat in the Lords?" asked Sofia.

"To tell you the truth, mother, I have not decided," replied Grenville.

"But you must, my darling," said Sofia.

"Why must he?" asked Sara.

"It's a matter of perception," said Sofia.

"Don't understand," said Sara.

"For Grenville's business to thrive as he wants it to, he must play the role of Duke of Hampshire," replied Sofia.

"I see," said Grenville, smiling.

"So, he plays the part of an upper-class aristocrat," said Sara.

"Exactly," replied Sofia, smiling. "Perception, people see what they want to see and imagine."

"Clever mother, very clever," said Grenville, smiling.

"It won't hurt to be part of the establishment and work within and outside of it, your grandfather and father were experts at it," said Sofia.

Next morning Grenville rang Lady Barnett and told her although his business commitments stopped him attending the Lords on a regular basis, she could rely on his support on important matters and could count on his attending when she requires it. Lady Barnett smiled as she replaced the receiver.

⁃

Grenville was sitting up in bed waiting for Sara to come out of the bathroom after her shower. "So what you think?" Sara said, coming from the bathroom, rubbing her hair with a towel.

"Sorry my love, never heard you, what was the question?"

"Your mother," replied Sara.

"What about her?" said Grenville.

"Grenville, you can be so dim sometimes," said Sara, smiling.

"Sorry, not with you," replied Grenville.

Sara sat on the bed and said, "Now your mother has lost your father, she feels in the way and lost."

"Never realised she felt like that," said Grenville, looking glum.

"Well, you need to reassure her she still has a part to play," said Sara, patting Grenville on the hand as she stood to get dressed. "See you down for breakfast," said Sara. "I am famished, don't be too long darling," she said as she closed the door behind her.

Grenville stood in the shower and let the hot water wash over him, pondering on what Sara had said. He did not give it a second thought what his mother was feeling or thinking, but Sara was right, she was no longer technically the Duchess of Hampshire, but the mother of the Duke. Grenville made up his mind and would let his mother and Sara have his decision at breakfast.

Entering the breakfast room, Grenville went to his mother and kissed the offered cheek. Looking closely in the smiling eyes, Grenville thought how much his mother was still a beautiful woman. Smiling, Grenville said, "Morning mother."

"Morning, my son," Sofia replied.

Grenville went to Sara and kissed her on the top of her head as she was eating a piece of toast. "Morning, my darling." Sara nodded in response. The conservation was light over breakfast, and once they had finished Grenville said, "Shall we retire to the reading room, need to have a chat with you both."

After they were seated, Sofia said, "This sound serious," smiling at Sara.

"Rather," said Sara, smiling back. Standing with his hands behind his back Grenville smiled at both his mother and his wife, and thought how lucky he was to have the support of two strong minded women.

"Mother," said Grenville finally.

"Yes, Grenville," replied Sofia, smiling.

"As you know, both Sara and I will be extremely busy with the business which leaves us a slight problem, which I hope you can help us with," said Grenville.

"Of course, if I can," replied Sofia.

"We would like you to carry on the day to day running of the Hall and the estate for us," said Grenville.

"If you are sure," replied Sofia.

"It would help us," said Sara.

"Knowing the Hall and estate are managed well will be a worry off my mind," said Grenville, smiling at his mother.

"It will be a pleasure to help," replied Sofia.

Grenville went across and kissed his mother on the cheek, and said, "I would only trust you with the Hall and estate."

After Grenville, had left the room, Sofia said, "Thank you, Sara."

"For what?" said Sara, smiling.

"You know for what," replied Sofia, smiling.

Sara went over and hugged Sofia and whispered, "Us Duchesses have to stick together," which brought laughter from both.

∞·∞

The only sound was from the air ventilation system from the bubble, as Grenville called it, as the board of S&T Imports sat around the conference table.

Grenville finally said, "Welcome, I know you are all busy people so we will crack on." This brought a smile from around the table.

Jonathan stood without being asked. "Chairman, fellow board members," Jonathan started, "I have looked over the contracts for the proposed purchase of the air cargo company, and have made a few suggestions to the legal team, but I do not see any forthcoming problems with the purchase." This brought smiles from around the table.

"Thank you, Jonathan," said Grenville, smiling at Jonathan, who nodded in acknowledgement. "Anything else?" asked Grenville.

"No, your new legal department are very competent, and will do you proud," smiled Jonathan, sitting down.

Grenville looked at Hugo, who stood. Hugo gave the same start as Jonathan. "The business is continuing to grow, with established business and new business," said Hugo which brought a "well done" from around the table. Hugo continued, "At present, with assets considered we have a working capital of just short of six hundred and forty million." This brought a few gasps from around the table. "If we carry on the way we are going, we will reach the billion mark hopefully within ten years." Smiling, Hugo sat down. The room once again was in silence.

Grenville said, "When we started out I never imagined in my wildest dreams we were capable of achieving this, and I put this down to you all."

Holding out his arms to the table, Hugo spoke for them all when he said, "We thank you, Chairman, for having faith in us all." This brought a round of applause from the table.

Grenville looked at Carole and nodded. Carole stood and smiled. "Our computer systems are now the envy of a lot of companies, and if the truth be told, a few government agencies around the world. Our new research and development department are making strides to better our security in this turbulent world, but we are still confident that if we require information we can obtain it, plus we are at present well protected from cyber-attacks and snoopers." Carole sat down and everyone in the room understood what Carole had just said. Grenville sat nodding, with a smile on his face.

Grenville smiled at Sara, who stood. "Mr Chairman, fellow members, the day to day running of the company is in excellent health, we have I feel the best management team in place who are committed to S&T Imports," everyone around the table nodded, "but I am afraid to say I must hand over most of my day to day workload to my very capable assistant," said Sara, smiling.

Grenville stood. "What? No way."

"Sit down my love," said Sara, which Grenville did.

"Let me explain, my assistant will take over my day to day workload for now, but she will obviously only do the S&T Import workload; I will remain on the board."

"I am confused," said Hugo.

"Men are sometimes stupid," said a laughing Carole.

Sara turned to Grenville who still looked puzzled. "Yes, my darling, we are going to have a baby," said Sara with tears in her eyes.

Grenville jumped to his feet and went to Sara, took her in his arms and said, "I am so proud of you, my darling." Everyone else came together to congratulate Grenville and Sara. "I want you all to join me at Hampton Hall this weekend to celebrate," said Grenville, smiling.

"When did you find out?" asked Carole.

"This morning. Five weeks along," said Sara.

"Wondered why you were acting suspicious this morning," said Grenville.

"I wanted the doctor to confirm it first before I told anyone, sorry I kept it from you darling," said Sara.

"You are forgiven, my love," said Grenville, laughing.

"Anything else?" said Grenville, looking around the room. "Good, see you all at the weekend." Grenville stood. Everyone else stood as well, as the cube hissed and started to open. "Carole, can I have a word before you go?" asked Grenville.

"Of course, Chairman," Carole replied, sitting back down.

Once everyone else had left, Carole re-activated the bubble again. Once it had finished its cycle Grenville said, "Carole, I have a small task for you, I need you to put a profile together on someone for me, if you don't mind?"

"Of course, Chairman," replied Carole.

Sliding a piece of paper over the desk, Grenville said, "Can you find out everything you can on that name for me?"

Carole studied the name and said, "Of course, Chairman." Without touching the piece of paper, Carole smiled and said, "As soon as I have the information I will let you know, Chairman."

"And Carole, I would like you to handle this personally, and keep it between us two." Smiling, Carole nodded at Grenville and understood Grenville's meaning.

Once back in his office Grenville took the piece of paper and placed it in his desk top shredder and smiled. Grenville then took the laptop from his bottom drawer and sent an email to Tom:

Pirate

Information of Simon Muscrat being processed.

Duke

Once Grenville had sent the encrypted email he sat back and closed his eyes. He knew the email would make Tom happy; Tom's quest was moving forward.

A few days later the desk intercom went and Michelle said, "Carole would like to meet you in conference room three."

As he passed, Grenville told Michelle that if he was required to please come and get him. Michelle smiled and said, "Of course, Chairman."

Grenville was the first one in conference room three. Moving to the control panel, he started the cube's descent. Once it had finished, Grenville stepped inside and waited for Carole. After a few minutes, Carole entered conference room three and stepped into the cube and closed the door. After a silent hiss, the room light went green, letting them know they were now secure. Carole placed the buff colour folder in front of her and smiled at Grenville.

"Here is a complete background check on Simon Muscrat, including his financial affairs," said Carole. Grenville smiled and nodded. "Was not easy," said Carole, "had to route the information via a few dummy IP addresses so the CIA would not get suspicious with someone asking questions on one of their ex field agents. But we got there in the end," said Carole, smiling. Carole slid the folder over to Grenville, who opened it and started to read the single typed page. As he was studying the page, Carole said, "Of course, this is the only copy and all search data has been erased, so if anyone was checking we are covered. But a quick overview: Muscrat is now out of the CIA and running a successful boat hire business out of Miami."

"Thank you, Carole, so much, for your quick and professional work," said Grenville, smiling.

"My pleasure, chairman," said Carole, standing up. "If there is nothing else?" said Carole, unlocking the cube and stepping out.

Back in his office Grenville scanned the documents into a folder on the laptop; once complete, Grenville shredded the contents of the folder. Grenville sat back at the email he had sent and smiled.

Pirate

Information on Simon Muscrat attached, will await your next commission.

Duke

A week later Duke received an email back with two names on it.

Duke

Next commissions are Colonel Jack Packer and James Landcourt, prefer Packer first, as he was the one who met with Max.

Pirate

୫୭·୧୨

The weekend was what Sofia needed, she admitted to herself as she sat alone in the reading room. The last few years had gone so fast, with so many changes, even by her standards; first, her first son tried to ruin the family, and his death, the return of her second son, his return a changed, better man, restoring the family before her husband James died. This brought a smile to her face. She was pleased he lived to see his estate restored. She knew the toll was becoming a burden on him and making him ill, but Grenville's return had helped and he had started to become himself again. Sara's father's death, Grenville and Sara's wedding, which was as everyone said what the place needed, and now she was going to be a grandmother, which to her was the best news she had received this year. Smiling to herself, she heard the door open. She was surprised to see Hugo enter.

"Hello, not disturbing you, am I?" Hugo asked.

Smiling, Sofia said, "Of course not dear, were you looking for me?"

Walking over and sitting next to Sofia, Hugo said, "Yes I was actually. The others have taken the dogs for a walk around the grounds, not really into the countryside," said Hugo, smiling.

Sofia had liked Hugo since the first time she had met him when he was a boy, he had been with Jonathan inseparable with Grenville, and she knew he was a loyal and a trusting friend. Sofia had always treated Hugo and Jonathan like sons whenever they stayed, always making them feel part of the family. "So, what can I do for you, Hugo?" smiled Sofia.

Hugo looked a bit flustered and tried to speak.

Sofia smiled and laid her hand on his and said softly, "It's OK, Hugo, you can trust me."

"I know I can, that's why I waited until we were alone to speak to you," Hugo said, with a strained smile.

Patting his hand, Sofia said, "How can I help?"

"It's Carole," said Hugo.

"I see," said Sofia.

"Do you?" replied Hugo.

"Of course, I might be old but I have eyes," said Sofia, laughing. Hugo stood up and started to pace. "You want to ask her to marry you," said Sofia quietly.

Hugo sat back down, and said, "How did you know?"

"I see you together, and I think you are perfect for each other," replied Sofia, smiling.

"You think so?" said Hugo, standing up again and getting flustered.

"Hugo sit down, before you have a stroke," said Sofia, laughing again.

Hugo sat down and said, "Sorry."

"Don't be silly, Hugo."

"I am not as confident as Grenville or Jonathan with women, I never know what to say to them."

"I understand Hugo, I really do," said Sofia. "Let me tell you a secret," said Sofia. "Grenville's father James was the same as you," Sofia went on.

"Really," said Hugo. "But he was an Earl then a Duke."

"Even Earls and Dukes can be shy with women," said Sofia. "It took him weeks to ask me to marry him, although I had dropped so many hints, in the end I said yes before he finished asking me, to put the poor lamb out of his misery," said Sofia with a giggle.

"Really, gosh," was all Hugo could say.

"I can tell she is very fond of you," said Sofia.

"Oh, you think so?" said Hugo. "But do you think she will marry me, if I ask her?" continued Hugo.

Sofia considered Hugo's pleading eyes and said, "I am sure she will, Hugo. And if she refuses you, ask me, I am free," said Sofia with a laugh. This made Hugo go bright red. Still laughing, Sofia said, "It will be fine, remember the saying Hugo, faint heart never won true lady."

Hugo smiled at Sofia, "Thank you, you have been most helpful," said Hugo, kissing her on the cheek before standing.

"Good luck," said Sofia, smiling as Hugo left the room.

After dinner that night everyone was in the lounge drinking coffee, when Grenville went up to Hugo who was standing alone by the windows. "Everything alright Hugo, you look pensive?"

"Yes, fine," replied Hugo too quickly.

Grenville smiled. Leaning in, Grenville whispered into Hugo's ear, "Go ask her, you fool."

Hugo looked shocked. "Don't know what you mean," said Hugo with a stammer.

Grenville smiled. "I can win fifty pounds off Jonathan if you do it," said Grenville. Hugo stared into Grenville's smiling eyes and only saw love, not ridicule or mirth.

Turning from Grenville, Hugo said in a loud voice, "Everyone, can I have your attention please." The room went quiet and everyone looked at Hugo. Sara went and stood next to Grenville and took his hand. Jonathan stood and went to the drinks table, leaving Carole alone on the couch. Hugo moved slowly over to Carole, kneeled down in front of her and said, "Carole, I love you, always have since the first day I met you here at the Hall. Please will you marry me?" Hugo took a ring box from his pocket and held it up.

Carole smiled down on Hugo and said, "Of course I will, Hugo." Hugo leaned in and they kissed. Taking the ring from the box, Hugo placed it on her finger. Carole helped Hugo to stand while the room was clapping and cheering. Hugo was going red as everyone congratulated him.

"About time," said Jonathan, slapping Hugo on the back.

"Knew you had it in you, old man," said Grenville, also slapping Hugo on the back.

"By the way Jonathan old bean, that's fifty pounds you owe me," smiled Grenville.

"Put it on my tab, old man," replied a laughing Jonathan.

Carole stood with Sofia and Sara and showed them her ring.

"Well done," said Sara, hugging Carole.

"So, pleased, my dear," said Sofia, adding her congratulations as well.

"You must hold the reception here," said Sara.

"You sure Grenville won't mind?" said Carole, looking shocked.

"Like he has a choice," said Sara, smiling over at Grenville who smiled back. Jonathan and Hugo noticed Sara looking over and smiling.

"Think you are being set up, old man," said Jonathan.

"Think you are right," replied Grenville, laughing.

∞•∟

Grenville looked out of his office window and smiled. He had a stroke of luck with Grace. Although she was settled into her new bungalow, the girl he had recruited to be her personal assistant had turned out to be a disaster; the girl had lasted three days before Grace had her running in floods of tears, and refusing to go back. But then Alice Mitchell found the missing document.

Grenville admitted the document was the only thing that gave him licence to run S&T Imports, signed by Tom before he had left Belize. How he had mislaid it was still a mystery but Alice Mitchell from the legal department had found it in an old filing cabinet and decided to translate it into English, something Grenville never did. Grenville could not remember Alice before their meeting, but during the interview Grenville knew that since her discovery Alice would have a thousand questions going through her mind. Grenville knew she was the right person for the job to look after Grace. Still smiling, he was sure Grace and Alice would get on like a house on fire. Grenville always had been a good judge of character, Tom had taught him that, plus when Alice said, "Of course I will meet with Mrs Backer. One thing has crossed my mind, Chairman, is this offer because I found the document or my sparkling personality?" Grenville put his head back and laughed. Yes, Grace and Alice have the same cynical outlook.

After reading Tom's new email, Grenville picked up the phone and asked Michelle to see if Carole was free to meet him in conference room three. After the bubble, had closed and settled, Grenville said, "Thanks for coming so promptly."

Carole smiled at Grenville in reply. Going on, Grenville said, "Got two further names for your personal attention Carole," passing over a piece of paper. "Please can you trace Packer first," smiled Grenville.

"Will get onto it as a matter of urgency," said Carole.

"Thank you, Carole, most kind," replied Grenville, standing to indicate the meeting was over.

A few days later, Michelle buzzed. Picking up the receiver, Grenville said, "Yes, Michelle."

"Carole to see you, Chairman."

"Thank you, Michelle, please send her in," replied Grenville.

On entering, Grenville went and met Carole half way across the room. Kissing Carole on the cheek, Grenville said, "Everything OK, Carole?"

"Yes," said a smiling Carole.

Grenville motioned towards the comfy chairs. Once seated, Grenville said, "So how can I be of help, Carole?"

"Won't take too much of your time, just wanted to let you know that the new commissions you gave me are going to take a week or so, due to a lot of red tape," said Carole.

Grenville understood exactly what Carole was saying. Smiling, Grenville said, "Thank you my dear for letting me know. I will pass on your concerns. How are the wedding plans going?" Grenville asked.

"Very well thank you, Grenville, now you have so graciously handed over the Hall for the reception," said Carole, smiling.

"My pleasure my dear, anything to help," replied Grenville.

"We will be down this weekend to finalise some details," said Carole. "Plus, not seen Sara for a few weeks and need a catch up," Carole went on.

"Wonderful," said Grenville, "she will be glad of the distraction."

"Not going well then?"

"Sara does not like sitting about doing nothing," said a laughing Grenville. Standing, Grenville said, "Until the weekend."

Carole stood as well. Grenville kissed Carole on the cheek, and Carole said, "Until the weekend," as Carole left.

Grenville sat and pondered on what Carole had told him. Obviously both names were still heavily involved with the CIA and the United States government, and although not insurmountable Carole was right to be cautious with the information. Grenville decided to email Tom and let him know the information would possibly take a little time to gather, but not to be concerned; all was in hand.

A few weeks later, Grenville was sitting in his office with his hands behind his head with a smile on his face. Before the phone had rung twice, Grenville had picked it up and before he had time to speak, Michelle said, "Chairman, Carole would like to see you in conference room three if you are free."

"Of course, Michelle, tell her I am on my way," replied Grenville as he replaced the handset. As he entered conference room three, the bubble was already in place with Carole sitting with the door open waiting for him. Smiling, Grenville entered the bubble and closed the door, waited for the hiss as the door sealed and sat down opposite Carole and smiled.

"So, Carole how is it all going?"

"Very well, thank you Chairman," Carole replied smiling. "I have the information of the two names you gave me," Carole said.

"Oh well done, thought you said there was a lot of red tape surrounding them," said Grenville.

"Not as much as I first envisaged considering one was still with the CIA, that is Colonel Jack Packer, but the second name was easy, even you could have found him," said a smiling Carole.

She passed the first folder over. "Colonel Jack Parker," said Carole, Grenville opened the folder and read the single typed sheet; while Grenville read, Carole continued. "Colonel Jack Parker is semi-retired from the CIA, only taking consultancy work, and he is living in New York."

"Sounds a nasty piece of work, but excellent work Carole, most impressed," replied Grenville.

Continuing, Carole said, "As for James Landcourt, Senator James Landcourt, Presidential candidate for the Democratic Party, and forerunner and the dead cert to get the ticket to the White House." She passed over the second folder.

As Grenville scanned the single piece of paper again he said, "Carole, you have excelled yourself as always." Standing, Grenville was keen to get the information off to Tom.

Back in his office once again, Grenville scanned the documents into a folder on the laptop; once complete, Grenville shredded the contents of the folders.

As Grenville stared at the blank laptop screen, he was worried Tom was getting close to the top people those in command, those who gave the orders. As Tom went higher, the people would be more protected and harder to, how did Tom put it, "chat to". This made Grenville smile. Shaking his head, he softly said to himself, "Stop being paranoid, Tom will be fine, he is no idiot and always has a plan."

Before sending Tom the information, he needed a few things in place first. Grenville picked up the phone. "Michelle, can you ask Hugo to meet me in conference room three, please."

"Of course, Chairman," as the phone went dead. A few minutes later the phone on Grenville's desk rang and Michelle said, "Hugo is on his way, Chairman."

"Thank you, Michelle," as Grenville replaced the handset. Hugo was already there with Carole when Grenville arrived in conference room three.

Before Grenville said anything, Hugo said, "Sorry Grenville had to ask Carole to come and use this dam contraption for me, I still don't like it."

Smiling, Grenville replied, "Don't worry Hugo, don't like it myself."

"What are you two like," said a laughing Carole. Once the bubble was in place, Carole turned to leave.

"As you are here, Carole, you can join us."

"Of course, Chairman," said Carole, smiling.

Once the bubble door was closed, Grenville said, "Hugo, got a small task for you, and I would prefer if you could handle it personally."

"Of course," replied Hugo, looking up expectantly with his pen poised.

"I want you to book in the name of a Mr Tom Jones a room in the Plaza Hotel, New York, also have a rental car in the hotel garage for Mr Tom Jones, then for the following month book a room at the Jefferson Hotel, Washington. And it would be appreciated if the payment could not be traced back to S&T Imports."

"Sounds easy enough," replied Hugo, smiling.

Back in his office Grenville sent Tom the email:

Pirate

Both files on each name are attached. Have booked Mr Tom Jones a room in the Plaza Hotel, New York, also have a rental car in the hotel garage. The following month have booked a room at the Jefferson Hotel, Washington, anything else let me know.

Duke

A month later Grenville received another email:

Duke

Finally found the last name coming home, arrive tomorrow morning. Have pre-booked a room at the Dorchester Hotel, London, grateful you could confirm booking and pay for the month.

Pirate

Grenville picked up the phone and Michelle said, "Yes, Chairman."

"Please can you ask Mr Thorpe and Miss Burke to meet me in conference room three, please?" asked Grenville.

"Of course, Chairman," replied Michelle as Grenville put down the phone.

As he enters conference room three, the bubble was already in place with Hugo and Carole sitting with the door open waiting for him. Smiling, Grenville entered the bubble and closed the door, waited for the hiss as the door sealed and sat down opposite Hugo and Carole.

"Tom is coming home tomorrow," said Grenville. Hugo and Carole did not speak. "I need you to do a few things in preparation," Grenville went on.

"And of course, old bean, you require no paper trail or traces back to S&T Imports," said a smiling Hugo.

"As always, Hugo, you read my mind," said Grenville, nodding. This made them both laugh which helped lower the tension in the room. "First, Tom has pre-booked a room in the Dorchester Hotel, in the name of Mr Tom Jones. Can you pay for a month for Mr Tom Jones at the hotel? Also, can we have a company flat prepared with a hire car in the underground car park if required?" asked Grenville.

Hugo nodded and said, "Leave it all to me, old bean."

"Thank you, Hugo. See you this weekend."

"Carole and I are looking forward to it, old man," said Hugo smiling.

Grenville looking at Hugo intently. Smiling, Hugo quietly said, "Grenville, we are not stupid, Carole and I. We did our own piece of detective work between us, and we know all about Tom Sharapova."

Grenville opened his mouth but no sound came out, he looked totally shocked.

"Don't worry," Hugo quickly added, "you have our total trust."

Grenville stood and went to the glass wall and stared out. Softly, Grenville, said, "I do not intentionally keep you in the dark," turning with tears in his eyes, "it was not that I do not trust you both. I was trying to keep everyone safe, so if ever it came back on us I would take the fall and only me."

"Who else knows?" asked Carole.

"Only Sara," replied Grenville, "but we both share each other's secrets, we do not have them between us." Grenville smiled.

"Of course," said Carole, joining Grenville at the glass wall.

Hugo hugged Grenville and said, "We always have trusted you" Gaining his composure, Grenville went and sat down. "I will arrange it all as soon as I am back in my office," said Hugo, smiling at Grenville.

"Thank you both," said Grenville.

"And what do you want from me?" asked Carole.

"Oh yes," said Grenville, "can you get me a mobile phone we can use only once?"

"You mean a burner phone," said a smiling Carole. "Of course, will drop it off as soon as I have it," replied Carole.

"Thank you both so much."

Pirate

Dorchester Hotel, London, booked for the month in the name of Tom Jones, will contact you when you arrive.

Duke

Once back in his office Grenville sat back at the email he had sent and smiled. Tom was finally coming back to England. Grenville lost his smile and realised the big risk Tom was taking coming anywhere near England after all these years, but Grenville knew that Tom had worked out some sort of plan, and Grenville knew that whatever his plan was, Grenville would be ready to help. Grenville smiled again. Just like old times again, and the thought gave him a slight shiver down his spine, something that had not happened in ages. But the truth was, Grenville knew he was excited at seeing Tom again.

Grenville picked up his desk phone and dialled Jonathan's private number. After three rings Jonathan answered. Grenville immediately said, "Jonathan my dear chap, how are you?"

"Very well thank you Grenville, to what do I owe this pleasure?" asked Jonathan.

"Wondered if you were free this weekend and you fancied a weekend away at Hampton Hall?" asked Grenville.

"Let me see," said Jonathan. After a pause, Jonathan said, "Of course old man, would love to."

"Wonderful, Hugo and Carole will be there and I am sure Sara would love the distraction," said Grenville.

"Looking forward to it, see you on Friday." Before Grenville had time to respond, the phone went dead.

Ᏸ·Ꮯ

Newton was waiting for Grenville as he came out of the railway station. Opening the door and saluting, Newton said, "Welcome home, your Grace."

"Thank you, Newton. How's it going at the ranch?" asked Grenville.

"Excellent," said a smiling Newton.

"Good, good," replied Grenville as the Rolls set off towards Hampton Hall. Back at the Hall Grenville went to find Sara and Sofia. He found them both in the reading room. Going over and kissing Sara and Sofia, he said, "Hope you are both well."

Sofia said, "As always, darling."

Sara said, "Will be once young Hampton here has made an appearance."

"Don't worry, the first is always the hardest," said Sofia, smiling.

Grenville said "I have invited Jonathan down for the weekend."

"Wonderful," said Sofia. "With Hugo and Carole, as well, should be a nice weekend," Sofia went on, "I will go let the Preston's know the arrangements," as she left the room.

Sara stared at Grenville. "What you up to, Hampton?" asked Sara.

"Don't know what you mean," replied Grenville, smiling.

"I am seven months pregnant, not senile yet," said Sara smiling.

"Need to get the team together, Tom is finally returning to the UK," said Grenville.

"Excellent news," said Sara, smiling.

"But we will discuss it once we are all together."

"Of course," said Sara, "now come and give me a hug if you can," she said, laughing.

After dinner, they gathered in the lounge. Once everyone had a drink in their hands, Grenville stood and tapped his glass. "Ladies and gentlemen," said Grenville, smiling, "thank you all for coming this evening, I have some important new to impart to you all. Tom is finally coming home," said Grenville, scanning the room. No one spoke. "But first let me tell you all the truth. I think you deserve that much from me. I know some of you know parts, and others have, through their diligence, worked some of it out," Grenville said while smiling and nodding at Hugo and Carole, who smiled back, nodding. "But before I start I want you all to take this opportunity to make up your own mind and if your conscience dictates, to leave, without any recriminations. It was never my intention to keep you in the dark; this was done out of love for you all, so there would be no comebacks if everything went pear shaped."

"Plausible deniability," said a smiling Jonathan. No one moved.

"Thank you all," Grenville said softly.

"As you all know, I first met Tom while I was backpacking in Belize with Jonathan here," said Grenville, indicating Jonathan, who nodded in agreement while smiling. "Tom saved my life and rescued Jonathan and me from a rather ugly situation which I must admit was of my own making," said Grenville, holding his hand out to Jonathan.

"Folly of youth, old man," said Jonathan, laughing, which made everyone else laugh.

"Absolutely, old bean. Once Jonathan had departed for home, and I decided to stay with Tom my life changed for the better. Under Tom's guidance he made me the man I am today, and I became a different man, more outgoing, confidence and at peace with myself. I had never known before I was happy with the work Tom and I were engaged in, albeit at time not totally legal," which made Grenville smile, "but as you know all good things must come to an end. I received the letter from Jonathan about the death of my brother the same time that a family member of Tom's and a good friend of mine was killed in Belize, Max was his name. Both incidents on their own were not remarkable but together triggered future events.

"I found out Max did not only obtain work for Tom and I, he also traced people for Tom. Why did he do this? Unbeknown to me, Tom had suffered a personal tragedy. Tom, although born in the UK, had to depart after he was accused at 14 of murder. He made his way to Odessa where he and his friend Sebastian created what we now know today as S&T Imports. After a few years, Tom married Sebastian's sister, and he changed his name from Tom Backer to Tom Sharapova, taking his wife's family name. Natasha and Tom had a daughter they called Grace.

"Sebastian was killed in a bomb explosion which left his uncle Vlad wounded. Whilst he was recovering in hospital, Vlad let Tom into the family secret: Vlad was the head of the biggest Russian mafia family in Odessa."

Grenville looked around and only saw wonder on their faces. Continuing, Grenville went on, "Tom took over the, shall we say, family business, while Vlad was recuperating. After Sebastian's death Tom had no enthusiasm with S&T Imports so concentrated on the family business. Once again, they tried to assassinate Vlad, but with Tom's intervention they missed again, but this time there were tragic consequences. Tom's wife Natasha and his daughter Grace were killed in the ensuing getaway by the assassins. Tom, as I think we can imagine, was distraught over losing his family, and over their grave made a vow of vengeance to track down the perpetrators and bring swift justice to them.

"The getaway car was abandoned at the docks and they found out the only ship that had sailed that day was a US cargo ship going to Belize, so that is where Tom went to begin his quest. Max managed to track down the passengers from the US cargo ship, and found one of the men responsible; that's where Tom first heard that his family had been killed by the US/ British intelligence agencies. Operation Blackstone was what they had called the operation. Max was killed while tracing the next name on the list. This is where my story begins with S&T Imports. I did not hesitate to offer Tom my assistance and between us we came up with the plan to re-activate S&T

Imports. So, with your help, we have made S&T Imports a worldwide company. I have kept Tom informed of our progress and he is most impressed by your loyalty and trust to me, and since we have been operational, we have traced several names for Tom, but now he is on the last name and that person resides in the UK, so he is homeward bound.

"Of course, the next part is a very dangerous time, so once again I ask if any of you wish to leave then I will not hold it personally."

Sofia slowly stood and moved towards Grenville. Placing her hands on his face, she smiled into his eyes and said, "You are my son and I am proud of you."

Everyone stood and went to Grenville. Sara hugged him and whispered, "You will always have my love."

Jonathan hugged Grenville and said, "Always here for you, my old friend."

Hugo hugged Grenville and said, "Always your servant."

Carole hugged Grenville and said, "Without you, I would not have been where I am now."

With tears in his eyes, Grenville said, "Thank you all so much."

Later that evening, Grenville took the burner phones that Carole had dropped off for him and rang the Dorchester hotel and asked them to give the following message to Mr Tom Jones when he booked in to the Dorchester Hotel tomorrow morning. Grenville asked the receptionist to repeat the message. Once Grenville was satisfied that the message would be relayed correctly he disconnected the call and placed the phone in his jacket pocket. He would keep the phone with him night and day, until it rang. A few days later, the mobile rang and all Grenville said was, "CC one two one," before the connection went dead.

Grenville removed the back of the phone and removed the SIM card and with his cigar lighter burned it in his ashtray. While Grenville watched, the SIM burn, he picked up his desk phone and rang the Carton Club to confirm his booking at 12.30 for a private lunch. Once Grenville replaced the receiver he smiled. He hoped Tom would work out the code. Just like old times, Grenville felt himself come alive again. He realised he had missed the danger that Tom brought with him. Grenville threw back his head and laughed and said out loud, "I sure hope you got a good plan, you old Pirate."

℘ · ℘

As Grenville approached the Carton Club, Forbes the doorman saluted and held the door open for Grenville and said, "Welcome, your Grace."

Smiling, Grenville placed a folded ten pound note into Forbes' hand and said, "Thank you Forbes, looks like rain later."

Still smiling, Forbes replied, "Looks that way, your Grace," as he closed the door on Grenville.

Grenville walked to the reception desk and said, "Morning Jenkins, all well I hope?"

Jenkins smiled and said, "Welcome back, your Grace."

"Good man," replied Grenville, smiling.

"Can I have a quick word, your Grace?" said Jenkins, looking slightly embarrassed.

"What is on your mind, old chap?" replied Grenville, but Grenville already knew his problem.

"We seem to have you double booked for two luncheon rooms today."

"How odd," replied Grenville, looking surprised. "I am sure I only booked the Waterloo Room," continued Grenville.

Jenkins studied the book in front of him, smiled and said, "Of course, your Grace, I have it here. I do apologise for any confusion," said Jenkins. Jenkins then said, "All is prepared for you in the Waterloo Room for your lunch, I will send Stephen up with the menu and wine list."

"Thank you, Jenkins," replied Grenville as he studied the members' book to see who was at the Club today.

Once Grenville had given Stephen the order for lunch, Grenville asked Stephen, "Grateful, old man, if you could open that window for me please, smells a bit stuffy in here."

Stephen went and opened the big bay window and turned and said, "Anything else, your Grace?"

"No thank you, Stephen," replied Grenville, "will ring if I need anything else."

Bowing slightly, Stephen said, "Will bring your lunch at one, your Grace," before leaving the room and closing the door quietly.

Grenville was feeling nervous. It had been ages since he and Tom had been together; yes, they had a brief few hours on his honeymoon, but this was the first time they had planned to meet since Grenville had left Belize, and Grenville could not get this uneasy feeling out of his head that Tom was making a mistake putting his head in the lion's mouth. But this made Grenville smile and he could hear Tom's voice in his head: "Duke, you worry too much, always have a plan." Grenville sipped his brandy and waited patiently for Tom's arrival. Grenville stood as the door slowly opened and Tom quickly came in the room, and closed the door behind him. Smiling, Grenville went to embrace Tom. "The years have been good to you, you old pirate."

Tom, smiling, said, "Being a Lord certainly agrees with you," tapping Duke's expanding waistline.

Both men hugged again and burst out laughing.

After lunch, had been finished, Grenville said, "So, how was it?"

Tom sat back and said, "Duke, I don't think I have had a better meal in years."

Grenville smiled. "Glad it met with your approval, old man," Grenville said, "let's sit on the comfy chairs. Down to business," as he pulled out a white piece of paper and passed it to Tom. Tom studied the piece of paper for a few minutes, then passed it back to Grenville, who by this stage had taken a cigar from his pockets and had begun to light it. As he did so, he also casually lit the piece of paper and dropped it into the ashtray and, with his cigar, made sure the paper ash looked like cigar ash. Tom smiled; he had taught Grenville well. Grenville raised his eyes to Tom.

"So, as you suspected, this is the last name of the people who killed your family." Tom nodded, and Grenville went on. "Ironic really, last name and they happened to be in the UK. Full circle, as we say," smiled Grenville. "Please be careful though, Tom," Grenville warned, "they will be well protected and by now will know you are coming for them."

"O ye of little faith."

"Not at all, I kind of like having you around," which made them both laugh again.

"So, what do you think?" asked Grenville, pointing to the folder that sat on the table between them marked S&T Imports.

Tom looked at Grenville for a few minutes, then smiled and said, "To tell you the truth, when you told me your plan in Belize I was a little uncertain you could achieve it all. But," continued Tom, "you have proved me wrong."

Grenville sat back and said, "I did not do it alone, I have the most amazing friends helping me." Continuing, Grenville said, "You remember Jonathan from Belize."

Tom smiled. "Of course, I do."

"Although he technically does not work for S&T Imports…"

"He was going to be a lawyer," interrupted Tom.

"Indeed, he has, going to be the youngest high court judge in the country," smiled Grenville.

"Excellent," smiled Tom.

"Plus, one of my oldest school friends, Hugo who is my right-hand man, and if I admit none of our success would have been achievable without him," said Grenville. "And," went on Grenville, "Carole, who has built the most amazing computer system known to man. I admit the two of them between them have made S&T Imports work, and I must admit together are the most amazing couple I have ever known," smiled Grenville.

"I would love to meet them both," smiled Tom.

"One day hope you can, old man," smiled Grenville.

"Anyway, forgot to ask, how is Sara?" said Tom.

"Blooming," smiled Grenville, "eight months pregnant and bored," which made them both laugh.

"Thanks for all the emails about mother," said Tom.

"My pleasure, old man. She was delighted when I contacted her and told her I had news about you, she was beside herself, and I know she is proud of the man you have become. She is so proud of her Tom," replied Grenville, smiling.

"Is she OK though?" asked Tom.

"Oh yes, Sara and I see her once a month and the new residential home is top class, plus I have someone looking in every day, Alice Mitchell is her name. Your mother has particularly taken a shine to her. Your mother is not the easiest woman in the world to please. A few have been sent packing, but Grace seems to like Alice, they get on like a house on fire. Alice takes her regularly to visit and lay flowers on your father's grave."

Tom smiled and was pleased his mother was in good hands. "Duke, I don't know how I can ever repay you," said Tom in a whisper.

"Don't be daft, old man," said Grenville, laughing, "you made me a near billionaire and head of a successful private import/ export business. It should be me thanking you," which made Tom laugh as well. Grenville went silent then said quietly, "I have the friendship of the greatest man I have ever known. You can take everything else away from me, but that I cherish that more than life itself." Tom leaned over and they both embraced again.

Grenville handed Tom a key with a tag on it and said, "New accommodation, no doubt they found the hotel by now."

Smiling, Tom said, "They sure have, had fun getting here."

Grenville said, "Please be careful, Tom."

Smiling, Tom was about to say something, when they both heard the commotion outside. Looking at Tom, Grenville said, "Time to go I think."

"Absolutely," smiled Tom.

They briefly hugged again and Grenville said, "See you soon, Pirate," as Tom went to the windows and Grenville went to the door. Grenville took a quick glance behind him to check Tom had gone, but all he saw was the curtain slowly rippling in the breeze.

As Grenville opened the door he was confronted with a man pointing a gun in his face. Grenville said, "Gentlemen, can I help you?"

"National security," said the agent, flashing his badge at Grenville. "Please go back inside, sir."

"How exciting," said Grenville, "but I don't care what security agency you are from young man, this is the Carton Club and never in all its two-hundred-year history has a firearm been brought past the statue of Lord Carton, the founding father of this club, which currently sits in the main lobby. It is one of the Club's founding rules." The men stared at Grenville.

"I am the twelfth Duke of Hampshire and a committee member." Just then, the doors to the Wellington Room opened and none other than the current Home Secretary came out. There seated behind him were three military high ranking officers all in full dress uniform. "What the bloody hell is going on out here?" said the Home Secretary.

"Looking for a fugitive, sir," said the lead man, showing the Home Secretary his badge.

"What, in the Carton Club? Ridiculous you idiot, you've been had."

"But we have sound intelligence, he was in the Carton Club and we had intelligence that he came to the Wellington Room," said the lead man, who was by now starting to feel uneasy.

"So, you think I am having lunch with your fugitive? I shall speak to your Director personally, this is outrageous," said the Home Secretary.

"Outrageous," said Grenville behind them all. "Now get out," said Grenville.

As the men were leaving, the Home Secretary turned to Grenville. "Do apologise for the confusion, your Grace," he said, smiling.

Grenville was not smiling when he said, "Not good, Fairfax. Men with guns. Shall have to report it to the committee."

"Whatever you feel is best, your Grace," said the Home Secretary, bowing deeply.

The three men put away their firearms, and as they passed Grenville said, "Not good, gentlemen, not good."

The men all nodded and said, "Your Grace," as they retreated the way they came.

Grenville turned on his heels and with a spring in his step and a smile on his face said, "Another brandy, I think." Sitting back down, he pressed the buzzer beside him, and a few minutes later there was a gentle knock on the door. Turning, Grenville said, "Stephen, another brandy if you please, and can you get someone to close that open window? It's turning rather chilly in here."

"Of course, your Grace," came the reply. "Straight away."

ଔ · ଓ

Grenville was sitting in his office when he noticed Alice Mitchell had made an appointment to see him at ten that morning, Grenville wondered what Alice could possibly want, but deep down he had his suspicions. At precisely ten am, the buzzer on his desk phone went as Grenville picked it up. Michelle said, "Alice is here for her ten o'clock appointment, Chairman."

"Excellent," replied Grenville, "please show her in." Grenville heard the soft knocking and standing watched as Alice entered. Smiling, Grenville went and met Alice and kissed the offered cheek and said, "Alice my dear, what brings you to my door this early?"

Alice replied, "Went to see Grace yesterday."

"Oh yes," said Grenville, and seeing the tension in her eyes, Grenville said, "how is the old dear?"

"She had a visitor," was all Alice said, smiling.

Grenville put a finger to his lips. Alice immediately understood the meaning. Grenville said, "Follow me." Alice followed Grenville from the room; he stopped at his secretary's desk and said, "Michelle, going to the meeting in conference room three," before striding off with Alice. Michelle looked puzzled and scanned the diary; she could not see any meeting in conference room three scheduled, but shrugged, and after all these years working for the Chairman she was not surprised it was not in the diary.

Once in conference room three, Grenville activated the glass bubble. Grenville smiled at Alice and waved for her to follow. The glass cube had fitted neatly over the small conference table and chairs. Once Grenville and Alice had stepped into the cube, Grenville pressed a button, and the door was merged into the glass cube with a hydraulic hiss. "Impressive," said Alice.

"An evil requirement, currently," replied Grenville, smiling. Grenville and Alice sat at the conference table, and Grenville said, "Shall we start?" with a smile.

Alice said, "I met Tom yesterday and I have a message from him."

Grenville smiling said, "Thought you might, what did you think of our Tom?"

"Nearly blew his head off, when I caught him snooping around Grace's bungalow," said Alice. This made Grenville put his head back and roar with laughter. Alice looked at Grenville with a puzzled look.

"Sorry for laughing my dear, I bet you made his day pointing a gun at him."

"Don't understand," said Alice.

"My dear, let me explain the enigma that is Tom Backer." For the next two hours Grenville explained everything to Alice about Tom: his life story, where he, Grenville, fitted into the story and the reason for the company. Alice just sat and stared at Grenville and what he was telling her, nodding and shaking her head at times, other times with tears in her eyes, and other times laughing out loud with Grenville; in fact, before Grenville had finished his tale, she had covered the entire spectrum of human emotion.

After Grenville finished, all Alice could say was, "What a man," and realised she was perhaps falling a bit in love with him. This thought made her blush, and Grenville picked up on it immediately.

"No, my dear, you don't have feelings for people like Tom Backer, he is on a mission of vengeance and he has given his life and soul over to it, you will never be able to deviate him from that path, you will only end up getting hurt if you get in his way."

Alice was silent for a bit then said, "After he has killed the last name on his list, what then for Tom Backer?"

Grenville smiled. "Never thought of that one, my dear. Perhaps between us we can come up with a plan."

Alice smiled at Grenville and said, "No doubt we can," which made them both laugh.

Once Grenville was back in his office, he thought about what Alice had just said: "After he has killed the last name on his list, what then for Tom Backer?" Grenville admitted to himself with everything that had been going on lately he had never given this a second thought, and he was sure Tom never looked past the names on the list. The future for Tom was never an option; he was blinded by his vengeance and Grenville knew he had never even considered returning to a normal life. Grenville smiled. "A normal life", whatever that was. But Grenville started to formulate a plan. He had decided to tell Alice about Tom not because she needed to know, but deep down Grenville knew Alice could be good for Tom. Yes, she was a beautiful lady, and no doubt had many admirers, but Grenville suspected she needed a certain man in her life to give her what she needed, and Grenville was in no doubt that Tom was the perfect candidate, although Grenville knew Tom would disagree. But Grenville sat back in his chair, smiled and said to himself, "What we need is a good plan."

࿓·࿓

Next day Grenville and Alice had agreed to meet at Tom's flat. Grenville was the first to arrive, getting the taxi to drop him off three streets away from the flat. It was not long before he noticed Alice coming in the opposite direction. Eventually Alice joined Grenville, and smiling, Grenville said, "How are you my dear?"

Smiling back Alice said, "Good, thank you."

"They smell nice," said Grenville, pointing at the bag Alice was holding.

Still smiling, Alice said, "Nothing like a morning treat."

Grenville said, "You look different this morning."

Alice went red and said, "Just a bit of makeup to make a girl feel better now and again."

Grenville smiled but did not comment. "Shall we?" Grenville said as he indicated toward the door to the block of flats' main door. Tom let them both in; he was surprised to see her, but he noticed Alice was carrying a large brown bag which had the most amazing smell of freshly cooked pastries.

While Alice went into the kitchen to make some coffee, Tom whispered to Grenville, "What is she doing here?"

Grenville held up his hand and said, "Tom, sometimes you've got to trust me."

Tom said, "Always will, Duke," before hugging him.

A few minutes later, Alice came from the kitchen with a pot of coffee and a plate of sweet-smelling pastries. While all three sat munching pastries, and drinking coffee, Grenville casually said to Tom, "Tom, I have explained everything to Alice here."

"What, everything?" said Tom, going tense.

"Yes, everything, and she is now totally on our side and part of the cause." Tom looked at Alice and saw her smiling at him; all Tom could do was smile back. When Alice took the tray back to the kitchen, leaving them alone, Tom took Grenville's arms and said in a whisper, "You told her everything?"

Whispering too, Grenville said, "Yes, my dear chap, everything, warts and all."

"Blimey," said Tom.

"I know," said Grenville, "and she still wants to know you, amazed me as well." He laughed as he patted Tom's face. Grenville watched Tom and Alice interact and smiled; he was sure they were both becoming close. They had a lot in common and the same outlook on life. Grenville knew if they did not yet, that eventually they would fall in love, and this to Grenville was another problem he had to overcome: how would he get them together?

"You listening to me, Duke?" said Tom.

"Sorry old man, was miles away."

"We could see," said Alice, smiling.

Tom said, "Let's all meet at mother's in two days' time. I will meet you there, and see if we can come up with a suitable plan of action."

Grenville and Alice both stood to leave. Grenville said, "See you day after tomorrow, and try and keep out of trouble," before giving Tom a hug.

Tom and Alice looked slightly embarrassed on what to do. Grenville broke the tension by saying, "Tom, for god's sake, give the girl a hug." Smiling, Tom and Alice embraced. Eventually Tom and Alice parted, both looking awkward. Grenville patted them both on the back and said as he laughed, "What are you two like?" Both Tom and Alice smiled, not sure what to say, as Grenville looked towards the sky and said, "Please lord, help us. Come on Alice, let's get out of here before Tom here turns to a gibbering teenager again."

Both Tom and Alice went red and Tom said, "Now you are being silly." Still laughing, Grenville took Alice by the arm and they left the flat.

Outside on the street, Grenville said, "Can I give you a lift, my dear?"

Smiling, Alice said, "No thank you, I could do with a walk." Grenville watched Alice walk down the street and smiled and thought to himself, *Alice and Tom, now that is part of the plan that needs serious finesse*, and he knew the right people to ask. Still smiling, Grenville turned in the opposite direction to find a taxi back to the office.

80·CB

Grenville was the second to arrive at Grace's. Grenville noticed Alice's car already in the parking bays. "Can you wait for me, Newton? Should not be long."

As Newton held open the car door for Grenville, Newton replied, "Not a worry, your Grace."

Alice opened the door to Grenville and smiled. "Hope you are well, Grenville," she said.

Kissing the offered cheek, Grenville replied, "Could not be better, my dear."

Grenville went to Grace and gave her a hug and said, "You are looking well, my dear."

Grace smiled and said, "Thank you my dear, things are looking up."

Laughing, Grenville said, "Indeed they are."

Eventually there was another knock at the door. Alice said, "I will get it," eventually returning with Tom.

Grenville smiled as Tom and Grace hugged, then Tom hugged Grenville and said, "How you doing?"

Grenville replied, "Good, thank you."

Grace said, "I shall make some tea," leaving the three of them alone to chat.

"So," said Alice, "where do we start?"

Tom said, "I need to get close to this bloody woman."

"Close enough to kill her?" asked Alice.

"Yes," said Tom, "she is the last one on the list, the one that gave the orders to try and kill me and Uncle Vlad, but ended up killing my family. I need to look her in the eyes and tell her why she is going to die."

Grenville and Alice were both nodded their heads; strangely, they both understood Tom's obsession. "So," said Grenville, "How do we get Tom close enough to Julie Somerville, Director of MI5?"

"I can," said Grace, standing in the kitchen doorway holding a tray of tea.

"Sorry," said Tom, "what did you say, mother?"

"I said, I can get you close to her." Grenville looked at Grace with astonishment.

Taking the tray from her, Alice helped her sit in her high back chair. Before anyone else spoke, Grace said, "Be a dear,

Alice, can you get me that brown box next to my bed, and bring it to me?"

"Of course," smiled Alice. When Alice returned, and placed the box on Grace's knee, she sat back down; Grenville looked at Grace opening the box. Grace looked at Tom and said, "What I am about to tell you might alter your perception on all of this, my son." Grenville noticed Tom looked confused. Grace handed him a faded envelope, which Tom took, and extracting the letter, Tom read it; still looking confused, he passed it to Grenville and over his shoulder Alice read it as well. Grace said, "Julie Somerville is your birth mother, Tom." The room went so quiet that you could hear the ticking of the clock on the wall. Tom sat and stared into space as Grace went on to explain Tom's birth. "Perhaps I should have told you when you were growing up; I always thought in my heart she would eventually return and claim you, and take you away from me. That was always my biggest fear, while you were growing up. At first I tried to stay distant from you but after a few years I loved you so much I considered you my own child, and knew I could never give you up, so as time went on, and you grew into a wonderful young boy, I never had the courage to tell you." Grace had tears streaming down her cheeks.

Grenville felt the tears fill his eyes. Tom went and knelt in front of her and hugged her. Grenville stood and with his hands on his head, said, "Well, this is a game changer."

"Sit down, Grenville," said Grace, "you are making the place look untidy."

Grenville sat down as ordered. Grenville's mind was in turmoil on Grace's revelation, about Tom's real birth mother, but he felt pride for Grace on letting go of her secret, but Grenville was not sure how Tom would take the revelation he thought he would properly let sleeping dogs lie but then again, he was not Tom. Grenville listened to Tom as he spoke to Grace and felt so much love for them both, the tears were now flowing before Tom had finished talking to Grace. Grenville looked at Alice and she also sat with tears in her eyes listening to Grace and Tom. Eventually Tom said, "She is still responsible for my family's deaths."

Grace wiped her eyes and said, "That's settled it then, you better hear my plan."

An hour later, Grenville was shocked on hearing the plan that Grace was suggesting and eventually Grenville said, "You are a devious old bird," to which Tom and Alice could only nod and confirm his sentiments.

Everyone was silent. Eventually Grenville said, "Well, I admit in principle it is a good basic plan, but it needs fine tuning to make Grace and her plan work." Alice and Tom both looked confused. Grenville said, "Of course, getting to kill her is the easy part but has anyone considered what comes afterwards?"

Tom was the first to say, "To tell you the truth Duke, never really gave it much thought."

Grenville looked at Alice, who had a concerned look on her face. Still smiling, Grenville said, "Do not worry, I have the best team to formulate a plan."

Alice said, "How long have we got to set it all up?"

"Three days, four tops," said Tom. "I think I am on borrowed time. The intelligence agencies are not stupid, and will be closing in fast."

Grenville said, "Not to worry, give me a day or two and I will have it all in place."

Alice stood and said, "If you need anything, let me know."

Alice kissed Grace then as both Tom and Grenville stood. Alice hugged them both but Grenville noticed the hug with Tom lingered longer than his. Once Alice had left, Grenville said casually, "Lovely girl, that, and so loyal."

"Stop it, Duke," said Tom smiling. "I know what you are doing."

"What, old man? I was only saying you could do far worse."

Tom punched Grenville on the arm, and said, "Behave. Seriously, can you get a plan formulated in the time frame?"

"How do you ever doubt me, my dear chap?" smiled Grenville.

"Never," said Tom, also smiling.

"Good, then let me worry about it, you spend time with Grace." As Grenville, hugged Grace he whispered, "Get him to see sense with Alice."

Grace whispered back, "Don't worry my dear, I always knew how to handle my boy."

Once Grenville was back in the car, he said, "Newton, the office if you don't mind."

"As you wish, your Grace," replied Newton as he headed back towards London.

∞·∞

As soon as Grenville returned to the office and before he entered, Grenville asked Michelle to see if Mr Thorpe and Miss Burke were available for a quick chat. Smiling, Michelle had picked up the phone before Grenville had closed his office door. As soon as Grenville had sat down, the phone buzzed on his desk, and picking up the phone Michelle said, "Mr Thorpe and Miss Burke are available now and will meet you in conference room three," before the phone went dead. Grenville closed his eyes and hoped Hugo and Carole could put a good workable plan together in the time frame which would allow Tom to complete his quest for vengeance and allow him to escape.

As Grenville entered conference room three, Carole operated the door, and then came across and hugged Grenville. "You look tired," said Carole, looking concerned.

Smiling, Grenville said, "Been a tense few days."

Hugo hugged Grenville and said, looking worried, "What can we do, old man?"

Smiling, Grenville sat down heavily followed by Hugo and Carole. Eventually Grenville told Hugo and Carole what had transpired over the last few days plus the plan that Grace had come up with. Hugo and Carole both sat and listened in silence, as Grenville told them. Once he had finished speaking, and after a pause, Grenville said, "I know I have no right to ask you, and of course I understand if you refuse my request, but if you could come up with a plan that helps Tom achieve this final act and escape capture, we would be eternally grateful. You two are the best minds I think I have ever known," said Grenville, smiling.

Eventually, Carole said, "Grenville, give me and Hugo an hour or two and we will come up with a solution." Grenville looked at Hugo who was smiling and nodding his head.

Standing, Grenville said, "Thank you both."

"Will call you in a bit," said Hugo, and he shepherded Grenville from the bubble.

Back in his office Grenville rang Sara, just to hear her voice, and after the conservation Grenville felt a little better. As promised, after a few hours, which to Grenville seemed like a lifetime, Carole buzzed his desk phone from conference room three. Grenville quickly made his way to conference room three. As he entered, Carole closed the bubble and went and sat next to Hugo. Grenville sat opposite them. Hugo smiled and said, "Carole and I have pondered your problem and we have come up with a workable plan."

Grenville smiled as Carole laid out the plan. Grenville listened and eventually with tears in his eyes said, "You two are amazing."

Hugo and Carole were both smiling and Carole eventually said, "Easy, really."

Grenville eventually said, "Please explain it all again to me again."

Smiling, Carole said, "Of course, Grenville. The first thing was we found nothing wrong with Grace getting into the hospital, after all a lady of her age will be easy. Alice will ring the ambulance and make sure she is taken to the correct hospital, and see her safely admitted, then she will ring Tom with the floor and room details that Grace is in."

"Why does it have to be that hospital?" asked Grenville.

"Because it is the one closest to the Thames," said Hugo, smiling.

Carole continued, "In the mean time you will ring from the hospital, to let Miss Somerville know Grace is in hospital, near death and wants to explain before she dies about her long-lost son."

"How do I get into the hospital and pass as a doctor to make the call?" asked Grenville.

Smiling, Carole said, "Funny you should say that, but I have just spoken to Sara, and Sara and your mother will come to town to do some shopping with you for the baby and while you are out shopping. Sara will have a sudden pain, and of course the closest hospital will be St Thomas'."

Grenville looked shocked. Holding up her hands, Carole said, "Grenville, don't look so worried. She will be fine and only in for a few minutes, but long enough for you to ring Miss Somerville and pass on Grace's message to her."

"It needs to be from St Thomas'," said Hugo.

"Why?" asked Grenville, looking puzzled.

Smiling, Carole said, "MI5 are not stupid and will monitor all calls coming in to their Director, so it must be from the hospital to make the call look credible. Alice will follow Miss Somerville and her security detail to the hospital and ring Tom once she has arrived, so Tom can get into place. We are convinced Miss Somerville has never told a living soul about having a child and being a mother. She will of course be most eager to enter the room alone to see Grace, and know what information she has about her long lost son. After all, she still would rather keep it a secret, if I have judged Miss Somerville correctly."

"Where Tom will be waiting," smiled Hugo, interrupting Carole.

Carole continued. "The next step is to get Tom safely away. We suggest that Tom is waiting in the room with Grace when Miss Somerville enters. I am sure Tom can pose as a doctor, after all someone in a white coat in a hospital is rarely scrutinised too closely. Once Tom has killed Miss Somerville, then Grace can pull the assistance cord to summon a nurse, who will obviously see Miss Somerville lying on the floor and will summon help.

This of course will have her security detail come running as well, and in the confusion Tom can slip out of the room, down the back stairs and out of the hospital."

Grenville smiled and nodded. Carole continued, "Hugo here has purchased an old speed boat and will have it tied up at the Thames embankment opposite the hospital, where someone will be waiting to speed Tom out to the open sea where it will meet up with the Red Star. As you know we have had the Red Star on our books for some time now and now it is at Milton Haven getting loaded. I have spoken to Captain Sharapova and he will sail a day earlier to make the rendezvous," said Hugo, smiling.

"I think I know who will pilot the speedboat," said Grenville, smiling.

"Oh, please tell?" asked Carole, smiling.

Grenville said, "Alice Mitchell."

"Really," said Hugo, looking surprised.

"Yes," said Grenville. "Tom and Alice are quite close now, and I am sure I can convince her," smiled Grenville.

"all ready ahead of you," said Carole, "I have already spoken to Alice and she has agreed."

"Blimey," was all Grenville could say.

"I think she has fallen in love with your Tom," said Carole, laughing.

"How did you work that out?" asked Grenville.

"Us women know these things," said Carole smiling as she looked at Hugo who had gone red. "All you need to do is to convince Tom to take her with him."

"I can try," said Grenville.

"Men, what are you like."

"And everyone has agreed to this?" asked Grenville.

"Of course," said Carole and Hugo in unison. Grenville looked stunned once again. The plan was brilliant, and worked out in every detail. He could find no fault with it, and the most amazing thing was everyone was involved and everyone accepted their part they had to play without any questions.

Grenville stood with his eyes full of tears and hugged Carole and Hugo, and was unable to speak as he left the bubble.

ჯ·ᏼ

Next day Tom answered the door and was surprised to see only Grenville standing there. "Hello," said Tom, looking surprised.

"I know, only me," said a smiling Grenville.

Tom went red as Grenville followed him into the flat. Tom asked, "Time for a coffee?"

"Of course, old man," replied Grenville. After Tom, had made the coffee and they were both sitting in the lounge Grenville smiled and said, "Just popped in to give you the final plan."

Tom sat and stared at Grenville as he explained the plan and afterwards all Tom could say was, "Wow, that sounds brilliant."

Smiling, Grenville said, "Hugo and Carole came up with the plan."

"Sounds a pretty good plan to me," smiled Tom.

"But…" said Tom.

Grenville held up his hand and said, "Tom, everything is in place and everyone knows the risks, but they are doing it out of love." Tom lowered his head before Grenville went on, "These last few weeks have brought back so many memories of our time together, it's made feel positively young again."

"You getting soppy on me, old man?" said Tom, smiling at Grenville.

"Properly am," said Grenville, smiling. "Can I ask a question, Tom?"

"Of course, Duke, ask away."

"Once you have killed Somerville, what next for Tom Backer?"

Tom stood and paced the room, eventually turning to Grenville and saying, "To tell you the truth I have never really given it much thought."

Smiling, Grenville said, "I thought you had not. Well, to my reckoning you have a few options."

"Really? Please tell, old wise one," said Tom, laughing.

"Well, you can go back to Belize and fade away into the sunset never to be heard of again, you can return to Russia and go back to your old life with your uncle and the family, or you can make a fresh start with someone new who has fallen in love with you, and you can spend the rest of your life having a second chance at happiness," said Grenville. "Anyway," said Grenville, standing, "just wanted you to know you had options. Listen, Tom, be safe and take care, and remember I am always here for you."

"I know Duke, you were one of the reasons I had the fortitude to carry on all these years."

"Now who is getting soppy."

Both laughing, they hugged and both had tears in their eyes.

"Need to go," said Grenville. "Just a few minor details to put into place and make sure the timings are all coordinated and everyone is ready to go," smiled Grenville. "Just wait for the call from Alice, to set the plan in motion."

"Then it is all up to me," said Tom, smiling.

Just as Grenville closed the flat door on Tom he said, "I want you to promise me something, Tom."

"Anything," said Tom.

"Think on what I said and do the right thing by Alice," said Grenville softly as he closed the flat door.

80·G3

As Newton drove along, with Grenville, Sara and Sofia, Sara suddenly said, "Newton can you be a love and pull into the nearest hospital, I have a pain."

Smiling, Newton said, "Of course, your Grace," turning left towards the Thames. No one commented on the fact that Newton had passed a hospital three hundred yards from their current location. After twenty minutes, Newton pulled up at St Thomas' Hospital, and Grenville, Sara and Sofia entered the hospital while Newton waited outside in the VIP parking space.

Sofia went straight to the reception desk and said, "I am the mother of the Duke and Duchess of Hampshire, and my daughter-in-law, the Duchess, is eight months pregnant and is having some pains." The nurse quickly picked up the phone and rang a number, and in minutes a doctor and a nurse arrived. "Good," said Sofia. As she explained this to the doctor, the nurse had gotten a wheelchair, and sat Sara down in it and Grenville tried not to laugh at Sara who was playing her part to perfection.

They all followed the doctor into a side corridor and down into a nurses' station with a set of double doors. The doctor said, "Please wait here, your Grace, while we examine your wife." Grenville nodded. The doctor smiled at Sofia and knew she was not going to wait; as they went, Sofia winked at Grenville as the doors closed behind them.

Grenville looked around, smiled and went to the nurses' station, picked up the phone and dialled the number for MI5 and once it was connected said, "Please may I speak to Julie Somerville."

"Regarding?" said the voice.

"I am Doctor Randall from St Thomas' Hospital, it is about a friend of hers, a Miss Grace Backer," said Grenville.

Grenville waited for a minute then the phone clicked and the voice said, "Doctor Randall, how may I help you?"

Grenville said, "We had an elderly lady admitted called Grace Backer and she wanted me to give you a message."

"Get on with it, doctor," said the voice, sounding impatient.

"Sorry," said Grenville. "Had to write this bit down," Grenville said, crunching a piece of paper near the handset. Grenville continued, "She asked me if I can contact a Julie Somerville at MI5 and tell her before I die, I want to see her and tell her about her son, sorry, don't know if it makes any sense, but that's the message."

"No, makes perfect sense, thank you for ringing, Doctor."

As the line went dead, Grenville replaced the handset his end and said, "You are most welcome, Director Somerville."

Just then the doors opened and the doctor returned with a smiling Sofia and Sara. The doctor said, "Nothing to worry about, your Grace, all is well, bit of wind probably."

Grenville tried not to laugh but said, "Thank you, most kind, doctor," as he shook the doctor's hand.

Back in the car, Sara turned to Grenville and said, "Now that piece of play acting is out of the way you can take us all to lunch."

Smiling, Grenville said, "If you please, Newton."

Smiling, Newton said, "Of course, your Grace," as he moved away from the hospital.

Grenville stood on the embankment of the Thames having despatched Newton in the Rolls to collect Grace from hospital and take her home. The sun had disappeared and a dark cloud had descended, plus it had just started to lightly rain. Grenville slowly removed a glove, placed his hand in his coat pocket and pulled out a mini pair of binoculars, and scanned the Thames estuary. He picked up the small speed boat heading towards the open sea, unable to make out the two figures clearly. One was a woman by the hair blowing behind her and the figure next to her stood rigid. Grenville gave a small laugh, and on impulse, he raised his hand in salute. Grenville left the hand hanging for a few moments then dropped it back down; he knew he had fulfilled his promise made all those years ago, to his best friend. He had finally helped him lay his ghosts to rest. He wished now Tom could start to live again and find happiness. Grenville knew he had done all he could to achieve this, but for now he had his own concerns. Smiling, Grenville placed the mini binoculars back in his pocket, replaced his glove, clapped his hand and thought, *hope Newton is not too long.*

Grenville spotted Newton and smiled. Newton pulled up next to Grenville and Grenville climbed in next to Grace. After closing the door and before Newton had pulled away, Grenville said, "How you feeling, Grace?"

"Much better, my dear," replied Grace, smiling.

After a long pause, Grenville said, "Do you think he will ask her to go with him?"

Grace replied, "Well, we've done everything to make it happen," which made Grenville laugh.

"You are right there, old thing," replied Grenville. After making sure Grace was safely back into her accommodation, Grenville said, "Back to the ranch, if you please, Newton."

"As you wish, your Grace," replied Newton. Grenville sat back and closed his eyes after a few hectic days. He thought of Sara and the birth of their first child; this made Grenville smile. This was his only concern now, anything else would have to wait.

Epilogue

Nurse Lisa McNeil enjoyed her job, especially when she was on nights at the secret government private hospital, somewhere in leafy Warwickshire. At present, there were only two registered patients; one was a man who had recently returned from Africa with malaria and one was a woman who was currently in a catatonic state, and had not responded to treatment for over two years.

Nurse McNeil had just completed her rounds of the two patients. The man was asleep and the woman's condition had not changed. Making a coffee and returning to her desk, she took out her new novel she had brought that day, to enjoy a few hours of peaceful reading until the day staff came on shift. After reading a chapter Nurse McNeil felt her eyelids droop, as tiredness began to take hold. From a distance, she heard a buzzer going off. At first, she wondered what it was, she then became wide awake and realised it was a room call buzzer. Rushing to the man's room, she was surprised to find him still fast asleep. Puzzled, Nurse McNeil went to the woman's room, and saw the call cord light was flashing. Moving to the bed, and leaning over, Nurse McNeil was surprised to find the woman's eyes wide open and she was trying to speak.

Nurse McNeil poured a cup of water from the bedside cabinet, and helped the woman to drink using a straw. The woman closed her eyes as she drank as if it was nectar. The woman tried to speak again but it was too weak for Nurse McNeil to hear, so she leaned in closer. As she did so, the woman gripped her arm and stared into Nurse McNeil's eyes and said, "Sharapova, call Corby MI6."

Nurse McNeil removed the woman's hand and, placing her own hand on the woman's arm, said, "Lay still, I will go fetch the doctor." The woman nodded in agreement and closed her eyes again, as if the effort of the last few minutes had been a struggle for her. Nurse McNeil returned to her desk and rang the on-call doctor and explained what had happened. The on-call doctor told her he would ring back in a few minutes.

A few minutes later the on-call doctor rang back. On hearing the doctor's reply, she placed the phone receiver down and looked puzzled, but doing as the doctor ordered she returned to the woman patient, and noticing she had once again fallen asleep, she took the chair next to the bed and waited for the on-call doctor to arrive. Nurse McNeil wondered who this woman was; she only knew her as Patient S, but she wondered what had the on-call doctor so worried that she had been told to sit with her and make a note of anything else she said. Nurse McNeil watched the woman sleeping, and pondered on what she had said and who she was.

Next Book – A Plan of Vengeance